# Devil's Snare

By: Laurie Wipperfurth

Thank you to all those who helped me to bring this novel to publication. Sandy, you have been with me since the beginning, patiently nudging me forward. Ant, Peter, Steve and London, your frank opinions have helped me through out. To all of you who have read the early versions, your insights were invaluable. Carol, your editing was just super. And to Dave, thanks for your constant support.

Wistman's Wood – Dartmoor – Britain
March, 920 Anno Domini

"Stay here, little lass—right here near the light."

Vala nodded solemnly. Her uncle gave her a hard look before taking his little rushlight and striding toward the rough wooden barn to feed Old Tom, their horse, two pigs called Auntie and Bill, and a few chickens who did not deserve names.

Vala stood in the warm glow that fell through the open cottage door. She looked about her and then off toward the barn. It wasn't that she meant to disobey her uncle. Surely, he must know that there were no twigs for the fire in the empty dooryard. Vala was four years old, and if life had taught her anything, it was that firewood fell from trees, and the trees were by the road.

Skipping off away from the cottage, Vala breathed in the sharp scent of dying leaves. She shivered a little in the cool night air, but small girls are hardy. Down near the road, she began to fill her homespun apron with twigs. It was nearly spilling over when the pounding of hoofbeats startled the child. Out of the gloom galloped a huge black horse, the mist of the rising fog shredded into tatters around its hooves. Vala noticed the horse particularly. The only horses she'd ever seen were plow horses, thick and slow. This horse was sleek and haughty, as was its rider.

The rider yanked up hard on the reins, bringing his mount to a halt at the edge of the roadway. The horse snorted, its breath a cloud hanging in the air. The horseman was nothing less than the exact likeness of the Devil or one of his minions. When he swept back his long-hooded cloak, Vala let out a tiny gasp as his icy stare fell on her. The bits of twig dropped from her apron. Vala was not a timid child, so she brushed herself down as though she'd meant to drop her tinder just here. Jutting out her little chin, she gave that man, or devil, back as good as he gave.

"You there, who are you?" she demanded in her tiny voice.

The man gave her a cold smirk.

"Child! Come away!" cried a hoarse voice far behind her.

Uncle Adrian came rustling through the leaves, limping noticeably, as he always did when he had to move quickly. He motioned her back, and Vala was torn between following her uncle's command and giving this interloper some more of her tight-lipped stare. Her uncle stepped between Vala and the horseman, so she could not see the looks the men exchanged before her uncle took hold of the horse's bridle.

"It's been years, Simon. Why now?"

In solidarity with her uncle, Vala put her fists on her hips.

"She appears to be growing and as healthy as could be wished," said the man, never taking his eyes from Vala.

Vala was fairly sure that 'she' meant herself. "I never get sick," she put in.

The stranger ignored her comment and looked archly at her uncle, "Is it safe?"

Her uncle nodded. There was a silence in which the horse stamped its hooves and both men stared at the ground.

"You know it's best this way," the horsemen finally said. Her uncle made a harrumphing noise, the one he saved for when he didn't agree but didn't want to say so.

"Will you come inside?" Uncle Adrian asked finally, as though hospitality and obligation required that he ask.

"No." The horseman's eyes rested once again on Vala's upturned face.

"Come nearer, girl," he said, bending down a bit, beckoning her.

Her uncle's expression told her nothing, so she stepped forward. "I'm not scared of you," she told the man. She was just a little afraid but refused to drop her gaze.

"That's good." The man's lip curled into what might have been a smile.

"Who are you?" she asked.

"My name is Simon."

Vala nodded.

"Hold out your hands," he commanded.

Vala cupped her palms and extended them.

The man reached into a pouch and sprinkled some dried things into her waiting fingers. Vala sniffed them cautiously.

"Ash berries," the man said, "It's Ash Moon tonight. Put these into the candles, and your house will be protected from mischievous spirits."

Uncle Adrian pulled Vala close. "Ash Moon," he growled, sweeping the berries away. "That's nonsense!"

The man simply turned his horse northward and spurred it away.

As he vanished down the road, Vala tugged on her uncle's coat. "Who was that man? Where did he come from? His horse was bigger than ours. Do you think it's faster, Uncle? Will that man come back?"

Uncle Adrian only grunted and steered her back to the cottage. Vala did not see the man again for many years.

Chapter One:
933 A.D. Feast of the Annunciation
*"A stumble may prevent a fall."*

Vala Crofter craned her neck, watching the narrow path that disappeared into the trees. Stephen was not in sight. At morning prayers, he'd whispered an urgent plea to meet him in the woods, and even though it was rather wicked to come unchaperoned, she'd agreed.

Heavy clouds were edging over the valley, the last vestige of March rains. The village of Wistman's Wood would receive a drenching before the day was gone. Vala lifted her chin, closing her dark blue eyes as a gust of wind wafted strands of honey-colored hair over her reddened cheeks. She'd come away without her cap, and she wasn't good at braiding her locks, so if she looked like a wild nymph, it couldn't be helped. Instead, she fussed with her woolen kirtle and wrapped her shawl tighter around her shoulders.

She was certain she knew why Stephen had asked her here. He meant to propose marriage. It was high time, for she was seventeen, well past the age when most girls wed, but more than that, she loved Stephen. Wistman's Wood was a small village, and everyone knew Vala to be outspoken, a trait most men would shun in a wife. Yet Stephen never upbraided her for her forward nature.

"Where is he?" she moaned, bouncing on the balls of her feet and staring at the empty path. She turned toward the stone monolith rooted at the turning in the path. A great finger of granite pinning the woods to the side of the valley, the villagers called it the Demon Stone.

Father Wulford insisted that the legions of hell issued forth from it in the black of night to snatch up unsuspecting souls and drag them down to the underworld.

It took a strong wager to coax the local lads to touch its cold surface.

It was such a fantastic story, how could it be true? Vala inched forward and then looked about her. No one was near. She stuck out her foot toward the base of the stone.

"What are you doing?" Stephen pounded up the path, his handsome face pinched in a scowl. "Vala, get away from that...thing!" he ordered.

She jumped back but then regretted having acquiesced to his command like a weak-minded ninny. Vala pursed her lips and put the sole of her leather boot firmly against the ancient menhir.

"It's just a rock," she stated tartly.

"It's the *Demon* Stone, girl." He panted, a stray lock of dark hair falling over light green eyes. "You ought to know better." Stephen pulled her out of the stone's shadow. "Your curiosity will be the death of you."

Instead of arguing, Vala swallowed her ire in favor of a buoyant mood.

Her beau was nineteen and the son of the blacksmith. Stephen trained at his father's forge. Soon, they'd call him Master Smyth, after his important role in the village's commerce. For her birthday, he'd fashioned a small iron whorl meant for spinning. It was meant as a practical gift, but instead of putting the whorl to use on the new lamb's wool, Vala carried it about in her pocket, fingering the edges.

Stephen tightened his grip on her hands, pulling her toward him. "I love you, Vala. You know that." He placed a tentative kiss on her lips, and she beamed at his brashness. Even though they were very much alone, he lowered his voice. "The priest is going to talk to Tessie Thatcher today. She hasn't named the father yet."

Vala cocked her head. It was not the remark she had expected, although it was a subject of great interest in the village.

Stephen shook his head. "She is an odd thing."

"Tessie is a bit empty-headed at times, but I'm sure there is no evil in her." Stephen huffed.

"Well, I feel sorry for her," Vala said. "If she hasn't told who the father is, she must have a reason."

"Vala," Stephen said with a quaver in his voice. "You know my feelings for you."

"Yes, of course, Stephen."

"And I'd like us to wed."

Although she wanted to say, 'I would too,' something in his tone held her back.

"I'd planned we would go to the church next Sunday."

Vala watched his face, disquiet rising in her gut.

"Do you recall the bonfire on All Saints Eve?" he mumbled.

"All Saints Eve?" Vala shook her head. "Are you feeling well, Stephen?"

He stroked her ring finger with his thumb. "That night, I was walking home by the mill pond. I'd drunk more ale than I should have, so I was taking some air." He licked his lips as though tasting the words.

"Most of the village had too much ale that night," she offered.

"I met Tessie Thatcher by the pond," he said, his voice quiet. He swallowed. "We...I..."

Vala blanched as his meaning hit her. She yanked her hands away.

"Tessie says I must marry her, but things are confused in my mind about that night."

"What are you saying?" Vala demanded.

"The spirits of the dead were abroad, Vala. The girl must have put an enchantment on me." Then, with absolute sincerity, he said, "Tessie might be a witch!"

Vala let his words sift through her, trying to breathe, trying to think. Tears welled in her eyes as her fingers found the whorl in her pocket. Many possible retorts sprang to her lips until one escaped. "Will you say she *forced* you?"

Stephen mumbled something, but Vala did not hear it. She let the whorl fly. "Tessie will need this to make your child's blanket!" It thudded hard against Stephen's chest as she spun and stumbled up the path. There'd be no happy betrothal today, no professions of undying love, only hot, angry tears. The bite of humiliation was nearly as sharp as the betrayal. "Won't the old women talk now!" she muttered bitterly.

The village women called Tessie Thatcher a vixen. Vala had no great love for the girl or her foolishness. Tessie had a way of looking at men, and perhaps she deserved her reputation. Yet, to suggest the girl was a witch? How spineless for Stephen to blame his own failing on Tessie.

Vala brushed low branches out of her way like a fallow deer shouldering through the underbrush. Her mind roiled with life's injustices and the capriciousness of men. It would be far better to end as an old unmarried woman than to cleave to a false beau, for how could she ever trust him?

One thing was clear. Tessie and Stephen *must* wed. It was only right. Yet, if Stephen declared that Tessie had put a spell on him, if he made a claim of witchery, the silly girl could be banished, or worse.

Vala hiked up her skirts and ran. Uncle Adrian would know what to do. He'd have soothing words for her. Even better, he'd flail Stephen for this treachery. Uncle Adrian always knew what to do, and he was well regarded in the village. He would know the best defense for Tessie, should Stephen press his claim of witchery.

Wistman's Wood, a village of nearly sixty souls, crouched in the mouth of a shallow valley. A stream pooled at its center, forming the village mill pond, before continuing its journey south. Vala slowed as she neared the village proper and wiped her face on her sleeve, composing herself before stepping from the trees. She dodged a flock of geese headed toward the reedy water, then quickened her pace. Ann Fuller and Old Jenny were leaning on the capstones of the well, hard at their gossip.

"Vala!" Old Jenny called. "How are you this fine day?"

Ann cocked an eyebrow. "Child, you look like someone stepped on your grave."

Vala faced them but could think of no fit reply. Instead, she spun away and hurried on. The forge was cold, and she was relieved that Stephen's father was nowhere in sight. The mill's creaky waterwheel churned the flowing stream murky brown beneath the rickety footbridge. Vala crossed it with care, clutching the edges of her shawl to hide her face. She gave a great sniffle as tears threatened to overtake her. Only a furlong more over the fields and she'd be home.

Belligerent voices rose above the sound of the mill's grist stone. She was nearing the Thatcher's cottage with its pole-roofed dugout that served as storage for Eldon Thatcher's harvest. In their small dooryard stood Tessie, with her mother and father facing her down like jailers.

"Daughter, there is little time left!" Tessie's mother cried, touching the girl's belly. "Just tell us the name of the father."

Tessie stared at the barren garden patch with a stoic expression. Her father aimed a kick at a large sheaf of heather he'd bound for sale. "I've lost my patience, daughter! The priest will soon be here, and you daren't lie to him!"

Vala didn't fancy eavesdropping on this conversation, but before she could flee, Tessie raised her red eyes to Vala and shook her head.

Vala wondered what Tessie was thinking. Was she protecting Stephen? Desperate to get away, she turned and collided with a wide, wool-cloaked body.

"Vala Crofter! A word, please."

Vala cringed under Father Wulford's dour gaze. "Yes, Father?"

Father Wulford was new to the village. He'd come in the dead of winter after old Father Cyril had succumbed to fever and flux. Father Cyril had been a stern, commanding presence, yet he'd known how to listen to folk. He'd been a good friend to her uncle, visiting often for cider and conversation. He had claimed to disapprove when Adrian decided to teach Vala some rudimentary Latin, but the old priest would quiz her if he caught her on her own, and would correct her pronunciation with a wink and a smile. Vala didn't think Father Wulford ever smiled.

"Let me bless you, child," the priest said, taking her bowed head for an invitation. He placed a heavy hand on her shawl-covered pate. "*Confitemini Domino, quoniam bonus: quoniam in saevidicus misericordia eius.*"

"Thank you, Father." Vala reasoned that she needed an extra blessing today, although Tessie needed one more. It would have been a good blessing too, 'Praise the Lord because He is good; because His mercy endureth forever.' The priest should have said '*saeculum*' instead of '*saevidicus*', but Vala was forbidden from issuing a correction.

"Take heed, child," Father Wulford continued, adopting his most pompous tone. "The devil is loose in this village." He glanced down the path to where Tessie stood. "Fornication is a great sin. Mind that you and your young man do not yield to temptation."

"Yes, Father," she replied, her jaw clenching.

The priest waggled an accusatory finger in Tessie's direction. "That one is most surely damned. I hope she will confess, for if she does not, there is little I can do."

"But—what about the boy?" Vala asked. "Why is Tessie the one damned? Surely the boy deserves a punishment too."

"*Woman* transgressed in the Garden of Eden. *Woman* led man to sin!" the priest pronounced.

Vala was spoiling for a fight and nearly blurted out a ripe retort; instead, she bit down on her lip, bobbed her head and turned to run.

"Wait, child," the priest commanded. "I've meant to mention something particular to you." Vala chafed to be gone from the vicinity of the Thatcher's cottage, but he continued. "Your name, child," the priest said. "Where did you get it? The baptismal records are incomplete."

Vala scowled. "My parents named me. They died just after I was born." Uncle Adrian had explained this much to her, but it wasn't a subject he liked to discuss.

"'Vala' is not a saint's name," Wulford sniffed. "It's some sort of pagan abomination. You ought to choose another."

Her name was all she had of her parents, and just now, it felt like so very little. She gulped a ragged breath as Father Wulford spun on his officious heel and strode toward the commotion in the Thatcher's garden. Vala bolted for home.

The freshly turned earth of her uncle's rye field filled her boots with loose dirt. It was just another annoyance in a dreadful day. "Uncle!" she hallooed toward the cottage, "Uncle Adrian!"

How dare Stephen have his way with Tessie, then, on the very next day, pretend he loved her? Why should Tessie refuse to name him?

"Uncle Adrian!" she bawled again. He was probably tending his pigeons.

She spotted her uncle down by the road, talking to a stranger. Uncle Adrian was a large man who gave off the air of command, yet he had a gentle streak. His hair was the color of frost, but his eyes were normally lively and bright. Today, he bore a look of tired resignation. He turned from the stranger and made his way toward her, his ever-present limp more noticeable than usual.

"Uncle," she breathed with some relief. She ran to him and took his hands. "I have to tell you something."

"Vala," he interrupted. "You must pack your things. I'm taking you on a trip, and we haven't time to spare."

His words did not register. "Stephen just told me—he said—" She paused to catch her breath.

Uncle Adrian began to hitch the dappled plow horse to the cart they took to market. "I have something to confess to you, Vala. Something I'd hoped never to say." Uncle Adrian clinched the old leather harness tight. "You've grown so," he mused. "Soon, you'll marry your Stephen and have a nice little cottage near the forge." His brow wrinkled. "Nothing needs to change. Remember that, Vala. You always have a choice." He limped to the far side of the cart and attached the harness to the shaft.

"But Stephen—" Vala faltered. They were having two separate conversations, neither hearing the other. "Where are we going?"

"We can talk as we ride. Go and pack. We must be away."

Vala looked at him dumbly.

"Hello, miss!" said an overly bright voice behind her.

Vala jumped. The stranger, a portly man with a wide-brimmed hat, was right beside her.

"I'm Farley... Farley the baker, from Bridestowe." He extended his hand. Vala looked at it, confused. Uncle Adrian nudged her away.

Farley the baker seemed not to notice. "As I said, friend, I can take her along to Bridestowe. You need not trouble yourself to come with us."

Vala was near to tears again as she looked to her uncle for an explanation.

"Vala, we're losing daylight. Go and pack your things."

"I don't understand!" she cried.

"For once, girl," her uncle growled, banging his fist on the cart and fixing her with a hard stare, "can't you simply obey?"

His words were like a hard slap. She couldn't recall her uncle ever taking such a tone with her. At age six, she'd demanded he call her 'Mary May Flower' for a full week. She'd spoiled a whole bin of millet once by leaving off the leather cover, inviting every rat and mouse in the neighborhood to a feast. She'd ruined his best knife trying to scratch her name on a stone. None of these had evoked such a response.

Confused and wounded, Vala found the cottage door and then the ladder to the little loft under the eaves where she slept. It was a bad dream—this entire miserable day. She prayed to wake while cramming her few possessions roughly into a sack, but as she stumbled outside, the cart and her uncle were as solid as ever. The stranger was there too, with an odd look on his pudgy face.

"Get in." Uncle Adrian avoided her eyes, just as Stephen had done before breaking her heart. Then he mumbled the strangest of words. "I'm taking you to your father."

Vala felt dizzy.

"I never meant for you to learn this in such a way. So much time has passed, so much that I believed he'd decided to leave you alone."

"My father is dead. You told me so."

Uncle Adrian shook his head. "Your father gave you into my keeping soon after your birth. Now he is ill and asking for you. In good conscience, I can't deny him."

Vala couldn't frame a question.

"She doesn't know?" Farley asked incredulously.

Uncle Adrian turned on the man. "We will meet you at the crossroads."

Farley backed away, his hands raised. "Certainly. I'll await you there."

Vala watched her uncle watch the back of Farley as he mounted his pony and trotted away.

Uncle Adrian sighed. "Listen, child. Your father is a hunted man. He knew you were better off here."

"Why must I go? What if I refuse?" she demanded. "And who is that fat man?"

Uncle Adrian raised an eyebrow and then lifted her roughly into the back of the cart. Straw poked at her through her woolen dress and cloak. Her uncle dumped several blankets onto her lap, avoiding her burning stare, then climbed into the cart. A man of plain words, he said what he meant and never uttered falsehoods. It alarmed her that he'd kept such a great secret from her all these years.

Stephen, too, had a bitter secret. Vala balled her hands into fists. The two men she trusted most had lied to her.

Chapter Two:
*"A person with a bad name is already half-hanged."*

The cart bounced and creaked along the path, making a wide arch around the low end of the valley where the stream ran shallow and the peat bogs could trap the unwary. Vala huddled with her back to her uncle, who was sitting on the narrow driver's bench. The moor was treacherous but also beautiful in its way, but she could take no joy from the freshening countryside. Her uncle had fostered her curiosity, contrary to the other good and sensible parents of Wistman's Wood. Vala was boiling over with questions; however, for the first time in her life, she was unable to pry her lips open to ask even one of them. Her uncle was a liar, her father a criminal, and Stephen had broken her heart. Betrayal was a confounding thing.

"Child, I'm sorry I kept this from you. Your father was in danger, and I feared you would be too, had I been more truthful." He didn't look back at her, nor did she turn toward him.

"Why hasn't he ever come to see me?" As she said this, an image of a handful of ash berries flitted through her head.

Adrian straightened in his seat. "He knew coming here would bring trouble down upon us." He sighed. "And now he is ill, and he asks this favor. It was dangerous for him to do so."

Vala spun toward him. "You say he is a criminal, but that I must do him a favor?" She stared down at the road beneath the cart, moving not much faster than she could walk. She could jump out and run away. She'd heard of the great cities to the east. In a great city, they might value a girl who could read and write.

Adrian yanked up hard on the reins, the cart bobbed to a stop, and her daydream evaporated.

"When your father gave you into my keeping, I was not sure how I'd manage. I was a single man, set in my ways. As things turned out, I've counted myself blessed these years. After you see Simon and hear what he has to say, you may do as you wish. Run away, or come back to Wistman's Wood—as you like." The corner of his lip trembled, and he rubbed a hand over his weathered jaw. "I hope you'll want to come back home, to me, and to Stephen too."

Vala pursed her lips. A part of her wanted to throw her arms around her uncle's neck and feel the protection she always had when she was close to him, but there was too much to take in right now.

They drove through the chilly water at the ford, and then back up the farther bank in silence. Soon, they reached the crossroads where Farley was waiting. To the east was the market town of Dartmeet. They took the west turning into country unfamiliar to Vala.

Her uncle waved Farley onward. "We'll be right behind you," he called. Farley seemed to want to ride alongside them, but the track was narrow, and he was forced to kick his horse into a trot.

"Your father named you," Adrian whispered. "In the Saxon tongue, 'Vala' means 'Chosen'."

"Chosen? For what?" How strange that he should mention this after Father Wulford's comment.

"I believe your father fostered the hope that one day you would join him in protecting the old ways—the old gods."

"What do you mean by 'old gods'? And why are we whispering?" Vala asked as she crawled nearer to the front bench.

"That baker doesn't need to know our business," Adrian said.

"Who is he?" Vala asked.

"A friend of your father's," Adrian muttered, then he turned to Vala. "The old gods were venerated and worshipped long before folk knew of the one God." He gave the reins a little shake, warming to the subject. "The old gods are ancient, older than the trees and the hills." He nodded into the distance. "There is one for rain, and one for harvest, a sun god, and so on. They are warriors and queens, spirits, fairies and the like. Folk who worship them believe they are magic. Your father and his friends still worship them."

Vala scowled toward Farley, who was bouncing like a plump chicken on his mount. "That is heresy."

"Wistman's Wood has a priest. Not all places have priests to tell them of the one God, and in some places, the folk worship both old and new." Adrian looked back at his niece. "The tales about the great stone at the edge of the wood come from stories of the old gods."

There was an obvious contradiction in this, and Vala edged closer to her uncle. "Do you mean the part about demons coming out of the stone at night? Father Wulford tells everyone to shun the stone. Does he believe in the old gods, too?"

A hint of a smile played over Adrian's lips. "He would never admit such a thing. He would say the demons are fallen angels."

"People talk about demons, but no one actually sees them." Vala's brow wrinkled. "I've touched the stone, but nothing happened, so I don't think the stories can be true."

Adrian shifted on the wooden plank seat. "Truth is a hard thing to judge. Each man carries his own truth in his heart. There may be demons in the stone, and there may not be."

"Uncle, do *you* believe in these old gods?" She was no longer certain she knew this man who had raised her.

"Father Cyril and I used to have some rousing discussions on the subject." That was her uncle sidestepping the question. "You are a clever girl, Vala. The time has come for you to decide for yourself. *Fortes fortuna iuvat.*"

*Fortune favors the brave.* It was the first Latin phrase he'd taught her. Whenever she was frightened, he'd repeated it to her. Now he was taking her to meet a mysterious man with heretical ideas who'd abandoned her as an infant. He expected her to be brave. It didn't bode well.

"We'll stop for the night at the inn at Mary Tavy!" Farley called back to them. Adrian raised his hand in acknowledgment.

The village of Mary Tavy was set at a crossroads in the bowl of a shallow valley. Mist shrouded the cluster of lantern-lit cottages grouped around a small market square. Vala rose up on her knees and rubbed the chill from her arms.

They rolled to a stop in front of a crooked stone structure where a weathered wooden sign swung from a pike. It showed a bird overlaid with a sprig of some plant.

"The Grouse and Gorse," Farley said with a flourish.

Vala wondered how the man kept such high spirits after so long in the saddle.

Uncle Adrian climbed to the ground and straightened his stiff leg with a painful wince. "Wait here," he said, heading for the door. Farley was already pulling his horse toward the stables.

Vala took charge of the reins, tugging her wool cloak over her hands. The bark of a lone dog echoed down the lane. The town was still but for the muffled voices drifting from the inn. Along with the sounds came the smell of roasting meat. It made Vala's stomach groan.

The door of the inn banged open, and three men jostled their way out, laughing and shoving each other. One of them wobbled toward the wagon. Vala looked warily at the man and then toward the inn, wishing her uncle would come out.

"Mistress!" the man slurred, making a broad bow. The other two grinned up at her. The first sidled closer. "I'm talking to you, girl. Are you too good to talk to me?" He threw his arms wide, the smell of sour ale strong on his breath.

She tightened her grip on the reins. "Please, sir, leave me alone."

He pointed to his chest. "I do as I please!" With a broad swing of his beefy arm, he made a grab for her leg. Vala shrieked.

Farley stepped from the stable and looked toward the ruckus. His features tightened and then slackened to a grin as he made his way toward the men. He slapped the loudest drunk on the back.

"My old friend!" he enthused.

The drunk man turned unsteadily and faced Farley with a look of confusion. "Do I know you?" he mumbled.

"I'm sure we've met. Last year in Bath, I think, or was it Exeter?"

The man and his friends looked from one to the other.

"We should have a drink together sometime," said Farley, steering the men away. They followed his voice like sheep. "Next time you come to town, all right?" The men were now aimed and moving down the road.

Farley turned to Vala and tipped his hat. She nodded, surprised at the baker's cool and clever head.

The door of the inn opened again. Uncle Adrian was talking to a stout woman as they walked toward the wagon.

"Erich!" the goodwife called out, and a brawny stableman appeared to take charge of their cart and horse.

"Are you all right, lass?" the woman asked, eying the retreating men and then Vala's pale face.

"Yes, thank you," Vala mumbled.

Uncle Adrian turned, but the men had melted into the darkness. Vala took her uncle's proffered hand to climb down. She gave him a reassuring smile, although inside she was angry with herself for being shaken by such louts. No one had ever accosted her so. The wide world was a more perilous place than she'd imagined.

"We've a nice fire inside, and a hot supper. That should put you all right!" the woman said, leading them toward the warm light pouring from the doorway.

A large, low-beamed room greeted them. There was a bright blaze in the hearth, the scent of chicken cooking on a spit, and the odor of sweet cider floating in the air. Several patrons were sitting at a table in the corner, laughing and talking together.

The woman bade them sit near the fire and sent over steaming trenchers of chicken stew. She, herself, fetched cups of cider with honey. Inhaling the fragrant steam, Vala reveled in the grand repast. The warmth and food soon had her nodding.

"I tell you," Farley said, waving a chunk of bread at Adrian, "I can take the girl on from here. You can return to your plowing in peace."

Adrian's brow furrowed. "I will deliver my niece to my brother, sir."

Vala thought that Farley had best leave off before her uncle said what he really was thinking.

The baker shrugged. "It's no business of mine. I was just offering to help." Farley finished his stew and took his cup to join the folk at the large table.

"Surely, having a guide is better than becoming lost in the wilderness," Vala whispered.

Uncle Adrian looked vexed as he lifted her by the elbow to her feet. "Surely."

Their traveling companion nodded to Vala and Adrian as they made their way to the innkeeper's wife. She pointed out a side room with a charcoal brazier for heat. Fresh rushes covered the floor, and she provided them each with a blanket.

"No need to fear," the woman said. "Just a few guests will stay the night, and my Hal will be on watch."

Uncle Adrian thanked the woman while Vala took her blanket to a corner. She knelt on the floor and made her nightly prayer for the health of her uncle and the salvation of her soul, then rolled up in the blanket and was soon asleep.

Vala was falling, falling, falling, from a great height. Just before smashing into the earth, she startled awake. Her chest tightened in panic until voices beyond the room reminded her she was sleeping at an inn. Several feet away, her uncle tossed in his blanket. He wasn't sleeping well, either. Vala sat still for a moment, letting her eyes adjust. The room was empty except for the two of them, but in the keeping room, tempers were rising.

"And furthermore, ye don't know of what ye speak!"

"But I've been there, friend. Been in the palace of the pope. It's not so very hard to get inside, and those inside know the truth of it."

"The pope is a great man—sent by God himself! You daren't speak of His Holiness as though he's a common whoremonger."

Vala got to her feet and padded to the doorway, the better to hear the discussion. On a bench in the far corner, Farley was snoring with gusto. Three others sat by the fire, hunkered down around a barrel. On top was a board marked with squares and crowded with wooden pieces. Some were dark and some light. The tallest of the pieces had a gilt top.

"Listen, friend," said the one nearest the hearth, a fellow with a leather cap trimmed in some sort of animal fur. "I know little about the new pope—John XI he calls himself. He might be a fine fellow, but his mother was often in old Pope Serguis's bed. It is known that this new Pope John is the old pope's bastard." He moved a dark piece and then gestured to his opponent to take his turn.

The man playing the light-colored pieces was the stableman she'd seen earlier. "You're a bloody liar!" he growled, lifting his own piece and slamming it down on a free space.

The third man, garbed in forester's green, noticed Vala in the shadows and nodded in her direction. "Let's keep our heads, shall we? There is a young lass present."

Vala blushed at being discovered and was about to go back to her bed.

"Even a child like that can see Rome is naught but base corruption," said Leathercap.

"So say you!" grunted the stableman, who crossed his arms and studied the board.

"Wait a moment, girl," called the forester. "I've a question for you."

Vala pulled her blanket around her shoulders and took a few tentative steps closer to the group. The two men stopped their game.

Leaning forward, the forester asked, "Lass, do you believe that God himself ordains our pope?"

Vala noticed that Farley had stopped snoring. She thought his one eye had opened a slit.

"Yes, of course," she replied.

The stableman cut in, "Leave the poor girl alone. Don't twist her with your questions."

"Just asking the girl's thoughts," the forester said with a shrug. "You ought to move there." He pointed toward a light-colored piece.

Vala loathed being disregarded, so she spoke up. "Our priest says God endows the pope with holiness."

The forester grinned. "If the pope is a bastard, would it make him less holy in the eyes of God?"

"You don't know he's a bastard!" the stableman hissed. "And why ask the opinion of a mere girl?"

Vala ignored this comment and took another step toward the hearth. "God is perfect, is he not? He would only allow the purest of souls to lead his church." The image of Tessie with her ripening belly came to her. If that child was a bastard, would it make the child evil? She shook her head as the men watched. "Any man, regardless of birth, whom God ordains as pope, deserves our respect."

The forester's lip curled in a sly smile. "What if a pope, ordained by God, is found to be a fornicator? Is he still to be obeyed and revered?"

Vala paled. "The pope would never—"

A hand took hold of her shoulder. "Excuse us, good sirs. We have a long ride tomorrow." It was her uncle.

The forester gave a polite nod. Farley seemed to relax back against the wall.

"But, Uncle—" Vala had decided to respond that God alone could judge a man or a pope, but Uncle Adrian was pulling her away.

"We don't want to draw attention," he whispered. "Come, get some sleep."

Morning arrived with the maddening crow of a cock. As Vala partook of porridge and some hard cheese, Adrian drummed his fingers on the oaken table in a nervous staccato, nearly as irritating as the rooster. Their guide winked at them as he made his way outside, and Uncle Adrian took the opportunity to lean close to Vala. "I have two things which must be said before we set out." His weatherworn face was pinched. "I am sorry now that I didn't tell this to you sooner. My only excuse is that I hoped this day would never come."

Vala blinked up at him. "There's more?" She had assumed she'd heard the worst, finding her father was a heretic.

Adrian rubbed at the stubble on his chin. "When we reach your father, he may mention your brother."

Vala thought she'd misheard. "I have a brother?"

"You *did* have a brother. Lugus was his name. I believe your father named him for the Celtic deity, Lugh." Adrian waved a hand in the air. "Lugus would have been about two years older than you, but I understand he died recently."

Vala was stunned. "Why didn't you tell me? How do you know he's dead?" It had never occurred to her that she might have any family beyond her uncle, and now this would-be brother was dead before she'd known he existed.

"Your father has his ways of contacting me," he replied. "Simon felt it was necessary to keep these things from you, lest you innocently repeat something to the wrong person."

Before she could ask who that wrong person might be, he thrust a small object into her hands, wrapped in a cloth. "This is something your father left in my keeping when he brought you to me."

Vala pulled back the linen wrapping. Inside was a wooden box the size of a man's fist. On every side, the maker had carved complex knots and spiral shapes, delicate and precise. Vala traced them with her finger, admiring the graceful patterns. She would have thought it a solid cube except that she could hear an object rattling around inside. She tried to see a way to open it.

Uncle Adrian stayed her hand. "Best to leave it closed for now." It was an unnecessary warning, for there were no hinges or a latch of any kind. "This has been in our family for many generations. There are those who would do harm to obtain it." He laid his fingers over hers.

"What makes it so dangerous?" she whispered.

"Some folk believe it is a thing of great power. Therefore, I ask that you keep it hidden, as I have."

Vala recoiled, but her uncle held her fingers firmly in place.

"Simon will explain it all," Adrian said. "It's his place to do so." He stuffed the box into her pack and then lifted her chin, looking into her eyes. "More important than the box, Vala, I ask you to make an effort to know your father. He ought to have come to you sooner; he ought to have claimed you as his own. Still, he is your family. He's made mistakes, which I'm sure he'd admit, but he can tell you about the past, and about why he hid you as he did."

Vala opened her mouth, then closed it as a cheery voice intruded. "Are we ready to proceed?" Farley was rubbing his hands in anticipation of another day's riding. "We can talk at leisure today, for the road is wide from here, all the way to Bridestowe."

She nodded, struggling to smile. "Is that where we are going?"

Farley hoisted their packs. "We are, indeed. I should tell you that I am considered the finest baker in Bridestowe. You'll find out once we reach our destination!" He grinned and tromped out the door to their waiting cart.

Uncle Adrian smoothed a stray lock of hair from Vala's forehead. "Say nothing of what I've told you to this man," he whispered.

Farley, the finest baker in Bridestowe, was all chivalry as he helped Vala into the wagon. As they rolled along through the countryside, Farley rode close to the wagon on his fat sorrel pony. "Simon is my great friend," he said. "Since I needed to come to this excellent little hamlet for some sacks of rye flour, I told him I'd fetch you back too. Did I mention I'm a baker? I think I did."

Her uncle raised an exasperated eyebrow.

Farley chattered on. "Bridestowe is quite small, and less than a day's journey away. You had a bit of a scare last night, but there should be no further trouble, not in Bridestowe. Yet the world is a complex place, is it not? Take my business. Even though I am the sole baker in the town, still, I try to offer only the best of hot water crusts, flat tarts, and, of course, breads..."

The man carried on without any encouragement, so Vala turned her thoughts to the odd box hidden in her pack. What sort of threat could a small wooden box hold, she wondered. What sort of father bestowed something dangerous upon his child? She gazed out at the gorse bushes and heather.

"Do you know my father well?" Vala blurted, interrupting the recitation of a pastry recipe.

"Oh my, yes!" Farley said. "A better seer, one is not likely to find."

"A seer?" She turned her full attention to the man.

"He foretells the future, among his other talents," replied Farley. "I do wish I had such a gift."

Vala crossed herself. Fortune telling was a great sin, but again, there was that look of warning on her uncle's face, so uncharacteristic, reminding her to remain mute.

The wagon lumbered on, and Farley barely stopped speaking, even to catch his breath. When Vala could no longer follow his prattle or keep her eyes open, she dropped into an uneasy slumber.

A misty glen full of mysterious boxes spread out before her. Each box had a voice. They clacked, chattered, and banged, combining into a din so loud that she could not hear their words. She jerked awake as the wagon wheel jostled through a deep rut.

"This is the crossroads," Farley called, pointing them toward the east road. "Not far now!"

The late-afternoon sun pierced banks of thick clouds as their cart lumbered into the village. Bridestowe boasted at least twice as many dwellings as Wistman's Wood. Most were of rough stone, giving the enclave a formidable presence. Smoke curled up through vents in the thatched roofs, heavy with the pungent scent of peat. Children raced about, calling to each other, while the livestock, tethered or penned up in yards, contributed to the smells and noise. The folk of the village were garbed in homespun and knitted caps, just like in Wistman's Wood; however, their faces were unfamiliar, and to Vala's mind, unfriendly.

In the center of the village, instead of a Christian cross atop a church, three large standing stones loomed. They were similar to the stone at the edge of the wood back home, but not so tall. Each was the height of a man, one leaning against the other two in a drunken aspect. They cast unwelcoming shadows across the road, and the position of the wagon ruts indicated that the villagers gave them a wide berth.

"Uncle, what are those marks?" Vala pointed toward a door lintel adorned with strange symbols.

"Those are runes, child," he said. "I don't know how to read them anymore."

Farley moved his horse closer. "I can read them, young miss." He began to point. "Ur, Algiz, Ingwaz..."

Vala squinted. "Do they protect the houses?"

Before Farley could answer, a villager hallooed to him from a garden plot. "So sorry, I have business with that man. It will just be a moment."

"We can find our way from here if you just tell me the way," said Adrian.

Farley seemed a bit annoyed but provided directions.

They steered onto a winding trail at the far end of the town. It climbed a hill into some woods, becoming a narrow track with the trees and bushes so close, they brushed against Vala like grasping fingers. The foliage gave way to a clearing on a shelf of land with a view of the village below. They had arrived in front of a dilapidated dwelling with thin, pale smoke rising from a crumbling stone chimney.

With a grunt of disapproval, Uncle Adrian brought their horse to a stop. Vala climbed down, wondering for the hundredth time why they'd come. Tangled vines encroached on the door. Green and black mildew had attached itself to the wood under a very small window. Cracked pottery shards crunched underfoot. Hanging from the low eaves were various symbols made of metal or wood, such as she'd seen in the village.

Adrian came to her side, handing over her small bundle. "Vala, if you decide you don't like living with Simon, he can send a message and I'll come and fetch you back. You'll always have a home with me."

Vala's throat tightened. "You mean to leave me with him?"

He only whispered, "*Fortes fortuna iuvat.*" Then he called out, "Simon!"

From inside came a hoarse cough, followed by a shuffling sound. The door opened. The man who peered out was stooped and pallid of face. It was hard to tell his age. His hair was black but salted with grey. He moved like an old man with no reservoir of strength. Vala thought he might have been tall, and perhaps he'd once been the tough, sinewy sort—maybe not so long ago. Whatever illness now consumed him had taken a horrible toll. She wondered if a seer, even a sick one, could detect fear.

Without a word of welcome, Simon Finn Negus beckoned them inside.

Chapter Three:
*"Death closes all doors."*


"Thank you for coming so promptly," Simon rasped, gravel in his voice.

"It is as we agreed, brother."

Uncle Adrian set her things on a table littered with dirty bowls and breadcrumbs. A bold rat scurried away, disappearing into a dark corner. There was but one room with a linen hanging, greasy and old, that curtained off the far end. The reek of spoiled food and filth filled the dwelling.

Simon sank down on a rickety chair made from deerskins stretched over rough wood posts. He stared up at Vala for an uncomfortable minute.

"She looks older than twelve."

"She is seventeen, Simon," said Adrian. "You've lost count of the years."

Simon turned his gaze to the dwindling fire on the hearth. "I had lost track. Is she still a maiden?"

"How could you ask that?" Vala said, firing up for a fight.

Adrian put a hand on her shoulder.

Simon eyed his brother. "Darian, as you well know, it matters."

"Leave off, Simon."

Simon shrugged. "Did you give the girl the box?"

"Yes, brother," said Uncle Adrian.

Vala shook her head in confusion. "Did you call my uncle Darian?"

Uncle Adrian opened his mouth to respond, but Simon spoke first. "What name do you know him by?"

"His name is Adrian Crofter, of course."

"Crofter is an occupation, not a proper name. There are things that have been kept from you, girl, in order to ensure your safety." Simon turned to his brother. "I ought not to have used your real name, even here. The illness has brought me low."

Vala looked to her uncle, seeking clarification.

"It's time to explain properly, Simon," Uncle Adrian said. "You've caused me to lie to the child all these years, but it has to stop." He put a hand on Vala's shoulder, "My real name, the name of my youth, is Darian. I wished for anonymity, so I reversed the first two letters. Darian became Adrian. I took the sort of family name the village expects—Crofter, a tiller of the land. Your father, who wishes to proclaim our heritage rather than to hide it, calls himself Simon Finn Negus."

Uncle Adrian gestured to Simon to continue the story, but he declined with a shake of his head.

"Our family is descended, in a long line, from the great warrior king Finn, leader of the Fianna," Uncle Adrian said. "Finn was the protégé of Tadg, a Druid seer of great renown. In the past, it was a prestigious heraldry, but to proclaim one's relationship to the house of Finn, in these times, was to take on the stain of heresy."

Simon snarled, "Heresy is the invention of the small-minded."

Arms crossed, Vala listened as the brothers discussed this odd deception. "There must be many people who are related to this king Finn," she said. "Are they all in danger?"

Simon raised an eyebrow in derision, or perhaps in approval. Vala met his stare, but the intensity in his eyes proved too much, and she looked away.

"Brother, you know, you look like the devil himself," Uncle Adrian interjected. "Your face is so grey."

"Some would say I *am* the devil," replied Simon.

"Save your japes for your followers," Adrian replied. "Vala is here as you requested. You must answer her questions. In return, she will nurse you. The girl has a prodigious knowledge of herb lore."

To Vala, the properties of plants and herbs, which she had learned as a small child, were a normal part of life and nothing remarkable.

Simon gave her a sidelong glance. "You hid this talent from the priests, I hope?" Then overcome with a fit of coughing, he spat copiously onto the dirt floor.

Vala took a step back.

"What ails you, brother?" Adrian asked.

"A flux—nothing more."

"A flux can kill."

Simon gave a dismissive wave. "It's nothing. I've been improving these past few days. However, my illness convinced me that I could wait no longer to indoctrinate the girl. I'm not a young man."

"Aye," Adrian replied. "Do you wish me to stay on?"

"It will be safest if you leave, lest there be talk in the village."

"You can't go!" Vala cried, grasping Adrian's arm.

"It will be fine, my dear."

Simon gave a painful smirk. "Are you afraid of me, girl?"

She *was* afraid, but she rounded on her father. "I don't know you, or why you abandoned me. I don't understand why I'm here."

"I did not abandon you. I kept you alive," Simon said. "Your uncle settled in your village because it is so remote. When I thought of it, Adrian's home was the best of choices—a good place to disappear."

"What of my mother?" Vala suddenly demanded.

Her uncle put a comforting arm around her. "She died when you were born, just as I told you."

"Don't speak of that!" Simon growled as a bout of pain twisted his face and doubled him over.

Uncle Adrian shook his head in frustration. "Simon, for seventeen years we have not spoken of these things. Now is the time to remedy it." He made for the door.

Simon straightened. "So, girl, are you worth all this effort?"

Vala pursed her lips with no idea how to reply. Her head was whirling with the mad revelations of the past few minutes. "Uncle! Wait!"

Adrian was in the yard, tightening the girth strap on their horse.

"Don't leave me!" Vala pleaded.

Her uncle hugged her and whispered in her ear, "I must go now before anyone takes notice. Hear your father out—it's all I ask." He pulled away and climbed into the wagon. "Once you've heard everything Simon has to tell, you may choose your own path. Due to the care we've taken all these years, I think it will be safe for you to return home if you wish it." He reached down and put a hand on her cheek. "Your father is a harsh man. He is rough at the edges, but not a monster."

As the wagon trundled away down the track, those parting words rang in her head. Vala wiped her damp cheeks, trying to control her panic. Simon was her father. He had asked for her. She took a deep breath and strode inside, ready to demand answers. She perched on a stool near the fire and faced the man.

"Do *not* sit there!"

Vala leapt to her feet in alarm and spun to look at the stool.

"That was Lugus's stool—your brother, Lugus. I keep it for him."

Vala thought she must have misheard. "But isn't he dead?"

"Spirits come back to the haunts they knew in life. I would have a familiar place for him to settle and be at peace." Simon returned his gaze to the fire.

Vala eased herself onto the hearthstone, realizing the dead son ranked higher than the living daughter. "I deserved to know I had a father and a brother! Why would you keep this from me?"

Simon raised one dark eyebrow, an unfathomable look creasing his face. He opened his lips to reply, but was taken with a spasm of pain that doubled him over. Once the paroxysm had passed, he sat taking deep breaths. As he watched the fire, she watched him.

It was hard to imagine this man as her father. He was rough, and he stank. His leather breeches and brown linen shirt were well-worn and dirty. His hair was greasy and unwashed. Around his neck hung symbols on grubby leather strings. One, made of copper, had a runic symbol such as she'd noticed on their way through Bridestowe. This one had a simple line with a cant at one end. She wondered what it meant but was loath to prick the silence.

Afternoon faded to evening, and the single candle on the table wavered and burned low until darkness surrounded the cottage like a misty curtain.

"You are not what I had expected," Simon said, rising stiffly. "You may sleep by the fire." Holding his gut, he hobbled to the curtained area.

Vala sat speechless. By the time a retort came to her, it was too late.

She rummaged about for bedding in the miserable hovel. Her uncle had thoughtfully left the old quilt she had used on the wagon ride. After fetching it over to the fire, she curled up as best she could on the hard dirt floor.

Why in the world had her uncle abandoned her? Simon didn't like her. 'Not as expected,' she thought.

Well, neither was he.

During the night, Simon stumbled in and out of the house, knocking into the clutter as he navigated his way to the door. She guessed he needed to relieve himself, but so often? The first time, it frightened her, but as the night wore on, it simply became an annoyance. Finally, she yawned and slid into an uneasy dream.

A forest of waving tree branches surrounded her. Smoky light filtered through their twisted trunks, and lichen covered them like ragged winter cloaks. The woods were very like Wistman's Wood, yet different somehow, darker and more impenetrable. A weighty malevolence hung over the trees as she clambered over gnarled roots and boulders. The acrid odor of the lichen overwhelmed her.

She leaned her hand against the closest trunk to steady herself. A branch began to twist around her arm, the bark scratching her skin. More branches grasped at her. Vala struggled as the massive trunk twisted and crackled. The branches forced her toward a large knothole. It gaped open, ready to swallow her in earthy darkness.

From within, the shadowy hollow rumbled a voice. "Tell me what you see!"

Vala's eyes flew open. A hideous face was inches from her own, her wrist held in a vise-like grip. She screamed.

"What did you see?" the face barked. Her father's face.

She ripped her hand from his grip and scrambled to sit up.

Simon crouched over her in the dark like a great bird of prey with overly bright eyes. "You had a strong dream. I saw that you did!" He had a wild gleam in his eyes even though he was holding his gut, his discomfort secondary to his need to question her.

"Yes, it was a dream."

"Do you often have them?" he demanded.

"Everyone has dreams." Vala wished he would back away.

Simon straightened with effort. "I want to hear it when I return."

Huddled under her quit, Vala watched him shamble outdoors. She pretended to be asleep when he returned and heard him grumble as he made his way back to his bed.

Morning did nothing to improve the look of the cottage. Dusty sunlight streamed through the board slats of the window and showed all the cracks in the mud walls. Vala rose stiffly from the floor and poked about until she found an earthenware basin and a bucket half-full of water. She cleaned the basin and then used it to wash her face and hands.

As she scrubbed the table, Vala mused about her brother. Had he the same hair color as she, the same eyes? She wondered about his life and his dreams as a hacking cough announced Simon's appearance. Bleary-eyed, with sagging skin, he struggled to get himself to the chair by the fire. There he collapsed, putting his hands over his bloodshot eyes.

"Father?" Vala ventured. The man looked far worse in the morning light.

"It will be safer if you refer to me by my name."

"But you're my father. I can't call you—"

"Don't question me, girl!" He winced, clutching his gut. "Later. We'll discuss it later. There is too much to explain, and I haven't the strength just now."

"Breakfast?" she suggested with as much contempt as she could muster.

"Don't bother. Farley will be here shortly with fresh bread. He comes every day."

Vala bent to stir the oat mash she had begun on the fire. If he would not eat it, she would. There was little in the larder, so plain mash would have to do. Some fat blackberries would have been an excellent addition, but it was too early in the year. At home, she would have added a few dried blueberries. As it was, there was only the mash.

"Tell me of your dream," Simon demanded.

"It was nothing," she replied, not looking at him. "I hardly recall it."

"I think you do." The edge in Simon's voice was dangerous.

Vala turned to him. "I dreamed that a tree trunk was going to swallow me."

Simon's lip curled. "It probably means you long to escape your past. How opportune that you are here. Your future will be quite different with me."

She scowled. Her past was quite fine, or had been until a day ago, and she did not intend to stay with this man.

"Was there more to your dream?" he demanded.

"That's all," she replied obstinately.

A booming voice called from the yard. "Simon! Good morrow!"

Vala opened the door to Farley, who smirked in a queer way.

"Good morrow to you, young miss. Is Simon up and about?" The baker removed his floppy felt hat and squeezed past her, a basket on his arm. There was flour in his bushy brown hair. The baker set down his load and removed two small loaves of bread. The loaves, like the baker, were dusted over with flour.

"Simon loves fresh bread, and as he's been feeling poorly, I've been adding a little concoction of my own to the recipe," Farley said with pride. "Meadowsweet and powdered knotgrass," he confided. "It helps to settle the gut and expel worms and the like."

Vala shuddered. She knew the properties of those particular herbs, but there were other, better options. "Back in Wistman's Wood, we use—"

The small man laughed. "Every place has its own remedies, does it not? You'll see, young miss, Simon will recover in a trice." The baker scrutinized Simon. "He's already looking better. Up and about! Perhaps you'll walk to the village this week."

The comment struck her as disingenuous. Never had Vala seen a living man who looked less ready for a walk than Simon Finn Negus.

"Thank you for the bread, my friend," replied Simon.

The baker waved a dismissive hand. "A bit of bread is a small price to pay for your good advice."

Simon's face twisted into a grimace of pain. "You are too kind."

After a few more forced pleasantries, Farley hurried off to his paying customers. Simon stood and watched him go. "He shouldn't be a problem. I trust him. But don't speak to anyone else unless you must. You must say you are my niece, or my whore—as you like."

Vala's mouth dropped open. "A whore? How could you suggest—"

"Don't be a simpleton," Simon rasped with a painful sigh. "This isn't about your virtue; it's about your life. I have many things to tell you—matters of grave importance. You must learn to set aside the small-minded rules you've been taught." He bent over and moaned, then straightened. "Just now, I need rest." He took a small loaf from the table and disappeared behind the curtain.

Oft-dubbed as quick of mind and sharp of tongue, Vala found she was out of her depth in the shadow of her father. She scowled at the filthy drape before stomping out into the yard. Why had he called her here if he meant to treat her with such contempt? What did he want with her? She stared at the hovel, hands on hips. He could rest for now, but tomorrow she'd hear him out and leave. That was firm. Her uncle could ask nothing more. She would walk all the way home if she had to.

The noise of chickens retreating beneath a rotting heap of fallen tree limbs caught her attention. Vala picked her way over the deadfall and found a great dark palfrey tethered inside a sagging lean-to. This horse was completely out of place under the crumbling thatch. He was sleek and well-muscled, with a white tuft of mane falling into his face. He eyed her suspiciously.

"I can't say that I like you, either," she told the horse as she placed some fodder within his reach.

Back inside the cottage, the smell of illness hung heavy in the air. Vala propped the shutters open to let in some fresh air. With little else to do, she made a slow circuit of the room, inspecting whatever dusty oddments she found. On a rickety shelf above the door, two small crocks were oozing something thick and oily. She sniffed bunches of dried herbs and discovered a cracked jar containing a pouch of coins.

Her most interesting find was a hempen sack containing a board and a small leather pouch of stones. The board had a shallow grid carved into its surface, seven squares by seven squares. She took it to the table and emptied the stones on top of it. There were nine white stones and sixteen black ones. The stones were smooth to the touch, probably gathered from a streambed. There was one stone different from the others, a large quartz crystal. Vala arranged the stones on the board and then recalled the game the men at the inn had been playing. It could be the same sort of game, she reckoned.

Vala set it aside and reached for the bread the baker had brought. She broke off a piece. She could ask Simon how to play the game, although he did not seem the sort who would play games. Maybe it had been her brother's. She popped the bread into her mouth and immediately wrinkled her nose. It was mildly acidic and bitter, with the faintest suggestion of ripe fruit. Farley had said he'd baked in some meadowsweet. She sniffed the loaf, and the characteristic scent of the herb was discernable.

She set the bread aside and went to examine a basketful of tanned and rolled skins. Vala selected one, its edges stiff and hard. Upon the cream-colored hide, penned in dark ink, were lines and symbols. Vala rubbed a finger over the ink. Old Father Cyril had taught her to make ink, and she was rather good at it. The priest had remarked that due to her efforts, he had more ink at his disposal than parchment. This ink was probably made from hawthorn bark.

She was studying the line drawings, trying to make sense of them, when she felt Simon beside her.

"Ever see a map before, girl?"

"What is a map?"

"Your uncle has neglected your education."

"Uncle Adrian is the best of men! He taught me to read and write! He taught me everything! He was the perfect *father*." She drove home that final word like an axe into soft wood.

He never flinched, just spread the map on the table. "This shows the lay of the countryside—roads, rivers, seacoasts." His finger traced the darkest ink lines. "Here," he said, pointing to a small symbol similar to a wagon wheel. "This shows the location of a sacred site of worship."

"A church?"

"No, girl, never a church."

With that tiny bit of intelligence delivered, Simon shuffled to his corner behind the curtain, reminding her not to disturb him.

The maps entertained Vala for the remainder of the morning. She pulled each out in turn and examined them, but without known points of reference or names she recognized, she could not tell what they depicted. She replaced the last one in the basket and picked up the little box her uncle had given her. The box proved as obstinate and enigmatic as it had done the first time she had held it. She was unable to see how one might lever it open.

Carvings adorned all the sides and sealed in some ingenious way. As she turned it over in her hands, an object clunked about inside. She replaced the box gingerly on the table, just in case the thing inside was as dangerous as her uncle had warned. It was just one more thing for which she needed an answer.

As darkness fell, Vala ventured outside for firewood. The air was fresh and pleasant after the stifling cottage. As she toted her armload of wood, movement near the corner of the cottage startled her. Vala dropped her burden and took up a single faggot in defense. The bushes rustled as she edged closer.

"Who is it?" she demanded.

Silence met her challenge. She pushed at the overgrown foliage with the stick of firewood. Nothing moved. Vala breathed deep in relief. "Just a squirrel," she assured herself.

The rest of the night was uneventful but for Simon's loose bowels.

The baker came again in the morning, bringing more bread, but Simon did not rise from his bed. When Simon refused to come forth, Vala made an attempt at courteous conversation. "Can you tell me your recipe?" she asked. "What grains do you use, and what herbs?"

"Oh, miss," Farley sputtered. "It's a family secret, my bread." He begged her pardon and left. After his previous verbosity, this seemed unlike him.

"Strange man," Vala muttered as he hurried away.

Later that day, Simon made his way outside to the bushes, moaning and clutching at his stomach. Vala offered to make him broth to settle his gut, but he refused.

"I am only trying to help you recover," she said.

Simon shuddered. "I am improving. This evening, I will explain that which you must know. There is much…" He broke off as a cramp hit him. "Much…to reveal."

Vala knew there would be no revelations until Simon was better, but he looked worse by the hour. She had vowed to leave today but decided she would wait just a bit longer. What harm could it do?

It was a wet, grey evening. As Vala stoked the fire, she heard a rustling outside. Taking up a candle and the fire poker, she strode to the door. Heart pounding, she flung open the door, intending to drive off the offending beast or man.

An old woman, short and plump, was standing on the threshold. "Is Simon here?" she asked.

"He's ill, mother," said Vala, lowering her fire poker.

"Ill? Oh, child, I'm sure you're mistaken. Simon can cure anything from warts to gout." Uninvited, she stepped inside and shuffled to the fire, where she warmed her hands. "Descended from warriors and seers, you know. Explains his gift of prophecy. Don't you agree?"

Vala peered at the little woman, who continued to chatter on without drawing a breath.

"I like to get a reading from Simon several times a year. I think it's good to find out what's coming in the new season. I especially like him to read my palm," she said, extending her hand toward Vala. "There are few men who can read a lifeline correctly, don't you agree? Are you a diviner, too? I've always wished I had the gift! But Simon, my word, what talent!" the woman said with a smile.

It dawned on Vala that her father made his living from fortune telling, and also that the residents of Bridestowe were a garrulous bunch.

The woman prattled on, "Have you ever used his mustard poultice? I use them for my back when I have a damp cough. Tonight, I made one for my husband, but then I received a premonition. I said to my Gordon—Gordon being my husband— I must go see Simon, I said, and he just nodded, as he does. Gordon can't speak, not since the ram kicked him in the throat. Simon cured him completely, all but his voice." She lowered her own voice and winked. "He never said much worth hearing." She gave an impish smile and squeezed Vala's arm. "But where is our Simon?" She scanned the room as though he might be hiding.

"I'm sorry, but he's been quite ill," Vala said again.

The woman's rosy smile changed to concern. "If what you say is true, you must give him warm goat's milk with dandelion or some beet leaf. That will put him right!" She waddled to the door. "I'll be back in a few nights. And remember, goat's milk and beet leaf." With that, she was gone, leaving Vala feeling breathless.

Vala was well-versed in plant medicines, yet she'd never thought of using beet leaves for flux. She set to work and made the concoction as instructed. When Simon staggered out of his miserable corner an hour later, she offered him a cup.

"Did you make this?" he asked, sniffing at it. Before Vala could answer, Simon grasped at his gut and hurried outside, leaving Vala holding the cup. When he returned, he waved the proffered cup away.

"You ought to try something," Vala sniped. "You aren't improving just eating that foul bread." She began to wonder if he would die.

In the darkest hour of the night, Vala woke to the now familiar clatter of Simon staggering into the room. She made to ignore him, but tonight it was different.

"Stand and fight, you dog!" Simon crashed into the wall, eyes wild, waving one arm as though wielding a weapon at an enemy only he could see. "Germain!" he screamed as he stabbed the air. "You sack of horse dung!"

Vala scrambled out of his way as he spun drunkenly around the small room. After he collapsed to the floor, she put a tentative finger to his chest.

"Father?"

Simon swiped weakly at her arm. "Sliced him up—sliced his foul face," he whispered.

"It's all right," soothed Vala. "It's naught but a dream." His skin felt hot. Bleary eyes stared at her. She helped him to his feet, but he wrenched away, staggering back to his bed without further comment.

Vala tipped a log onto the fire. Slumping to the floor, she rubbed the chill from her arms. She watched the embers glow orange and red. It seemed unlikely that her father would ever reveal why he had wanted her to come. He spoke as though he had great mysteries to reveal, but he'd had years to disclose them. Ill as he was, he continued to refuse her help. On the morrow, she would gather her things and leave. She would walk if she had to.

A painful groan broke the silence, waking Vala where she sat dozing. After it subsided, a weak whisper drifted out from behind the curtain. "Girl, come here."

Vala leapt to her feet and took a step backward. She had a sudden, unreasoning fear of what lay behind that grubby curtain.

"Vala, daughter! Obey me!"

Vala took up the dish holding a nub of a candle, then crept to the curtain. A vile smell assailed her as she drew it back. Her father was lying on a low pallet of straw along the wall. She moved toward him, each step more reluctant than the last. His eyes were closed and his face deadly pale. She bent closer, holding her candle over him. A cold hand snatched her wrist, and her candle toppled to the floor where it guttered out. Moonlight streamed through a hole in the roof, lighting her father's face with a ghastly pall.

He pulled her closer. "They will come for me. They will come for you!" he croaked. "They will know. The little box...very, very powerful. Magical." His face was shining with fever. "Yours. It is yours by right. Do not allow them to take it!"

Vala tried to twist out of his grasp. "Who wants it? What's inside it?"

Simon's breath was putrid as he spat out his anxious words. "I've saved it...for you."

Vala yelped as his nails dug into her skin.

"Young Ethan," he gasped. "Find him."

"Who is—"

"Promise me," he rasped, ignoring her queries. "Promise." He licked his cracked lips. "Burn this house once I have died. Leave my body here and burn it." He clenched his teeth and arched up, tightening his grip on her arm. She couldn't wrench it free.

Vala was near tears. "The priests say you should be buried."

"I don't care a whit for babbling priests." He took a shuddering breath. "I ask—I *demand* one thing of you." His eyes were bright, and spittle flecked his chin. "Promise to burn me."

"Yes," she agreed, terrified. "Yes, if that's what you wish."

"Swear it!"

Fear pounding in her chest, she whispered, "I swear."

He spat a glob of dark blood onto the floor, then slumped back on his pillow and shut his eyes. As his claw of a hand went limp, Vala scrambled out through the curtain, rubbing at the red welts rising on her wrist. She watched the curtain the rest of the night, not daring to drift off to sleep in case he was dead—in case he wasn't.

As soon as the first light of morning, dim and pale as a ghost, illuminated the room, she ventured closer. "Father?" she called. "Simon?"

There was no answer, so she steeled herself and brushed back the curtain. He was lying still as stone, eyes open, staring blankly at the ceiling. His skin was grey, his reeking clothes were grey, and the blanket covering his thin, bony frame was grey. It was as though he'd already turned back to dust. She let the curtain fall and staggered outside, where she retched. Fresh air eventually cleared her lungs of the stench of death.

Were her father's final words the ravings of a madman? She didn't know him well enough to judge. If they were true, she was in danger.

"No!" she said into the stillness. "I can't think about this now." Things needed doing. Burning a dead body was a great sin, and a promise to do such a thing could never be taken seriously. She'd go to the village. Someone there would help her lay her father to rest.

As it was, no one in the village wished to help bury Simon Finn Negus.

"I'm sure you are a nice, decent girl," said the old woman who had come to Simon's house just two nights past. She set her basket on the ground and pulled her cloak around herself. "The man was a sorcerer, as of course, you know." She looked left and right, then whispered, "A brilliant one—I shall miss him." Then she straightened. "Folks went to him for maladies they couldn't cure, and readings of the future, but they went by night." The old woman shifted nervously. "The church doesn't hold with the old ways, and these folk want a real priest to come here someday. In truth, Sunday mass would be good for business. My Gordon and I could sell lambs for the twice the price on a market Sunday."

"Don't you think the church would happily send priests if there were people who needed converting?" Vala replied.

The woman picked up her basket. "It's best if you just bury him, lamb, don't you agree? The ground is soft enough this time of the year."

Farley was her father's best friend. Vala decided to try his stall, but it was deserted. Tears of frustration welled in her eyes. Nothing like this would have happened in Wistman's Wood. Neighbors would have rallied around. The body would be 'prepared' by the village women, and the men would dig a proper grave. The priest would come. Her village would not leave the entire task to a young girl.

The weight of the last week crashed down on Vala as she stumbled out behind the market stalls, not bothering to wipe away her tears. Why had her uncle left her with a madman, a man no one wanted to know in the light of day? He must have known the kind of man Simon was. Shaking with anger at the foul situation in which she was trapped, she collapsed under a wide elm tree. The rough old trunk dug into her back. Fields ready for harrowing stretched away to the north. Vala pressed her hand into the earth, which was soft and damp. She could probably dig the grave herself. Her fingers tightened on the handful of dirt. She felt a little sorry for her father, who would not be receiving a proper interment.

Hushed voices interrupted her reverie. Vala sniffed and peered around the tree trunk. Two men had stopped between the stalls, just yards away from where she crouched.

"About them scrapings you've been taking from my wine casks," said a thin man wearing an apron. "All that white powdery stuff."

"Shut up, you fool. I told you I had all I needed. The job is done." It was Farley.

"Well," said the wine seller, "I figure I deserve a share of the profits."

"Profits!" hissed the baker. "There's no *profit*."

The wine seller raised his eyebrow. "I figure it has to do with old Simon and you bringing him bread each day." The wine seller clasped his hand to his chest and simpered, "Oh, no charge to you, Simon. You give me those wonderful predictions!" The man laughed. "Farley, I've known you for too many years. You are against fortune telling and such nonsense. You're kin to that rough-looking monk—"

Quick as a fox, Farley grasped the man's tunic and put his nose inches from the man's face. "There are others in this business, as you've guessed, others who'd pay you with a blade 'crost your useless throat if you speak out of turn."

The thin man shrugged out of Farley's grasp and gave him a sly smile. The baker's eyes darted about before he reached beneath his apron and shoved some coins into his blackmailer's hand.

"Simon's daughter is with him up there." Farley jerked his head toward the copse of trees. "And who can say what she knows or has guessed. Might have to do something about that too. Mind you keep quiet and forget about the scrapings." He spat on the ground at the wine seller's feet and stomped off.

The wine seller chuckled and counted his coins.

Vala huddled behind the tree, praying she would go unnoticed. Farley was responsible for her father's death in some way and was willing to pay off the wine seller to keep him quiet. The business about wine casks and scrapings made no sense, but she now knew who had been making noise outside her father's cottage at night. Perhaps her father had had a good reason to wish the house burned down around him.

Chapter Four:
*"Keep counsel of thyself first."*

Instinct is a powerful thing. Adrian Crofter, known in his old life as Darian Finn Negus, never ignored it. The subtle prickle on the back of his neck put him on alert. He shaded his eyes against the pale spring sun. A messenger bird was coming.

Three neighboring farmers were loitering in his yard, jabbering about the miller's recent demand for a larger portion of grain for his labor. They were deep in their discussion, and he couldn't just shoo them away. He glanced at the barn, then hefted his axe and shifted the helve until the iron head was resting in his palm. There was the very real possibility that if he didn't see to it now, both bird and message would fly away.

Instinct was not a thing to ignore, and therefore Adrian let the axe head slip and the honed edge slice into his palm. Blood oozed forth. His neighbors cried out and offered a barrage of well-meant treatments. Adrian scorned his own clumsiness, excusing himself to see to the wound. Behind him, the men dispersed as Adrian hurried toward the barn in search of something to staunch the wound, along with whatever news awaited him.

Chapter Five:
*"Despair doubles our strength."*

Flames licked the doorway and the windows of the hovel. Vala shielded her face from the rush of heat. After dousing the contents of her father's dwelling with oil and splashing a goodly amount on her father's body, she'd set it all alight. Black smoke billowed above the sagging thatch. Perhaps the townsfolk would come to have a look once the smoke rose high enough.

She thought of saying a prayer for him, but she doubted he would want one. How could she pray for such a vile man, even though a vile deed had felled him? Vala didn't want to cry for him, so she wiped at her damp eyes.

Her pack lay at her feet, and she was keen to flee. Her father had warned that danger was upon her, and she now had good reason to believe him. But there was one more thing to do.

She weighed the cube of carved wood in her hands. Her father had died before enlightening her about the box. It was important to him, but not to her, so it should be an easy thing to pitch it into the flames. She shook it, feeling the familiar rattle, and then raised it over her head, ready to lob it into the conflagration.

What if the fire didn't destroy it?

Vala lowered it again.

What if some unsuspecting soul should pick it up? The box was dangerous— both men had told her so.

She couldn't afford to dither. The smoke would rise, men would come to look, and she had to be away. The blazing fire would surely burn the thing inside. She raised her arm again, but it dropped to her side. Her Uncle Adrian said this box was her birthright. He had saved it for her, whether he believed in it or not. He and her father had protected it for years, and her family for generations. Vala balanced it on her palm. She would take it home and demand that her uncle explain it. There would be time to burn it later.

Scooping up her pack, she shoved the box inside. She fitted it in alongside the pouch of silver, a few apples she'd saved from the larder, and the game board with its sack of polished stones. Without a backward glance, Vala ran to the rickety lean-to that housed her father's horse.

She'd been raised around horses and mules, but never one as spirited as the palfrey her father kept. Still, she did not hesitate. She flung a blanket onto the animal's back, hoisted the leather saddle into place and then tied her satchel to it. After hitching on the leather bridle, she mounted.

She found herself a moment later gasping for breath, lying in a puddle on the ground.

Vala climbed to her feet. The horse eyed her haughtily. She ignored the raw patch on her elbow where it had slammed into the ground and grasped the reins again. The horse reared his head, but she held him with a fierce stare. She was done with this place. She wanted to be gone, and no dumb animal was going to stop her.

As she hoisted herself back into the saddle, she wondered if the fire had frightened the horse. Vala patted its neck to steady it, but the stallion was not soothed. He jumped and bucked, spinning about in an effort to throw her again.

Vala kicked him hard in the sides and felt the obstinate beast shiver down his withers in irritation.

"You may not want to carry me," she said. "But you *will*."

The heat of the burning hovel hit her as they raced past in a wild gallop to the main road. The horse made every effort to dislodge her, but she yanked hard on the reins to assert herself as master. Vala needed her uncle, and this devil's spawn of a horse would take her to him.

She would have liked to avoid the village but there was no other way back to the main road. A small press of women conversing on the green blocked her path. Tense moments passed as they ambled out of her way. Vala fidgeted, her eyes darting to the tree line where dark smoke mushroomed and wafted away on the breeze. It was madness to have burned the house. Soon, someone would notice it—would realize it was more than a cooking fire.

The woman began to shuffle aside when the cry of "Fire!" rose from several directions at once. Men dropped their loads and began to run toward the blaze. There, standing directly in her path, was Farley, the baker, shading his eyes, looking toward the smoke. Vala tried desperately to turn her horse. When Farley looked up at her, his malice washed her in icy terror. Vala lost her head and whipped the horse, who bolted past the old standing stones and out onto the road.

The foul stench of her father's burning corpse clung to her. What was worse, the wooden box bouncing against the horse's flank was the very sort of devilry she'd meant to leave behind. For all she knew, Farley had been waiting for Simon to die so he could steal it. As the horse's hooves pounded along the road, the conversation she had overheard pounded in her head. "Who can say what she knows... Might have to do something about that too..." She glanced over her shoulder, expecting to see a troop of men following her, but the road behind her was empty.

"Calm yourself," Vala whispered, then took a deep breath. Her uncle knew much more than he had told her. When she got home, he would know what to do. "All I have to do is get home in one piece."

Around the next bend, they came to a split in the road. Vala forced the stallion to the south fork. The big palfrey began to buck and neigh in agitation. Frustrated with the high-strung beast, Vala dug her heels into his flanks. He moved tetchily a dozen yards down the road and then came to an abrupt stop. He raised his sleek black head and snorted.

"Wicked beast," Vala hissed.

It took some coaxing to get the horse to obey, but soon they were jogging along the cart path. Heavy grey clouds rolled in, promising rain. At least the road ran straight to Mary Tavy, and Vala was eager to reach the little inn where she would have a safe refuge for the night.

She expected to be pursued, although she couldn't imagine why Farley would do so—except for the box. She put a hand on her pack, then looked up just as the heavens opened and rain pelted down.

The horse splashed through muddy puddles forming in the wagon ruts as the downpour increased to driving curtains of water. The cart path narrowed. Vala had been sleeping during much of the trip to Bridestowe and did not remember the road closing in like this. After a time, the way had winnowed down to a sheep track.

Shivering in her wet wool cloak, water dripping into her eyes, Vala realized she had come the wrong way. The only turn she'd taken was at the split in the road, which meant she had turned south too soon. Vala wondered if the horse had known this was the wrong road when he had balked at the turning.

She couldn't go back, not toward a known enemy. "We have to go east and south," she muttered, squinting out at the terrain through the wild spring deluge. She yanked the horse to the right, and he veered out across a field. They threaded their way through the open country for an hour or so as darkness began to fall. The cold rain, driven by whipping winds, refused to let up. Vala gave the horse his head. Her chilled fingers could do little more than hang on.

A grove of fir trees appeared at the edge of a soggy meadow, and she pulled up hard on the horse's reins. She dismounted and pulled the horse beneath their boughs. He resisted, and she snapped at him, "Well, we can't go on, can we?"

"Stubborn beast," she muttered as she tied the horse to a low-hanging branch. "I need to rest, even if you do not." Vala wrapped her wet cloak tightly around herself and sank down into the relatively dry bed of needles. Rain dribbled through the branches onto stiff fingers as she fumbled in her pack for any comfort it might offer.

She dared not start a fire, for it would smoke significantly, giving away her location. In her pack were a few winter apples. She tossed several to the horse before biting into one herself. The apple skin was wrinkled, but it was sound and sweet. After her meager repast, she curled up on the ground, hoping for a few hours' sleep. The horse pawed at the earth for a few minutes, and then he sank down on his haunches, lowering himself to the ground near her. Vala could feel warmth radiating from his body, and she moved closer to lean against his back.

Her dreams were full of riders chasing her through field and fen. They cornered her, circling their horses around her, and drew long shiny swords. As the blades drew in, closer and closer to her neck, she jerked upright with a gasp. All around her was blackness, but the warm flank of the horse was solid and reassuring. Vala patted the beast and tried to sleep again.

Hours later, groggy from a restless, miserable night, Vala got to her knees. Pale morning was peeking over the tree line. The horse bucked up to his feet, and Vala followed. She was hungry, but she had no more food. She was cold and damp, but there was nothing she could do about that. She patted the horse's neck and combed her fingers through his white forelock. "Things will be better when we reach home," she muttered.

Their progress was slow as they picked their way through woods, streams, and rocky hills. The countryside was rousing itself from winter hibernation, with new green shoots poking up through the dead brown undergrowth of the previous summer. Would that she could enjoy it, but fear hung heavy over the fine spring day. The mysterious box was the cause.

The day brightened as the sun shone in a watery blue sky. With no sign of pursuit, Vala's spirits rose. Before long, they reached a wide, well-traveled road. She hoped it was the one she sought.

They were a bedraggled pair by the time they reached the Grouse and Gorse in Mary Tavy. Vala dismounted and walked the horse around to the stable. She did not see the stableman about, so she led her mount to a stall. He regarded her with a black, penetrating eye and fought her efforts to tether him.

"Please, stop struggling," she said, feeling the soreness of the road. "Look, there are oats to eat, and it's dry." It seemed he did not share her optimism for this place.

Once she'd tied the horse and wiped him down, Vala set off for the inn proper and pulled open the door to the familiar keeping room. It was midday, and the inn was nearly empty of patrons.

"My dear girl!" the innkeeper's wife cried. "Back to see us so soon?" Without awaiting a reply, she ushered Vala to a table. "Some food, lass?"

"Yes, please. And a bed for the night. I put my horse in the stable—"

"We'll see to him. We've plenty of room and a nice mutton pie. Will that do?"

The woman hurried off before Vala could reply, so she simply sat and soaked in the warmth of the fire, the tang of fermenting grains, and the scent of roasting meat. Tension melted away. She was safe.

The promised mutton pie was set before her along with a cup of cider. Vala dug a spoon into the crust and inhaled the herb-scented steam. She lifted a spoonful and blew on it. The flavor was reminiscent of home.

As she ate, Vala noticed the stableman enter. He stopped when he spotted her. She nodded, but he scowled at her and didn't look away. Vala dropped her eyes. What had caused the man to look at her thus? When she glanced again in his direction, he was speaking to the innkeeper's wife, all the while keeping an eye on Vala. The woman shook her head in uninterested dismissal, and the stableman stalked to the door.

A knot formed in the pit of Vala's stomach as she stared at the door. She tried to take another bite of the pie but found she could not. "Mistress," Vala called to the innkeeper's wife. When the goodwife came near, Vala was unsure what to say. "The stableman," she began. "Was he angry I left my horse in the barn?"

"Oh no," the innkeeper's wife said. "Erich has some strange notion that you are a heretic, or a witch, or some such vile thing. He claims someone was looking for a witch. I told him you'd been here just a week ago with your charming uncle. Such a lovely man, your uncle," she continued. "Now, don't you mind him. Erich is just suspicious by nature." She gave a knowing wink.

Vala stabbed at her mutton. She felt queasy. The 'someone' who had spoken to Erich had to be Farley. Who else? She swallowed and looked around the room. The baker could walk in at any time. If he accused her as a heretic or a witch, would the villagers allow him to take her away? The comfortable inn no longer felt like a refuge, but a trap. Vala set aside her spoon and rose slowly. Her damp clothes clung to her as she slipped out the door and bolted for the stable. She stopped long enough to peer through an open window. The stableman was not about, so she made for her horse. He was restless, shifting about and snorting.

"Not happy here?" she whispered. He whinnied and stomped his feet. "I agree," she replied, untying him and pulling him from the stall.

"Good horse, that," a voice growled. Erich had been waiting in the dusty shadows.

"He is," Vala mumbled, keeping her head down and leading the horse past him.

The stableman stepped to block her way. "A man came here yesterday. He said you were wanted by the Church."

"The man you spoke to killed my father and wants me dead," she replied.

"Witches ought to die," Erich grunted. "He offered silver for information—more if I seized you."

Vala pressed back against the horse's bulk. She daren't scream. The possibility of a reward might tempt others, making her plight worse.

Erich made a grab for her just as the horse's huge head snapped around. He bit the stableman hard on the arm, and the man yelped, stumbling backward. Having created the needed diversion, the stallion trotted into the yard with Vala close behind.

The bleeding stableman let fly a string of curses, but Vala had thrown herself into the saddle and was galloping for the road. As they splashed through muddy water standing in the wagon ruts, she tried to decide what to do next. She knew they should leave the road to avoid capture, but she was loath to do so. It would slow them down, and she was desperate to get home.

With a muttered curse, she veered off the road to the east. Vala's panic, combined with her lack of knowledge of this countryside, soon conspired to get them well and truly lost.

"Yes, we're lost," she told the horse with a sigh. He didn't offer a helpful flick of the tail to point the way.

Vala gave a laugh. "I should at least give you a name, horse." She gave it a moment's thought before saying, "Thistle!"

The horse snorted.

"No, it suits you," Vala said. "You're beautiful, but prickly." She patted his neck, and this time, he didn't attempt to bite her.

Chapter Six:
*"Common sense is not so common."*

There was no way know how far south she needed to go, or how far west. Vala felt foolish as they picked their way through tall bracken and around treacherous bogs that dotted the landscape. It had only taken her uncle two days to reach Bridestowe in their slow-rolling cart. She was already two days out, with a good horse, and not likely to reach Wistman's Wood before dark.

Within an hour, Vala had dismounted and was leading Thistle on foot. Peat bogs were tricky. Some of them floated over underground streams or ponds, and the unsuspecting who put a foot wrong could sink beneath the surface with frightening speed. She didn't want to risk the horse to a misstep, but it was slow and soggy going. The horse cropped grasses, his jaws grinding at the tough vegetation, while Vala longed for the hot mutton pie she had spurned at the inn.

They reached firmer ground as evening settled. Vala's legs were weak from miles of hiking through the mossy wetness. She was just about to mount up again when she put a foot wrong, into a sludgy hole that sucked her leg in up to the knee. Vala fell back onto the solid path with a gasp. She tried pulling her leg from the sucking mud with little success. Tears filled her eyes as she struggled. The horse bent his head over her, and Vala grasped the proffered reins. Thistle began to back up slowly. Vala wrapped the reins securely around her arm, letting the horse drag her free.

Vala considered the beast as she stripped the icy muck from her leg. "Good horse," she said. Thistle tossed his head, and Vala laughed.

It was full dark when they struck the road. Luckily, the sky had cleared, and the moon rode high. Vala knew the landscape and the familiar valley which rolled down toward her village. Soon, she'd see her uncle. He would comfort her and explain the wooden box. There would be a hot meal and a familiar bed. Excitement replaced fear as she spurred the horse toward home.

Going through the village was the fastest way home, but she was riding a strange horse. If she met someone, which was likely, what story would she give? As Vala considered her options, Thistle jerked to a halt and refused to move. "Now, why have you stopped?" she hissed. Thistle snuffled the air, his head high. Smoke was floating in the air, but not the smoke of chimney fires. This was heavy and acrid.

Vala slid from the saddle and ran full-out toward the village. This amount of smoke meant something large was afire. Rounding the bend, she saw the cause of the smoke. The miller's house was a mass of orange and red devouring flames. Villagers were frantically dumping buckets of water upon the conflagration. Flames leapt high into the air, and burning wisps of thatch floated on the breeze, threatening to set other homes alight. Fire was one of the greatest fears the village faced, for it could consume years of building or an entire season's harvest in minutes.

Shouts and sweating faces showed the effort the village men were expending to save the house and the grist mill. Nick Thatcher was raking burning bits away from the building and stomping out the glowing embers. Oswald Tailor cradled a bleeding arm but was yelling at the others to keep up the pace, moving buckets from the millstream to the blaze. The mill wheel was still turning, water spilling into the stream unaware of its imminent danger.

Smoke rose from a cottage downwind of the flames. The thatch was smoldering, and a gang of the younger boys heaved water onto its roof. The blacksmith's house was nothing but charred wreckage. Stephen's father was sitting, head in hands, in the midst of smoking timbers and broken bits of household goods.

The elderly women were huddled together in the dark, praying loudly and crossing themselves. Younger women beat out hot embers while siblings held back crying toddlers. Some pigs and chickens had gotten loose during the panic and were running about, adding their voices to the confusion. Father Wulford hurried amongst the villagers, urging them to the church to seek comfort in God. He would probably lay the blame for this tragedy upon them and their sinful ways.

Wulford stopped beside a distraught young woman and pulled her away, patting her back in a comforting manner. This kindly action left Vala with a tiny pang of guilt for her unkind thoughts. In the glow of the fire, she saw the girl's silhouette. It was Tessie.

"Lass, what are you doing here?" barked a gruff voice. Gilbert Wright, the town's carpenter, flanked by Robert Gallows, pulled a cartload of new timbers up beside her. The carpenter was huffing and puffing as he and Robert eased the yoke to the ground.

"I've been—" Vala began, trying to invent a plausible story.

"Good thing ya missed this," Gilbert said, waving a hand at the village.

"Good thing the robbers didn't set your house alight, what with Adrian off to the market in Dartmeet," said Robert. "I thought you went with him, girl."

"Well, I—" Vala said, then stopped. "He went to Dartmeet?"

Gilbert cut in, "Those damned robbers! They lit up the smithy and the mill when they couldn't find who they were after."

"What do you mean? What robbers?"

Robert wiped his forehead with his sleeve. "Six men on horseback. They came riding down the road and started calling for 'the cursed spawn of Simon Finn Negus'." He looked to Gilbert for confirmation. Gilbert nodded.

"Finn Negus?" Vala felt as though she'd been punched hard in the stomach.

"Young Stephen says to them loud and clear, 'There's no one here of that name. Now, get you gone!'" Gilbert spat on the ground, black gritty spittle. "The leader didn't like it, though."

"Nasty bit of work. Great gash on his face," said Robert, drawing his finger from his own eye down along his jawbone. "His men grabbed Stephen, and when no one could answer, they knocked the boy on the head!"

Gilbert chided his companion, "This child was near to marrying Stephen herself until he wed Thatcher's girl."

Robert gave an uncomfortable shrug. "You'll find another lad, Vala."

Gilbert nodded his agreement, and then he pointed toward the easterly road. "We all grabbed our spades and rushed 'em, but the scum set the mill alight."

"It was nothing but pure mean spite!" Robert replied in agitation. "We pulled one of them from his horse, and Stephen's father took his revenge."

"We gotta get these timbers down to the mill before the far side caves in." Gilbert took up the yoke and strained against the bar.

"Wait!" cried Vala. "What happened to Stephen?"

"Were you not listening, lass? His body is there—where he fell." Gilbert put his own weight into the yoke and began to push.

In the center of the road near the well, she could see a lump with a blanket thrown over it.

"Killed?" she whispered, finding it hard to draw breath.

"Killed dead!" Robert said without a backward glance.

The finality of it rang in her ears, and she felt she would retch. The riders had come here looking for her and her uncle, and when their search proved fruitless, they'd murdered Stephen.

Vala stumbled toward the church as the riot of voices began to die down. The fire was losing to the village folk. In the road was a body with an iron poker through its neck. Vala would have been glad if it had been Farley. She would have given the body a second impalement herself, but the bloody face was unknown to her. The other body was Stephen.

Vala stepped away and hurried for the church. She found Tessie inside the cool darkness, seated on the altar's step, rocking back and forth. Her eyes were blank. Vala sank down to the floor next to the very pregnant girl and put an arm around her. "Tessie?" Vala whispered through her own tears. "Speak to me, Tessie." The rocking continued. "Tessie!"

"I am pleased you harbor no ill will for this child. She needs our prayers," said Father Wulford from the shadows. "Just five days wed," he sighed.

It was a shock that Stephen and Tessie had wed, but hardly as much as Stephen lying dead.

The church door burst open, and Tessie's relatives surged in. They surrounded the girl, speaking comforting words as they shepherded the young widow outside. Shame and guilt rooted Vala to the spot. It was her fault that Stephen had died. The burning of the village was her fault. Her legs had gone weak, and she clutched at the wall for support. "The men who did this. Who were they?"

Father Wulford fingered the crucifix at his neck. "I do not know, child. It all happened so quickly. I didn't see the devils. Of course, God sets us tests, and we must show our faith."

This was no punishment from God. The riders were seeking her and the box. She was sure of it. Vala looked at the priest and felt an intense pressure to unburden herself and confess. Could there be absolution for the stain of being a child of Simon Finn Negus, for burning him in his house, for somehow bringing death and destruction down on her own village? Vala tried to speak, but no words came forth. Instead, she pulled a coin from her pouch. The silver gleamed as it dropped into the priest's hand. "A mass for Stephen," she muttered before fleeing.

The only thing to do was to find her uncle. He was sure to know how to stop all this. If she acted quickly, perhaps no one else would die.

Chapter Seven:
*"Give the devil his due."*

"How can we have lost the wench?" growled a man who lurched around the fire with long, determined strides. He glowered toward a heavy little man who was fiddling with his pack.

The little man blinked stupidly. "She is clever, that one. Why, back in Bridestowe..."

"We lost her, and those stinking peasants killed one of ours, you blathering idiot!"

All the men went silent as their leader spun toward them.

"Tomorrow, you two go back north," he said, pointing at the upturned faces. He turned toward the new recruit. "You will go with me."

"I would wager the wench is dead," the young recruit offered, scratching at his sparse beard. "A woman on the road, alone?" He looked to his fellows for confirmation.

The other men hunched in silence, eyes avoiding their unfortunate companion.

Two quick steps and the leader had the youth by the throat. "Remind me what your name is, boy."

The young man croaked out, "Roman."

"Roman, do you recall the story of your patron saint?"

Young Roman seemed unsure if he ought to reply.

"He had his tongue cut out!" snarled the leader. "If you do not wish the same, keep your thoughts to yourself."

The youth swallowed hard while the others edged farther away.

Their leader spun to the fire. "I'll go to Exeter alone. Caspian, take this pup with you. He annoys me."

"And where should I go?" asked the plump man.

"Go to the devil, Farley."

Chapter Eight:
*"It is an equal failing to trust everybody and to trust nobody."*


Vala raced back for Thistle. If Farley's gang of thugs discovered that Adrian Crofter was really Darian Finn Negus, they'd kill him. She had to find her uncle before they did.

"We can't go through the village," she told the horse as she scrambled up onto his back. "Too many eyes about. And Stephen..." Vala bit her lip. He was lying bloody and broken in the dust. She wiped her eyes on her sleeve. Now was not the time to break down.

She steered Thistle around the far side of the woods. Even in the dark, Vala was able to find the edge of her uncle's field. She tied the stallion under the trees and hurried to the cottage. Robert had told her that Adrian had gone to Dartmeet, but he rarely stayed away overnight, preferring to return to his own bed.

"Uncle?" she called, pushing the door open.

It was dark as pitch inside, so Vala had to grope her way to the fireplace. Though she knew the room by heart, she suddenly found herself sprawled on the floor. Vala got painfully to her knees and felt around. The table and stools were up-ended. She scuttled to the hearth and managed to ignite a small rushlight. The wooden blanket chest stood open, its contents strewn about the room; the kettle and the cooking pans were lying in the middle of the floor. This was not the act of a common thief, for nothing seemed to be missing. Her stomach twisted into a knot as she realized *they* had done this—Farley and his lot.

Vala prayed her uncle's absence meant he was still in Dartmeet. She quickly righted the room. Her fondest desire was to start a roaring fire in the familiar hearth and settle down in front of it, but that would be foolhardy with the riders about. For tonight, it would be another night outside in the cold. She took a wedge of cheese and some limp carrots from the larder and wrapped them in a blanket. Then she ran back to Thistle. The palfrey allowed her to rub his neck.

She sighed, pressing her cheek against him, then offered him a carrot. Once he had enjoyed his treat, Vala walked him along the familiar path toward the only place no one would come or look for them—at least after dark.

A patch of tender young crocuses surrounded the huge standing stone. Vala eyed the monolith, cold and silent. She prayed that the rumors of demons hunting for victims in the woods were no more than children's stories as she led Thistle deeper into the woods to find a place to sleep.

Sunlight filtering through the hulking arch of branches stabbed her eyes. Vala moaned, straightening up. Her back ached from the tree root she'd lain on all night. Her clothes were damp, leaves sticking to her skirts. Thistle, however, seemed primed to travel.

The road to Dartmeet was familiar to her, and under normal circumstances, riding such a fine horse on such a day would be a treat. But with fingers tightly knotted in the reins and eyes constantly scanning the road ahead and behind, Vala barely marked the gentle spring air or clear blue skies.

After a few hours, the village of Dartmeet appeared around a bend in the road, and relief flooded through her. Soon, she would find her uncle, and all would be explained.

The marketplace was full of sound: clucking chickens, children's squeals, tinkling bells and braying mules. Carts crowded the road as men hurried about loading sacks, stone crocks, or livestock they'd bartered for. Women called from stall to stall, and colored fabrics flapped in the breeze. Vala loved the bustle of the market town and eagerly waded into the throng, moving from stall to stall in search of her uncle. When she was unsuccessful, she tried the public house. The innkeeper listened patiently, scratching his scruffy beard. He'd not had a patron of Adrian's description during the last few days.

She traipsed the length of the market once again with a growing knot of anxiety twisting her gut. The merchants and customers hadn't much patience for her queries. By the time she'd interrogated the woman tending the last stall, she was frantic.

Vala searched for a vantage point above the thinning crowd. The village church sat upon a little rise, so she hurried toward it. From its stone steps, she could view the entire throng, but he simply was not here. Needing a quiet place to think, Vala turned and pushed the door open,

Much like the church back home, this one had a small open nave with shuttered window slits and a small altar draped in a white linen cloth. Candles were burning on wooden stands in the corners. Dried lavender mingled with the rushes on the floor, scenting the musty air. Vala walked to the wooden railing stretching between nave and altar and fell to her knees. She clasped her hands together and began to sob.

The sound of a creaking wooden door roused Vala from her misery. Through wet eyes, she watched a figure approach.

"Can I help you, child?" The man bent to help her stand, and the wooden cross at his waist grazed the floor.

"Thank you, Father," she muttered.

"Tell me what is distressing you, daughter."

"It's my uncle," Vala began. "I must find him, but no one has noticed him, and I *need* him."

"Tell me about this uncle. Perhaps I can help."

Vala took a shaky breath and, for the hundredth time that day, began to describe her uncle. As she spoke, the priest's brow wrinkled. "Was he wearing a brown hat with a wide brim, stitched around with leather?"

"He has a hat like that," Vala replied hopefully.

"Come with me, child." The priest rose and led Vala outside, across a rough yard, to a small house set back against the trees. As he opened the door, he said, "Three nights ago, a traveler brought a body to me for burial. He'd found a man along the road with a broken neck. We believe that horse threw his master. The horse broke a leg and had to be killed."

The priest retrieved a small bundle and handed it over. Vala shook her head, unwilling to accept this blunt end to her search.

"I saved his things in case someone should come looking for him." The priest pressed them into Vala's arms.

With trembling fingers, she unrolled the saddle blanket. It was the one Adrian had cut from a sheepskin. Inside was a worn bridle similar to the one her uncle used. However, it was the hat that brought her low. She ran her fingers over the patched edge along the brim. She remembered how she'd used black thread to mend it. She fingered that thread. If her throat had not been so tight with anguish, she would have been screaming. The priest helped her to a stool and patted her back as she gave in to overwhelming grief.

"Where is he now?' she asked when no more tears would come.

"I buried him in the graveyard behind the church. Would you like to see?"

Vala nodded and followed the priest out into the late afternoon sun.

The graves were marked with small cairns of stones. The priest stopped next to a freshly turned mound, her uncle's final resting place.

"His name was Adrian Crofter." As the words left her lips, she recalled his real name was Darian. Should she tell the priest? Did it matter? After staring at the mound for some time, Vala said quietly, "I don't know what to do."

"There is nothing to do, my child, but to pray for his soul," replied the priest.

With a movement honed by years of repetition, she dropped to her knees, clasped her hands together, shut her eyes and began to pray. Beside her, she knew the priest was kneeling too. She couldn't imagine the world without her uncle—his laugh and his voice. It was too much to take in. She prayed fervently that God would look kindly upon the man who had raised her—the best man she'd ever known.

"Father, you've been very kind. May I ask you something... something important?"

"Certainly, my child."

The priest assisted her to her feet and then stood quietly next to her. Vala stared out across the valley, where green was beginning to replace the dull grey of winter. "If someone had an item that might be magical, where should it be taken—so that it could be examined?"

"Magical?" He crossed himself. "Do you mean something cursed, something which demons have possessed?"

Vala's brow knitted. She hadn't thought of the box as cursed, but more in the line of something that might be turned to an evil purpose, like a poison.

"Is magic always evil?"

The priest's face flushed. "We are taught that magic is an abomination of God's holy miracles. Magic is the devil's attempt to mimic the power of God to lead man astray."

His explanation accounted for both her uncle's concern and her father's warnings.

"Do you have this object?" he asked.

Vala nodded.

"And you believe it is cursed?" he asked.

"There are men who will kill for it," said Vala.

"Men will kill for things other than magic, child. However, if it is truly cursed, we might burn it."

She could have left the box to burn with her father's body. She had taken it because she thought her uncle would explain it. Now, she had no trusted ally or safe haven, but instead of fearfulness, she was aflame with a reckless urge for answers.

"I don't wish to destroy it without knowing if it needs destroying." She was sure her words made her sound foolish and contrary. "Is there someone who could tell the difference, someone who might advise me? If necessary, destroy it properly, so it could never hurt anyone?"

The priest's brow furrowed. "I do not know the answer, my child."

She could sense the man was out of his depth. A few moments passed before he spoke again.

"The bishop, the one called De Roche, is at Bath, by papal command. He is a learned man who may know of such things. A pilgrimage to Bath would show God your faith, and it would be a tribute to your uncle."

Vala had not thought of making a pilgrimage. Her choices were to give up and ride home or take the box and her tale to Bath.

"If you go, Exeter is your next stop. From there, you go north another few days' ride." The priest put a hand on her shoulder. "It is a hard and dangerous road. Men of the road prey on travelers."

This priest had no idea how dangerous the road would be. The trip was doubly treacherous for her because the men who had burned her village were still about, but she couldn't risk going back and bringing more destruction down on her village.

"It would be better to burn the thing now rather than risk it," said the priest.

Vala lowered her eyes. "Father, you've been most kind. Thank you for your advice."

The priest allowed her to spend the night on the floor of the church. Early the next morning, Vala paid a visit to her uncle's grave. She gave the priest several silver coins to pray for Uncle Adrian's soul.

Before she mounted up, Vala pulled her uncle's old hat from her pack and held it to her face for a moment. It held the woodsy, musty smell of him. Grief, if she allowed it, would immobilize her, so she whispered, "Fortune favors the brave, Uncle." She would seek out this bishop and hope to the heavens that it would not mean her doom.

The road was good, running straight and level for miles. The steady rolling gait of the horse settled Vala. If her funds held out, and if she met folk along the road who could direct her, the journey shouldn't prove too difficult. The sun appeared through an opening in the clouds and shed a warm, welcome light on the countryside, chasing away some of the dark thoughts of her father's putrid body, her dead uncle, and of young Stephen, face-down in the road.

When evening fell, Vala settled into a hollow beneath a hillock. She fed carrots to Thistle and dined on the cheese she'd brought from home in front of a small blaze. Perhaps a fire was a mistake, but she needed a little warmth. Before lighting the bits of dry sedge and sticks, she'd watched the road for nearly an hour. No one appeared from either direction. Thistle stood, head bowed, one back leg drawn up in sleep. The horse had relaxed, and that alone should have allayed her fears, but when she finally drifted off to sleep, nightmare fiends wielding knives hunted her.

Vala crawled out from under her blanket as rosy morning light streaked the sky. She found herself whole and unscathed. It was a hopeful sign. Perhaps she'd made a wise choice.

The day's ride was uneventful. Vala encountered small groups of travelers but kept to herself. Thistle was happy to trot past any wayfarers with his head held high. It was for the best, for those close to her were dying at an alarming rate.

Vala pictured Exeter as a large, neat, and well-ordered village, but it was nothing like her imaginings. Exeter was a city. Buildings crowded together and perched at odd angles and a powerful stench assailed her. She pulled her cloak up over her mouth and even Thistle's nostrils twitched. The streets were a repository for all manner of offal. In her own village, the folk fed the leavings from meals to their livestock, while waste went to fertilize the fields. They discarded little, unlike these folk.

The streets were chaotic. Children darted between wagons, horses, and people. Smoke twirled from chimneys, adding sharpness to the sour smell in the air.

"Fresh butter, honey, goat's milk!" an old gamble-eyed crone sang from a ramshackle stall. A horde of flies buzzed was buzzing about, walking in the butter and thickly crowning the lip of the open crock of goat's milk. No one was bothering to shoo them away.

Vala hailed a man idling next to a smith's forge. "Excuse me, sir. Is there an inn nearby?" She was bone-tired from four days on the road, and the little bit of afternoon light remaining would not take her much farther.

The man cocked his eyebrow and then sauntered over and put a grubby hand on Thistle's mane. "Maybe so, maybe so." He patted her horse. "The closest is The Bard, over yonder." He waved his thick-fingered hand toward the east. "Got cheap ale, but the food is slop." He squinted at her. "You don't look the sort as would go there." He picked something from his teeth with a blackened fingernail, then spat. "The Bard's got rats aplenty."

Vala grimaced.

"Then there's The Ram's Horn," he said with emphasis. "A bit cleaner, but the old hag who runs it is a thief. She's cheated me out of a few coins in my time. Mostly when I was in my cups." He winked.

Vala didn't intend to become drunk, so it seemed the better of the two choices.

The man pointed ahead. "The Ram is down this lane. Turn by the fishmonger's stall."

Vala nodded her thanks.

A weathered sign showing a ram's head on a pike swung over a wooden gate. Inside was a small dirt courtyard. A single dusty horse was tied to a ring in the wall. The inn itself was a dismal affair, and Vala wondered how much worse The Bard could be. She dismounted and tethered Thistle next to the other horse.

A young man with a grease-stained tunic stretched over a chubby belly lounged in the shade of a hay wagon. He eyed her dully as she approached the inn's door, whose door handle was a ram's horn tied on with jute. Before she could enter, a small, bony woman came roaring out, nearly knocking Vala flat. Her glare was frightening, her tongue was sharper still, and she used it to fill the courtyard with ringing curses.

"Will Planke! Where are you, you great lump?" she bellowed. "Get the water now, or I'll rip out your liver!" With much screeching and whacking from her stick, she chased her servant from the hay wagon and sent him off to his chores.

Vala slipped inside the inn, shutting out the commotion. The common room was a dark and dank disappointment, smelling of stale mead and sooty smoke. The hearth was cold, with no promise of a hot meal. A small pig snuffled in the debris on the floor, munching old apple cores.

The wrinkled old woman came grumbling through the door and stopped, fixing Vala with a scowl. "We ain't hiring any maids." She pulled an old shawl tight about her shoulders.

"I'm not looking for a position. I wanted a meal and a bed for the night."

The woman's face changed immediately, as did her attitude. "So sorry, my dear. We don't often get such pretty young guests here. Please, come in, come in!" The old crone patted down her apron, sending a dusty cloud into the air. "You are free to sleep anywhere in the common room. There are blankets by the fire. Just the one night, then?" the proprietress asked. "Because I charge a silver coin a night."

When Vala raised no objection, the woman continued, "Is that your horse outside? Because it's another coin to stable the horse."

Vala had no idea what proper payment was for a night in an inn. She had a goodly sack of coins, but this room was full of cobwebs, and the blankets were so filthy, she would not have used them for the horse. She was unsure what to do.

"It's not very—" Vala was about to say 'clean'.

The old woman cut in quickly. "I have better accommodations just down here, miss. How silly of me! A well-bred girl like yourself wants the best." The woman led her toward small alcove, curtained off from the main room. It had a pallet in the corner, more comfortable than the floor. Hoping to seal the deal, the woman added, "I'll have some hot water brought in for you. How will that be? And I'll have fresh rushes put down."

"I'll just get my things," Vala sighed and turned for the door. Behind her, the innkeeper screeched for her harassed servant, Will.

The sun had disappeared behind a mass of huddled buildings, bathing the courtyard in long shadows. The serving boy, ignoring his mistress's shouts, was lingering over-long at lighting a torch outside the door. He doffed his hat to Vala, fumbled it, and then disappeared inside.

A few scruffy-looking boys were loitering near the gate, and a nervous Thistle was stomping his feet. Vala stroked the horse. "It's just one night," she murmured.

With a reluctant glance at the inn, she unknotted the sack in which she'd stowed her extra clothing and set it on the ground. The leather pack containing the box was harder to undo. Vala dropped her money pouch next to the sack and worked at the tight leather thong. The sound of running feet caused her to look up. One of the boys bowled into her, shoving her toward the wall. He snatched her sack from the ground, but Vala lunged forward and managed to get hold of one corner.

"Thief! Thief!" she shrieked as they tussled for control. With a loud rip, her belongings scattered over the ground. The boy stumbled backward as his partner joined the fray. With a blow that hit true, Vala's ear exploded in pain, and she crumpled to her knees. Kicking out hard, she connected with the first boy's leg. He cursed as Vala scrambled to save her silver, but not before he spied her money pouch and dove for it.

The second boy deftly snatched up her things while the first wrestled with Vala over the money pouch. Vala bit his hand as his knee ground into her side.

"Help me, someone!" she screamed in pain and exasperation.

Vala rolled and groped wildly for her pouch. Then she had it! She could feel the coins through the leather. The thieving boy tried to pry her fingers off. She resisted, even though his fingernails were digging mercilessly into her skin. Coins spilled into the dirt, dribbling past the drawstring. The boy released his hold on Vala, seizing as many as he could rake together.

"You there! Stop!" Will was waddling toward the melee.

"Run!" one of the boys cried.

The two young rogues scrambled to escape, but Thistle saw his opening and kicked out with his hind legs, knocking the first boy to the ground. Vala staggered to her feet and gave chase. The boys dashed through the gate, one cursing and clutching her clothes, the other laughing over a fistful of her silver. By the time she reached the gate, they had disappeared into the shadowy labyrinth of streets and alleys.

"Oh, my! Oh, my!" the old innkeeper croaked, hobbling into the yard.

Will reached Vala, huffing too hard to pursue.

"Did those nasty beasts rob you, girl?" The old woman had the air of a merchant afraid she'd lost a customer.

"They took my clothes and money." She stalked back to the spot of the attack and began searching the ground for any remains the thieves had left behind. There were a few coins scattered on the ground among the shreds of her clothing sack. A handkerchief, a shawl...that was all.

The side of Vala's face was stiff and painful. She wiggled her jaw back and forth, testing if it was broken. Then she remembered the wooden box. The leather satchel remained securely tied to Thistle's saddle. Vala removed it, wondering if luck was with or against her.

The old woman eyed the remaining coins in Vala's hand with a certain amount of relief. "Let Will take care of your horse, my dear, and come inside. You need a cup of barley water, or perhaps something stronger."

Vala limped along behind the innkeeper. Once inside, she dumped her remaining possessions on a table and sat. Her hands were scratched and dirty, and she wiped them on her torn skirt. She spread out the coins she had rescued and counted them. Only eleven remained from a much larger hoard.

The innkeeper brought her a wooden trencher of thin soup, some stale bread, and a small cup of mead. The trencher had bits of dried food stuck to the edges, but Vala was too hungry and exhausted to care. She wondered what sort of fare Thistle had received. She owed him a nice apple for the kick he had administered to the young thief.

While she ate, several men trailed in, ordering up ale. After finishing the bland soup, Vala hobbled off to the relative privacy of the sleeping alcove. Eyes followed her, and she realized that unmarried, unchaperoned girls did not visit inns alone. It occurred to her that this would make her more memorable if someone asked after her. It was a very foolish mistake.

Lowering herself to the sleeping pallet, she rubbed her temples. She'd have to get cannier, or such errors would mean her death. Vala examined the great purple bruise on her shin. Just a little rest, she decided, then she would leave. If she got away soon, in the dark, perhaps it would not matter that she'd made such a clear target of herself. A little nap couldn't hurt, though. She was so very tired. She laid her head down, and she was asleep in moments.

Vala awoke with a start and clambered to her feet, still sore from her battle with the thieves. To her dismay, it was fully daylight. She splashed water on her face and shoved her remaining possessions into the leather satchel. If the men who had fired her village had trailed her here, she needed to be gone.

The old woman sidled in. "Girl, why are you traveling alone?"

Vala balked at the question she didn't wish to answer. "I'm not alone," she lied. "I'm... meeting my family."

The old woman sucked her lips over her rotting teeth, "I'm no fool, girl. If you're running from a bad husband or a master who beats you, you must know traveling this way is dangerous. Those boys last evening are nothing to the men out upon the road."

Vala's telltale flush told the old woman all she needed to know. "There's nothing I can do about that," she snapped. "I have to go to Bath. Can you direct me to the right road?"

"I can tell you the way, but why not avoid trouble altogether?"

"What do you mean?"

"A disguise, girl! You need to appear to be someone less easy to overpower."

Vala frowned.

"If you were to dress as a boy, no one would bother you. As a woman, you make an easy target."

Vala spread her skirts. "I have only these clothes."

"I have some old things that I could let you have, for, say, two silver pieces. It might save your pretty neck," the old crone cackled.

Vala blinked. It was a reasonable idea. She reckoned her silver would do her no good if she were dead in some roadway ditch. "May I see the clothes?"

The old woman grinned and hurried off. She returned with a pair of rough-knit leggings, a large shirt, an overtunic with a hood, a jerkin of a heavy fabric and a battered cloak. She dumped these on the floor and added a pair of boots nearly worn through at the soles. The entire lot hadn't been washed in an age.

"Try them on," urged the old woman. "I'll help you tie up your hair."

Vala cinched the overly large leggings around her waist with a cord. The old woman produced a length of cloth which she instructed Vala to wrap tightly around her bosom to hide her female traits. By the time Vala had donned the shirt, tunic, and jerkin, the old woman was exclaiming rapturously how unlike a girl she appeared. Vala topped off her disguise by pulling her uncle's old hat over the hood, which helped to hide her face. The effect was good.

After some haggling, the old woman agreed to take one silver coin and Vala's dress in trade. Even though her kirtle and tunic were homespun, Vala knew it was a bad bargain. She scratched at the leggings and hoped they were not flea-ridden.

The transaction complete, Vala stowed her small knife in her belt, hefted her satchel and strolled into the common room, affecting an exaggerated swagger. She was pleased to note that none of the patrons gave her a second glance. She went looking for Thistle.

Will was cleaning the stables as she entered.

"I'll take my horse, boy," she said in a demanding tone.

"But, sir, you don't look a bit like the person what owns this horse," said Will, stiffly standing his ground.

She patted Thistle's rump. "A good beast!"

Will flapped his arms like a disturbed goose. "Sir, you cannot take that horse." The boy's words turned to a yelp as he stepped into a bucket and fell spectacularly.

"You met me yesterday," Vala laughed, pulling the stable boy to his feet.

Will squinted. "I'd'a recalled meeting you, sir."

Vala was about to reveal her face when the old woman stormed in.

"There you are, Will. Take this lass to the north road, and then get back here double quick. Do you understand?"

Will looked, if possible, more confused. He touched the brim of his cap as Vala mounted and then led the way through a few winding streets until they reached one of the main roadways.

"This here road will take you to Bath, good sir, or miss," Will panted.

"Thank you," Vala replied, tossing him one of her precious coins. She was feeling quite generous and confident, swathed in her new disguise.

"Thank you, mistress, or—" he bumbled, doffing his hat in a fluster.

Vala grinned and coaxed Thistle into a gallop, her goal near enough to taste.

As Will waddled back toward the inn, rubbing the coin between his fingers and thinking of all the hot meat pies it would buy, a man wrapped in a long black cloak approached him. After they had exchanged a few words, the man vanished down an alleyway, leaving Will looking confused once again.

Chapter Nine:
*"A smooth sea never made a skilled mariner."*


Bright white moonlight filtered through the overhanging trees, casting a ghostly pall upon the narrow road. Bright eyes winked from the underbrush, but the passing horseman was too weary to care if it was rabbit or wolf. Even the monk's horse did not shy away from the sudden rustling in the verge but kept plodding doggedly forward.

Brother Phillip had been traveling this accursed river road since before dawn. The shadowy river bent away to the right as though it would go on forever. He sighed and decided to look out for a spot to camp. At this pace, he would never reach Hemyoch tomorrow, and after that, he had another village on his list. Brother Cuthred, the abbot at Glastonbury, always grew agitated when Phillip was late in returning from these assignments. Phillip thought of Glastonbury as home or the nearest thing to it. However, home and hearth had to wait. His Excellency the Bishop was his true superior, not Brother Cuthred, and the bishop was a demanding man. Far from being vexed, Phillip counted himself blessed for the opportunities the great man provided.

"Lord, if it be your will, grant your servant patience," he prayed. Phillip was not blind to his own faults.

A muffled shout ended Brother Phillip's musings, and he yanked up hard on the reins. Shadowy figures were grappling at the river's edge. One of them raised an arm, and something glinted in the moonlight.

"Stop there!" Brother Phillip roared as the pair pitched into the water. He spurred his horse down the incline, through a gap in the dense thicket and toward the river. A hulking form, black against the eddying stream, was bending over the other figure.

"Stop at once!" bellowed Phillip, leaping from his horse and pulling a short, thick staff from his travel sack. Without fear, he ran toward the fray. The good brother, normally a man of peace, was not a stranger to defending himself.

"In the name of Our Lord, stand back, villain!"

The ruffian stumbled from the water, dodging Phillip as he sprinted toward a steed standing ghost-like near the trees. The man flung himself into the saddle and drove his horse toward the road. Phillip could hear the pounding of hooves as the thief vanished into the night.

There was no time to pursue the scoundrel with his victim's body sliding into the black river water. Phillip flung aside his stave and splashed into the river, soaking the bottom of his robes and filling his boots with chill water. He heaved the lifeless body to the shore, surprised to find it was a youth, thin and light. The monk did not hold out much hope for the poor wretch. Bandits were notorious for leaving few survivors.

The youth had made a small camp with a meager fire, more smoke than flame. Phillip suspected the villain had intended robbery as he hauled his patient toward the dim flicker. A great black stallion tethered to a tree stomped the ground, whinnying and pulling his lead taut. He eyed Phillip with suspicion.

"Calm yourself," he crooned to the horse. The beast snorted again but settled down, fixing Brother Phillip with a wary look.

Phillip touched the dark, warm ooze spreading around a slash in the youth's jerkin. The bandit's knife had found flesh, but the youth was still breathing.

"Grant me the skill to mend this, your child," Phillip prayed. A devotee of the healing arts, he was clever with herbs and medicinals, and somewhat of a specialist with wounds, although it would be prideful to admit this talent.

The bedraggled youth stirred and began to shiver violently. Phillip suspected the boy had taken a blow to the head, for he was mumbling incoherently. A few pieces of deadfall on the fire increased the heat. Phillip's own feet were numb, but the lad was wet to the skin and needed warming. If he didn't act quickly, the boy would die from a chill, even if the wound was stanched.

"Blankets," Phillip muttered. "And something for a bandage."

After removing the two blankets tied to his own saddle and some medicinal ointment, Phillip approached the other horse.

"There's a good boy," he crooned, patting the beast's flank.

The sack carried by the other horse held little: a blanket, a box wrapped in a thin linen garment, and a few other oddments. Phillip balled up the linen and grabbed the extra blanket before hurrying back to his patient.

"Now there, lad." He knelt down. "Let's get you warmed up and that wound dressed."

The youth was incoherent, head lolling from side to side. Phillip pulled off a tattered leather hat and slid down the hood which was clinging to wet, matted hair. He felt the skull through a mass of soggy locks. A large lump was forming at the back of the head.

Phillip tugged free the sodden coat and jerkin. Once he'd managed to strip off the dripping wet shirt, Phillip saw, to his confusion, that the youth already wore a bandage wound around his chest. The bandit's knife had sliced through it, and blood was flowing freely. The cut had split the flesh just under the arm, across the rib cage.

"Boy, you have amazing bad luck!" Phillip examined the bandaging, looking for the stain of dried blood. He found none. The sweet scent of coneflowers and comfrey reached him from the little crock of ointment he'd set near the fire. It was a concoction of Phillip's invention, and its healing properties had been tested and deemed successful many a time. It would have to work a miracle tonight.

Phillip sliced away the old binding and made to rip a new bandage from the linen garment when a curious thing caught his eye. The firelight played across his patient's pale white torso, and he peered more closely, unwilling to believe what he was seeing.

Phillip grabbed hold of the youth's wet leggings and peeled them off. "Not a boy," he whispered, his weather-toughened face flushed. "God save me, what sort of mischief led to this?" Phillip rubbed his temple with a finger. The girl was in desperate need of attention, so he shook open a blanket to cover her body, crossed himself, and then gave his attention over to her wounds.

Vala fought to open her eyes. The weak sunlight was blinding, and her head was throbbing with pain. Perhaps she was dead and gone to hell. If so, she didn't want to force her eyelids open just yet. There was a burning sting across her chest under her right breast. She remembered a hooded figure in the dark. Before she could recall what had happened, she drifted back into darkness.

Someone lifted her head slightly, and cooling water dribbled into her mouth. She gulped at it, coughing and sending water down her chin. A gentle hand wiped it away.

"Try not to move just yet."

Vala tried to open her eyes. Every bit of her body ached. Even her fingertips felt painful as she rubbed her eyes. A disembodied face hovered over her. It was a man with light brown hair and blue, hopeful eyes. Vala tried to speak, but blackness washed over her and the face was gone.

When Vala next awoke, the sun was low in the sky. Wood smoke filled her nostrils, and she fought queasiness as she levered herself up on her elbows.

"Are you cold, lass?"

Before she could answer, the weight of another blanket was draped around her shoulders, and she clutched at it for warmth.

A kind, intelligent face bent next to her. "Water?"

Vala nodded. "Please," she whispered.

A strong, warm hand wrapped her trembling fingers around a wooden cup. She sipped at it.

"What happened?" she rasped.

"I was hoping you could tell me that," said the figure crouching next to her.

Vala tried to gather her wits. Blinking across the clearing, she saw clothes hung on tree branches, ragged and limp. It took a moment for her to realize that the clothes were hers, traded for in Exeter. She moved her hand beneath the blanket and felt her skin. "My clothes!" she gasped, snapping her head toward the man. She instantly regretted the rapid movement. Pain sliced through her head, followed by a wave of nausea. She took several slow breaths, pressing her fingers hard against the throbbing.

She focused on her savior. Taking in his habit, she lowered her eyes. "You're a monk, aren't you?" Her gaze returned to the clothes hanging on the branches.

"My name is Brother Philip." The monk's tone was kindly. "You fell in the river and hit your head when that bandit attacked you. Can you tell me your name?"

"Vala," she whispered. "My name is Vala." She put a hand to her side, the source of most of the pain, and found a thick pad bound against the spot.

"He dealt you a rather serious knife wound."

Vala pulled her hand away, feeling awkward under the good brother's gaze. "I stopped here for the night. I tied up my horse and gathered some wood for a fire." A tight, sharp pain jabbed at her, and she rolled onto her uninjured side with a moan. "A rider came along," she said, wincing. "He attacked me."

Vala could see the outline of the box through the sack still dangling from her saddle. The black-cloaked attacker had demanded the 'relic', and when Vala gasped out, "I don't know what you mean!" he had come at her with his knife.

Vala sipped her water. Sluggish as her brain felt, she was sure the man had wanted the carved box. Perhaps she ought to set the wretched thing in the middle of the road and ride away. She'd had nothing but ill luck since receiving it.

The monk watched her with interest. "Vala," he mused. "It's an unusual name." He waited a moment. "Why were you dressed as a boy, Vala?" he asked.

Someone in Exeter must have known she'd come this way disguised as a boy and followed her. How else would the rider have found her? Thinking made her dizzy, and the monk was waiting for an answer. She wanted to trust him. His hair had the tonsured cut worn by most monks, and his robes were neat and well-kept. He was young, no more than two or three years beyond her own age, she guessed.

The weight of the past days' events crashed down upon her like the felling of a tree. She hugged her knees and began to weep. The monk hunkered down beside her and placed a hand on her back.

"I have to go to Bath and find the bishop there," she said through her tears. "I have to take him something... Something my father left me when he died. I think it's magical, or cursed," she whispered. "The man who attacked me wanted it." She dared not disclose any more, even to a kindly stranger—even to a monk.

"I hardly think the villain was hunting you specifically." Phillip pressed a cool hand to her temple for an instant, and his eyebrows contracted. He was looking at her as though she were addle-brained.

"I've been followed for days!" Vala replied, gritting her teeth against the pain slicing through her head.

"This road is treacherous, and thieves are bold. You were alone—a good target."

"He was after the box, and I don't even know what's in it." She hadn't meant to tell him any of that, but somehow she had. She could feel his eyes on her as she edged closer to the fire. She must sound a complete fool.

Brother Phillip climbed to his feet and dusted off his robes, then circled the fire and felt the damp clothing. "These rags will never do. They certainly won't dry hanging out today. Have you other garments, girl?"

"No," she replied, trying to rake her hair out of her eyes. "I traded mine for these in Exeter."

Brother Phillip pursed his lips to suppress a grin. "Not the best trade." He stared at his horse for a long moment, then strode to his pack and brought it round to where Vala huddled near the fire. "You say you are bound for Bath, to see the bishop?"

She nodded.

"I would be honored if you would travel with me for a few days. I am going in that direction, and I'd feel better if I could look after your injury until it shows signs of healing. You've received a bad blow to the head and ought not to be alone. Will you do me the favor of riding with me? As we travel, you can tell me more of your cursed artifact."

Vala felt heartened, but just as quickly, she deflated. "What if the man comes back and brings others? I couldn't bear the thought that I'd caused a monk to be killed."

"*Accipere quam facere praestat injuriam*," Phillip said.

"Better to suffer an injustice than to do an injustice," Vala translated automatically.

Brother Phillip's shock was obvious. "You know Latin?"

"My uncle taught me," she replied. "What do you mean by doing an injustice?"

"Uhh... Well, I meant that it would be wrong of me to leave you alone, no matter what might happen to me."

Vala nodded, still feeling quite thickheaded.

"But... few people study Latin, outside of the church. Not many of my fellows could have translated so smoothly. And the gentry may pretend an understanding but rarely recognize but a word or two."

The monk's words bespoke compliment, and Vala blushed.

Phillip held out his pack. "Inside, you'll find a spare robe, cowl, and hood. If you put them on, you will appear to be a monk. It's a better disguise than your previous one."

Vala fingered the warm woolen robes. They would indeed be an improvement over her pathetic rags. "Wouldn't that be a sacrilege, Father? I'd be impersonating a monk."

"Please, call me Phillip. I'm not so much older than you," he replied, extending the pack to her. "I don't think Our Lord will mind if you wear dry clothes."

Vala accepted the pack and climbed stiffly to her feet. Wincing and clutching at the trailing blankets, she hobbled to a clump of bushes feeling very light-headed.

The bandaging around her chest was tight and firm. A small stain of blood showed near where the knife had cut her. She ran her fingers over the spot. Trying not to dwell on the monk's ministrations, Vala bound the brown woolen robe closed with a piece of cord from the pack, giving a firm tug on the knot. She donned the scapular, letting it drape down her front and back. The hood and cowl went over the top, but as her shoulders were so small, the cowl hung down past her elbows. She ran her fingers over the cloth, soft and finely spun. This monk must have come from a wealthy family. Cloth such as this was costly. She peered over the thicket to where he was sitting by the fire.

"Will you take some of this bread to eat?" he called. He was toasting some on a stick.

Vala approached in her new disguise.

"Ahhh!" Phillip remarked as he climbed to his feet. "Hood up, please."

Vala raised the hood.

"Pull it farther down over your face," he suggested.

She obeyed.

Phillip strolled around her, giving her an appraising look. "Very good," he said. "You make a fine monk, Vala. The robe is a bit too long, perhaps, but otherwise very proper."

"It's kind of you to help me like this." Vala grinned under the voluminous hood. She accepted a hot piece of bread and sat down across from Phillip to eat it.

Birds twittered industriously in the brushes, and the river splashed as it tumbled over the rocks along its banks. The hum of nature calmed her and cleared her foggy head. Vala took small bites at first, her insides threatening to rebel, but they did not. After a time, Vala ventured a question. "Where are you traveling?"

"I have some villages to visit on the church's business."

"What exactly is it that you do in each village? Do you say the Mass?"

Phillip raised his head, "No, not the Mass. I have a different function." He sighed. "I investigate miracles."

A dozen half-formed questions burst to the surface inside her painful skull. She put a hand to the lump on her head and winced. "What does that involve?"

Brother Phillip laughed, his blue eyes crinkling at the corners. "Sometimes, a person will report that the Blessed Virgin, or some saint, or perhaps an angel, appears on a certain spot each day, or there may be a pool of water believed to have healing powers. The Church must investigate such things to see if they are real. Then, if they are found to be genuine, we must decide if they are the work of the devil, or of Him." Brother Phillip raised a finger heavenward. "The bishop is desirous to sort the true miracles from the frauds. Britain's standing will rise with the Holy See if we can confirm that God has blessed this isle with corporeal—physical signs of His presence." The monk's eyes were alight with feeling as he spoke.

"And you see these miracles?" Vala asked. "It must be wonderful. I'd love to see one."

A slight frown passed over Phillip's face. "I, too, would love to see one. I fear I have yet to find a true miracle, one that can be proved to the satisfaction of the Church," he said. "And to me."

"Oh," said Vala, sitting back, a little disappointed.

"Some of my fellows claim to have seen them, and it gives me hope."

"Do people call on you to identify the devil as well? Our village priest said that there are monks who go about the countryside exorcizing the devil."

"Some say the devil is easier to find than a saint," laughed Phillip. He passed a cup to her that contained a steaming, sweet-smelling liquid. "It's a bit of watered mead, heated up. It should allow you a good long sleep."

"But I've just slept."

"We'll go on tomorrow if your wound can tolerate it. Drink."

Vala sipped the soothing liquid, her anxiety slipping away. She eased herself down and curled up, setting her cup aside. "Watch out for men in black cloaks," she mumbled as she slipped into a dreamless sleep.

The next day dawned bright, with fat white clouds gliding overhead. Vala was still stiff, but her head was clear. As they ate some hard cheese, she queried Phillip about their route.

"Hemyoch, a village just along this road, will be first," replied Phillip. "Then Bruton, and finally, the abbey at Glastonbury. Bath is about a day's journey farther on."

"What miracle will we see in Hemyoch?" To Vala, the prospect was exciting.

"We visit a woman whom the local people revere as a saint. It is a serious business." Phillip's voice took on a more commanding quality, "Your role will be as my assistant—a silent and invisible assistant."

Vala nodded, solemn concentration on her face.

"You'll have to keep your hood pulled down. It wouldn't be proper for a monk to travel with an unchaperoned maid, much less one disguised as a monk."

Vala marked his instructions with a serious nod, but he winked at her. "You will make a fine assistant."

They collected their possessions, preparing to leave. Vala didn't fancy riding with her robes flapping around her legs, so she slipped into the bushes and pulled on the old leggings she had brought from Exeter, and then strode to her horse.

They rode at an easy pace that day. Vala refused to complain of pain, though the bouncing of her mount was wearing. The disguise was a comfort, for who would suspect two monks? Of course, she'd thought the first disguise quite good. She twisted to look behind them and was repaid with a stab of pain, so she settled back in her saddle. No matter what happened, she couldn't allow Brother Phillip to be hurt because of her.

Vala was sore and tired by the time they reached the small enclave of houses that formed the unremarkable little hamlet of Hemyoch. The dozen or so houses were stick and mud daub construction with thatched roofs. There was no inn, marketplace, or even a church, just dogs, chickens and the tang of peat fires on the air. Phillip asked at the first dwelling to ensure they had reached the right place.

"Yes, indeed, this is Hemyoch," chortled a plump woman, her hands dripping with wash water. "You'll want Ellesmae, Your Holiness. She lives just down the way. She's the daughter, you see. She's expecting you!" The woman began to lope down the main road, calling after them, "Come! Come! I'll guide you!" Holding her apron from flying up in the breeze, she cried, "Ellesmae! Ellesmae!" her voice rising to an insistent screech.

Other women emerged from other houses and joined the procession. They stopped outside one of the dwellings, where a woman bustled out, hands over her mouth. The others fell silent. Introductions were unnecessary. Ellesmae lifted her hands toward Phillip as though he were her savior as all the women began chattering at Phillip. He slid from his horse, handing the reins to Vala.

"Please, one at a time," he said as Vala pulled the two beasts toward a nearby tree.

Vala stayed next to the horses, her heart beating fast in expectation. If she played her part well, she might soon meet an actual saint.

"I was afraid you might not arrive in time. My mother won't last much longer, I fear," Ellesmae said mournfully. "She's very old and can't rise from her bed."

A thunder of hooves came around the bend. Three riders cloaked in black and riding fast galloped through the small hamlet without regard for man or beast. The women shrieked in terror, pulling small children from their path. Others shook their fists and called out, but the riders took no heed.

The lead man stood up in his stirrups and scanned the area, slowing only slightly as he did. He glanced briefly at Phillip and Vala before urging his group onward. In seconds, they were gone, leaving nothing but a lingering cloud of dust and a trampled chicken in their wake.

Vala did not take note of the buzz of disgust from the womenfolk of Hemyoch as Ellesmae chivied Phillip toward her door. She followed woodenly, her heart in her throat. Those riders had been looking for her. The monk's disguise alone had saved her.

Phillip and Vala stepped into the modest dwelling. It smelled of pease porridge and a baby's acrid changing clouts.

"What is your mother's name?" Phillip asked.

"It's Judith," whispered Ellesmae. She said something else to Phillip, but the jostling and chirruping of the crowd of women drowned out her words. "Mother is just in here."

Ellesmae threw the villagers a reproving look before pulling aside a curtain and leading her guests into a small alcove. The room had a dim golden glow about it from the sackcloth curtains covering a small window. A very old woman was lying in bed, her skin pallid, blue veins standing out on the gnarled hands.

Ellesmae touched the woman's arm. "Mother, two monks are here to speak to you."

The old woman opened her eyes, sightless and milky. "Sir priest, you ought to look to your horse," said the woman in a hoarse whisper. "I fear he has something in his hoof. He will go lame if you ignore it."

Phillip raised an eyebrow. "Thank you, Mistress Judith."

"She says things like that all the time," the excited daughter confided, nodding significantly to Phillip. "She predicts all manner of things: diseases, storms, everything."

"That is all I have to say," the old woman interrupted in a civil tone but with definite finality.

"But, Mother," began the harassed daughter. "These men are here to establish your claim to sainthood. You must convince them."

"I'd like to have a drink of water," said the old woman.

Forgetting she was to remain in the background, Vala picked up a cup sitting near the bed and put it to the woman's lips.

"Perhaps we could speak to your mother alone," suggested Phillip.

Ellesmae curtsied reverently and retreated from the room into the huddle of waiting village women. Phillip drew up a stool close to the bed. Vala edged away against the far wall while Phillip began speaking to the old woman in a whisper. As he spoke close to her ear, the woman did not move, staring upward with a vague smile on her lips. Without warning, she raised her head and held out a shaking finger toward Vala. "Why do you hide your true self, lass? The Lord is not deceived, nor am I."

Vala blanched, and Phillip spun to look at her. The daughter and the other women had retreated outside, so they had not heard. Vala moved a bit nearer the bed, fascinated by the old woman's shrewd words.

"I could tell by the tread of your foot as you came in that you were not a man, and therefore not a monk," the old woman explained. "My daughter said two monks had come, so I knew you were wearing the habit to conceal your identity."

Vala tried to form a response, but Phillip put a finger to his lips. He waved a hand in front of the woman's face, but she did not flinch.

"I'll keep your secret, child," said the woman, her face sublime. "Though I'm sure the story is a good one. And, you, sir monk, please stop your hand-waving."

"You have a nimble mind, mistress," said Phillip. "And a fine set of ears."

"Was this my test?" she cackled.

"No, I wouldn't try to trick you," Phillip replied with a kind smile.

"I might be blind and old, but I pay attention," she said with a touch of pride. "Sometimes one can see the truth better without eyes. The wind has a smell when the rains are coming. Sounds have a feeling that vibrates inside you, like the way the ground feels when horsemen pass by. These things tell me much."

Vala stared at Judith, fascinated.

The woman tipped her head. "The riders who just came down the road—" She turned her face toward Vala. "You fear them?"

Phillip jerked his head toward Vala, who stared in amazement at the woman. His brow furrowed. "Please, lady," he said, trying to turn the woman's attention to the issue at hand. "Stories of your gift have come to our notice. Your daughter feels you are blessed with the spirit of God because of your purity of soul. I cannot judge, however, unless you have something to tell me of a prophetic nature."

"My daughter is a good woman, but don't trouble yourself, sir monk. If I come back from my grave with news of heaven, then perhaps you'll come again. For now, tell Ellesmae the bread is about to burn." She closed her eyelids, thin as parchment. "I'd like to rest."

Phillip patted the woman on the hand and drew away.

After rescuing her nearly burnt bread from the community brick oven in a flutter of screeches and commotion, the daughter joined them by their horses. "She never wants any payment when she helps someone, and she's helped many. She can say the most remarkable things. I wish you could hear," said the daughter with obvious regret.

"I am sorry too," said Phillip. "But sainthood requires documented miracles. The interrogation process is very long and grueling. I fear she wouldn't survive it. It may be best to let her go to her final rest in peace. She is an extraordinary woman."

Ellesmae nodded in sad resignation.

Phillip took his horse's reins and noticed it shying away from him. The horse scuffed its back foot against the ground. Phillip examined the hoof and wrested a sharp stone from it. The old woman's words had proven true. Had the woman simply heard the gait of the horse and surmised that it carried a stone in its hoof? Phillip stared at the house for a long time and then mounted, motioning for Vala to follow.

"How did you find the lady, Judith?"

"I don't understand how she could *hear* that I was a girl," Vala said incredulously.

"She is a very gifted listener," began Phillip. "Her blindness has heightened her other senses. She notices things that most of us ignore."

"She isn't a saint?"

"No, she is not, although her gifts of perception are impressive."

Vala tried closing her eyes and attempted to make out Thistle's hoof beats compared to those of Phillip's horse. It was disorienting, and she almost lost her balance.

Around midafternoon, Phillip halted and insisted on a rest. He laid out some bread and dried meat for their meal. Vala accepted water and ate a small piece of bread but could not stomach the meat. Relieved to be out of the saddle for a bit, she curled up on the grass and closed her eyes. Her side was sore, and it felt good to allow her bruised body to relax. In moments, she had drifted off to sleep.

When at last she awoke, it was dark, and a good fire was burning nearby. A folded blanket lay beneath her head. Brother Phillip was sitting quietly across from her.

"You should have wakened me," Vala said, sitting up too quickly and paying for it with a new wave of pain and a grimace she could not disguise.

"I was a fool to think you could ride so soon," said Phillip. "Forgive me."

"But you'll be late for your next miracle," said Vala.

Phillip grinned. "A true miracle will wait."

They talked comfortably for a while. Brother Phillip was an educated man who had seen much in his travels. After a time, Vala glanced up at Thistle, who was snuffling in the grasses under a nearby tree. The box was hanging in the satchel. Perhaps Phillip had seen something like it somewhere. He had been very kind to her. What was more, he was a sensible and knowledgeable person. If the box was dangerous, maybe Phillip could advise her.

She rose and retrieved it from her pack. Holding it made her skin crawl as she remembered her father's fetid body going up in flames.

"This is what they gave me," said Vala. "My father and my uncle."

"The cursed box?"

She nodded.

"May I?" Phillip examined it for a few minutes, turning it over in his fingers. "I believe I recognize what this is. I saw one of these many years ago. My father brought a thing like this back from a voyage to Calais."

"Your father had one too?" Vala was aghast to think that magical boxes were a common commodity.

"My father was a merchant and an adventurer. He traveled the world to bring goods to the rich and the powerful. He saw many things—unique and sometimes strange. He brought one of these home, and we children were allowed to attempt to solve the puzzle." Phillip smiled. "It's a puzzle box, or that's what we called it."

"What sort of puzzle?" Vala sat near him, the better to see.

"The puzzle is in the construction." He held it up and peered at each side in turn. "The box has secret panels that slide or move in an unexpected way until the contents of the box are revealed."

Vala watched with new interest while Phillip pushed and turned the box in different directions. Holding it very close to his eyes, Phillip screwed up his face and pressed his thumb against one of the sides. It moved. Vala leaned closer as a small panel slid open, revealing smooth wood underneath. Phillip studied the box for many more minutes but was unable to move any other piece.

"I'll try, shall I?" Vala was eager to attempt to open the box herself. The prospect of solving the puzzle overrode her fear of whatever sort of item the box might contain.

Minutes of fruitless examination and frustrating pushing and turning made no change to the enigmatic cube. Discouraged, she hissed, "Maybe we should just break it open."

"It's your property to do with as you please," said Phillip. "However, smashing it could damage the contents. In fact, some such boxes are designed to destroy the contents if someone breaks into them." He nodded toward the cube, "This one is of very fine workmanship."

Vala sighed. "What was inside the puzzle box your father gave you?"

"My elder brother finally succeeded with it," said Phillip. "The box contained a small horse carved from ivory. I was very jealous, as I recall." He laughed at the memory.

Vala laughed too, but she was sure her own box held nothing as innocent as a carved horse. "How many brothers did you have?" Brothers were of some interest to Vala, having discovered she'd had one.

"Three," Phillip said, holding up a finger. "I was the youngest. The other two died before they were grown."

"I'm sorry," said Vala. She cast about for a change of subject. "When did you know you wanted to be a monk?"

Phillip gave a tight laugh. "I am an oblate, Vala. My father gave me to the monastery at the age of eight."

"He gave you away?"

Phillip tilted his head. "When my father's business began to go badly and one of my brothers was taken ill, Father decided he needed God to look more kindly upon him. The priests told him he ought to give a son to the Church, and that God would bless him for it. So, I was sent to the monastery. Father died within the year, and so did my brother."

Vala frowned. "Why didn't you leave the monastery? You didn't choose it?"

"I respected my father's will, and it's been a good life, too, for the most part. As a merchant seaman, or even as the captain of a ship, I would not have been educated as I have been." Phillip rose to put another log on the fire. "Wealth can be a burden, you know. It never brought my father real happiness."

"You can't marry, though, or have a family."

"It is a small sacrifice." Phillip's voice sounded strained even though his face remained passive. "I have seen many things, and I have been privileged to read the books in the libraries of the abbeys I visit."

Traveling the countryside and reading books sounded like a very romantic life. Vala gave the box a final twist and shake, then closed the one sliding panel that Phillip had found. She had avoided handling the box before. Now she fantasized about what it would feel like to solve its secret puzzle. Perhaps it was like the stone in Wistman's Wood, not as harmful as legend reported.

Vala allowed her fingers to glide over the warm wood, mellowed by age. "Is it of oak?"

Phillip leaned closer, touching the surface. "Most likely ash."

"What will the bishop do with it, I wonder?"

"I'm not sure, Vala. He might try to have it opened. You should prepare yourself. He will probably tell you it isn't cursed or magical."

"Both my father and my uncle told me it was dangerous, and my uncle never lied to me." Vala didn't like to tarnish her image of her uncle, but the man had hidden her entire history from her. He *had* lied.

"Come, Vala." Phillip's tone lightened. "Why do you believe in this curse? Tell me the full story."

Since Phillip had shared his history, Vala felt compelled to relate hers. It poured forth like the breaking of a storm. Phillip seemed aghast as her tale unfolded. They talked into the night, until Vala could keep awake no longer, slipping into sleep next to the fire.

Chapter Ten:
*"All are not friends who speak one fair."*

A log cracked and fell, sending a small puff of fiery sparks into the air, and Phillip jerked upright, staring wildly into the blackness. Glowing cinders floated up into the air, lighting Vala's sleeping face. Phillip exhaled shakily as he recalled where he was.

The damnable dream had come again, and it took a moment to slow his breathing. He pulled his knees up and wound his blanket around himself. It was just a dream—just an old memory twisted by his slumbering brain. He could not drive it out, not by prayer, nor fasting, nor hard riding, nor did falling asleep exhaust. Nothing made a difference; the dream in its many variations would come of its own volition.

Phillip scrubbed at his eyes to wipe away the offensive scene. He'd been no more than eight years old. Brother Hollis and Brother Gregory were both sixteen. The three shared a cell in the abbey. Hollis and Gregory had come to the abbey with a calling, or so they claimed. The monastic life provided a bed and regular meals, a better life than that of a peasant farmer in many ways. Whether their vocations were real or not, they had *chosen* to come to Glastonbury and then sullied the place with their sin.

"Come along, my dear. He's nothing but a little boy."

"But, Hollis," she had argued in a whisper, "I don't like him being here."

Hollis turned to Phillip. "Be a stout little fellow, won't you? Just sit quietly like a good lad."

Phillip had nodded. Hollis was his hero, the cleverest of fellows. He stood up for Phillip and got him extra helpings at dinner.

The girl lived in the village. Phillip had seen her carrying milk pails. Hollis had remarked on her just that morning, and now he was coaxing her into their cell. Phillip wanted to tell Hollis that such a thing was not allowed, but Hollis was older and also his friend, so Phillip held his tongue.

Hollis kissed the girl easily, whispering in her ear, making her giggle as he pulled her down onto his straw pallet. Phillip fidgeted and tried to focus on the nub of candle burning in the holder. It wasn't right to have a girl in the monastery. He bit his lip but remained silent.

"Hollis! Stop it!"

Phillip stole a look. The bodice of the girl's gown was open, but her voice sounded more playful than anxious.

"You're a real beauty," Hollis soothed as he pushed her skirts up.

"But I don't want—"

Hollis covered the girl's mouth with his own, smothering her words. Phillip looked away and held his breath. There was a whimpered cry, but he was too embarrassed and confused to go to the girl's aid.

Hollis moaned, and then the struggling ceased. "You were wonderful, Bessie."

"My name is Beth," the girl said, her dark eyes flickering between longing and distress.

Hollis rolled off, his robes hanging open. The girl scrambled to cover her bosom and her pale legs as Hollis straightened his habit.

The door to their cell opened. "Done yet?" Gregory whispered, peering into the room.

Hollis smiled at the girl huddled on his pallet. He laid a few coins on the table. "For you, Bessie." He grinned as he passed Gregory, who slapped him on the back in a collegial way. At the door, Hollis put a finger to his lips, reminding young Phillip to stay quiet.

The girl pushed herself back against the tumbled stone wall. "Hollis?" she cried pitiably. "Hollis, I don't want to!"

"None of that now," Gregory said, untying his own robe. "We're paying you well, girl."

He was on top of her in a second, his hand smothering her cries. Phillip saw the tears wetting her cheeks as Gregory used her. When Gregory had finished, the boys bundled Beth into her cloak and hurried her away. She was still weeping, with their silver coins clutched in her hand. Gregory stayed behind long enough to say, "Little Brother Phillip, report anything of this to the abbot, and you're dead."

The memory dissolved into the cool darkness, but Phillip felt the stain it left on his soul. He had not told. That was his bane and his shame. No amount of confession could purge him of the memory. His penance was the recurring nightmare, where sometimes he watched the girl's humiliation dumbly, but other times he was her tormentor. The angry, guilty, and even lustful feelings that the dream provoked terrified him.

Phillip shivered as he got to his knees. He clasped his hands and began the prayer *Nocturna Tempora*. He believed God would exact a terrible levy on the souls of Hollis and Gregory, but what of his own culpability?

Chapter Eleven:
*"The worth of a thing is what it will bring."*

Phillip crouched beside the fire in the damp morning. "How is your wound?"

Vala pushed at the slice in her side and winced. It hurt extraordinarily, but it wouldn't do to appear frail or fragile. "I can tolerate it."

"It needs re-bandaging. It might fester and become a putrid, weeping sore if not tended to."

Vala began to argue. The village women in Wistman's Wood believed in leaving wounds covered.

"I've found that injuries which are bathed and dressed heal more quickly," Phillip stated. "If it becomes inflamed, a fever will follow, then death."

He went in search of his small kettle. As he heated water, he cut a fresh bandage. "I have an ointment which is very good on wounds."

Vala pulled off the cowl and opened the front of her robe far enough to slide her hand inside and feel the bandage. The linen was stiff with dried blood.

Phillip handed over the padding and bandage material and then set the warm water and ointment next to her. "I'll turn around, then you can sit by the fire where it's warm and I can lend a hand if need be." Phillip turned his back.

Vala lowered the robe and unwound the old bandage with an occasional twinge of pain. The wound was an angry red slash surrounded by blue-black bruising. It wept a bit of bright red blood and clear fluid. Vala took up a scrap of cloth and used it to clean the wound. It stung terribly before the heat of the water spread comforting warmth down her side.

"It seems fine," she said.

"Any pus? How does it smell?"

"No pus." Vala bent her head toward the wound and sniffed. "I don't smell anything."

"What about swelling?"

"None."

Phillip nodded to himself. "Good."

With some effort, she managed the bandaging herself.

"It's going to be interesting when we reach Bruton," Phillip offered, trying to take her mind off the pain of the proceedings. "I think we may see a real miracle if the accounts are true."

Vala winced as she tied off the linen and shrugged back into the robe.

"What sort of miracle does Bruton have?" she asked as Phillip helped her mount Thistle.

"According to a letter from the village priest, the Bruton church has a statue that cries tears of blood."

"How can that be? How often does it cry? How large is it?"

Phillip grinned at Vala's rising enthusiasm. "When we arrive, the priest will show me the statue and the proofs he has that the miracle is real. I'll examine the statue..."

"And we'll see a true miracle," Vala chimed in.

"And you will hold the horses," Phillip said pointedly.

The village of Bruton was set on a slope running down to a river valley. As they came over a rise, Vala saw it spread out before them, as pretty a place as she'd ever seen. There were about three dozen dwellings. Spirals of smoke reached up into the air from the many home fires. A dovecote stood on the hill just off the road, a sort of sentinel overlooking the village. Chickens and pigs squawked and squealed in agitation as a group of children raced down the road to greet the two monks. At a gesture from Phillip, Vala rearranged her hood and straightened her cowl. They followed the growing throng toward the center of the village, where a small church stood.

Solid grey stones, hewn and hauled here with some effort, formed the walls of the church. The roof was thatched, and it appeared that a rectory of sorts adjoined the church at the back. Next to the rectory door was a small vegetable patch. The entire thing reminded Vala strongly of the little church in Wistman's Wood. This one was larger, to be sure, but designed on the same principle.

The congregation of villagers looked up at the newcomers with expectant faces. Judging from the market day excitement in the air, their visit was happily anticipated. Phillip slowed his horse, giving a blessing to the eager, upturned faces. Vala fell back and let the throng surround Brother Phillip. She ran his instructions over in her head: hold the horses, don't speak, keep your head bowed.

A village elder stepped forward. "Thank you, Brother, for making the long journey to see our Virgin. Bruton is proud you are here," he proclaimed, sweeping off his hat.

"I am happy to come, sir. The church wants to document such mysterious events and is always glad to find a place where God shows himself to mankind."

Vala could hear snatches of conversation in the general clamor, recounting the miracle they had all witnessed.

"...and there have been several cures. I don't know if that was told to you, Your Excellence?" the elder continued over the din. "A lame man was healed, and a boy who was mute now speaks!" The crowd cheered his words. "If our claim is proved, will the bishop come and build a cathedral here?" the man wanted to know.

"Sir monk," interrupted another man, "if a cathedral is to be built, we could come by as much timber as might be needed, or even stone. Over yonder..."

Brother Phillip cut them off with a raised palm. He called loud enough to silence the crowd, "I want to see those healed by the statue, and after I witness the miracle of the weeping Virgin, I will convey my findings to the bishop, his Excellency the Bishop De Roche, who will decide how to proceed."

In response, the voices of the townsfolk rose, hopeful and excited. If a bishop commissioned a cathedral, the town would grow in size and prosperity.

Vala dismounted and stepped forward to take the reins of Phillip's horse. With head bowed, she led the horses to a nearby tree whilst the rest of the company crowded around the steps of the church.

A small man scurried over to her and doffed his hat. "I'm the priest's assistant. I'll tie 'em up for ye, sir monk. You should go and watch the miracle." He took the reins, flapping his hands to shoo her toward the church. She watched him secure the horses and then scuttle away around the side of the church.

The village priest, arrayed in fine vestments, parted the crowd and made his way to Phillip. Vala squinted at him from under her hood. He was very pale of face, and his hands were smooth and unmarred by physical labor.

"I am Father Junius!" The priest clasped Phillip's hand with both of his. "Thank you for making this journey. You are about to see a wonder! One beyond the capabilities of a poor, ignorant priest like myself."

She couldn't say why, but Vala was certain this priest was well up to having a miracle under his nose and basking in the glow of celebrity.

"Where is the statue, Father?" asked Phillip.

"It is more of a carving on wood, a relief or 'Soulagement de Bas', as the French say." The priest laughed airily. "It depicts the Virgin ascending into heaven."

Vala saw a flicker of irritation in Phillip's eyes.

"First, you must hear about the miracles our precious Lady has wrought."

Father Junius turned to his flock. In a carrying voice, a sermonizing voice, he said, "Tell the bishop's representative what Our Lady has done for you, my children."

The villagers quieted to a low buzz while he spoke and then erupted in a noisy clamor.

"I touched the tears, and my headache was cured!" shouted a woman.

"And I had a lump just here…" was drowned out by, "…my son's leg!" Many more such claims showered down upon Phillip.

"So many miracles," Father Junius exclaimed, hooking his arm through Phillip's. It was time to tow him inside to view the miracle.

Phillip's expression never changed. He disengaged himself from the priest and stepped down into the crowd. A look of vexation flitted over the good father's face as Phillip pulled a woman forward, asking her to tell her tale.

"Your Honor," the woman began in a rusty voice. "I touched the blood, and then I went home and rubbed the head of my ewe. A week later, she gave birth to twin lambs, and her not even expecting as far as we knew. Then, to top it off, that very night, my youngest son, who we thought was lost and dead, came home to us safe and sound!" The woman wiped a tear from her eyes.

"I'm sure the return of your son was a joy to you," Phillip said kindly. "How old was the child? Where had he been lost?"

"He was eighteen, by my reckoning. He went off without a word last year," said the woman. "But now he's come back."

Phillip's face fell. "Eighteen. I see." Then he forged on, "Was the ewe kept in a separate pen from the rams?"

"Oh, no, Your Honor, no. We wanted her to have lambs, but she hadn't dropped a lamb in four seasons."

Father Junius shooed the woman back.

"Sir monk?" An old fellow bowed toward Phillip. "I fell off my hay rik, and from that day I've had a lump on my leg, just here." He touched his knee. "I was almost unable to walk. But I touched the Virgin's tears, and now I'm cured!" The man smiled as he limped back into the crowd.

Phillip shook his head and raised his hands for quiet. "Please, listen carefully. Can anyone tell me of a person, blind or lame *from birth*, who has been cured by the tears?" There were whispers and expectant looks amongst the crowd, and then silence. Phillip raised his voice. "Has the harvest doubled since the Virgin began her weeping?" Silence. "Have the wolves avoided your flocks?" Some questioning murmurs, and then more silence. Phillip pressed a finger to his temple.

Father Junius touched Phillip's elbow before all his evidence of the miraculous fell flat. "Please! Come! See the weeping Virgin for yourself, and you will know it is a true miracle."

Phillip allowed the priest to lead him into the church. The crowd surged forward and tried to push inside. Vala was desperate to see the weeping Virgin, so she edged in behind the crowd and worked her way forward along the wall in the tightly packed little church. The pompous voice of the priest rose above the shuffle of bodies.

"About a year ago, the Virgin began to weep blood. It was during a Mass, and I threw myself down before her and thanked the Lord for blessing our small church."

Vala pulled her hood more tightly over her face and watched the crowd as the priest droned on. Old women were weeping and praying. Faces were alight with fervor. These people believed their village had been blessed by a miraculous manifestation, and it filled them with pride. It felt as though the small church could fly straight up to heaven.

Something began to trickle from the eyes of the Virgin, and the priest cried to heaven in ecstasy. The crowd gasped. Vala stared at the wooden relief, where two small rivulets of crimson trickled down the Virgin's face. Father Wulford had spoken of miracles, but she had never imagined how uplifting it would be to witness one.

The crowd surged forward, eager to see, and Vala found herself forced toward the back of the throng. She stumbled into a box set upon a stand. It was the church's coffer, and its weight hinted at a goodly quantity of silver—more than the church at Wistman's Wood could have collected in a year.

Vala allowed the tide of villagers to surge past her until she was able to step outside. She'd just seen the miracle, a real miracle, and she couldn't wait to tell Uncle Adrian.

With a jolt, she realized there would never be a chance to tell him anything again. Vala fought the flood of emotion that threatened to overwhelm her. She walked slowly around the outside of the church. A few deep breaths of fresh air steadied her.

Sweetpea and columbine grew along the edges of the church, clinging to the cracks in the stone. Their faint scent drew Vala along the little path, right to the rectory door. It stood slightly ajar, and she could see a sliver of the room inside: a cross on the wall, a sleeping pallet, and a small hearth. There was movement inside. A man was fiddling with something, rifling the priest's belongings while everyone was inside the church. Vala rushed in, intent on catching the thief.

She recognized him at once. It was the priest's assistant, the man who'd tied their horses. Red-faced, Vala was on the verge of uttering her apology when the man bolted from the room.

"Pardon my intrusion!" Vala called before remembering she was not to speak. Her hand went to her mouth.

She moved to follow him but stopped in the doorway. Why, in the name of the devil, had the man run off? She looked back at the small table where he'd stood, and her question changed. It took a moment to put it together.

Vala touched the wall. Two small holes were visible through the mortar. With her fingernail, she lifted the ends of the wicks that protruded from the holes. She picked up the vial and the little reed standing on the table, and her eyes narrowed. She set the vial down and placed her hand once again upon the wall, which was cool and slightly damp in the spring air. Vala strode off to find Phillip.

She had to wade through the chattering throng now moving back outside. A man was telling the woman next to him, "It just starts up for no reason. I wonder what the Virgin is trying to tell us."

The woman shook her head. "I can't believe our luck to have such a thing here."

A man behind them put in, "All the world will want to make a pilgrimage here to see our Lady!"

Vala shouldered her way to the center of the church. Brother Phillip was trying to get close enough to examine the relief while Father Junius jabbered away, blocking his path. Vala cleared her throat and gestured to Phillip. He frowned and strode across the nave to meet her. Father Junius sighed in decided relief.

"What is it?" Phillip hissed. "I have work to do. I need to examine the eyes, but the priest keeps blocking—"

"Do you want to see how the miracle is done?" Vala whispered, keeping her hood low and her head bowed. "Come and look." She led the way with Phillip behind and Father Junius jogging after them.

"Is your examination complete?" he called. "Will you be telling the bishop about our Lady and her tears? I could send some with you in a vial."

Vala guided Phillip resolutely to the rectory door.

"Wait!" she heard the priest call. Then, more urgently, "Stop! Where are you going? We should go back inside! She may weep again! Wait!" His voice rose in desperate panic.

"Where *are* we going?" whispered Phillip.

Vala did not speak but went straight inside the priest's quarters, Phillip and Father Junius at her heels. The priest's face was sickly grey. Vala reached the table and lifted the vial. She pointed to the dead chicken hanging near the cook fire with its head cut off and a bowl set beneath to catch the blood.

"On the other side of this wall is where the carving of the Virgin hangs," Phillip said slowly, sizing up the wall. The comment was unnecessary. Everyone in the small room knew the truth.

Vala lifted the little reed and dipped it into the vial, then touched it to the strings extending through the small holes in the wall. They watched the liquid being pulled into the damp wicks.

"The Virgin weeps," Phillip growled, turning to the priest, cowering in the doorway. "Father Junius, you have tried to deceive the emissary of a bishop of Rome."

"Please, Brother." His voice took on a conspiratorial tone. "You must understand the difficulty of keeping the common people interested in the Church. There is a good deal of silver in my coffers. I could give you a nice offering. You could do with it as you see fit." The oily priest lowered his voice. "*Manus manum lavat.*"

Vala's brain was on fire with the discovery of the fraud, but she had wit enough to understand the words—*a favor for a favor.* "You vile man!" she blurted.

Phillip's booming voice covered her outburst. "Contemptible wretch! You cannot buy silence nor forgiveness from me. I will be reporting this to my superiors. I suggest you repent." Phillip's words crackled with suppressed rage. "You can begin by confessing your sin to the good people of Bruton."

"I can't tell them something like this," moaned the priest, who'd shrunk from pompous prelate to broken man in a matter of minutes. "They would kill me."

"At least you would leave this world with a pure soul," Phillip said coldly. He strode from the rectory, Vala at his heels. A feeling of righteous indignation swelled in Vala's chest as they made their way to the horses.

A group of expectant villagers clustered in front of the church, waiting for Brother Phillip's judgment of the weeping Virgin. He slowed his mount next to them and made the sign of the cross over their hopeful faces, mumbling a blessing. He finished with "*Dum vita est spes est.*" Without another word, he spurred his horse toward the road.

Vala followed Phillip as he galloped off. He'd said, 'Where life is, hope is.' It was a long while before he spoke again.

Chapter Twelve:
*"To deceive one's self is very easy."*

"Brother Phillip?"

"Vile worm," muttered Phillip. "Offering me silver to ignore his deception." A thin smile crossed his face. "I might never have discovered his trickery without your aid."

Vala blushed. "You would have found him out. His helper wasn't very discreet."

"You were observant and fearless. You'd do well in my line of work," Phillip said.

"Those poor people," Vala said. "Duped by their own priest."

"A crowd will sometimes go violent when riches are at stake." Phillip shook his head. "I've still not witnessed a true miracle."

"How can you keep your faith in them?' asked Vala.

"If I found one true miracle, no one could doubt the power of Our Lord," he said, unspoken yearning in his words.

The path broke out from the trees and merged onto a wider road over open countryside. Phillip kicked his horse into a gallop. Vala did not follow.

Phillip stopped and turned in his saddle. "What's wrong?" he called.

Vala looked left and right before moving slowly toward Phillip. "Those riders who came through Hemyoch—"

"No one is following us, Vala," said Phillip, and with a nod, Vala followed him across the grassy downs.

"We'll reach Glastonbury Abbey tomorrow," he said after two hours of riding.

Vala nodded.

Phillip was unsure about what he was about to propose. Did she really look like a monk? The hood of her robes swayed as the horse trotted along. He didn't think anyone would guess her true sex, but would it be good enough?

"There is a splendid library in the abbey. Would you like to see it?"

Vala looked up. "A real library?"

Phillip grinned. "The only problem is that women are not allowed inside, so the disguise is crucial. You would have to be very careful while we are there."

"Pretend to be a monk?" she began.

"You are very convincing," Phillip said quickly. "There will be no problem."

Taking a woman inside the monastery was madness. Phillip had no idea what was driving him to take the risk. Vala was bright and intelligent, and she would appreciate seeing the books, but was that reason enough?

"I would love to see the books, of course, but should we risk that?" she asked.

"After your cleverness and bravery?" he replied.

She *was* brave. She had confronted the corrupt priest. She was determined to journey to Bath on her little quest. He smiled wryly. Her daring and innocence were a dangerous combination. It encouraged those qualities in him.

"Ought we try to fool the brothers at your abbey?"

Phillip knew he was suggesting perpetrating a deceit. Somehow, he did not feel sinful. He was still feeling the anger at a lying priest. "You'd find the monastery interesting. But we would need to disguise your voice too."

Phillip was silent for a bit. "A vow of silence!" he shouted. "The key is silence. Never speak. Just nod or shake your head. Do you understand?" No matter how innocent, this was a foolhardy deception.

"I could just stay at an inn. I could put on my other clothes," Vala suggested.

"It will be an adventure," Phillip said in reply. Why risk so much for so little, he wondered—just to show her some books? Was he any better than Father Junius, tricking his flock? Phillip tried to turn his focus to prayer. He touched his forehead, his heart, and each shoulder in turn, but instead of finding the words to the Lord's Prayer, his mind drifted back to Vala. She was far too intriguing.

Twilight had washed the color from the fields and trees before they halted for the night. A large hazel thicket shielded their camp from the road.

"Tomorrow, you shall need a monk's name."

Vala slid from Thistle's back and stooped for a moment waiting for the pain to subside so she could straighten up. "Could I be Brother Adrian, after my uncle?"

"A more common name, a saint's name, I think," replied Phillip. "Perhaps John, a name that doesn't draw attention."

Vala was unimpressed by its lack of imagination.

"Good. Brother John it will be." Phillip heaved his pack to the ground. "And

I'll say you've taken a vow of silence."

Vala couldn't imagine choosing such a vow, but if Phillip wanted her to do it, she would be as silent as a corpse.

Phillip rummaged for what food remained to them.

"We have something from one of the women in Bruton," said Vala. "She handed me a sack as we were riding away. I nearly forgot." The sack held a mortrews of smoked eel wrapped in cheesecloth and a small loaf of bread. It proved a feast after hours of riding.

Full of the thick paté and warmed by the small fire, Vala retrieved the wooden box. Phillip watched her work at it, trying to solve the mystery. Suddenly, she gave a yip of glee.

"I did it! I found another one!" she cried.

Having achieved a small victory over the enigmatic box, Vala laid it aside and drifted off to sleep.

Chapter Thirteen:
*"Ale in, wit out."*

It was the following afternoon before they were in view of the wide, slow-moving River Brue and Glastonbury Abbey beyond. A few round thatched houses dotted the land around the river—tenants of the abbey. The ground was marshy, and even though the season was early, small swarms of midges buzzed around the fresh green shoots.

"It's a bucolic life for most of the monks," Phillip explained.

"Don't your brother monks travel, as you do?" Vala asked.

"I am unusual. The church has chosen to send me far afield, but most of my brothers stay behind the abbey walls, tending the grapevines in the nearby fields. The monastery's wine is of excellent quality, widely known and desired. A cask resides in the cellar of the pope himself. It is an accolade that brings great pride to Brother Unus, the monastery's vintner."

They approached a gate tended by a small boy, garbed in novice's robes. He pushed up his over-long sleeves and grunted as he swung the heavy wooden doors open.

"Brother Phillip! At last!" a grey-haired monk cried from across the courtyard and hurried toward them, his arms flung wide in welcome.

"Brother Cuthred! It's good to see you, my friend," said Phillip, leaping from his horse and striding forward. Vala dismounted and adjusted her monk's habit, concealing her face under her hood. She waited, trying to remain inconspicuous as Thistle tried to nuzzle her neck. Brother Cuthred clapped Phillip on the back and then faced her. Vala froze with her head and shoulders lowered like a dog whose status in the pack is in question.

"This is Brother John," Phillip lied, "We met on the road, and he desired to visit Glastonbury before traveling on to Bath."

"Welcome, my son," said Brother Cuthred.

Vala nodded deeply and said nothing.

"Where you are from, Brother?" Cuthred inquired. Vala fidgeted nervously and prayed that Phillip was going to intervene.

"Uhh...he's come from Exeter," Phillip said. He was already struggling with the deception.

Brother Cuthred smiled from Phillip to Vala and waited for the newcomer to elaborate. "A man of few words, Brother John?" he asked.

"He has taken a vow of silence," Phillip supplied.

"Oh, of course!" said Brother Cuthred. "There are those in our order who choose silence too. They prefer the contemplative life. Welcome, Brother."

With that, Brother Cuthred grasped Phillip's arm and drew him inside with many questions about his trip and nary a backward glance at Vala.

The monastery proper was composed of thick stone walls, trailing ivy and moss. Brother Cuthred led them through a low passage, jabbering and laughing. The walls were cool, and their footfalls slapped noisily in the dim space. The passage with its moist scent gave way to a stone-flagged courtyard. There they found many monks, working or in prayer.

"Brother John hoped to see our fine library," Phillip said.

Brother Cuthred smiled. "I hope you enjoy your visit, Brother John. Phillip, please join me at table later."

After Cuthred had left them, Phillip touched Vala's arm, indicating another passage to their right. Vala became conscious that her gut was unclenching for the first time in days. The thick walls would protect them from the terror of the riders. Even though she was impersonating a monk and at risk of discovery, it was less dangerous than the open road.

At the end of the passage, they walked down a number of steps that twisted to the left. Phillip took a lit candle from a small alcove in the wall next to a heavy wooden door. He pushed the door open and ignited a torch. Inside the large, square, windowless room, a riot of scents assailed Vala, leaving her feeling euphoric and lightheaded.

"I like to think of this as my kitchen," Phillip said. He circled the room, lighting more torches until a warm orange glow suffused the space. Wooden shelves lined the walls, and a long table filled the center of the space. Upon it sat a set of scales and a heavy mortar and pestle. Copper pots and kettles hung on pegs flanking a small hearth, and an industrious spider had woven a web between a few of them.

The shelves were laden with hundreds of bowls and jars containing tree bark, dried mushrooms, and fungi. Bunches of herbs hung from the rafters. Some of them still bore faint colors of yellow, purple or white, a testament to their original glory. Vala reached up and plucked a leaf, rubbed it between her palms, then sniffed. "Marjoram," she said as the scent rose around her. "Do you make your medicinals here?" she asked. "If I had such a room, I would never leave."

"I gather remedies during my travels and then try to reproduce them here. I've been blessed to discover some successful ones." Phillip's face shone with pleasure as he pulled two crocks from a shelf. "Look here." He removed a linen cloth from the top of the first crock. "This one aids particularly in breathing, making the chest feel free when a patient is overwhelmed with phlegm."

A strong scent arose from the jar, filling her nose, throat, and lungs. It left her feeling wonderfully refreshed. "It's very nice," she said.

"Unfortunately, the plant is hard to procure. A merchant ship brought it here from the Holy Lands."

He sealed the jar and then opened the second. It was half-full of a lumpy, glutinous substance. Vala bent over it but did not touch.

"This makes moderate burns heal faster, and the scarring is not so great. It must stay cool, though, for if heated, it loses some of its healing properties. I am still refining the formula."

"How useful. People suffer so from burns," said Vala. She dipped a finger in the jar and rubbed the balm on her palm.

Phillip busied himself with some bunches of herbs. "This is a very good physic," he said, handing her a stalk to smell. It is *Pimpinella anisum*."

"My uncle always used *Ricinus communis*." Vala touched the tiny flowers. "Is this better?"

"*Ricinus communis*? Do you mean castor beans? I've never thought of them," Phillip said.

"It works quite well. He liked it for headaches too, I remember."

Phillip scratched a note on a slab of slate with a small lump of chalk. "I know of some uses for the oil from the beans, but I've not tried it for headache. I must experiment with it!" He reached for a crock from the shelf. "I've meant to ask you more about how you came to understand Latin. You are extraordinarily good at it."

"My uncle started showing me words when I was about seven. We didn't have writing implements, nor a book. He'd just draw out letters in the dust. I thought everyone could do it. I mean, we heard the words every Sunday in church," said Vala, warming to the subject. "Uncle Adrian used to make up silly phrases to test me. It was fun to try to guess. Then the priest..." Vala stopped herself. It might offend Brother Phillip if she told him about Father Wulford's abysmal Latin.

"Your village priest?" prompted Phillip.

"Well, yes," said Vala. "Our old priest was good at Latin, but Father Wulford makes mistakes during Mass." She had gone too far, and she knew it.

Phillip sighed. "Yes, that happens far too often, I fear. Not everyone has the gift to understand a language different from his or her own, and the training is often lacking. The Church will take in the zealous regardless of their ability to learn."

Vala had never heard a cleric make such a statement. Men of God were inviolate, regardless of their faults, a point her village priest had emphasized many times.

Brother Phillip gave her a wry smile and turned the subject back to his original query. "Your uncle sounds like a rather extraordinary man. Was he a scholar?"

"He was a farmer."

"Not many farmers are also Latin instructors. How did he come to be educated?"

The question stopped Vala. It was a part of him, like his battered hat and the wrinkles around his eyes. She had never thought to ask, although she had asked a thousand much less important questions.

"I thought I knew my uncle, but perhaps I didn't," Vala said softly. "I thought I knew how I came to live with him, but that story was a lie. I don't know how he learned it."

"He must have been a good teacher, though, or you were an apt pupil."

Vala grinned.

Phillip rummaged in a sack on the floor and filled a small pouch with brown powder. "I love to putter about in here, but there will be no time this trip." The longing in his voice was clear.

"It would be a fine place to pass the time," Vala said as she sniffed plant buds and crushed seed pods in her fingers, asking what certain ones might be. Phillip replied to each query with an amazing knowledge of herb lore. She reached a small jar of white powder. It had an "X" on it struck through with a line. "What is this one?"

"Beware of the jars with an 'X' marked on them," he said quickly. "They contain poisons and the like." He came to look over her shoulder. "That is a crust of sorts. We gather it from the insides of wine casks. It's called tartar, or beeswing, a substance that can purge the bowel if used very sparingly. Do you know the term 'repurgo'?"

Vala nodded, examining the white powder. The words of the men she had overheard behind the market stalls in Bridestowe came back to her: 'About them scrapings you've been taking from my wine casks...' She sniffed the powder.

"It's not toxic in small amounts," Phillip said. "The novice need not have marked it so."

Vala dipped the tip of her little finger into it, touching it to her tongue. It was mildly bitter, but with the hint of fermented fruit—grapes, to be exact. She spun to face him. "Could this kill a person?"

Phillip glanced up. "Many things in this room are deadly if used indiscriminately."

"Could someone use it to murder?" she persisted.

Phillip took the jar, considering it. "Well, yes. I imagine that if a person received a heavy dose day after day for a week or two, they would weaken and might succumb to death."

Vala's voice was barely audible. "This is how they killed him."

"Pardon?" asked Philip.

"My father was killed—murdered. This powder is what they used."

"You must be mistaken, Vala. Why would a person go to such trouble? Other poisons are faster."

"It would be hard to discover, wouldn't it? Even if the victim knew his herb lore?"

Phillip scratched his chin. "I know you're distressed over the loss of your uncle and your father, but murder is such a heinous crime—a crime against God." Phillip set the jar back. "You should apply more of the coneflower ointment on your wound. I'll get you some."

Vala nodded vaguely, starring at the benign jar of beeswing resting on the shelf.

Phillip's satchel was bulging with a fresh stock of medicinal ingredients as he led the way back up the stairs toward the living quarters. After several turnings, they reached a small wooden door at the very end of a dark corridor.

"We'll stay here," Phillip said, and pushed open the door.

The small monk's cell was bare but for two raised sleeping coves, one on each side of the room, a wooden crucifix, and a small wood table that held a single candle. Someone had placed fresh rushes on the beds, filling the space with the scent of newly mown hay. Although sparse, it would be much more comfortable than sleeping on hard ground. They left their packs inside the door.

"Now for my treat!" Phillip whispered. "I know you'll like this. Follow and keep that hood down."

Back into the labyrinth of passageways they went, turning many times until they reached the foot of a narrow stair. They climbed, getting an occasional view of the valley below through cross-shaped arrow slits in the thick stone. At the top were a narrow landing and a door. Phillip grunted as he pulled the door open, then stood aside for Vala to see. Inside was a long, low room, illuminated by candles. On each side of the room were shelves and cupboards full of books, scrolls, and piles of manuscripts. The smell of parchment and old leather hit her as fully as the herbs had done two levels below.

"It's amazing," she whispered, putting her hands to her face.

Phillip's eyes shot to hers in warning, and she shoved her hands beneath her scapular. Two monks at the end of the room squinted up from their stacks of parchment, quills, and pots of ink. One nodded politely at Phillip and whispered something to the other.

Vala followed Phillip along the table and watched as the monks embellished pages of text with painstaking and artistically drawn letters. Using a tiny brush, one brother was painting a bird with its wings spread. The other brother was applying gold leaf to a book of psalms.

"Brother Thaddeus, what are you copying?" Phillip asked the eldest monk.

The monk painting the bird blinked his tired eyes and focused on Phillip. He stretched and pushed his hands into his lower back. "It is a Bible," he replied. "The entire compilation of the writings of Moses, Ezra, Solomon, and the others. I am very satisfied with the Book of Genesis. Here, look." He gently turned back the pages, and Vala saw the words *'In principio'* penned much larger than the rest upon the first page. The picture that accompanied them was rich in detail and illuminated by minute brushstrokes of gold.

Vala could have watched the monks for hours, but Phillip drew her away. He pointed out various books as they made a slow progress around the room. Some were heavy, with large hasps closing them, while others were small and so fragile, one dare not touch them.

"Many of these are gospels or writings of saintly scholars," Phillip whispered. "But some are stories men have written down for pleasure or instruction." He pulled a small book from one shelf. *"De Excidio et Conquestu Britanniae,"* he read.

Brother Thaddeus grunted as Phillip handed the book to Vala. She had never held a real book before. Her lips moved over the words *De Excidio et Conquestu Britanniae*—The Ruin and Conquest of Britain.

"It's the treatise of Saint Gildas on the history of Britain," said Brother Thaddeus. "He also discusses monastic life and chides monks and priests for their behavior. We have several of that." By his tone, he didn't think much of Saint Gildas or his comments on history.

"As we have several, might Brother John borrow this?" asked Phillip.

Brother Thaddeus waved a hand. "Take it, take it, Brother, but don't expect enlightenment."

Phillip quirked an eyebrow, then turned to Vala. "Brother John, this must be returned within the year. That is the rule of the library of Glastonbury. You should wrap it in oiled cloth when not in use to keep the dampness away. Books are very precious things."

Brother Thaddeus interrupted, "That copy is one which young Brother David penned for practice. You can see he made the cover for it, too. His pen work is not lovely, but his enthusiasm is great." The monk gestured to the small volume in Vala's hand. "As it is not fine enough to archive, you may keep it if you like, Brother."

Vala couldn't believe her luck. She was the owner of a real book. She clutched it to her chest, afraid they'd demand it back.

A new monk bustled in, eliciting another grunt from Thaddeus. "Ahhh! Brother Phillip!" the newcomer said without acknowledging the scriveners.

"Brother Niles," Phillip replied without enthusiasm.

Niles strode with purpose to the scribes' table. "Here are the changes we wish to make."

He shoved a sheaf of papers under Brother Thaddeus' nose. Thaddeus replied with a cough and pointed to the far end of the table. Brother Niles eyed the pile of accumulated work there, noting that Thaddeus hadn't enthusiastically embraced his project.

"When can I expect it?" the monk sniffed.

"Soon, I expect," Thaddeus replied off-handedly. Brother Niles scowled and strode from the room. Once the door had closed, Thaddeus muttered, "They're changing it again."

"Your beautiful gospel of Mark?" Phillip said.

The two eyed each other in a moment of understanding.

Thaddeus pulled an elegant volume toward him and ran his fingers over the cover. "They wish to re-word the story of Christ and the withering of the fig tree. They believe if the tree wilts immediately, rather than the following day, as was written, it would be a more convincing miracle. So, they will have me alter the original passage."

Phillip groaned and patted his friend on the shoulder. He nodded Vala toward the door, and once they were on the stairs, answered her question before she could ask.

"Scholars pour over sacred books looking for ways to clarify the words, but I don't think they ought to change what the writer witnessed."

Vala frowned. "Why would they do that?"

"I think they are too eager to clarify the mysteries of our faith."

On the surface, it sounded like a wholly noble idea, yet to change the words a writer had put down might change the meaning. Vala's brow furrowed as they descended the stairs. "Phillip, they are changing the Bible?"

Phillip only sighed.

As they emerged back into the stone courtyard, a tiny novice with a runny nose came panting up to them. "Brother Phillip, Brother Cuthred said to find you and bring you along. Brother Amos has arrived from Rome, and he wants a word."

"Thank you, Tyrone. I'll be along."

Tyrone nodded, backing up a step or two. "Brother Amos brought the rib bone of St. Wilfred."

"I'll be right along," Phillip reiterated.

"Brother Sebastian says the saint's relic will give us miracles," young Tyrone continued. "The abbot is having a golden reliquary made and everything!"

"Tyrone, I thank you. Please go tell the abbot I am coming," replied Phillip. "Now, off with you!"

The boy jumped and hurried away.

Phillip muttered, "They buy these artifacts from peddlers who swear they are real. Often, they aren't even human bones!" He glanced at Tyrone, running across the courtyard. "I must go. You'll need to keep out of the way until I return. Perhaps the garden." He motioned for Vala to follow him to a nearby gate. "There is a bench over against the wall." He pointed across the garden. "You should be safe until I can come for you."

"I'll be fine," Vala whispered before Phillip hesitantly left her.

A substantial garden lay beyond the gated archway. How she wished it had been summer, for it would be glorious in full flower. There were plants of all varieties peeking out in the weak spring sun. Rows of woody bushes bore fat green buds. Dead brown herbs left from the previous fall stood in orderly rows or else ringed the bases of fruit trees whose new leaves were just starting to make their appearance. A few monks were tending the plants at the far end of the garden, paying her no heed. She made her way to the bench along a path lined with bright purple crocuses. She smiled, recalling that the same flowers had been in bloom at the standing stone in Wistman's Wood a scant week before.

Vala settled herself on the weathered bench, adjusting her hood again, then drew out the small book she'd been given. She opened it with great care. It would be difficult not to love the book itself, with its smell of new leather and crisp parchment. Her fingers moved over the pages, feeling the texture of the inks and paints. It took a few moments to decipher the hand, for the letters were of somewhat irregular size.

*Whatever in this my epistle I may write in my humble but well-meaning manner, rather by way of lamentation than for display, let no one suppose that it springs from contempt of others, or that I foolishly esteem myself as better than they; —for, alas! the subject of my complaint is the general destruction of everything that is good, and the general growth of evil throughout the land...*

Vala was completely absorbed when someone coughed. She lurched and noticed a pair of worn leather boots standing in front of her. Since she could not look up, she clambered to her feet, head bowed and eyes downcast.

"I'm sorry, Brother. I did not wish to disturb your reading," the voice said sounding eager rather than sorry. "I'm Brother Samuel. We saw you come in with Brother Phillip."

Another monk was standing behind Samuel, wearing thick-soled sandals. "This is Brother Ignatius," said the first monk.

Vala bowed toward the sandals.

"Is it true you have taken a vow of silence?" asked Samuel.

Vala nodded deeply, hoping the confirmation would cause these two to go away and leave her to her book. Brother Samuel however, went on.

"Brother Phillip is always off on some interesting mission. We were wondering what this one was about, as you were his traveling companion."

Vala shrugged.

Brother Ignatius cut in, "Samuel, he can't answer a question like that if he can't speak."

"I know he can't speak, but he could nod or make hand gestures," replied Brother Samuel.

"Well, then, ask a proper question," retorted Brother Ignatius.

Brother Samuel rose up on his toes. "Did Phillip talk about where he had been?"

Vala shook her head.

Brother Samuel searched for some other line of attack. "Brother Phillip is often called to counsel the bishop. Was he in Bath?"

Vala shook her head.

"Brother Amos arrived today. Did Phillip say what that is about?" Ignatius said.

Vala shrugged, indicating her ignorance on the subject. She wished these two gossips would go away.

"He can tell us nothing," Samuel muttered, and the two retreated, thwarted by Vala's lack of information.

Before she could sit again, bells began to toll. The monks tending the garden rose and headed toward the gate. She was unsure what to do, but Brother Phillip appeared, sidestepping the tide of brothers.

"It is the dinner bell." Phillip sounded out of breath. "The monks dine together in the common room. You will have to sit at the low end of the table. I must sit with Brother Cuthred. Just keep to your dinner and nod. After we dine, I'll make our excuses."

Vala nodded soberly.

Benches scraped the floor and lively chatter met her ears as they entered the common room. Vala had anticipated a quiet hall, like a church, with someone reading prayers while the company consumed a meager fare. By a slight nod of his head, Phillip directed Vala to a bench at one end of the largest trestle table. She hastened to her seat and hunched over her trencher of stewed chicken, waiting for the signal to start eating. Monks jostled onto the benches, filling the seats around her, talking to their neighbors. Vala shifted uncomfortably. She hadn't bargained on having to blend into such a large company at table.

The final monk seated himself, and the room quieted while one of them said a prayer of thanks for their repast. After a hearty "Amen!", the monks fell upon the plates of bread and stew, and the conversation resumed. A fat monk to Vala's left filled her cup from a large flask and then passed it along the table. Vala tasted the rather sweet wine, the first mouthful warming her all the way to her stomach.

Vala gave only nods or a shake of the head when asked a question. Finally, Brother Samuel explained to his neighbors. "Vow of silence."

Soon, those around her began to ignore her, and Vala glanced down the table toward the end, where Phillip was in deep conversation with three older monks.

"You always complain about who they send as bishop," Phillip was saying.

"Saxony is not Italy," replied Brother Cuthred. "Nor is it France."

"He makes a fair point," said the balding monk to Phillip's right. "Britain needs men of the people, and these recent popes—" He leaned toward his dinner companions, and his next words were drowned out by the belly laughs of Vala's tablemates.

"—and young Brother Tyrone was at the gate when they came riding up. Nearly pissed himself when they demanded to see Brother Cuthred." There was general laughter, and young Brother Tyrone blushed.

"You didn't see the one who cursed at me," the boy retorted. "He'd an ugly gash on his face, and he looked like a demon!"

"Watch your tongue, Brother!" someone said.

Vala went cold inside at the mention of a scarred man at the abbey gates. She looked around, half-expecting to find a black-robed villain at the table.

"More wine?" the fat monk next to her asked, topping up then filled up her cup. She downed it in a gulp. Her pursuers were still searching for her. Vala wanted nothing more than to pull Phillip away from the company to tell him, but he and his table companions were engrossed in their discussion. She watched him wave his spoon as he clarified some point.

"De Roche is a wise and progressive man—"

The balding monk next to him shook his head with a sour expression.

Brother Cuthred replied, "He may be all that—" then spoke in a low voice while the other two gave him their attention.

Vala sank back against the wall in despair.

"You must drink faster, Brother John, if you wish to keep up," said Brother Samuel, giving Vala a good-natured poke. She looked at her cup and could not recall when it had been re-filled. She took an obliging drink as the table toasted the fine weather. Brother Samuel leaned over and topped off her cup again. The noise in the dining room had risen as the wine flowed, and Vala could no longer hear anything from Phillip's end of the table.

"To our reverend bishop," said the fat monk on her left.

"To Bishop De Roche!" they all cried.

Vala drained her own cup, not wishing to draw attention. Brother Samuel passed the wine jug once again. Vala tried to refuse, putting her hand over her cup.

She had no experience with wine, and it was making her dizzy. Her fingers slipped off the rim of the cup, and quick as that, it was full again. Her fellow diners made another new toast, and she was obliged to hoist her cup again. Around her, monks were laughing raucously and telling bawdy rhymes. Through the smoke floating in the air and the haze in her brain, she heard singing in a jumble of basso voices. Loud guffaws and much pounding on the table hailed the end of the song. Vala's head thrummed from the oppressive smell of peat smoke and sweating monks.

She felt a strong urge to escape the room. She needed air and a place to lie down. The room was spinning and she gripped the table to make it stop, but it was not enough. She slipped sideways off the bench onto the floor.

A voice overhead laughed, "The lad can't handle his spirits!"

Vala tried to get to her knees, and with several awkward attempts, she managed it. Someone grabbed the back of her robes and hauled her to her feet, then slung an arm around her to support her.

"I'm sorry," a voice whispered over the general din. "I shouldn't have stayed at the table so long. Just keep your head down."

That, at least, was easily done. Vala's head felt like lead.

"Young Brother John has barely given up milk, and you lot have gone and gotten him drunk," Phillip chided the table with a laugh.

As Phillip dragged Vala away, there were calls of farewell and quips about a monk who couldn't hold his wine.

Vala tried to use her feet, but they became twisted in her robes or confused about which one was to step next. It was rather funny, she thought, and she giggled.

Brother Phillip shushed her.

"I have to tell you something," she whispered, but she could not recall the important news she'd desperately wanted to deliver. She focused bleary eyes on him. "I'm sorry."

"It's my fault," he said. "I was so engrossed in conversation, I forgot about you. I fear you'll have a terrible headache in the morning."

The words washed over Vala, but she could not capture their meaning, and the monastery's dark labyrinth of passageways only added to her confusion. Phillip guided her faltering steps passed endless identical doors. Finally, he stopped.

"What's this?" she mumbled dully.

"Our cell," he said, pushing open the door.

The room was dark except for a small stream of moonlight coming through a high window. Phillip leaned her against the doorframe as he lit a candle. Vala clung to the stonework as the floor began to pitch under her feet. Phillip chivvied her inside.

Phillip closed and barred the door, heart pounding, and leaned heavily against it. They had barely escaped discovery. In the morning, they would slip away, no harm done.

Vala lurched toward one of the beds before he could move to help her. She pushed off her hood and then tugged off the cowl.

"It's so...warm," she mumbled, struggling to pull off the scapular. It, too, fell to the floor. Last, she wrestled her way out of the woolen robe before collapsing on the bed. The cell was silent but for her deep breathing.

Phillip stared at her, back pressed against the door, anchoring himself to something solid. The girl's skin glowed warm and smooth in the flicker of the candlelight, her hair spilling across the fresh rushes. He swallowed and tried to look away, but he could not. The taut linen bandaging covered her chest. He remembered applying the first bandage the night near the river, his fingers grazing her skin as they did their work. His eyes flitted to the knot of cord holding the old brown leggings in place. The nubby fabric was a contrast to the pale flesh of her belly.

His fingers splayed out on that cool skin, barely touching it, his palms hot as they slid along the curves of her waist and then her hips. She breathed slowly and evenly, with never a flicker from her closed eyelids. He lifted one of her knees so he could kneel between them. Phillip's body rumbled with lust. The animal fought for control.

"Help me, Lord," he whispered.

He squeezed his eyes closed and sucked in a ragged breath. When he opened them, he was still standing with his back against the door, his fingers clutching hard at the bar. He had not moved. Vala lay sleeping, unmolested in any way. The fire in his gut still raged, but he pushed the animal roughly back into its place, where he thought he could begin to fight it once again.

From somewhere in the depths of the abbey, a single bell clanged, dull and heavy. It was the hour of Compline, the monks' call to prayer. Phillip crossed himself, wrapping his fingers around the crucifix at his chest. He raised a façade of cool detachment, and approached the bed, then pulled a blanket quickly over the sleeping girl. With only a momentary pause for regret or guilt, he opened the door and made his silent way through the darkened passages of the abbey.

Chapter Fourteen:
*"In for a penny, in for a pound."*

A cock crowed under the window, and Vala roused herself with difficulty. Her head felt like lead. She forced her tongue away from the roof of her very dry mouth and sat up. Disentangling herself from her blanket, she struggled to her feet.

"The wine," she groaned. Holding her head, she vowed never to drink it again. Vala blinked against the light and realized Brother Phillip was not in the cell. That was for the best.

Her clothes, for the most part, were in a heap on the floor. She pulled them on, reckoning that she and Phillip should have been on the road by now. She was reminded of Brother Tyrone's report of the scar-faced man who'd come to the abbey gate. She must tell Phillip immediately. She hoisted her pack to her shoulder and looked about for Phillip's satchel. It was gone.

Vala picked her way along the passageway, hoping to avoid notice. The cool morning air was refreshing after the stuffy sleeping chamber. It eased her pounding head a bit. Thankfully, she met no one as she slipped out the stone passage to the place where the horses were stabled.

The sun was a pale disk that slid in and out of view through wispy grey clouds. She was glad for the overcast day, for even this dull morning light hurt her eyes.

Vala located Thistle, but Phillip's horse was missing. She couldn't imagine where he had gone, for the plan was to continue on today.

An old withered monk hobbled toward her as she saddled her mount. "He rode off at daybreak, Brother John. Our Brother Phillip said your paths diverge here at the monastery, and that you would be going on alone."

Vala pulled her hood low to hide her face and her disbelief. Phillip had failed to tell her they were parting company. She had come to rely on him, so much so that it felt like a betrayal for him to leave her without a single word of farewell. Why had he done it? Out on the road, a murderous company was seeking her, yet there was nothing to do but ride for Bath, and the bishop.

The old monk handed over a cloth sack containing some dried lentils and a skin bulging full of cool water. She first shook her head, declining the food. It made her stomach roil to think of eating.

"You can't be riding off without victuals. Young men are too hasty and most end up suffering for their rashness." The old monk grinned, shaking a finger at her. Vala nodded her thanks and tied the food bag to her saddle.

The wind whistled around the walls of Glastonbury Abbey, driving iron-grey clouds to the southeast. The road was deserted, and Thistle broke into an effortless canter. When he sprang over a large pothole, unprepared, Vala lurched forward. Her stomach lurched too, and she was almost sick on the spot. She squeezed her eyes shut in an attempt to counteract the stabbing pain behind them.

"Wine," she muttered. "Never again!"

Vala was miserable from the vestiges of drink and forsaken by a man she counted as an ally. She tried to call to mind the events of the evening before. Her drunken fall could have proved disastrous for Phillip. If her idiocy had turned him against her, she guessed she deserved it.

Rain threatened, presaged by a strong wind that buffeted girl and horse relentlessly. By midday, Vala's cheeks pinked so much that they burned. A copse of trees behind the lee of a hill provided a respite, and Vala decided to take shelter there. Thistle grazed on the new shoots of grass while Vala drank from the waterskin. She didn't know if they'd reach Bath by evening. Phillip would have known. She should have asked him, but she had set far too much store in his help and protection.

"It's my mission, not his. The box is my responsibility," she muttered, knowing it was up to her to see her mission to its conclusion.

Thistle's ears flicked at a sound from down the road, and Vala cursed as she hurried her horse into the trees. She imagined the black cloaked riders coming upon her in the wild where she had no chance of defending herself or outrunning them. Hoofbeats approached, and Vala crouched, holding her breath. Over the hill, a cart rumbled along, driven by an old man hauling bags of wool. The man did not notice her and soon disappeared around the bend. Vala crumpled against a tree trunk, letting Thistle go back to grazing.

Hot, angry tears welled up. She was alone, frightened of any sound, and she hid from innocent old men going about their business.

She took out the food sack given her by the monk. She opened it with a sniff. Dried lentils. She'd need a fire and a pot to cook them, but she had no pot. She chewed on a few, crunching through their hard skins as she ran the back of her hand over her damp face. The dust of the road left a dirty smear across her fingers.

A tiny stream gurgled below the grove of trees, and Vala climbed down to it. She stripped off the monk's robe and bathed herself in the cold water. Chilled and dripping, she pulled all the garments she possessed from her pack and considered them. Seeking an audience with the bishop of Bath whilst impersonating a monk would not do. The only other clothes she possessed were the boy's clothes she had traded for in Exeter, and they were a poor and shabby substitute for the fine woolen robes Phillip had lent her; however, they were her only option.

Thistle proved a good horse. Vala didn't need to attend to their course as long as there was a road to follow. It left her free to consider what she'd say when she met the bishop, how to present her case without sounding a fool.

"I brought this from Bridestowe," she tried aloud. "Murderous thieves were after me the entire time, Eminence... or Your Grace?"

She cleared her throat and tried again. "My father was no Christian, sire. I'm worried about the inheritance he left me. I'd be obliged if you could examine it and assure me that it's safe, or help me to destroy it." It sounded pompous spoken aloud. If Phillip had been here, he could have guided her.

In the afternoon, the country lane merged into a larger way, big enough for two carts to pass unimpeded. They were nearing the city. Travelers became more frequent, galloping fast on errands or plodding along wearily, anxious for home and hearth. Vala watched ahead and behind for signs of her pursuers, and by pure force of will resisted the urge to dive into the trees when she met a cart or a rider. It was not long before she got her first glimpse of Bath.

Coming out onto an open paddock, the road dipped down toward a slow-moving river. Bath spread out along the bank on the far side. Just as with Exeter, the smell of the city reached Vala before she neared the first buildings. It was a river smell mixed with the scent of animals, cooking fires, and offal. Vala pulled her cloak up over her nose and mouth until her senses became acclimated to the invasion of odors.

A sturdy-looking bridge of stone and timbers spanned the river. Once they had crossed, Vala and Thistle found themselves in the midst of the city proper. Dwellings surrounded them, and sellers were barking out their wares. The buildings were clustered together so tightly that one appeared to be holding up the next. Rounded stones paved the roadway. Thistle did not like the slippery, uneven surface and shied sideways, snorting irritably.

The crowded thoroughfare curved to the right, and soon Vala saw a tall structure, grand and imposing. Not a style she'd seen in Exeter. The façade was tall, with huge stone pillars marking the entrance. Above the entrance was a round window adorned with a carving of wild fern. Mist rose from behind the high walls and then settled down on the street with a smell like water washing over the rocks near the millpond at home.

Could this be the cathedral? Crowds of people were milling around, looking agape at the structure, just as she was.

A balding man called, "Taking the waters? Pay here!"

Eager people pushed through the crowd to the man. He collected coins and led a group off through the main doors.

Vala stopped a passing youth. "Is that the church?"

"That there?" He looked amused. "That's the old Roman baths. People come to bathe in the waters. The water is hot, you know. Costs silver to get in," the youth told her. He began to walk away, but turned. "Church is up yonder."

Vala dismounted and patted Thistle, who was dancing in agitation from the press of the crowd. She stood for a moment, taking in the majesty of the baths. High up on a pediment, another stone carving caught her attention. It was a fierce face chiseled into the center of the sun. Vala could almost feel the intense eyes following her as she pushed past the throng toward the church.

The Roman baths were grand, but to Vala's mind, the church was much grander. She wondered why there were fewer people marveling at it. Fronting the great portico was a low wall that enclosed a courtyard. An open gate admitted the faithful to the church precincts. Vala approached in awe. Liveried guards attended the gate, and one of them barred her way as she attempted to pass inside.

The tall man raised his spear. "State your business."

His companion hurried over and pushed the spear tip down. "We don't threaten visitors unless they come bearing weapons, you stupid ox. Anyone can come into the church who is civil and not drunk."

The tall man reddened, and his eye twitched.

His superior continued to chide him. "Do you see a weapon on this boy? No, you do not!"

The spear wielder's shoulders slumped.

"You are here to keep the peace and to answer questions, not to intimidate the visitors." He faced Vala. "Where can I direct you, boy?" Then, jerking a thumb at his companion, he said, "This one here is new to his post."

Vala fumbled in her sack and brought forth the wooden box. "I have something to give the bishop."

"A box?" said the guard. "You know the bishop doesn't actually see commoners."

"It's something cursed," Vala muttered. This had an effect on the guards, but it was not the effect she'd anticipated.

The tall one burst into laughter. "What, a shriveled griffin's claw? Or perhaps it's a dragon's heart?"

Vala pulled the box to her chest. "It's nothing like that!" But of course, she didn't really know.

"Go in if you like, boy. You can tie your horse by the stable yonder," said the second guard, waving a hand toward the far side of the courtyard. "It won't matter. It's too late to see His Grace today, and the bishop ain't likely to see you anyway, nor will he be wanting your old box. Best burn it and go back home."

Vala pulled Thistle across the courtyard. She hadn't come this far to give up at the bishop's very door. She tied Thistle and stalked back to the front of the church, but she had no idea what to do next.

"I overheard you say you wish to see Bishop De Roche."

Vala turned. Behind her was an elderly priest. He was leaning on a cane and squinted at her through rheumy eyes.

"A very good friend of mine bade me look out for a youth riding a black horse like that one." He pointed a gnarled finger toward Thistle. "A person wishing to see His Grace?"

"Was it Brother Phillip?" asked Vala, suddenly hopeful.

The priest indicated a stone bench under a spindly tree. "I sit over there, you know," he said as though he hadn't heard her. "I sit and think, and sometimes pray. It's wonderful when the sun is shining." He hooked her arm with his. "But come along now and let's get you to the bishop."

Vala couldn't believe her luck and was just about to say so when one of the gate guards shouted toward them.

"Father Guillard!"

The old priest waved at the man.

"Father, you know the bishop won't like it if you bother him. He says no peasants. I don't like to think what he'll say to you."

The old priest grinned. "Not to worry, Jonathan. I'm sure the bishop will be happy for the diversion."

Vala saw the guard shake his head.

"Yes—my friend told me to watch out for you, and here you are!" chortled the priest. "And, as you suspected, he does collect relics and curiosities used by the old Celts and such. Heathens, he likes to call them."

Vala frowned. "Brother Phillip doesn't collect..."

"No, no! Dear me, no, child!" the priest said with a chuckle. "It's His Grace who does that." He winked at her. "I said to him, I said, 'Your Grace, why do you bother with these oddments? Surely, they aren't worth the effort.' And he said, 'Father Guillard, you should wear a hat. The sun is addling your brains.'"

The old priest cackled until he began to wheeze. Vala steadied him, but he patted her hand to indicate he was fine.

"The bishop said that to you?" she asked.

Father Guillard gave a dismissive wave and began climbing the broad steps toward the arched doorway of the massive church. "Come, my dear, and I can put you a step closer to your goal."

Vala's eyes moved upward until she was in danger of toppling backward. The immensity of the church was awe-inspiring, rendering her and her petty problems insignificant. She followed Father Guillard inside, where hundreds of tallow candles lit the inner sanctum. Vala spun to take it all in.

"Remove your hood, boy!" barked a prelate on his way to the courtyard.

Vala swept it back before remembering she was a woman and therefore required to cover her head. Her face reddened as she drew it back up. She hurried after Father Guillard, dipping her fingertips into a carved stone font of holy water as she passed.

The nave of the church was magnificent. Its vaulted roof and tall columns marched stolidly toward the altar. Beyond the columns, half-hidden nooks and alcoves tantalized her, while the smell of frankincense hung in the air, giving the space an ethereal feeling. There were hundreds of candles, illuminating the polished marble floors and the wealth of golden statuary surrounding the altar.

"It is very grand," Father Guillard said, as though reading her thoughts. "A worthy tribute to Our Lord."

How had they raised those high stone arches? It had taken all the healthy men and boys in Wistman's Wood to set the new roof timbers for their small church. Vala longed to explore every nook but instead fell in behind the old priest, who shuffled off toward the aisle on the far right. The light was dim and the ceilings were lower as they passed folk kneeling at small shrines where votive candles lit the faces of the hopeful and the hopeless.

"It is a bit intimidating, is it not?" the old priest whispered. "I confess, I prefer the small chapel behind the ambulatory." He gestured for her to follow him into the south transept.

Vala paused. "There's a chapel too? May we see it?"

"I'm afraid not," said the old man with a smile. "Only the priests may use it."

His walking stick tapped along the empty passageway. Even here, there was much to see. The ceiling abounded with elaborate paintings. Vala kept stopping to look and then hurrying to catch up.

"... and so that is how I came to meet him. You know, he is a real pleasure to talk to."

Vala had missed what Father Guillard had been saying, so she muttered, "It was very kind of you to help me."

"It's nothing, my child."

Vala wanted to inquire about Phillip, for if he was in Bath, she wanted to see him and apologize for her stupidity back in Glastonbury. Before she could ask, the elderly priest led her through an open archway.

It was a square room with dark stone walls containing little niches. In each was a statue of a saint or angel. Behind a bulky wooden table, a squat man with a sour face and a very large quill pen sat hunched over sheaves of paper. A great crucifix adorned the wall behind him. His ornate robes were made of fine quality black wool, and upon his head was a round black hat with no brim. A liveried guard stood on each side of the table. Neither one smiled as Father Guillard ushered Vala forward.

Vala fell to her knees. She had expected that it would be difficult to obtain an audience with so great a man.

"Your—Your Excellency," she stuttered. "I mean, Your Grace."

The sour man gave a loud "Humph!" and continued to write.

"Not yet," whispered the old priest. He tugged at her sleeve, and she clambered to her feet. Sniggering erupted from a knot of monks huddled in the corner.

"Boy, why is your head covered inside the church?" boomed the man behind the table.

"I'm a girl, Your Honor," she replied. "I mean, Your Grace."

"Take off that hood!" he demanded.

Vala froze with indecision, but one of the monks strode forward and yanked it off her head."

"Thank you, Brother William," said the man behind the table as Vala's long hair slid down around her shoulders. "I suppose that proves it. Put your hood back on, girl. Throw her out of here."

"No, Your Grace, wait!" cried Vala. "I've come a very long way to see you."

Father Guillard patted her arm kindly. "This is not the bishop, child, but his secretary. Tell him your business, and he will arrange for you to meet with the bishop."

Vala edged forward. "I've traveled a long way, sir. I come from Wistman's Wood. I carry something that I believe is cursed. I would have the bishop decide what should become of it."

The secretary glared at her, beady eyes never blinking. "Show me," the man said.

Vala held forth the box, which the secretary gave only the most cursory of glances.

"Do you imagine His Grace has time to meet with every rustic who passes through Bath? Leave the thing here and go away." He gave a dismissive wave and then rounded on the old priest. "Father Guillard, don't you have some pigeons to feed?"

The monks dissolved into appreciative snorts.

Vala's ire rose, not on her own account, but for the rough treatment dealt to the kindly old priest. However, Father Guillard was off in a world of his own, gazing at the ornate crucifix over the secretary's head.

"Hurry up!" barked the secretary, "Set your box down and go!"

It didn't feel right to lay the box on this table and just walk away. What about Farley's men? What of the attack on her village? She lifted her chin, "My lord," she began, lifting her chin, "I must show this to the bishop himself. Men have died because of it."

The secretary regarded her with a grimace, and she knew she had gone too far. The box was shaking in her hands, the accursed contents rattling as Brother William moved in closer. Vala pulled the box to her chest before the monk could snatch it from her. Instead, the monk gave a jerk of his head, sending one of his fellows off through a side door. The brother sidled past her to whisper in the secretary's ear.

The secretary's scowl never altered. "Follow this man," he said brusquely, and he bent over his parchment again.

Father Guillard clapped her on the shoulder with a satisfied grin. "You see, everything will be fine. The bishop will help you, child!" He gave her arm a squeeze before shuffling away.

Vala trailed after the monk, not feeling at all reassured.

Brother William's robes swished as he led her through a side door onto a covered cloister that encircled a huge garden. Priests were strolling at their leisure, lost in contemplation or prayer, but not so Brother William, who hissed at Vala to keep pace with his brisk stride. The monk's boots had seen hard use, and his face bore the look of someone who spent his days in the wind and the sun.

Vala plucked up her courage and ventured a question. "Are you taking me to the bishop of Bath?" Her voice sounded to her own ear small and shrill, but she wanted to be certain they weren't simply throwing her out.

The monk turned his disdainful gaze upon her. "This church was not given to Bishop De Roche as his seat. He is merely stopping here for a time, on papal orders. Therefore, he is not the bishop of Bath."

Vala suppressed her other questions and instead whispered, "*Fortes fortuna iuvat.*"

The cloister ran straight on toward another large stone building, but the monk led her to the left. Under the cloister's sheltering roof, an ornately carved door stood ajar. The monk stopped abruptly in front of it. Vala nearly ran into him.

She could hear men talking inside the room. Two men paused in their conversation as her guide pushed the door open, bowing low as Vala took a timid step into the well-appointed room. The room's occupants sat near a blazing fire, one dressed in a monk's garments and the other in lavish green robes with a short cape embellished with elaborate embroidery. A golden crucifix hung from the man's neck.

Her guide approached the monk, whose black habit was similar to his own but for a hood pulled low over his face. After a few words, the hooded monk dismissed her guide.

"What are you waiting for?" Brother William hissed as he departed.

The man in green lounged in a large wooden chair, feet perched on a footstool. The black-robed monk was perched on a stool. Vala took a step forward, glancing at the heavy tapestries adorning the walls. She felt every bit the foolish rustic as she cleared her throat to speak. The brilliant speech she'd prepared had flown from her head.

The man in green rose a bit stiffly. "What is it you want, my child?"

"Your Grace." Vala's eyes fixed on a splendid crucifix of gold that stood upon the table. Encrusted with gems, it radiated dazzling colors in the fire's light. "I mean, you are him—the real bishop?"

An impressive figure, tall and thin, the bishop nodded with a warm, engaging smile. "I am." His black hair was flecked with silver, and high, arching eyebrows set off intelligent eyes.

Vala pulled down her hood, allowing her hair to spill out. "Your Grace, my name is Vala Crofter, from Wistman's Wood. A good priest in Dartmeet told me that you collect things of the old gods lest they fall into the wrong hands." She knew she sounded like a terrible fool.

"And so I do, my child."

His height was imposing, and she took a small step backward, but he took her hand in his in a comforting gesture.

"You're trembling, child. There is nothing to fear here." He looked deep into her eyes. "Show me this thing you've brought—this thing of the old gods."

Vala pushed the box forward as though mesmerized, and the bishop took it.

He turned his back on her, showing it to the hooded monk, manipulating the box in his hands. Vala tried to see what he was doing but was afraid to edge any closer. The bishop held out the box for the monk so he might see inside.

The monk nodded appreciatively before the bishop shut each of the open panels. He placed the box in the monk's hands.

"You opened it!" Vala said.

The bishop faced her. "How did you come by this thing, child?"

Vala swallowed. "My father—he was called Simon Finn Negus. He gave it to me. An heirloom of our house, he said. He told me it was dangerous, but he died before he could explain. I think he was murdered," she whispered, as it was a sin to speak of such a crime in front of a holy bishop. "I tried to take it home, but riders came and burned my village. They killed—" She choked on the words.

The bishop cut in. "Your father didn't tell you what this is? Nor how to open it?"

"No, Your Grace," Vala mumbled. The bishop had opened the box without hesitation, while she had been unable to succeed in over a fortnight.

"Your family is descended from the heretic warrior, Finn, you say?"

"Yes, Your Grace, but my father didn't raise me. I only just learned of him a short time ago."

The bishop took her arm and steered her out of the room into the cloister overlooking the gardens. "Thank you for bringing this to me, Vala. You have done well. It is something very wicked and evil. I will take care of it so you need have no further worries about it," his voice comforting and fatherly.

"But, Your Grace, there are riders after me—after the box," she said, her voice shrinking to a mere squeak.

The bishop raised an eyebrow. "I have just been informed that a band of fanatics was apprehended mere miles from the city. We will make certain they don't trouble you again. After all, you cannot be held accountable for your heritage."

"The box is a sort of family heirloom," Vala said, but the bishop had already turned to the hooded monk, who whispered to him urgently. The bishop responded with an irritated shake of his head.

"Now, my dear, you cannot go about dressed as a boy."

"Your Grace, it was a disguise."

"It is a sin to deceive in such a way, but I grant you absolution because of the circumstances." He made the sign of the cross over her head. "I will have one of the good sisters take you to a room where you can rest and have a decent meal. We will find you some suitable clothing." He placed a finger to his cheek in thought. "How does this sound? You will spend the night here with our fine sisters, then you will attend Mass tomorrow morning in the cathedral before beginning your journey home."

It was more a command than an invitation, but Vala was sure he meant it kindly. The prospect of food and a warm bed was welcome. She reckoned she ought to give thanks, and what better place than this magnificent cathedral? Vala nodded, but the bishop was already striding off across the gardens with his monk.

A nun soon arrived to fetch her. "Are you the girl who is to spend the night with us?" asked the plump woman.

Vala nodded.

"This way, please."

The nun led Vala along the cloister, then across the gardens toward an ivy-covered wall which enclosed a small courtyard. Columbine clung to the cracks and crevices of the wall and framed a wooden gate. The nun opened it and nodded Vala inside. They were facing a number of plain doors set in the wall under a portico, and Vala was escorted to one of these.

"You may rest here. I will return with a change of clothing, as the bishop ordered. We should have something suitable in the charity basket." The nun looked Vala over as though measuring her. "You may dine with the nuns once you've changed. A bell will ring when the meal is set."

"Thank you." Vala gave a grateful sigh.

The nun left Vala inside a small chamber with a narrow palliasse, a candle in a dish set upon the floor, and a crucifix. Vala sank down on the cot. It was over. The box was the bishop's worry now, and she could go home.

Uncle Adrian believed that time would heal all wounds, and Vala hoped it was true. Home would not be the same without him, but even if the house was empty, she could go there and then decide what course to take. She would see how Tessie was faring. Vala thought she'd even like to see pompous Father Wulford. She missed them all. This adventure had made her appreciate the safety and stability of home. It might not be exciting, but it was far better than sleeping in ditches and evading capture by faceless riders, or feeling a cold knife's edge in the darkness. Vala giggled in giddy relief.

There was a soft knock, and the nun entered, handing over a bundle of clothes.

"Thank you, Sister. Might I ask your name? I was very rude not ask it before."

"I'm Sister Hilda," the nun replied. "And there is nothing to apologize for. An audience with Bishop De Roche is daunting. It's enough to put anyone into a state. He's so lordly."

"I brought the bishop a cursed thing." As Vala repeated the word 'cursed' again, it nagged at her.

"Oh, my!" replied Sister Hilda, her eyes wide. "That is serious business. Did the bishop place it with the rest of the things to be burned?"

"Burned?" said Vala.

"Yes, lamb. The man is a saint! He works tirelessly to stamp out idolatry and heresy. He has a room just above his audience chamber where he collects pagan things," she said. "Every month, the lot is carted out to a field beyond the church and burned. Tomorrow is a burning day."

"I suppose burning would be best," Vala said, although she had pictured a more romantic ending for the box. She envisioned learned priests inspecting it. Perhaps a powerful prayer could drive the evil out of it. Now that she knew its fate was burning, she wished she'd had a look inside.

Vala thanked Sister Hilda for her hospitality, and the woman left.

The charity garments were patched but clean. Vala pulled off her old things and stuffed them in her pack. She fingered the knife wound briefly before slipping into her shift, now considerably shorter having served as bandaging material. She donned a plain brown kirtle, some nubby stockings, and ties. The nun had also left a very nice cloak dyed with wode, voluminous and warm. Vala tried it on and spun around to see the effect as it floated about her feet. It would serve her well on the long ride home.

Dinner with the nuns was a quiet affair. They ate in silence while an elderly sister with a rusty voice read psalms. Back in her room, Vala lit the single candle and tried to say a prayer of thanks for the way things had worked out, but one final thing gnawed at her. The bishop had opened the box, yet he hadn't shown her the contents.

Vala tried to think about the trip home but kept returning to the object within the box. It was ridiculous to waste a moment's thought on it, but she longed to know what was inside. She reasoned that the bishop wouldn't have wanted a young girl exposed to something evil.

She pulled out her book as a distraction and settled down near the candle to read.

*Britain hath priests, but they are unwise; very many that minister, but many of them impudent; ... certain of them are deceitful raveners; ... wolves prepared for the slaughter of souls for they provide not for the good of the common people, but covet rather the gluttony of their own bellies."*

It was a shocking admonishment coming from a saint.

She snapped the book shut and began pacing back and forth across the small room, scuffing her boots on the rush-strewn floor, trying to convince herself that the thing inside the box did not concern her. The longer she paced, the more she found that, in fact, she did want to know its contents.

Vala opened her door onto the darkness now settling over Bath and gave in to the powerful urge. She'd find His Grace, the bishop, perhaps in that pleasing room where she had met with him. Would he refuse her a quick peek? A man of intelligence such as the bishop surely could not begrudge her curiosity. These were her thoughts as she made her way back through the gardens and into the cloister that led to the bishop's receiving room.

A single torch lit the far end of the cloister, its reddish glow illuminating a circle of stone and leaving all else in darkness. Vala moved along from pillar to pillar, feeling like an intruder in the sacred inner sanctum of the church. Even though she told herself she had a right to be here, she stepped as softly as she could, not wishing to be stopped or sent back to the nuns' quarters. As she approached the torchlight near to the bishop's receiving room, she heard voices.

"You placed it yourself, with the other things?"

"Yes, Your Grace."

There was movement, and Vala flattened herself behind a pillar. Two men came out into the cloister. She peered at them through the gap between pillar and wall.

Bishop De Roche gazed out over the garden. The other man was the black-cloaked monk. As he joined the bishop, he lowered his hood. A long scar creased the monk's cheek from eye to chin, an ugly scar, exactly as Robert Gallows had described it back in Wistman's Wood.

"This whole business has gone badly," said the bishop.

"You have what you wanted," the monk replied. "You've no reason to complain."

"You think not?" said the bishop. "You never actually captured Simon Finn

Negus, only a pile of smoldering ashes. You killed a bystander in front of an entire village. Burning hovels and murdering peasants will not endear them to us." The bishop's voice turned low and deadly. "In the future, save your recklessness for a situation where it is warranted."

"I was not responsible for the fire, and as to the killing of a peasant, I was forced to it," the monk growled. "That baker botched everything, and I needed information."

The bishop slammed his book down upon the stone railing. "You disobeyed my direct orders!"

"I thought I was following Your Grace's wishes, if not his specific orders."

"I want the entire event kept quiet," the bishop said, calm returning to his voice. "Make sure your men understand this."

"I've always have kept your little secrets, and I will continue to do so," the monk replied acidly.

The bishop sighed. "Tomorrow, the box will be burned with the rest. The girl will attend morning Mass and then set off for home."

Vala strained to hear as he lowered his voice.

"I trust you know what to do from there?"

The monk nodded.

"No loose ends, Brother Germain," said the bishop. "But wait until she's crossed the river. Do it quietly. Just kill her, and let the beasts of the forest gnaw on her corpse."

"While your hands remain clean," the monk said in a condescending voice.

The bishop ignored the comment. "We make a good team, Brother Germain. Tomorrow, you will finish off the last of the descendants of this so-called Celtic divinity."

Vala sucked in her breath. Her father had called out the name Germain in his delirium. Was this the very man he had cut? She peered out at the scarred profile.

"Why do you condemn the murder of some boy in some miserable village but condone it for the girl?" asked the monk.

"It's all perception. A quiet death is nothing, but a public one is trouble. The Holy See needn't know the methods we employ in bringing about the results they crave. Simon Finn Negus was the sole force holding those little bands of heathens together. His avowal that the souls are reborn again after death is a problem for us. If a man doesn't risk the fires of hell, why give alms to the Church?" said De Roche. "Without a bit of fear, the common man cannot be controlled."

"The man was nothing more than a rabble-rousing rustic," muttered Germain.

"But dangerous," said De Roche. "I'd have preferred to see him swing from the gallows. He would have made a fine example of the fate of heretics."

Germain's face twisted at the veiled rebuke. "That idiot from Bridestowe took matters into his own hands, but you could make an example of the girl."

"She doesn't appear to know anything." The bishop's gaze flicked to Germain's scar. "But the father is dead, and your blade took the son. Now, dispatch the daughter."

Vala covered her mouth with trembling fingers.

Germain rubbed his disfigured cheek. "Simon got in a lucky stroke."

The bishop smirked as he placed a small pouch into the monk's hand. "A contribution for services rendered."

The monk shook the pouch once, and as the bishop strode away, the monk stalked off in the opposite direction.

Vala flattened herself against the wall until the footsteps died away. The riders who had pursued her were monks—holy monks! The bishop had ordered her death and that of her father and brother.

She had to get out now. She would collect her things, find Thistle, and flee. The few coins she had left would not last her long, but there was nothing for it. She was alone and homeless, for she could not return to Wistman's Wood.

Vala crept back across the gardens and eased back inside her little room. She stood for a moment, dazed and confused, trying to think. She fingered the spot where the monk's knife had nearly taken her life, only now understanding why her father had hidden her away.

Riding in a dress, was not practical, not when she was fleeing for her life. She stripped it off, then rifled through the pack for the old leggings, torn shirt, and overtunic. Dressed again as a boy, she pulled on her cloak and put a hand to the door but didn't open it.

For the first time since the wooden box had come to her, Vala wondered if it needed her protection rather than her loathing. Without her uncle to advise her, Vala had been certain the box carried a curse, but there was a reason her uncle and her father had guarded the thing for years, though she didn't yet know why. Her mad father might have offered her some insight, but he hadn't. Maybe he'd not been so mad after all.

Vala shook her head. "Open the door and run, fool!" she ordered herself, but her feet did not obey.

She let her fingers drop from the latch and backed a step away. She had one advantage. They didn't know she had discovered their plan. They would be looking for her on the south road after Mass in the morning.

A wild notion swirled in her head, a risky notion that might get her killed.

Vala grabbed from her pack an empty cloth sack. She hung it from the rope belt at her waist. She would need her hands free. After gathering up her pack, Vala slipped out into the dark, silent garden. She breathed deeply, letting the fresh air clear her head. The great church with its high walls, porticos, and attendant buildings loomed like a giant beast about to devour her, but she could not allow fear to sabotage her quest. She had something vital to do for the sake of her family name.

She meant to retrieve her box.

Chapter Fifteen:
*"If thou canst not see the bottom, wade not."*

The cloister garden was deathly quiet, waiting for something: a shout of alarm or the discovery of a would-be thief. Vala tried to ignore her fears as she slipped through the shadows toward a shrine overgrown with periwinkle vines. She tucked her pack inside. After she pilfered the box, and if her luck held, she would collect it before she fled Bath.

She bolted the remaining few yards to the walkway and melted into the darkness between the pillars of the cloister. She was shaking as she slid along the cold wall. The sound of feet tramping over the stone floor was heart-stopping. With nowhere to run, Vala flattened herself in a niche in the wall and waited for doom to fall. Three liveried guards marched past, never looking right or left. She leaned out far enough to watch their retreating backs. Relief was brief as a finger touched her shoulder. Vala spun, eyes wide with terror.

"Good evening, child," said the mellow voice of old Father Guillard. "Beautiful night for a stroll, isn't it? And what a pleasure that I should run into you again."

"Father, you startled me," gasped Vala.

"I was just admiring the statues. I think they are extraordinary, don't you?" he mused. "When I can't sleep, I stroll about the grounds and look at my favorites. Here, you must come and see." He pulled her by the arm toward the torchlight and opened his hands, palm up, toward just such a statue.

"Yes, Father," Vala replied hurriedly. "It's very beautiful. But can you tell me—"

"Do you know," said the priest, lowering his voice to a creaky whisper, "they move sometimes, the statues do." He pointed a shaky finger at the one before him. "When the light is just right, you can notice it. But you must be very still."

Vala looked at the stone carving and then back at the sweet old man. "Father," she said gently, ignoring his ramblings, "do you know where the bishop stores items to be burned, like the little wooden box I brought him?"

"Ahhh... yes," he replied. "The bishop and his men are always busy with their collecting and their burning. I wonder at its value." Guillard shrugged. "I suppose it doesn't matter, though." He stared at the statue benignly for a long while.

Vala was not sure he remembered her question. She pulled her cloak tightly around herself, her stomach twisting in an anxious knot. "Father Guillard," she tried again. "Can you tell me where those things are kept?"

He startled, as though he had only just realized she was there. "Oh my, yes! Just there," he said, pointing down the dark passage. "Round the corner and up the stairs, and then a big wooden door with an iron ring. Of course, no one is to go inside. Sometimes they set a guard." He patted her hand. "Will you be staying in Bath, my dear? I do enjoy talking to you very much."

"No, Father," she replied. "But thank you."

He turned to the statue again.

Vala hurried to the side passageway. At the end of the shadowy walk, she found the stairway. A faint light glowed yellow at the top. She could detect no movement or sound, yet her feet refused to ascend those steps.

"I came here for the box, and I won't leave without it," Vala murmured as she fought to regain her recent bravado.

Step by step, she climbed to the top, where she found a wide landing which gave way to a passage on the left. Vala peered cautiously around the corner.

No more than five feet away, a guard was slumped over a small table, blocking half the hall. Bits of his dinner lay on a wooden plate near his nose. One arm drooped down near the floor, where a limp finger hooked the handle of a pitcher. A noisy snore rattled the table, and Vala jumped back.

She leaned around the corner again. The man was breathing slowly and deeply, the reek of ale and onions surrounding him like a cloud. As quiet as a cat, Vala edged past the dozing man toward the only door, one with a large iron ring and heavy iron hinges. Taking hold of the ring, she pulled. The hinges creaked, and the sleeping guard stirred. There was nowhere to hide. Before Vala could devise an excuse to fool the drunken guard, things got much worse.

"Move along there, boys!" called a raspy voice from the passage below. Footfalls rang out, and Vala moaned in panic. More guards were coming. The man at the table raised his head a few inches. Vala watched it wobble and then drop back onto his plate.

She grabbed the ring and prised the door open just enough that she could slither through. The room was dark, and Vala dropped to hands and knees, then scurried for a hiding place. She found a table draped in a heavy cloth and scrambled underneath. She curled herself into a ball just as the men reached the top of the stairs.

"Steady, there," said the deep voice of the leader.

"I don't know why we have to store it away, just to haul it out again in the morning," complained a second voice. "Couldn't we just leave it here?"

"Bishop's orders," grunted a third. "He don't want this sort of thing lying about." Much scraping and grumbling filled the landing as they maneuvered something bulky.

"See here! Tuck has drunk his ration of beer as well as ours," complained the second man. "Look at the old sot!"

"And he's gone and left the door open! Tuck, you fool, wake up!" bellowed the leader.

Through the crack in the door, Vala watched two men juggle a very large tapestry or rug, while the other tried to rouse the sleeping guard. The drunken man refused to be revived.

"The devil take him," the leader snarled, opening the door wide.

Vala could see his stout legs as he fumbled with something just inside the door. A torch flared overhead, and the others grunted and shuffled inside with their burden.

"Set it down and let's get going. I want my supper," said the leader.

"This pagan devilry," said the third. "It gives me the shivers."

Vala held her breath as the men wrestled the heavy tapestry into the corner, then the various booted feet shuffled back out the door.

"We'll need a load of kindling in the morning to burn this lot," said the nearest man.

"And a score of men to move all this to the fire pit," chimed in the next.

The leader snorted, "Be lucky to get six or seven."

The light was extinguished and the door swung closed, leaving the room as dark as pitch. Vala relaxed her knees and shoulders as she listened to the sound of footfalls descending the stairs. It was a narrow escape, and she was far from safe. The drunken Tuck was just outside, and she had yet to find the box. She climbed shakily to her feet.

A small glowing ember remained in the torch holder. As Vala groped her way toward it, her fingers brushed a candle nub lying on the table. She touched the wick to the smoldering cinder, puffing on it to encourage a flame. Luck was with her, for with a little effort, the wick blazed to life.

Vala held the bit of candle aloft and surveyed the chamber. The tiny light did not carry into the corners of the room, but the reason the guards hadn't noticed her was apparent. The room was full to bursting with the oddest assortment of articles she'd ever seen. There were figurines depicting humans, part-humans, and animals of fantastic shapes tossed in amongst stacks of ragged books and scrolls. There were symbols of various sizes wrought in metal, ivory, stone, and wood.

Vala picked up a heavy round medallion. Someone had gouged out the gemstones, leaving empty sockets. She recalled the beautiful crucifix she had admired in De Roche's study, studded with gleaming gemstones. Perhaps the bishop put some of his finds to use.

Vala allowed the candlelight to fall upon the items stacked nearest the door. There, amidst the disorder, sat the wooden box she had carried for so many perilous miles. It was a recent acquisition, so it had been set just inside the room; otherwise, it might have taken her hours to locate it in this jumble of artifacts. Vala picked it up. It still rattled as before. She dropped it into the bag hanging from her belt.

The gilt edging of a book caught her eye. It was lying open on a table, and Vala couldn't resist turning a few pages. She could not read the text, but the elaborate paintings scattered throughout must have taken countless painstaking hours to create. It was a terrible shame to burn a book. After a moment's hesitation, she placed it in the sack too.

She knew she ought to leave, but a few minutes remained on the burning stub of wax. She set it down and unrolled a piece of fine linen cloth, heavily embroidered. The work was magnificent. It portrayed a woman surrounded by a border of symbols. In the dim light, she was not sure of the subject, but with a greedy joy at thwarting the bishop, she shoved the needlework into her bag.

Buoyed by the items in her sack, Vala swept her tiny light a final time around the room. The gleam of silver caught her attention. It was a knife, long and thin, with an embossed hilt of vines and other decorations. She had a small cooking knife, but she might need a weapon before this night was done. She stowed the knife in her belt where it would be easy to reach.

The witless guard was snoring as Vala stole past him. She scurried down the steps, checked for guards, and then flew along the cloister and out into the garden. In no time, she was pulling her pack from its hiding place. Vala felt euphoric at having beaten the bishop at his game. She was as good as riding free across a dark fragrant meadow, flying far from Bath.

"You, there! What are you up to?"

Vala spun.

A dark shape approached along the path. Behind her, a dull bell tolled from the chapter house, and the sound of chanting drifted over the garden, soft and melodious. Vigils would bring the priests to the church for prayer. Vala slid the knife from her belt and clutched it beneath her cloak as she sought an excuse that would allow her to escape. The gravel crunched under the feet of the approaching figure, while along the cloister, hooded clerics with candles moved in procession toward the church. Just as she thought she'd won, everything was going badly wrong.

Vala held her breath. A man stepped from the shadows in front of her.

"Phillip?"

"Vala! It is you?" cried Brother Phillip.

"Are you alone?" she asked softly, replacing her knife and pulling him into the darkness of the shrine. "I'm so glad to see you, but we can't stay here long. There are guards."

Phillip drew back. "Aren't you staying with the sisters?"

"Yes, but—" She stopped and peered at him. "How did you know that? How long have you been here?"

"I'm here on business for the bishop. I had to report to him about the miracles."

"Why did you leave me in Glastonbury if you were coming directly here?"

Phillip looked away. "I sent Father Guillard to watch for you."

Vala's joy at seeing Phillip drained away like water in a leaky bucket. "You're angry with me, aren't you? You didn't want to travel with me after the way I behaved in Glastonbury."

"Angry?" he said. "No. Why would I be angry? I was the one who was wrong, leaving you like that." Phillip caught her hand but quickly released it.

"I can't stay here, Phillip." It no longer mattered why Phillip had left her. She sucked in a ragged breath. "The bishop wants me dead; he wants to burn the box. I have to get away before dawn. You ought to come with me. They might think you were helping me."

"What do you mean? The bishop would never want you dead."

"Quiet!" hissed Vala. She scanned the darkness for signs of the patrol. "Speak softly."

Phillip raised an eyebrow. "Vala, calm yourself." He took hold of her arms. "The bishop is a godly man. You are safe here."

She could see the procession of priests wending their way to the chapel. Did the holy priests know what sort of master they served? Could they all be blind to the designs and intentions of the bishop? Could Phillip be that blind?

"Vala!" Phillip hissed. "I'm sorry I left you in Glastonbury. I was wrong. But I can assure you that you are perfectly safe now."

Vala laughed mirthlessly. "You have no idea how mistaken you are." She turned to go.

Phillip held tight to her arm. "Explain," he ordered.

His face was so very earnest. She sighed.

In a hushed voice, she told him, "Father Guillard helped me get an audience with the bishop. De Roche opened the little box, and then he gave it to a monk dressed in black and ordered it burned. He never showed me what was inside. He told me to stay the night and leave after morning Mass."

"That was kind of His Grace," interjected Phillip. "If the bishop burned the box, it is probably for the best. And, Vala, you ought to refer to him as Bishop De Roche."

Could Phillip possibly be a party to the bishop's plan? It made no sense. He could have taken the box from her at any time, and he'd had many chances to kill her.

She forced down her disloyal thoughts. "De Roche is the devil himself, and deserves no better title," she spat. "I went back tonight to see him. I was curious about what was in the box. I thought he might tell me. I overheard De Roche tell his monk to wait on the road after Mass and kill me. He said they had already killed my brother and father. I saw the face of the monk. He was the same man who killed Stephen from my village."

"You can't have heard them properly, Vala. The bishop would never—" Phillip rubbed his temple as though to rub the evil idea away.

"It doesn't matter what you believe. That monk, Germain, went off with his men to ambush me. They were the ones who've been pursuing me, and attacked me by the river." She fingered her wound through her tunic.

"Vala, I cannot believe this."

"Goodbye, Phillip." She twisted out of his grip and started off again.

"Brother Germain is the right hand of the bishop," Phillip muttered. "Germain does have a rather nasty air, it's true, but murder? I can't imagine it."

Fury welled up, burning in Vala's eyes. She turned back and poked her finger into Phillip's chest. "You know nothing! Go back to your books, or your precious bishop, or whatever else this place holds for you!" Vala turned and tried to steady her breathing as she headed toward the cloister.

Phillip grasped her wrist, but she shook him off. "Wait," he breathed, his face contorted. "Wait, and I'll come with you."

"No, Phillip, just let me go!"

"I can see you're in trouble, Vala. I can help sort this out."

Shadows played over his face in the darkness. Vala felt torn. It would be good to have a companion in the wild, but Phillip did not believe her, and that rankled.

"Do what you will," she said at last. "I'm going to the stables."

"I'll just get my pack. I'll meet you there. Wait for me!"

He hurried off toward the Chapter House. Vala took a long look around and, espying no one, sprinted toward the door into the cathedral.

Inside the church, the massive walls magnified every little sound. She feared someone would hear her, but the chanting of the priests echoed off the walls, covering her footfalls. The altar itself was dark, but lights from the chapel in the apse filtered into the nave, spilling onto the floor. She no longer desired a closer look, so she edged around it and made for the front doors.

It was difficult to budge the tall, heavy doors. Vala wedged herself against one of them and heaved it open a few inches. She could see no one in the outer courtyard. The moon was high, but a wispy mist obscured it, turning its brilliance into a murky yellow glow. The stable was not too far from the door, but there was no cover between the two.

The dim church lay behind her, and the priests continued to chant. She'd give Phillip a few minutes, and then she would go. Vala wondered why he wanted to come at all. He didn't believe her; she could see it in his eyes.

A sound from within the cathedral startled her, and she drew the knife. Phillip came puffing into sight, making far too much noise. Of course, if they found him leaving in the night, they wouldn't kill him.

"I'm ready," he announced. "But we ought to discuss this."

She ignored him, leaning her shoulder into the door with a grunt. Free of the church, she sprinted toward the stables. She could hear Phillip's feet pounding over the flagstones behind her.

The boy who tended the horses and mules was fast asleep on a pile of straw. She crept past him and along the line of horses to Thistle. Perhaps he sniffed danger on the air, for he kept very quiet as Vala guided him out into the yard. Once Phillip had brought out his own mount, she led the way out of the church precincts.

The exhilaration of escape diminished as Vala searched for a bridge across the river, one that would take them east, avoiding the southern road and its murderous party of monks. The road they finally found was so inconsequential that the tiny guardhouse at the narrow footbridge was deserted. They galloped out beyond the city boundaries, a clear route to freedom stretching in front of them. The buildings dwindled in size and density until the road became a bumpy cart path and then a sheep track through wild country. It was the dead of night, and the cool wind on her face wiped away some of the terror of Vala's death sentence.

When a road crossed their path, they pulled up their horses to a stop.

"I think this goes to the village of Bradforde on Avon, but we can't go on in the dark like this," Phillip said. "We are risking injury to the horses. Couldn't we rest in some glade of trees until morning?" It was the third time Phillip had implored her to stop for the night.

"It's not your life, is it?" Vala replied, but of course he was right.

An opening in the trees led to a hollow screened from the road. It was the best they'd do. She dismounted and unburdened Thistle, who nuzzled her neck. She was aware of Phillip tying his horse and rustling around in his own pack but ignored him. Vala wrapped herself in a blanket and flung herself down on the ground to sleep. Tired though she was, sleep did not come easily, with the bishop's words still fresh in her head: *Just kill her and let the beasts of the forest gnaw her corpse.*

Vala startled awake. She pushed up to hands and knees feeling stiff and groggy. A grey sky stretched overhead, and fog lay thick beyond the hollow. Phillip had kindled a small fire and was warming his hands. Vala crawled closer to the fire to shake off the morning's chill.

"A fire might give us away," she said, feeling rebellious even though the fire's warmth was welcome.

"I suppose it might," Phillip sighed. "If someone were looking for us. Perhaps you could tell me in more detail what happened in Bath. Then we can decide how to proceed."

It was irritating beyond words to hear the calm in his voice, as though he were placating a child. On the other hand, he had dropped everything and come with her. She owed him the facts, at least.

Vala recounted all that had happened and all she had overheard until she met him in the garden. She spoke in a tired, flat voice and kept her eyes on the fire.

"It's not that I doubt you, Vala," Phillip said, his face screwed up in concentration. "I believe you, but—"

He did doubt her. She knew it. At least, he didn't want it to be true.

"Perhaps Germain acted on his own. You said the bishop admonished him."

"De Roche admonished Germain for killing Stephen *in front of witnesses!*" Why wouldn't Phillip accept the bishop's duplicity? Vala wanted to rage against his comfortable little world.

"The bishop is a learned man. He is influential in Rome, and he has been most diligent in trying to discover true proofs of miracles. How a man like that could do such a thing?" Phillip rubbed his forehead hard.

Vala sighed and closed her eyes. "It's simple. In Bruton, when we discovered the trick the priest had played, you confronted him. He was sinning against God, and he was failing in his vows. This is no different. Warn De Roche's superiors!"

"It's not the same thing!" snapped Phillip.

She gave him a contemptuous look.

Phillip caught her glare. "I mean that there are issues of hierarchy."

"That makes it worse!" Vala cut in. "All my life, I've obeyed the commandments as the priests taught me. I asked for forgiveness when I sinned. When I accepted the box, when I believed it was evil, I sought help from the Church. I came on a long journey to find your bishop, only to discover he is the real evil. Why should I pray to a god whose champion is a man like that?" Vala's words surprised even her, but it was the logical conclusion, and the set of her jaw dared him to argue the point.

"Vala, not all men are good. Not all priests or monks are good. They are men."

"They are ordained to do God's will!" she shouted over his response.

"Certainly they are—certainly. But even the ordained are tempted by power, or comforts, or pleasure." He could not meet her eyes. "Temptation to stray is great, and all men face it."

"I didn't stray," said Vala. "And now I'm being hunted by your Church."

She leapt to her feet and stomped across the clearing. It was too much, hearing Phillip defend the bishop. How did one excuse murder or forgive a crime that the criminal did not repent?

Vala opened her pack and pulled out the woolen monk's habit. The small treatise of Saint Gildas fell to the ground. She picked it up, recalling the words she had read just two days ago: *Britain hath priests, but they are unwise; very many that minister, but many of them impudent...* She stuffed the book back into her pack and strode to where Phillip was sitting. She flung the robes at him without comment.

Phillip gathered up the garments, bringing them to his nose as though he was taking in her scent. He closed his eyes for a moment before he got to his feet and stowed them deep in his own pack.

They sat in silence for a long time. Vala wanted to lash out at Phillip, but he was not the enemy.

"I don't have any answers, Vala," he finally said. "I'm a sinner too."

"Phillip, what sin have you committed?" she sighed. "You should go back to Bath. I'll be fine. It was kind of you to accompany me this far."

Phillip chewed on his lip. "I'm not returning just yet. We can travel together for a while."

"I have my own mission," she replied, nodding toward her pack, which contained the wooden box. "Perhaps I can find someone who can tell me why De Roche wants the box badly enough to kill off my family."

"You can't travel the roads like a vagabond," Phillip replied. He was thoughtful for a moment, and then snapped his fingers. "I have an idea. Beckhampton is not very far. I know a good woman in the town who weaves very fine cloth. She sells her goods to the ladies of the great lords. Perhaps you could apprentice yourself to her. Since you don't wish to return home, you might find weaving a profitable profession as well as an art."

Phillip was the voice of reason against her passionate outrage. Outrage would not feed her or her horse. She got up and moved doggedly to retrieve Thistle, recalling how much she disliked weaving.

Vala stood holding Thistle's reins. She would never learn the secret of the box if she was making cloth all day. She'd chucked away the iron whorl Stephen had given her, a portent that her days of cloth making were done. She realized that she needed to be free to search out answers. Eventually, she and Phillip would have to take separate roads. The sort of folk who would understand the box would certainly shy away from a monk.

Phillip was watching her, and she found it difficult to look into his earnest face to tell him so.

The midday sun burned off the fog as they made their way toward

Beckhampton. There were few travelers on the road, so they risked a rest next to a stream near the road. There, they took a bit of food and water while the horses grazed. When it was time to push on, she collected her things and went to retrieve Thistle, now slurping the cool water. The stubborn animal balked. She yanked at his reins, but he continued to lap water from the steam.

"I'll follow in a moment," Vala said crossly. "Once I get this willful horse to move."

Phillip nodded and allowed his own horse to wander off down the road at an amble.

"Come, Thistle," said Vala. "You've drunk your fill and more. Let's go."

Thistle continued to ignore her, so Vala tied her pack to the saddle and then checked the ground for anything they'd missed.

The rustling of the tall grasses and the babbling stream must have muffled the approaching hoof beats. All Vala heard was, "Whoa, there!"

The deep voice startled her, and she found herself flat on her back. Vala flailed her fists at the man pinning her to the dirt.

"Where did you get that horse?" he demanded.

"He's mine!" she shouted as she struggled to get free.

"Don't lie!" growled her assailant. "I know the person who owns him. Same white feet, same white forelocks, exactly like this one," he growled. "Merlyn!" he called, and Thistle chose that moment to throw up his head and whinny, as though agreeing that he was called Merlyn.

"He's mine, I tell you," said Vala, gritting her teeth. "He belonged to my father, and now he's mine!"

"Who is your father?" her attacker demanded, eyes piercing her like a knife.

Vala stared into those eyes, deep brown and intense, shot through with flecks of gold. Tangles of his dark hair brushed her cheek, and she jerked her head to the side. "What business is it of yours?"

Then she blurted out, "Simon Finn Negus!"

Leaping up, eyes wide, he wheeled around, looking for something. "Where is it?"

He strode to Thistle, who stood calmly munching grass. The man was younger than she had thought, perhaps nineteen. He appeared very tall from her spot on the ground, but she wasn't going to let his size stop her as she scrambled to her feet.

The man grabbed her pack.

"Stop, you thief!" she screamed, scooping up a large stone. She flung it hard, and the rock glanced off the side of the rogue's head. He yelped, stumbling back against Thistle, but did not cease rifling through her things.

She fumbled for the knife at her waist. Her hand shook as she raised it and charged. With an easy block from his forearm, he thwarted her attack. As she staggered backward, she realized with maddening certainty that she was not prepared to kill another person, however ill-used she felt.

"You have it!" he breathed. "You have it!" He drew out the little wooden box, and with sublime reverence, he held it up. "You are Vala. I couldn't be certain. Dressed like that, like a boy, I wasn't sure. I thought you'd be younger."

Vala scowled. "Who are you?"

His clothes were stained by mud and bleached by the sun, so it was difficult to tell what color they'd been when new. Grime-caked boots and a cloak stuck through with brambles completed his attire. "I'm Ethan. I was a pupil of your father's and a friend to your brother, Lugus."

"You knew them?" Vala reeled as though she had drunk too much wine.

Ethan nodded, rubbing the spot where her rock had struck him. "I knew them very well. Simon was like a father—" He hesitated. "His bones were still smoking when I arrived in Bridestowe."

Vala recalled her father's last words: 'Find Ethan.' Fear and curiosity assailed her in equal measure. "I have a lot of questions."

Ethan scanned the road. "There isn't much time."

"Was he really a fortune teller?"

"A—what?" Ethan asked.

She cut him off. "What was my brother Lugus like?" With barely a pause for breath, she gestured toward the small box. "And what am I supposed to do with that?"

Ethan closed his mouth and regarded her.

Returning at a gallop, Phillip thundered toward them. "Vala!" he called. "What's going on? Are you all right?" He leapt from his horse, brandishing his wooden staff.

Ethan turned a suspicious eye on Phillip as he replied, "I'll answer each of your questions. Just not *here*." He put a good deal of emphasis on the last word.

Vala backed up a pace, her common sense finally overcoming her curiosity. "Why not here? How did you find me?"

"It was a lucky chance, I guess," he said. "To tell the honest truth, I'd given up. I've searched for many days. I tried to find your uncle but without success. I heard rumors of you in Dartmeet, but I lost the trail. I decided to find the others of my company and renew the search with more people. But then, providence stepped in, thank the goddess!"

Vala's brow knitted. "But why did you come looking?"

"Simon entreated me to seek you out should he perish. He said the box would be in your keeping, and of course it would condemn you to death if certain people should catch you with it." The man cradled the thing against his chest like a treasure. "Forgive me for throwing you to the ground." Ethan bowed in Vala's direction.

"Who is this person?" demanded Phillip.

"Why should I believe you?" Vala inquired, ignoring the monk, seething at her side.

Ethan ignored Phillip's question too, never taking his eyes from Vala. "I can give you any proof you desire. Ask me something specific about Simon or Lugus. I will happily answer." There was a cheeky edge to him that made Vala nervous. She knew far too little about her father or brother to be able to put this man to the test. She was sure he knew that, too.

"What is my uncle's true name?" she ventured.

"Darian Finn Negus," he replied. "But he calls himself Adrian these days."

"What are your intentions, sir?" Phillip insisted, thumping his staff in the dirt to accentuate his words.

"Why are you traveling with this cleric?" Ethan asked.

"He befriended me," she replied.

Ethan inclined his head. Finally ready to acknowledge Phillip's question, he said, "Well, sir monk, here are my intentions. I will take Vala to a safe place, give her whatever she needs, and introduce her to her father's friends who can aid her."

Vala felt a strange sensation, as though an entirely new world had appeared out of nothing and all she needed to do was to step inside it. "You know a place where I'll be safe? Safe from the bishop?"

"Has De Roche learned of your father's death already?" Ethan asked.

"He was the one who had my father killed," replied Vala.

"You are assuming that," said Phillip, but his words were drowned out by Ethan's roar of anger.

"Bad enough that Simon is now spirit, seeking a new form, but murdered, and by that pissant De Roche?" Ethan growled.

Vala put out an arm to stop Phillip from coming at Ethan. Ethan did not appear to notice or care. "If you wish to live, you had best follow me now," he said. "This cleric can't save you if they catch you. This one might even be in league with them." He nodded toward Phillip.

"How dare you!" Phillip cried.

Ethan stared hard at Vala. "Choose!"

Vala pursed her lips. She'd felt a moment of doubt, coming upon Phillip in the cloister's garden, but those concerns had evaporated. She could only hope her voice would convey calm certainty and not the exhilarating fear she felt for what she was about to do.

"Phillip, I'm going with him. He can tell me about my family, and perhaps he can open the box." She eyed Ethan. "Do you know how to open the box?"

Ethan's brow furrowed. "Yes, of course, but not here."

"Vala," pleaded Phillip. "You don't know this man. Don't go off with him.

It's dangerous. It's foolhardy!"

Vala took Phillip's arm and pulled him several paces back. She lowered her voice. "Going to Bath was foolhardy, but I didn't know it. This man knows my family. I have to find out what he knows."

"Vala, think! He could be planning to harm you as soon as you are alone in the wild. You said yourself that your father was a frightening person. This man is no better."

Everything he said was very true, but now was the moment for risk. "I appreciate all your aid. I would have died if you hadn't rescued me, but this will never be over until I know why it happened."

Ethan kept an eye trained on Phillip. "You, priest, must swear not to follow. I cannot take you, nor can I protect you."

"My name is Brother Phillip, not 'priest', and I don't require your protection. God is my protector, sir."

"Then I wish your god well, and you also, Brother Phillip," Ethan replied.

"Let's be off," Vala said as she mounted up. The sooner they were away, the less chance of a brawl. "Phillip, thank you a thousand times. I'll never forget you. And please don't worry about me." She sincerely meant it, and regret washed through her at wounding him this way.

Ethan bestowed a smug look on Phillip as he handed the box to Vala and then mounted his own horse. With no more than a backward glance and a wave, Vala galloped off down the lane with the stranger.

Phillip watched wretchedly as a cloud of dust blossomed in their wake. When it settled, only an empty road remained.

Chapter Sixteen:
*"Zeal without knowledge is like fire without light."*

Thistle followed Ethan's horse in an uncharacteristic show of congeniality. After about a half-mile, Ethan slowed and swerved off the main road into a narrow lane deeply overgrown with bracken. It twisted and curved over ridges and down into little hollows. Since their progress had slowed, Vala took the opportunity to try for some information.

"Until you came along, I wasn't sure where to turn. No one was helping me."

"Hmm," was his reply.

"I'd like to know all about my father."

"He was an amazing man. I mourn his death," Ethan replied with an air of preoccupation. "The way ahead will be rough. Are you accustomed to riding?"

"Yes," she replied. "I'm a good rider."

"We'll try to reach my home before nightfall. Stay close." He clicked his tongue, and his horse broke into a trot. Thistle matched his pace.

"The box?" she asked.

"Not now, not here."

Vala felt its edges through her leather pack. "Why does it matter so much?"

"It's everything, isn't it?" he replied as he scanned the woods. "It can't be replaced."

Vala felt a rising exasperation. "Would you have taken it from me if I refused to come with you?"

Ethan didn't reply.

"Would you have?" she demanded.

"Possibly."

Vala pulled up on Thistle's reins, and he stomped to a stop.

Ethan spurred his horse back to where she had stopped. His face was dark with anger. "What are you doing?" he demanded. "We must keep moving!"

She stared at him, trying to manage her fear. Having grown up among trusting folk, she had overestimated her ability to judge the intentions of people in the wider world. It was very tempting to turn tail and run back to Phillip.

"How did you meet my father?" she asked.

Ethan's square jaw set in a hard line. "He saved me—when I was a child." The words caught in his throat. "I'd be dead, or worse, if not for Simon." He tipped his head back and sniffed. "Now, come along."

It wasn't his words but rather the tone of his voice and the look in his eyes that convinced her. There was old pain there. Ethan had loved her father and honored him as she honored her Uncle Adrian. She nudged Thistle to fall in behind Ethan's horse and stifled her questions.

They rode for hours over the wild countryside. At first, Vala tried to map their route in her head, but soon her concentration slipped. She was hopelessly lost. When she could tolerate the silence no longer, she asked, "Do you truly believe anyone could be following us?"

"That priest of yours had a deceitful look about him," he said.

"Phillip would never harm me. I'm sure of it."

Ethan reined in his horse. "Priests are dangerous. They've set aside their humanity in favor of commandments and vows that they twist to their own purposes. I've never met a trustworthy priest."

Vala gulped back a retort, for she'd just shouted the same thing at Phillip. "Phillip saved me from De Roche's henchman and healed my wound."

Ethan snorted but said nothing further.

By late afternoon, Vala was scratched, covered in brambles, saddle-sore, and her patience was nearing its limit. To top it all, as evening came on, it began to rain. Dark, roiling clouds came in from the west, and heavy sheets of rain pelted down, drenching them in minutes. The path became a muddy stream, slick and treacherous. To avoid their becoming separated in the darkness and the downpour, Ethan tied the horses together. Through the dark torrent of rainwater, he kept pushing on.

"It's not far now," he shouted over the rumble of thunder, pointing up a steep ridge. Rain filled Vala's eyes as she squinted toward the top. "We'll go on foot from here."

"On foot?" she cried.

Ethan motioned toward a path that hugged the side of the ridge. "I'll bring the horses," he shouted.

Vala was in a murderous rage as she slid from Thistle, but the storm was too loud and she was too cold to argue. She handed the reins to Ethan and started up the path. Footing was treacherous, leaving her to grope with numb fingers for a handhold among the muddy tree roots and branches. A thorn sliced her palm and she jerked her hand away, losing her tentative balance. A strong hand under her arm stopped her sliding off the edge. She turned to thank Ethan, but he motioned for her to keep moving.

Vala's boots were full of water, her clothes were sodden, and still the storm-ravaged skies doused them with endless rain. She wiped a bloody palm on her cloak, squinting through the darkness to try to get her bearings. She felt Ethan take her elbow and pull her forward. They had reached the top. Tall grasses whipped around their legs as they trudged across the spongy ground of an open meadow.

"Where are we?" she called. "When will we reach shelter?"

Ethan let go of her arm. "Just there!" he shouted, pointing ahead. He loped toward a dark patch, almost indistinguishable in the rumbling tempest. A cottage appeared, almost hidden by trees and bracken. Water streamed from the roof as they reached the eaves. Dark and cold as it appeared, at least it was shelter. Even if it was infested with rats, she wasn't about to complain.

They pulled the horses into a grubby little barn at the side of the dwelling. Vala wiped the water from her face while Ethan rummaged in a wooden box for a torch and a small flint.

"Welcome to my home," he said as he skillfully struck a fire. "Tie the horses. I'll get hay."

Vala's teeth were chattering too much to allow her to form words. After tying each horse, she unburdened them of dripping blankets and packs, then wiped them down while Ethan filled the manger.

A harsh caw startled her. Perched in the rafters, staring down at them, was a beady-eyed raven. It flapped its wings and rasped, "Intruder!"

Vala gaped. Birds did not talk.

"It's me, Lugus, bringing a guest," Ethan said, addressing the bird. "How are you keeping, my friend?"

The bird gave a jaunty tip of its head and squawked.

Vala looked from Ethan to the bird.

"Your brother Lugus was gifted, but not as a seer. He was good with herbs and potions," Ethan said. "But his real talent was with animals. He could communicate with them. I think that's why he came back as a raven."

Vala looked up at the black bird. "I don't understand."

"Lugus was my true friend, my brother." Ethan patted the horses in turn. "We lived together and studied together. Simon was planning to take us both with him to Anglesey. It's in the north, you know. He was planning to flee there to safety when it became too dangerous here."

"What did you mean about Lugus coming back?" she asked. Her brother

Lugus was a phantom to her, without form or substance.

"That particular raven carries your brother's soul," he said with such calm certainty that it took Vala a moment to grasp his meaning. "The night Lugus died, I was very sad, and as I sat grieving, the raven appeared. I recognized him immediately as Lugus." Ethan smiled then. "An apt name, Lugus."

"It's a *raven*," she said slowly, as though she were talking to Old Michael Ferrier back in Wistman's Wood—a nice fellow, but slow and given to whimsy.

Ethan did not waver. "That bird is Lugus, returned. In the old lore, Lugus is a god skilled in the arts, just as your brother was, and is depicted as a raven."

Vala was too tired to argue with this man who was her savior, and also, possibly raving mad. She was as good as his prisoner in this place.

The light in the barn wavered and failed as Ethan leapt out into the rain, sprinting for the house, the torch held aloft. Vala watched it splutter as the rain beat upon it. She took a last look upward, but the bird had blended into the blackness. She stumbled out into the downpour after Ethan.

After closing the cottage door against the rain, Vala dropped her pack on the floor. The single room was small and musty-smelling. A pool of muddy water formed at Vala's feet, soaking into the hard earthen floor. Ethan was just visible in the darkness, kneeling next to a rough stone hearth, building a fire.

In a moment, the flames rose up, illuminating the walls. "There's enough dry wood for the night." Ethan rubbed his hands on his breeches and faced her. "We'll hang the wet things by the fire. I have some clothes you can use until yours dry."

"That—that would be welcome," Vala stuttered, shaking with cold. She shrugged out of her cloak as Ethan scurried around lighting a few candle nubs with a burning stick.

If possible, Ethan's home exceeded her father's in its oddity. The focal point in the room was the large image of the sun emblazoned on one wall. It was crudely painted, and its wild face was strangely frightening. Vala edged nearer the hearth while Ethan rummaged in an old chest. He turfed out several pieces of clothing, considering each garment in turn. He offered one to her.

"I'll hang a blanket, and you can change," Ethan said as he draped a ragged quilt over the low rafters.

Vala's boots squelched as she disappeared behind the makeshift curtain. She pulled off tunic, leggings, and shirt, all muddy and wet, while Ethan clanked pots and puttered around near the fire. She hoped the sounds meant there would be something to eat. Food and sleep were all she desired.

"Throw your wet clothes out to me."

Vala pushed the sodden pile under the curtain with her foot. The borrowed garment was a nightshirt with a tie at the neck. It smelled fusty, but it fell to below her ankles and was blessedly dry. Vala snatched down the quilt and swathed herself in it. Once she had perched gingerly upon a rickety stool by a table set near the fire, she felt nearly human.

Ethan had donned doeskin breeches that bagged at the knees. His chest was bare, and his unruly dark hair was plastered down around his face. "I'm heating some braggot for you. It should take off the chill."

"If it's something hot, that would be wonderful."

Thunder rocked the dwelling and Vala jumped, pulling the blanket closer.

"My house is solid," Ethan said, pounding his fist against a low beam. One of the shutters banged open, and Ethan cursed as he threw himself at the thudding boards. The wind blew rain and wet leaves inside before he got it closed, and it continued to rattle against the sill in protest.

Ethan wiped the wet locks of hair off his face. "I'm afraid there are only a few vegetables and some dried venison. No bread or cheese."

"Anything would be welcome." What else could she say? She was miles from any other people. While the gale raged outside, she was trapped with this strange man. It was every maiden girl's fear or dark desire. Vala guessed most girls would think Ethan handsome. He had a strong jaw and dark eyes.

She shook her head to dislodge these frivolous thoughts. She was on a serious quest. Ethan might be comely, but he seemed deranged. Perhaps grief or anxiety had caused him to speak as he'd done, harshly one minute and crazily the next.

Vala searched for some conversational gambit. "The picture of the sun on your wall—did you paint it?"

"I did." He handed her a lopsided wooden cup full of pale, steaming liquid. "Belenus brings me solace."

"Who is Belenus?"

Ethan frowned. "The sun god, of course."

She hadn't realized the sun was so frightening. She stole another look at Belenus, then took a gulp of the drink. "This is very good."

Ethan shrugged his thanks as he filled bowls with his hasty soup. He sucked burned finger as he delivered the bowls to the table. "I'm not the best cook."

Vala took a taste, the odor of rosemary and barley rising in the steam. "It's tasty," she said, so ravenous she barely swallowed before she answered. She swirled the dregs in her empty bowl. "The braggot is good too. It reminds me of a drink that the women in my village make at Easter. I was only ever allowed a small taste. People brought jars as gifts to the priest."

"Of course they did. Damned drunken clerics," Ethan growled. "Braggot is a fermented drink made from honey."

Vala kept her head bowed over her cup. Ethan had such sharp, strange opinions. All she could hope was that a good night's sleep and some daylight would make conversation easier.

She glanced up at Ethan. He possessed that untamed, dangerous look a wicked girl might desire. A tingle shivered up Vala's spine, and she swallowed.

"You are dry now, and fed," said Ethan, rising from his seat. "It's time to substantiate your claim."

"My claim?"

"I must see it. If I am to bring a Christian into the Dumnonii camp, I must be certain you are not a spy."

Vala brightened. "You'll open the box now?" She stood, about to retrieve the box.

Ethan narrowed his eyes. "If you are truly Simon's daughter, you bear the mark. We all know of it."

Vala blinked. "What mark?"

Ethan raised his hands, palms out, as though trying to gentle a startled beast. "I hope you can understand. I must see the mark. Just turn around and lower that shirt."

Vala twitched between fight and flight, like a nervous goose. "I haven't got a mark."

"If not, then we have a problem." His voice was low and menacing.

Panic overtook Vala. There was nowhere to run except out into the downpour. She gathered the fabric of the nightshirt at her neck.

"I only need to see your back. Your shoulder, really. Just loosen the neck..."

"I will do no such thing!"

Ethan reached out a hand, and Vala lurched toward the door.

Faster and stronger, Ethan grasped her around the waist, flattening her against the wall. She kicked and flailed as he yanked at the neck of the old shirt and whimpered as the cloth ripped.

"If you're the real Vala, cease your struggling!" He twisted her shoulders toward the firelight.

"Who else would I be?" she cried, prying at his hands.

Ethan's fingers fanned out beneath her shoulder blade, then he released her.

Vala shook her clothing back into place as she shrank away from him. With tears choking her words, she screamed, "You're a barbarian!"

Ethan sat down hard on the floor. "You really are her."

She grabbed up the fallen quilt and scrambled to the door, her hands fumbling with the heavy bar. She had been so wrong, so foolish to come here. Tears clouded her eyes as she jerked at the bar, which refused to budge.

Ethan was panting from their struggle. "Well, it's good to know you're a virgin."

Vala ignored him, pulling frantically at the bar.

"When we met on the road, I was convinced you were Simon's daughter, but you were traveling with a cleric. It was very suspicious." Ethan looked up at her. "And just now, saying you don't have the mark. I couldn't risk bringing you to the Dumnonii settlement unless I was sure. But it's truly you!"

Why couldn't she get the damnable thing to move?

"It's all just as Simon told us." Ethan stood.

"I have no mark!" she screamed, still jiggling the bar.

"Of course you do. On your left shoulder, just here." He moved his fingers to a spot below his own shoulder blade. "Shall I show you?"

"Stay back!"

Ethan raised his hands again.

Vala pounded on the door in frustration. "Let me out of here!"

"Did you think I meant to molest you?" Ethan asked, abashed. "Truly, I would never do that."

"You ripped my shirt!" she hissed.

"It's really my shirt. I've only lent it to you."

Now she was angry. "How do you know?"

Ethan gave her a quizzical look.

"That I was... That I hadn't..."

Ethan brightened with understanding. "If you weren't a virgin, you wouldn't have fought me as you did. And it would be foolish for me to ravish you. If I did that, you might not be able to use it."

Vala opened her mouth to reply but stopped. Exhausted, she slipped down to the floor against the door. "Please, let me go," her words a piteous whine.

Ethan's brow knitted with concern. "I...apologize." He squatted down near her. "I didn't mean to frighten you so. I'm often accused of being brash. Perhaps I am, a bit." He placed a tentative hand on her shoulder.

Vala scuttled away from him with a cry.

Ethan sank down next to her. "It's only that Simon is dead, and Lugus is dead. Now, it's all on my shoulders."

Vala looked at him warily.

He ran a hand over his beard stubble. "I have handled this badly, but I had to see the mark. I should have realized you are young and have led a sheltered life."

"I am not so naïve as you believe," she snarled.

Ethan lifted an eyebrow. "As you wish. I only meant... I had to see." He rose. "This is how the bar works." He pulled an iron pin free and lifted the bar.

Vala knew she ought to have seen the pin, but she had panicked. Now, her weariness overwhelmed her: too tired to fight, too tired to run off into the storm. She wanted to cry. Instead, she reached over her shoulder and tried to feel the mark she didn't believe was really there.

Ethan lifted her pack onto the table. "Let's have a look at the box, shall we?"

"I can't stop you." Vala moved her hand under her arm with no more success.

"Do you want me to stop?" Ethan rummaged amongst her things. "Ahhh... You have Lugus's Tafl board!" The board and game pieces dropped onto the table. "He loved that game!"

Vala craned her neck. "It's called Tafl?"

Ethan held up the box. "When you asked if I could open this, I assume that was a ruse to fool the monk?"

Vala gritted her teeth. "No. I can't open it."

Ethan set the box aside and looked down into her eyes. "I've said I'm sorry for handling you so roughly. It's just that you were acting strangely. I expected you would wish to reveal the mark."

"*I* was acting strangely?" Vala spluttered. "And I *don't* have a mark."

Ethan reached down and pulled the girl to her feet. Vala rubbed her arm to wipe away his touch and quickly put the table between them.

Ethan made a noise deep in his throat and retrieved a small leather pouch from a shelf. He upended the bag, sending rounded pebbles clunking and tumbling across the cracked boards of the table. The stones had symbols scribed into their surfaces, and Ethan sorted through them, turning some over, pushing others out of the way. He offered one to her. Vala took it with guarded curiosity. It had a simple symbol etched on its surface.

"These are rune stones, used for divining the future. Your father gave me this set." His voice caught, betraying his feelings. He touched the small stone in her palm. "This rune is Ansuz. It represents wisdom." He picked up the box and worked the panels until the box revealed its contents.

Vala gaped. Inside was a fiery green stone set with silver and hung on a chain. She reached a hand toward it, but Ethan blocked her fingers.

"Emerald is a symbol of Ansuz. When you were born, your father had a vision that you would be a great seer—a wise woman. He called you by the name that means 'Chosen', yet he knew you were in danger. There had to be a way to identify you to the true believers and to link you to your birthright, so he marked you with the symbol of Ansuz, using his own amulet."

The curious symbol her father had worn about his neck flashed into Vala's head as she fingered the small rune stone.

"Simon heated his amulet in a fire and pressed it into your skin. The mark shows you are destined for this talisman, and it for you."

Ethan pushed the table aside and took a purposeful stride toward her. Vala shrank back, but he grasped her arm and pushed a finger below her shoulder blade. "Here," he said. "Just here is the mark."

Beneath his finger was the old scar she'd gotten when she was a wee child. She'd nearly forgotten it. "I fell as a child." Vala tried to pull away.

"No, it's the rune Ansuz," he said with galling confidence.

Vala twisted to examine her scar. "You're wrong. What sort of father would brand his own infant? It's perverse!"

Ethan turned and lifted the stone from its box. There was a symbol burned into the wood at the bottom of the box. It was the same simple design.

Vala's fingers dug at the old disfigurement. "That crazy old man!" she cried. "He gave me this?"

"Simon knew you'd have magic in you, even if it was not manifested at your birth."

She took a deep, shuddering breath. Uncle Adrian had always looked askance at the superstitions of the villagers. He did not hold with the idea of magic.

Ethan kept speaking, but his words made little impact on the flurry of her thoughts.

"It's in the air, in the water, in the earth itself. We can call it out at need. Magic can aid us, give us power and knowledge. It can give us the truth, Vala. Your father knew this. Your brother knew this, and soon, you will see it for yourself."

Vala sank onto a stool. "My father never told me any of this. He may have taken you in, and schooled you in his beliefs—"

"He kept you safe."

"Yes," Vala agreed, "but he abandoned me."

"Think what you will." Ethan rose from the table. "I need some air." He drew a knife from his belt and drove it into the wooden table. "At least I won't need this tonight."

Vala stared at the knife, and then at the back of the man who had been prepared to kill an imposter this night. He rapped his knuckles on the doorframe to ward off the evil spirits before stepping out into the rain-drenched night as Vala slipped her fingers under the edge of her smock and felt for the puckered ridges of the brand upon her back.

Chapter Seventeen:
*"Every path has its puddle."*


**February Sixteen, the Year of Our Lord 932 Anno Domini**
**To: His Eminence, Bishop Francis De Roche, Bath, Britain**

*A great deal of time has passed, old friend. We find we sorely miss your presence in Rome, your good counsel and person, being so many leagues away. Please know we hold you in high esteem and are eager for your return. There is an enterprise well-suited to your particular skills here at the Vatican.*

*You may be aware that Marozia Tusculani, dearest of mothers, has married Hugh of Arles. Her new husband is an entertaining fellow; however, she still finds the time to interpose herself in the affairs of Rome. With the best of intentions, Mother has taken to giving orders in our name. We need not tell you how discomfiting it is to be constantly stymied by one's own mother.*

*I desire your immediate return to Rome, where your particular gifts of persuasion, coupled with your perfect discretion, can bring about a resolution to this tedious tangle.*

*Needless to say, the city of Bath cannot be left without a champion. To this end, we have corresponded with the British monarch, King Athelstan, who is content to allow us to suggest a candidate for bishop of Bath. Ponto Bertelli is a worthy prelate, anxious to follow your lead. God willing and with favorable tides, Bertelli will arrive sometime in early May. Instruct him in your processes, and then return to Rome with what haste you may. We look forward to welcoming you home.*

*From the seat of St. Peter – The Vatican*

### *His Holiness – Pope John XI – Dominus Apostolicus*

De Roche smoothed the surface of the parchment and read the letter again, smiling to himself. This correspondence had been a long time coming. When the pope ordered him to this godforsaken isle of ignorant peasants, he knew his task would be difficult and tiresome. De Roche's mission had required a sound strategy in order to bear the fruit he desired, a summons back to Rome. His methods had finally paid off. Better yet, if he succeeded in the task the pope had alluded to in his missive, Pope John would be greatly in his debt.

A sound out in the cloister disturbed his reverie. "Father Guillard, is that you skulking outside the door?"

A faint shuffling of feet, and an old, bent priest hobbled to the doorway. "Can I be of assistance, my lord bishop?"

De Roche shook his head. He would have gotten rid of the damned old priest if he could, but Guillard was a filial legacy. "Since you are loitering about, Father, make yourself useful and find Brother Germain."

Guillard nodded and shuffled off.

The bishop settled back, watching the flames on the hearth, playing with the gold ring on his finger and relishing the supreme sense of satisfaction at his triumph.

With a swirl of dusty robes and mud-caked boots, Germain burst into the room. A black look made his scarred face even uglier. "We never saw her!" he growled. "She never passed us. We searched the woods and then checked with the bridge wardens, thinking she had gone off some other way, but no one saw her!"

"Keep your voice down," threatened De Roche. "How is it you let one silly peasant girl slip your grasp?"

Germain scowled. "I have men out looking."

The bishop's face twisted in annoyance. He did not like his schemes thwarted. "She knows nothing. However, I meant to tie up the loose ends." He mulled the options over in his head.

"She may hear something back in that village of hers. She might realize who I am," said Germain.

"My dear monk, the lass stood just here, telling her little tale, and never gave you a second glance. She was too flustered to give a thought to you," replied De Roche. "The box was the main thing, and that has been burned."

Germain frowned. "If she reaches her village, they will describe me to her. They have little else to do, these peasants, but repeat their tales over and over. Even the dull-witted will eventually put the pieces together."

De Roche rose and paced across the room. "Ride to her village. This time, be more discreet. Take her at night, quietly. Only her! Then return with your men as soon as you can. We are leaving this place within the month, assuming Ponto Bertelli can find his way here."

Germain gave him a quizzical look. De Roche raised the folded parchment, displaying the papal seal.

"Has our young pope found the fortitude to stand up to his mother and recall you?" Germain smirked.

De Roche chuckled. "No one stands up to Marozia and comes away unscathed. She controlled his father, Pope Sergius, and she put the papal mitre upon John's head. Now, she's married herself to royalty."

"How has the whore managed that?"

"She married the King of Italy. You have to admire her ambition."

"The king will require a proficient food taster." Germain laughed. "He'll wind up cold and worm-ridden, like the others before him."

De Roche carefully folded the letter. "And now she meddles in her son's affairs." He tapped the letter on the table. "The poor little puppy cries out to us for help. I believe he wants his mother dead. Too bad, in a way. Marozia is more a leader than her son will ever be."

Germain flicked a cockroach from the arm of De Roche's favorite chair and plunked himself down. "Are you going to help the mewling idiot?"

"Brother Germain, what a way to speak of His Holiness!" said De Roche, his lips curled into a cunning smile.

Behind the men, an ear moved silently away from a chink in the stone masonry, and a stone slipped back into place. Silently, the listener stepped from a deep alcove and blended into the bustle of the cathedral.

Chapter Eighteen:
*"Raw leather will stretch."*

Ethan split the final log, then wiped at his chest and face with his wadded-up shirt. He sauntered over to where Vala was sitting. In her village, men never went about bare-chested, so she felt a twinge of embarrassment. She had avoided looking at him or speaking to him since last night, but that could not continue.

She steeled herself and asked, "Would you really have killed me?"

Ethan shrugged. "I'm sworn to protect the Dumnonii. There are few of us left."

He hadn't answered her question, but she didn't pursue the issue. Ethan sat down next to her on a flat stone outcropping. The rocks were damp, but the sun was pleasant. He was a bit too close for comfort. Vala shifted away and set the box between them.

"This box is made of ash," he said. "And ash is the wood element for the rune, Ansuz. Runes are linked to elemental forces: earth, water, air, and fire." He lifted the box and opened it. "This stone is of the air. Simon told us there were other such stones given by the gods."

Vala sat up, alert to this new information.

Pointing to the side of the box, Ethan said, "This circular design represents the cycle of life, which is never-ending. Just here is the trinity symbol. As you know, the world is governed by the triad of gods for earth, sea, and sky."

She didn't know, but nodded.

"And here is a symbol of protection. It shields the contents from evil."

Vala took the box and examined the carving. The design was more than a decoration, just as the emerald was more than a pretty bauble. She lifted the green stone. "How did my father get this?"

"That's a fine question. The gods fought over the stones of power. In the end, the stones were hidden away, given to men, lest the war consume the world." He lifted out the stone, which glittered in the sunlight. "This stone was gifted to the warrior prince, Negus, and Simon was his heir, in a direct line." Ethan watched the stone swing on its chain. "Some of those who received it into their keeping found they were no match for its magic. Some went mad when they tried to use it."

Vala gave a small gasp.

"Or so the legend says," Ethan continued. "The desire for magic turns some hearts black. Blood has been shed to keep this from hands greedy for its secrets."

The small box felt uncommonly heavy in her hand. "It sounds quite dangerous."

"Your family has protected the stone for generations, so it could come into your hands."

"Each generation used it?"

"Of course they did, or tried to."

"And my father wanted to make certain that this dangerous object—over which you say gods warred—my father made sure this came to me?"

A loud caw sounded from the barn.

"Lugus is reminding me to water the horses." Ethan jumped to his feet and loped up the hill.

Vala sighed in exasperation. In her lap, the green stone glittered. A thin vein of coppery ore wound through the center of the stone. It was a pretty thing, in its way. The miller's wife back at home had a bauble she wore on holy days—a dull cat's eye cabochon on a thick chain. It was the woman's pride and joy, for her husband had given it to her as a marriage pledge. This stone was far more beautiful, albeit deadly. She pulled the chain over her head.

"It looks well on you." Ethan stood over her with the raven perched on his head, and Vala burst into giggles. The bird squawked, taking flight. It settled in a nearby tree, where it rustled its wings and strutted back and forth on the branch. "Now you've done it," Ethan grumbled. "He's angry. He thinks you've laughed at him."

Vala choked back her amusement into a tight-lipped grin. It had felt good to laugh in the sunlight.

"Come, Lugus," he coaxed. "She didn't mean to give offense."

The bird turned its back to them.

It was then that Vala noticed a small piece of metal strung on a leather thong and tied to Ethan's ankle. "What is that for?"

"My amulet for good fortune?" He ran his finger over the metal. "It's lead, with a spell pressed into it. The lead is folded to keep the luck inside."

Vala fingered the emerald again. "It doesn't sound as though this amulet would give good luck."

"Your stone is not an amulet," Ethan said. "An amulet is a thing of the earth. It is for spells, like healing, or luck, or love. An amulet helps us acquire things we want to possess. A talisman is a thing of much greater power. It is a thing of the spirit!" He lifted the chain with reverence and held it up in the light. The cool green stone shimmered like beads of dew on the forest moss. "This is a talisman," he said quietly.

Vala sat silent for a minute. The difference didn't mean much to her. "I don't believe there is anything mystical about the scar that Simon gave me." She ignored Ethan's frown. "He wanted to show your people that the stone belonged to his child, so he marked me."

"He had a vision!" Ethan insisted. "The *vision* told him the stone was meant to be passed from him to you."

"Did he have a brand on his back? I'll wager he didn't. Did any of my forbearers have a brand?"

Ethan glared.

"But he marked me," she said. "What foolishness!"

"He did it to prove your claim!"

"He did it because he was mad!"

"You didn't know him. Simon was a great man."

"He couldn't use this stone himself, could he? How do you know anyone has the gift? Perhaps the stone is a fraud too."

"He... Well, not everyone has the gift." Ethan was shouting now. "You Christians! You pray to statues. Have those statues ever answered your prayers?" He took hold of the talisman around her neck, his eyes dark and frightening. "This stone has protected your uncle's house, and you, since your birth. Without it, you would be long dead." Ethan's face had gone crimson with fury. His voice lowered dangerously. "So, if the stone has no value, explain why the clerics hunt it, and you."

Vala wanted to fire back a cutting retort, but she couldn't think of anything.

"Ah! You see it now," Ethan gloated. "De Roche knows the stone is magical. He probably wants it for himself. He had Simon killed for it. And that monk of yours could be part of their plot."

It was Vala's turn to scream. "De Roche was going to *burn* the box, with the stone in it. Moreover, Phillip isn't like that. He saved my life."

"Who is his master?" Ethan shot back.

"Brother Cuthred at Glastonbury," Vala began, but that wasn't really the way of it. "De Roche," she murmured. Although the bishop's men had nearly killed her, in her heart she was unable to put Brother Phillip into the same basket of villains. "If the stone is real," she said in a shaky voice. "If Simon was right, then I have the gift of divination. If he was mad, then I won't be able to foresee anything."

"Now you understand," said Ethan, as though he had finally succeeded in convincing her. "Tonight will be best. Night eliminates distractions, and the sensations are stronger."

Vala felt that she had lost this argument. Ethan had worn her down with his crazy, twisted point of view. She sighed.

"You must promise to really try," said Ethan. "It is what Simon would expect of you."

"Of course I must try!" she barked at him. She had come away with Ethan to learn about her family. She hadn't expected to be dragged into her father's insanity, but how would she know the truth if she didn't try? She got to her feet. "But Simon deserves nothing from me!" She stomped off toward the stable, holding the stone against her chest.

Thistle whinnied as she entered and she patted his flank, running her hands over his strong back as she moved forward. She laid her head against Thistle's neck.

"It's all too strange," she said, gulping back a sob. "One minute, I think I understand Ethan, then the brute opens his mouth. And tonight, he expects me to try to see into the future." The stallion pushed against her. "He believes the bird is my dead brother."

"Merlyn!" a voice squawked.

Vala nearly toppled into the manger. Up in the rafters sat the raven, looking down at her with an unblinking eye. It leapt from its perch and floated down, its wings fluttering, and settled on Thistle's rump. Her horse allowed it.

"Merlyn," it cawed again.

"Your father thought 'Merlyn' was a good name for this horse."

Vala whirled around. Ethan was standing in the doorway.

"Merlyn was the greatest of all the magic wielders," he said, "and Simon admired him very much."

"I prefer Thistle," she hissed through clenched teeth.

"Allow me." Ethan stepped up to the bird. "Lugus, your sister has given this horse a new name. We must respect her choice."

There was silence for a long moment.

"Merlyn!" cawed the bird. It flapped its wings and retreated to the barn's rafters.

"I'm sorry. He's quite stubborn."

Vala didn't know whether to laugh or flee in fright.

"All of this," he said, spreading his arms. "It must be quite upsetting. I should not have lost my temper. You don't know our ways." His voice was gentle, and his eyes had lost their fanatical gleam.

Vala sighed. "I've prayed to a finger bone. Father Cyril brought the bone of St. Loaran to our village church. And once, I prayed to it."

Ethan nodded thoughtfully and held a hand out to her. "I have a pheasant for our supper, and I'm rather a good cook when it comes to pheasant."

While Ethan cleaned the bird, Vala poked about the shelves, looking into jars and crocks. The far corner of the dwelling held a table overrun with jars and bowls. A rickety apparatus perched above them. Liquid was dripping gradually through a metal vessel with small holes hammered into the bottom. Below that was a soggy cloth full of something black and gritty. Fluid seeped through it into a basin, a dark, murky effluent.

"What are you making here?" Vala asked, catching a drip on her finger and sniffing.

Ethan's face lit up. Wiping his fingers on his breeches, creating a distasteful smear of blood and entrails, he hurried over to her. "It's very interesting!" He flourished his hands in front of the equipment as though he were a jester in a village fair. "This apparatus can make a magical powder." He took a small jar from the back of the bench and carried it cautiously to the table. Inside was a dark substance with a dead toad lying atop it.

"What does it do?"

He did not answer as he began to paw through the pile of firewood. He settled on a twig and wet the end in his mouth before slowly dipping the twig into the jar. Black powder clung to it.

"Stand back," he commanded, pushing her against the wall. He leaned forward and tossed the twig into the center of the hearth's flames, then lurched back, shielding Vala from a sudden explosion of unnatural green flame and a spray of burning ash. Vala shrieked in alarm as the hearth expelled an odor of rotten eggs and a cloud of black smoke which hung in the air like a threatening storm front.

"Good, isn't it?" Ethan rubbed his hands together. "Shall I do it again?"

"No!" Vala gasped as she rubbed at a tiny burn on her arm.

Ethan stomped glowing cinders that had settled on the pile of sheepskins before a fire could catch hold. A greasy, acrid scent spiraled up from them.

"What *was* that?"

Ethan smiled. "It's a powder distilled from soil! Can you believe it? From the very earth! I've tried it several times, but it never worked. This time, I was successful. I think the difference is the toad. I took great care to collect it from the same garden patch where I took the soil." He repositioned the toad atop the jar. "I've known two alchemists, and both of them could make this powder, but after I failed so many times, I thought it hopeless. Simon would encourage me to keep trying. He said each failure was a step nearer to success, and he was right."

Vala considered the jar and then the apparatus. "What purpose does it serve?"

"It is magic most elemental. That, alone, is reason to make it," Ethan said in full flow. "First, you distill out the essence of the soil and crystallize it. The material must be strained many times through this wood ash." He pointed to the cloth beneath the bucket. "The water must be allowed to dry up. After the crystals form, you wash them with strong wine and dry it again." Ethan laughed. "I'm not telling it just right. There are more steps, and it took months to make. At the end, you must add ground copper and brimstone. You can see the bits of yellow and brown in the powder." He stared at the jar fondly. "Then, of course, you must catch the toad."

"Why do you need a toad?"

"It's part of the magic of the powder. Perhaps the toad's death gives it life. All I know is that the toad imparts power to the substance."

"And how did you learn to do this?"

"Ahhh!" replied Ethan. "I have it written down. The formula came from a merchant who makes arms for a nobleman. Would you like to see?" Without waiting for a response, Ethan began rummaging on the bench and produced a piece of parchment, crumbling on the edges and stained brown in places. He handed it to Vala.

The heading read *Confloare*.

"Of course you would need to know Latin to read it." Ethan reached for the paper.

Vala withheld it. "I know some Latin," she said, and she began to read aloud. "*Confloare*, or to blow up into flame." She gave him a smug look. "The next part tells about the bucket of soil and the *sacco*, or filter of ashes. Then the part about drying and more distilling and drying. And then it tells about the sulfur powder. The last part says *buxus* and *operculum*. That means to protect with boxwood. I think it means a boxwood lid of some sort."

"No." Ethan grabbed the paper from her hand. "*Buxus* is a toad."

"*Bufonis* is 'toad'," Vala replied, her lips curled into a smile.

"That can't be right. How do you know?" Ethan demanded.

Vala thought back to her early Latin lessons. Uncle Adrian had drawn in the dirt with a stick as Vala asked him the words for 'duck' and 'cow'. Then she had asked about the stick itself. Adrian had winked at her. "Stick is *ramulum*, and this stick," he said, holding it aloft, "is *buxus*, or as we say, boxwood." The memory brought a lump to her throat.

"I remember my lessons on trees," she told him. "Which means the toad is neither magical nor required to make the powder." Vala handed back the parchment, and Ethan began reading, his lips moving silently.

She felt good having bested Ethan, for it put them on even ground. His exploding powder was interesting but probably not magical. As he had explained it, the stuff was made of common substances. It did not rely on intervention from spirits or demons, which was how she had perceived magic would work.

She took a seat in front of the hearth, hugging her knees. What if magic was a complete invention instead of a real mystical force? If magic did not exist, her father and his followers were fakes.

Phillip's miracles were a similar thing. The weeping Madonna had been a fake, but it had fooled an entire village. Vala wondered how many miracles were tricks or misunderstandings. Phillip believed that he would find a real miracle, and Ethan longed for real magic. Both men professed to believe, but each sought proof.

"I agree the toad doesn't matter," Ethan said, intruding on her thoughts. He dropped down next to her, folding his arms over his knees. "I wish I knew Latin, as you do," he admitted. "No one really taught me."

Vala could hear the yearning in his voice.

"But you have to admit the powder is a wondrous thing," he said, brightening.

She had to grin. "It is wondrous," she sighed. "Only, I think you ought to use it outside the house in the future."

They sat companionably for a change, eating their meal in silence. Outside, darkness fell. Vala felt they had reached a stalemate. She fingered the stone that hung heavy around her neck, thinking about what she was going to attempt. The Church would count her a witch if she tried. Vala wrapped her fingers around the stone.

Ethan climbed to his feet. "It's time."

Vala rose and followed him out into the night.

Ethan had laid a bonfire. Twigs had been tented over tinder, and over them, larger sticks, and finally, logs. He motioned her to sit. After touching torch to tinder, he crouched down in front of her with his hands pressed together in front of his face. "What you must do is hold the stone toward the firelight. You must allow your spirit to flow into it." Ethan put a hand on her shoulder and asked, "Are you ready?"

Vala blew out a breath. She had expected more instruction or ceremony. She nodded and raised the stone up to eye level.

Ethan scratched some symbols into the dirt with a stick and tossed a bundle of herbs into the flames. The calming scent of chamomile filled the air. He looked back at Vala before adding a few more aromatics to the flames, and then he retreated into the background.

Thin grey smoke billowed out between the logs, so acrid that she wanted to cough. It stung her eyes until tears flushed the harsh pain away. The light from the flames flickered across the emerald's facets, igniting its heart with fiery green rays. Vala's eyes slid in and out of focus. She felt her mind wandering over dark meadows of waving grasses and fiery hilltops with deep green skies.

"That's right," Ethan crooned in a soothing voice. "Let the stone speak to you."

The smoke wafted about her, but Vala forced herself to keep her breaths slow and deep. It was several minutes before something happened.

The stone slowly grew larger and heavier in her hand. Flames danced around the stone, reaching out for it and encircling it. Vala realized the flames had faces. Their dark eyes and mouths spoke to her, bidding her to join them. As if she were floating upward on a hot wind, Vala found herself on her feet. The earth tipped, wild and unbalanced, beneath her. She wove unsteadily, circling the fire, amidst the flame people. They were marvelously colored: orange, blue and yellow. Vala longed to commune with them but could not make out their strange, harsh words, which sounded like bark cracking in the searing coals.

Wishing seemed to make it so, because the hissing whispers began to make sense. Vala frolicked with abandon in the warmth of the cunning secrets they revealed. They spun patterns in the flame, coalescing into one fiery spiral that grew and grew like a woman twisting her long hair into a coil atop her head. The spiral formed a vortex and the spirits twirled around it, disappearing into it, beckoning her to follow.

Ethan stood well back from the fire. He would be there to help her when she was finished but would not disturb her until then. For long minutes, she sat cross-legged, staring into the stone. Then she shambled to her feet, shrugging off the cloak and then kirtle, and spread her arms to the blaze. Her forehead beaded with sweat as she danced round the bonfire, her shift clinging to her body in the hot fervor of her trance.

Ethan's heart drummed in exhilaration. The flames were speaking to her, and she would tell him what she'd learned. Simon had predicted this. He had known she would unite the old tribes against the onslaught of the Roman church. The others thought she was lost to them, but he had believed, and he had found her. Now, he was watching a true seer come into her own.

When she finally slumped to the ground, exhausted, Ethan hurried forward, gathered her up, and wrapped her in her cloak. The spell of the fire would fade quickly, and she would feel the sharp chill of the night air when it did.

Vala's face hit the ground and she dug her nails into the moist earth, unable to form a notion of where she was, or even who she was. Something warm enveloped her and she realized she was shivering violently. The fire was dying back and she cried out in despair as the fire spirits vanished amongst the flames.

"It's all right," said a voice. Arms were pulling her in; hands were rubbing her back and her arms. Vala wanted to escape this false warmth and leap after the retreating fire spirits, but she had no strength to pull away. She wondered who was keeping her from the brilliant fire people.

"What did you see? You danced in the spirit world. Did you see anything of the future?"

Vala struggled toward the flames, but she was so very weak. Then Ethan's face swam into focus through the haze. She'd seen the future and the past all twisted together.

"I might have seen something. I just can't recall it." Her head was beginning to pound. "A fiery circle, I think..."

"The Sun Cross!" said Ethan. "It's a great wheel that tells us of the eternity of the soul. What else did you see?"

"There were spirits made of fire. They told me things—in my head." Vala rubbed her temple.

"Was it Aedh? The lord of fire?"

"I don't know," she said weakly.

"It doesn't matter. You have the power. There can be no doubt."

"I feel wretched."

"Your father was never wrong about these things. And now it is proved!"

He tucked the cloak around her, and she closed her eyes against a rising pain in her temples and a nauseating sense of lightheadedness.

"In a few minutes, you will feel better." He smoothed her tangled hair.

The world stopped spinning, and when Vala opened her eyes, she realized her nausea had passed. She sat up and saw her kirtle balled up on the ground. "How did..."

"You cast it aside," Ethan said. "To dance with the spirits."

The Church burned women as witches for dancing round a fire unclothed. "No decent person would do what I did here tonight," she said, knowing she ought to feel guilt and remorse, but she had needed to test her prowess with the stone and had done so.

"The Dumnonii do not agree with such narrow-minded thinking." Ethan was trying to wrap her in the cloak. "You'll take ill in this night air."

Vala tried to get to her feet. She wanted to escape, to think. She took a few wobbly steps.

"Vala, wait!"

She felt the ground fall away, and Ethan's words were drowned in muffled darkness.

When next she opened her eyes, Vala was inside Ethan's house, lying on a pile of sheep pelts in front of the warm hearth, wrapped in several blankets. Ethan approached, candle in one hand and a steaming cup in the other.

"Willow bark tea." He held out the cup.

Vala knew the properties of willow bark to cure headache, and she accepted it gratefully.

"You should get out of your shift. I'll lay it out to dry. Can you manage it?"

Vala nodded groggily, and after he had turned his back, she shimmied out of the unpleasantly damp garment. Ethan hung up the shift and then wrapped another blanket around her like a thick cocoon. Orange firelight from the banked hearth flickered on the ceiling, reminding her of the fire spirits. The stone of Ansuz hung heavy around her neck. She pressed shaky fingers to it. There was no way to deny the experience, or ignore it. She had seen the apparitions, and she was certain the spirits had talked to her. She could not recall what they had said, but she remembered the sensation.

Vala sipped the hot liquid. Ethan had softened the bitterness of the bark infusion with honey and clover flowers. He was so very annoying at times, but also uncommonly kind. As she downed the remains of the cup, she heard him let out a loud snore from the corner.

They hoisted their packs onto their horses while Lugus swooped overhead.

"Avebury is not too far. We should find the Dumnonii camp by nightfall."

"I'm so tired," she complained.

Ethan wasn't listening. He had chattered since dawn and kept hurrying her along, eager to get back to his people. "They will be so glad to find you are alive! You'll like them, I'm sure, but you might find some of them a bit odd."

Vala squinted at Ethan, wondering how anyone could surpass him in outlandishness.

"There is a woman named Isolde," he said. "She can do powerful magic, and she wants to take Simon's place. I don't think we can allow this." Ethan mounted his horse and passed his fingers over his good fortune amulet.

Vala waited to see if he would say more on the subject, but instead, he turned his horse and cantered toward the path.

Her head hurt in the way it had done after the banquet at Glastonbury. She caught Thistle's reins and swung herself stiffly into the saddle, then followed him.

"Ethan," she called. "What about this Isolde..."

Chapter Nineteen:
*"The old ox plows a straight furrow."*

Dusty grey light seeped in through the high, narrow windows. The great cathedral at Bath held many beautiful and inspiring niches, but this forlorn little chapel was not one of them. The chapter house chapel was an afterthought—a builder's miscalculation resulting in an orphan space. The narrow orchard path that ran along an outer wall led to the entrance. The path was muddy in spring and overgrown with weeds in summer. In winter, bitter winds whistled along with it, coating everything in a layer of ice. The monks avoided it, favoring the handsome chapel in the apse.

Today, the dingy chapel had visitors. Two men stood together in the tiny nave, looking toward the altar. Above it hung a heavy iron cross brought all the way from Spain. The cross, originally commissioned for the main altar in the cathedral, was truly repugnant. Christ's face was twisted in an odd sneer. The architect had wisely banished it here. Like everything else in this space, it was a cast-off.

"Do you see how the artist has depicted the face of our Lord?" Father Guillard asked.

"It's an ugly likeness," Phillip said.

"It may be," mused Guillard. "But I've always preferred this chapel, for it feels more truthful for its ugliness than a serene and perfect visage on a dying Christ."

"Father, not now," Phillip sighed. He had failed in every way and had no stomach for idle contemplations. Vala might be in danger, and it was his fault.

"You are too hard on yourself, my son," Guillard said, reading his thoughts. "You say you saved the girl from Germain's henchmen, bound up her wounds and gave her your protection."

"But I left her when—" Phillip bent over in an agony of self-revulsion.

Guillard raised an eyebrow. "You had feelings you could not understand."

Phillip shook his head in denial, but Guillard waited calmly.

At last, Phillip snarled, "I knew well what I felt. I knew it! I feared I couldn't control my desires." The admission tasted bitter on his tongue.

Guillard knew confession alone would not give the young monk relief. Some form of penance would help, but Phillip would impose that upon himself. It was not for Guillard to meddle or to judge. Instead, the old priest pulled a sheaf of parchment from beneath his robes. "This is all the information I could glean."

Phillip accepted the documents and scanned them quickly. Father Guillard's spy had recounted the incriminating words, clear proof of De Roche's treachery. The bishop had sent his cur, Brother Germain, to do murder, just as Vala had said. The spy reported a letter suggesting De Roche was in league with His Holiness in mischief and murder. "I'm to blame for this—me alone!"

"That is ridiculous, self-centered rot. De Roche is to blame," Guillard replied.

Phillip crushed the parchment in his fist. "But I didn't believe her. She went off with a heathen because I didn't believe her!" Phillip dug his knuckles into his eyes. "God has deserted us." Perhaps his beliefs were a sham, just as Vala had suggested. Phillip reeled, dropping to his knees on the cold stone floor.

Guillard shook his head. "The young are so rash." His expression became whimsical. "There once was a crow. It was terribly thirsty, for there had been no rain for many days. Near death from lack of water, the bird spied a pitcher upon a table. He perched next to the pitcher and dipped his beak inside, but he was not able to reach in far enough to drink. The crow began to bemoan his fate. 'There is nothing to be done!' he cried. 'I will surely perish!' A small mouse regarded the crow. 'Sir crow,' said the mouse. 'See the pebbles on the ground? Try putting them into the pitcher.' The crow understood, and his desperate situation suddenly became hopeful, for after dropping enough pebbles into the pitcher, the water level was high enough that the bird could drink."

Phillip stared at Guillard, contemplating the fable.

The old priest grasped his friend's arm with a palsied hand. "I'll go to my room and send this information. Who can tell, my son, what a few pebbles may do?"

Leaving Phillip to his thoughts, Guillard hobbled back to his cell. It was not the spartan accommodation endured by the other priests. He had his books and his pigeons, along with several fine old tapestries that warmed the bare walls. De Roche feared him a little, which accounted for the insults, but preferred to ignore him.

*Too old*, he thought as he climbed the last few steps, bracing himself against the wall as he went. Espionage was a game for younger men.

Father Guillard closed the door to his cell and sank onto a stool next to a small writing table, clutching his chest. Old men ought not to be scurrying about.

As the pounding in his heart subsided, he poised his quill over a small bowl of ink only to find his mind was a blank. He knew he'd hurried back to write an important note, but the reason for the note escaped him. The quill sagged between his bony fingers. He gazed around the room, hoping for a clue, something to spur his brain back into action.

In his day, he had been revered and reviled for his sharp wit and cool intelligence. Those were the days of the Vicomte Arnaud De Roche, his patron and friend. Oh, the deeds they had done!

"*Noblesse d'épée*," he murmured, recalling the old glories. A deathbed promise and the stricture of the Vicomte's written will kept Guillard attached to the retinue of his old friend's son. Bishop De Roche could depend on the substantial legacy from his father only as long as he kept and provided for Guillard. In his turn, Guillard had tearfully pledged to provide guidance for the boy.

Sensing a tendency toward deceit in his old friend's son, Father Guillard paid a little network of spies to obtain information on the bishop's private doings. Guillard had been able to thwart a few of De Roche's nastier plans over the years, with the bishop none the wiser.

The cooing of Windsinger, perched prettily in her wooden hutch, stirred the old priest's recollection. He was to pen a letter to an old friend. He shook off his dusty memories, and, after dipping his quill with conviction, he began to write.

Chapter Twenty:
*"A full cup must be carried steadily."*

It was difficult for Vala to shake the muzzy feeling she felt after her attempt at scrying. She barely noticed the miles they traveled. It wasn't until late afternoon, as the sun painted long shadows between the trees that the dazed feeling subsided.

Ethan had rattled on and on about her abilities and her potential as a seer, but she couldn't decipher his babble. All she knew was that using the talisman had been uncommonly draining.

"What of my brother?" she asked. "How did he die?"

"I've no evidence, but we all feel certain that Germain waylaid Lugus on the road and there slit his throat. I brought his body back to Simon."

Vala huddled in her cloak, chewing over her growing hatred for Brother Germain.

They wound their way in the blackness along a narrow forest path. A bird chittered sharply off to their left, and an answering call came from in front of her. With cupped hands, Ethan's dark silhouette repeated the sound, then he took hold of Thistle's bridle and veered from the clear path. They ducked beneath a low branch, then down a rocky incline. A large clearing opened in front of them.

It looked like an encampment of vagabonds, those homeless travelers who sold trinkets and offered to mend pots for the price of a meal. Wagons covered with canvas and makeshift huts of wood and thatch ringed the clearing. Animal hides covered doorways and window openings. A large fire was blazing in the center of the compound. The greasy scent of roasted meat hung in the air.

Ethan slid off his horse and Vala mimicked him, grateful to set her feet on firm earth.

"Ethan, you dog!" snarled a voice from the shadows.

"Manning!" Ethan flung open his arms, and the men exchanged an exuberant bear hug. "This scoundrel is our best hunter and my friend," Ethan said presenting a stocky man about his own age who had a ruddy, weathered face.

"I should have known you were kept away by a pretty girl," Manning said with a smirk.

Ethan grasped his friend's arm. "This is Vala, Simon's daughter."

"No! Are you certain? Can she really be?"

Ethan nodded.

Manning took her hand. "Pardon my jest. No one believed you lived, goddess."

Vala frowned. "No! Please, just Vala."

"She has the sight, Manning. See here." Ethan pointed to the stone hanging around her neck.

Manning put a hand to his heart. "May the protection of the stone be upon all of us." Then he hallooed to the entire settlement, "Ethan's come back! He's brought Simon's daughter!"

Heads turned and popped out from inside the huts. People around the fire rose to their feet. Buzzing with the excitement of a hive of bees, faces converged around them, astonished and skeptical, all jostling for a look. Ethan greeted many of them, asking after their families and introducing Vala, who tried to follow the names. She found she was so exhausted, she could remember only a few.

The crowd parted for a slender woman, confident and regal. A hush fell over the assembly, not even the night creatures presuming to rustle the grass.

"Ethan," the woman said in a low, husky voice. "I see you have finally decided to join us. You should have come at once, after Simon's death." She gestured to the group. "You know we crave your opinion."

Something in the tone of the woman's voice told Vala that she did not desire anyone's opinion.

Ethan offered her a slight bow. "When I learned of Simon's demise, I went in search of his daughter, and I've found her." He took Vala's arm and pulled her into prominence.

"You've forgotten your manners, Ethan," said the woman, shifting her gaze to Vala.

Ethan coughed. "I apologize. Allow me to present Vala, daughter of Simon Finn Negus." He doffed his hat in a parody of a courtly bow. "And Vala, this is Isolde."

The woman raised an eyebrow, and the group watched her nervously. Isolde was an old woman, even though she walked with a straight spine and showed no mark of disease. Her hair was swathed in the same fabric as her dress, so it wasn't possible to see if her locks were greying. It was the woman's eyes that gave the impression of great age. They were pools of hoarded secrets.

"How wonderfully unexpected." Isolde took Vala's hand, turned it over, running a pointed nail over her palm, her features tightening before she let go. "So nice of you to join us, my dear," she said sweetly. "Ethan," she called over her shoulder as she glided back to her makeshift dwelling, "I'd like to see you in my lodge."

As Isolde disappeared inside, the world snapped back to life. Vala balled her hand into a fist to squeeze away the woman's touch, and in the thicket, a nightingale warbled. The group, sensing the entertainment was over, drifted back to their huts or the fire.

Ethan sighed. "I'm sorry, but I must go to her. If I don't, she might turn me into a toad." He chuckled, but Vala thought he believed it a possibility. "Sit by the fire and warm yourself. I will be back soon."

He found her an upturned log to sit upon, and she gratefully spread her fingers in the fire's heat. Ethan vowed to return quickly.

Chapter Twenty-One:
*"Foul water will quench fire."*

"Ethan!" cried a hunched woman with flyaway grey hair and wide-set eyes that looked in two directions at once. "You've returned!"

"Hello, Ragnell. How are you keeping?"

Ragnell simpered flirtatiously, "How are *you* keeping?" She held a struggling rabbit by the ears. Isolde's constant companion, this woman was equally deadly. Luckily, Ragnell was not her mistress's match when it came to intelligence.

Isolde's dwelling was a crazy quilt of materials with lodge poles set at random to support the roof. The room was arranged around a large table chock full of herbs, wooden casks, and jars. Isolde was a devotee of herb lore. She practiced her potions on the small animals imprisoned in woodbine cages who squeaked and cawed at the disturbance. The din included an occasional loud snore coming from a dark corner where the goddess's massive son, Borghild, was sleeping on a rug.

"Ethan," Isolde said, appearing from behind a drape.

He ignored her proffered hand and made a little bow. "Isolde," he replied.

She pulled back her hand. "Still mourning your misguided mentor?" she asked.

Before Ethan could respond, two loud whacks made him flinch. Ragnell had loped off the rabbit's rear legs with a cleaver. "Try hopping away from me now!" she tittered at the poor squealing animal. Isolde threw her a filthy look, and Ragnell dispatched the creature by chopping off its head.

Both of the old crones were completely mad.

"Ragnell, take young Vala a nice cup of hot cider."

Ragnell eyed her mistress and nodded.

"I could be your new mentor, Ethan," Isolde offered, running a thin finger along his cheek.

"You're more of a motherly figure," Ethan said, and turned away. His own mother had grasped his small hand and drawn him into the crowded marketplace with the promise of a sweet cake. He recalled her slender fingers around his shoulders as she shoved him away from her before she disappeared into the throng. He had been four years old when his mother had left him to survive or die.

Isolde sniffed, unsure how to respond, and then became businesslike. "Are you positive it is her?"

"I saw the scar," said Ethan. "She holds the talisman of Ansuz, and I tested her. She has the power to use the stone." He had to struggle to keep his voice devoid of the enthusiasm he felt.

"You say she used the stone?" Isolde asked. "Do you know the lore of this stone?"

Of course Ethan knew the lore. He shrugged.

Ragnell stepped back into the lodge. "The little virgin seer has her special tea."

"Quiet!" Isolde growled.

"Think of the power a virgin could wield with the stone!" Ragnell mused.

Ethan looked at the woman suspiciously.

"That is quite enough!" Isolde ordered.

Ragnell grinned and turned back to her butchery.

Isolde composed her face. "No one has seen the stone in many years. Why assume her stone is the true one?"

"It is," said Ethan.

"She might be an imposter. I wish to view the scar tonight."

Ethan ran a hand over his face. "We've been riding all day. Perhaps in the morning, if Vala consents."

"Tonight," said Isolde. "And I do not wish the girl to know. Ragnell has given her a draught—"

"What?" cried Ethan. "What did you give her?"

"Nothing lasting," said Isolde. "Take her to your hut. We will come within the hour. She will not remember."

"You had no right!" Ethan spun and started for the door, knocking several jars to the floor as he did so.

"Careful, Ethan," Isolde smoothly said. "Don't make matters worse."

Ethan stepped out into the night. He had a low regard for trickery of this type. He'd shed his blood to defend the Dumnonii and preferred a straight-on fight, not such underhanded tactics. He knew Isolde meant to use Vala in some way. It would have been better for the old witch if the girl had never been found. Now, she would try to benefit from Vala's power. Ethan's mind churned the problem over as he loped toward the fire where Vala was sitting.

A cup lay on the ground at Vala's feet, and the girl herself was slumped forward.

"Vala!" Ethan shook her. "Vala!" He picked up the cup and sniffed. The cider covered the scent of the sleeping draught Ragnell had given her. At least, he hoped it was just a sleeping draught.

"Is she all right?" a man across the fire asked.

"Just tired," Ethan lied, hauling Vala to her feet.

"I had some cider," Vala said groggily.

"Yes, I know," Ethan said. "Try to walk."

Vala stumbled along as Ethan half-carried, half-dragged her toward his own hut.

Isolde's penchant for the black arts was well-known. Simon had provided the ethical conscience for the group, and without him, Isolde was unleashed to perform her dark spells. A young seer, a *virgin* seer, would be a temptation, for to sacrifice such a one would release enormous power.

Ethan cursed. He hadn't thought things through, hadn't suspected Isolde would move so quickly against Vala. Once she had seen the mark on Vala's back, proving Vala's claim, how could he protect her? Ethan needed a way to thwart the old hag.

An idea bubbled up, a clever idea, simple and easy. It could work. He looked back over his shoulder as he hurried Vala into his hut.

"Where are we?" Vala asked weakly.

Ethan steered her to a straw pallet and lit a small fire beneath the central chimney hole.

"You're sort of handsome," Vala said, her words slurred.

Ethan raised an eyebrow. "Is that so?"

"My old beau was handsome," she said.

Ethan stripped off his cloak and then his shirt. "Simon, if you are watching, please forgive me," he whispered toward the roof. He went to the pallet. "Let's get your clothes off, shall we?"

Vala giggled as Ethan pulled her to her feet and unlaced her kirtle.

"My clothes are off," she announced, twirling free of her dress.

Ethan wondered again what they'd given the girl. Just then, her eyes rolled back, and she went limp. Ethan was just in time to catch her before she toppled into the fire.

He deposited her onto the pallet, then found a blanket and draped it over her, then pulled off his boots. Again, he asked forgiveness of Simon for what he was about to do as he lay down on the pallet with Vala. Beneath the blanket, he loosened the string on her shift and pulled it down off her shoulder. Relaxing into the rushes, Ethan held her against his bare chest. With gentle fingers, he pushed her hair aside, exposing the scar.

This simple trick would put an end to the old witch's avarice. His solution was genius. Ethan placed a light kiss on Vala's forehead.

There was a soft knock at the door, and Ethan levered himself up on one elbow, composing his face into a sleepy demeanor. Let the farce begin.

Two women entered, Ragnell in front, shielding the light of a small lantern, followed by Isolde, wrapped in a cloak. Ethan beckoned them forward with a yawn. The look on Isolde's face was clear to see, even in the dim light of the swaying lantern. The implication of two people sharing a bed was clear, and her sharp features contracted, purple with rage. Ethan pretended not to notice.

"She's deep in sleep, as you wanted." He invited them closer. With Vala held tightly against him, he slipped the blanket down.

"Ansuz," Ragnell muttered, reaching out a tentative finger toward the scar, a look of awe on her wrinkled face.

Isolde slapped the woman's hand away and jostled in front of her, eyeing the mark. "Ethan, you son of a cur. This girl should have been left a virgin!"

Ethan allowed his face to take on a look of shame and surprise. "Trust me, she is no worse off now than when I found her. Look at her! Seventeen, and pretty enough to have had several beaus." He ran a finger down her back. "She mentioned a stable boy, or a blacksmith, something of the like. Virginity aside, it's the scar that's important. Touch it, why don't you?"

Isolde grunted, pushing a cracked fingernail into the disfigurement, and Vala shuddered in her sleep.

"It's real enough," said Ragnell. "We can tell the others this girl is truly Simon Finn Negus's daughter." She clapped her hands together, obviously forgetting her mistress's scheme.

Isolde glowered. "Yes, it appears Simon's daughter has come home to us. What about the stone?"

Ethan gently settled Vala on her back. He lifted the stone so they could examine it in the lantern light. The girl's eyes fluttered, and he prayed she would not wake.

"It is an emerald, but whether it is the stone of Ansuz, who can say?" Isolde said, fingering the treasure.

For all her feigned disinterest, Ethan could see she coveted it. "Simon explained the lore of the stone to me," he offered. "Bad luck will befall a person who claims one of the stones without inheriting it in the direct line from the gods. And good luck will come to the stone's true master." There was no such lore, but the story sounded fine. "Vala has been exceptionally lucky since she acquired it. She remained hidden from the enemy all these years, and then escaped Germain and his men with nary a scratch." He watched the old witch's eyes and saw that he'd hit the mark.

"A direct line..." Isolde muttered. She was the most superstitious of women. Her talon-like fingers dropped the stone and disappeared beneath her cloak. "I want a word with you in the morning, Ethan."

"Another word?" he yawned.

She shot him an icy look before sweeping from the hut, Ragnell bobbing behind. As the lantern disappeared through the doorway, Ragnell poked her head back inside and wiggled her fingers at Ethan in a coquettish farewell, then the women were gone.

Ethan sank back in relief. People heard what they expected to hear and saw what they expected to see. He rolled to his side and allowed himself a long look at the girl, peacefully unaware of her near brush with death, for Isolde would have killed Vala for the stone, if not for his concocted lie. He'd also disabused her of the idea that the girl was virginal—and quite cleverly, too, he thought. Just like that, Vala was safe from Isolde.

"I saved her, Simon," he whispered in triumph, tucking the blankets around her.

The other pallet was cold after the warmth of a body pressed against his, but he quickly drifted off into a satisfied sleep.

Chapter: Twenty-Two:
*"Birds of a feather flock together."*

Shadowy figures loomed over Vala, full of menace as they poked at her and muttered. She wanted to twist away but could not make her limbs move. Then the stone sparkled before her eyes. Its radiance pulled her free of the darkness and propelled her into the light as pure spirit, flying up and away from her earthbound body, just as Lugus had done when his spirit soared as a bird.

The sky lightened from darkest night into a sun-drenched expanse of white clouds. She soared, effortlessly riding swelling currents of air. She had snow-white feathers that fanned out to ride the warm updraft. Something was tied to her leg, and her destination lay just below. Reveling in the sensation of wheeling downward, she spiraled toward her goal.

Someone approached. Hands removed the paper tied to her leg, then fumbled, tying a new paper there. Hands tossed her back into the air. The roof disappeared below as she stretched out her wings, climbing back toward the blue sky and white clouds and the bright, bright sun.

The dream was vivid, but, as dreams are like to do, it slipped away from Vala as she woke. When she opened her eyes, she found the hut was empty and the dream fully gone. She lurched to her feet and pulled her kirtle on over her shift. She struggled with the lacings, wondering how she'd removed the garment the night before.

A clean linen towel lay on the table next to a stoneware bowl of cold water. After splashing her face, she raked her fingers through her hair to tame it.

Ethan was sprawled on a bench against the outer wall, long legs stretched in front of him. "Good morning," he said. "Or perhaps I should say, good day. You slept the morning away."

Vala looked to the heavens, where the sun rode high.

"The women made mash. There's a bowl for you." He lifted two bowls, one partly consumed, and extended the uneaten one to Vala. "It's cooled off a bit."

"Thank you," she said, accepting the dish.

He looked her up and down. "You look nice."

Vala tried to cover her blush by shoveling mash into her mouth.

Once the bowls were empty, Vala accompanied Ethan in a stroll around the encampment. Men stood guard on small flets anchored in the trees.

"Are we likely to be attacked here?" Vala asked.

"The clerics are always looking for us. We are in constant danger."

Ethan always spoke as though opinion was stone-carved truth, but in this, he was probably right.

Each person they passed had a warm greeting for Ethan. A few of the Dumnonii stared at her, but for the most part, they treated Vala with stiff deference.

"Kale of Anglesey... Ann Worthy... Foderick and his son..." Ethan said, making introductions.

Vala smiled and struggled to remember at least a few of the names.

Manning emerged from one of the huts. "Good morning, goddess," he said, then he bowed grandly.

She grimaced. "Please don't call me that."

"You look very pleased, Manning," Ethan said. "Had a good evening?"

Manning turned a shade redder.

"He fancies a milkmaid in the village of Avebury, just yonder," Ethan said.

Wearing a broad grin, Manning punched Ethan's arm.

Across the compound, a mountain of a man shambled toward Isolde's lodge. He swatted at the air, mumbling as he walked.

"Who is that?" Vala asked.

Manning rolled his eyes. "That's Borghild."

"He's simple-minded, isn't he?" she said. "We had a boy like him at home. He was a good lad, just a bit slow to understand."

"I wouldn't say Borghild was a good lad," said Ethan.

"More ogre than man," Manning said.

Vala scowled at them both and then looked back at Borghild. "He can't help the way he is." But they were ignoring her and whispering together.

Manning nodded. "I'll come find you when all is ready." The men exchanged a significant look before Manning trotted off.

"Only a spineless dog kills with poison," Ethan muttered as he smiled and waved to a pair of women walking toward them.

Vala was about to ask whom he was speaking of when his face broke into a genuine grin. Grasping her arm, he pulled her toward a downhill path leading away from the camp. Vala squealed as green willow branches whipped against her. The path opened into another clearing where sat a dwelling built of fieldstones and topped with a timber roof. Below a deep overhang sat a man who jumped to his feet at their approach.

"Ethan!" cried the man.

Ethan gave the man bear hug. "Fletcher!"

"This is her—Simon's daughter." The man took Vala's hands in his own calloused ones. Deep wrinkles lined the old man's face, framed by the stubble of a beard and close-shorn hair. He had the look of a powerful man who'd lived a hard life, but his bright blue eyes sparkled when he smiled.

As Fletcher squeezed her fingers, Vala was surprised to recall the feeling of her uncle holding her hand as a child, which brought sudden tears to her eyes.

"No need to cry, little one," the man said with concern. "You are safe here."

"It's not that," she said, wiping her eyes. "It's just that you remind me of someone." She couldn't say why she had said that to this stranger.

"You miss someone close to you," said Fletcher, squeezing her hands again. "No, that's not quite it. You grieve?"

"Fletcher can read a person's thoughts," Ethan said. "He holds your hand, and he can see things about you."

"Impressions, no more," said Fletcher, stepping back. "I was a great friend of your father's. I was there just before he took you off to your uncle. You've grown into a lovely young woman."

Vala wiped her face with the back of her hand. "Can you tell me about him, sir? I never knew my father."

"Of course, little one, but you must agree to call me Fletcher."

Just then, Manning burst into the clearing. "Ethan, we're ready!"

"Good man," Ethan said. "Vala, I must go. I expect we'll be gone a fortnight. You will be perfectly safe here. I've fixed it." He put a hand on Fletcher's shoulder. "Watch out for her, won't you?"

Fletcher nodded.

"Wait!" Vala cried. But Ethan and Manning were already running back up the path. Ethan threw her a confident wave before disappearing into the trees. She started after them.

"No sense following," Fletcher said. "He's gone to do what he couldn't do until he'd found you."

Vala hesitated, torn between pursuit and the calming words of the old man. She felt like a piece of baggage hauled along for a time but dropped off when she became a nuisance. Phillip had left her behind at Glastonbury, and now Ethan had done so too.

Fletcher seemed to sense her thoughts. "They are going to avenge Simon," Fletcher said. "I wouldn't want to be that man."

"Farley," whispered Vala.

Chapter Twenty-Three:
*"To who we love best, to them we can say least."*

"You can't fault the boy wanting revenge," Fletcher said. "Simon was like a father to Ethan. He sucked in every word from the man's lips as though it were mother's milk."

Vala felt the flush of anger again. Ethan knew her family better than she did.

Fletcher took her arm. "Come into my house, Valora. I'll make us some braggot, and we can have a nice long talk."

She pulled her eyes from the path. "My name is Vala."

"I am sorry! An old man forgets." He chuckled and tapped a finger to the side of his head. "'Valora' is what your mother wanted to call you. It means 'brave'."

"You knew my mother?"

"I did."

Fletcher's home didn't have the temporary look of the huts in the clearing. There were rugs of sheep's skin on the floor and sturdy benches by the hearth. At the back of the main room was a worktable littered with tools. Fresh wood shavings scented the air with tree sap.

A short, heavy woman with rosy cheeks gasped as they entered. Her hands flapped in the air in front of her. "It's her, isn't it?"

"Vala, this is my sister, Meg," said Fletcher.

"The gods be praised you're safe, my dear." She pulled Vala into a hug and then dug into the pocket of her apron and produced an acorn. She pressed it into Vala's hand.

Unsure why the woman had done it, Vala smiled tentatively at Meg.

"You'll stay for the evening meal, won't you?"

"Do stay," urged Fletcher. "We're having partridge."

"I'd like that," Vala replied, and Meg hurried off to pluck her fowls.

Vala spotted a heavy wooden case. "You have books!" There were eight volumes, an unheard-of number for a person to possess. They were battered and well-thumbed, and Vala touched them reverently.

Fletcher fiddled with a pot of hot water hung on the hearth. "I enjoy reading, and I sometimes copy volumes, if I can get parchment."

"I have two books," Vala said proudly. "One was given to me by the monks at Glastonbury, and the other—" She stopped herself from saying she'd stolen it. "—is in a language I don't know."

Fletcher handed her a steaming cup. "If you'd like, I could look at it, and perhaps we can decipher its secrets."

Vala smiled at him and then opened her hand to consider the acorn.

"You don't know the meaning of Meg's gift, do you, child?"

"No, sir."

"The acorn is a good luck token. The spirit of the oak tree lives in its seed. It's a strong protective force."

"In Wistman's Wood, we have some oak trees. The priest says demons live inside them." Vala rolled the acorn in her fingers.

"Priests," Fletcher said with a dismissive wave.

"Tell me more of my mother and father," Vala asked, sipping her drink. "That's what I'd really like."

"Simon spent his life keeping your parentage a secret." Fletcher sat and stretched out his legs, motioning Vala to a bench. "When did you learn the truth?"

"The day I was taken to see him, just before he died."

Fletcher frowned, tapping his fingers on his cup. "Your mother, Madelyn, used to speak of her hopes for you as she awaited your birth." He took a sip. "She was convinced you were a girl and planned to name you Valora. Your sweet mother died giving birth to you. Simon was beside himself with grief. In that state, he had a powerful vision in which he glimpsed your future. He modified your mother's choice and told us your name would be Vala."

"My uncle said it means 'chosen'."

Fletcher nodded. "Of course I was shocked by the brand Simon put on your back, but the man was overcome with a terrible grief."

Vala twitched her shoulder.

"I should begin nearer the beginning," Fletcher said. "It was at Bodmin Moor, just before your birth, where we were betrayed by one of our own. We never discovered who it was."

Meg re-entered the room and upended a bowl of dough onto the table. She began to knead.

"Soldiers attacked in the night," Fletcher said, then took another sip. "They trampled the crops and burned our homes. Meg took Lugus and fled, but your mother was too far into her labor and couldn't be moved. As you were born, your mother expired."

Vala listened, spellbound.

"Simon refused to let you go, and he would not leave Madelyn. We had to pull him from the house. The soldiers were close, setting everything alight as they went. Simon grabbed a flaming brand and set fire to the house, shouting that they would not touch his wife."

The room was still but for Meg's rhythmic kneading of the bread.

"We escaped into the forest dragging your father, who was wild with grief. While we watched the destruction from a safe distance, he went off with you. We didn't notice at first, for all was chaos. When we found him, he was huddled by a small fire, rocking you and mumbling to himself. The brand on your tender little back was an angry red welt, and you were crying so hard, you could barely get a breath."

Fletcher set aside his cup. "Simon had the little box that contained the talisman. He was determined to take you and the box to your Uncle Darian that very night. We let him go, and we prayed to the gods that nothing else would befall the two of you before you reached safety."

Meg's pink cheeks had gone pale. "It was for the best. Your father was in no fit state to care for an infant. I kept Lugus with me until the poor man was back in his right mind." Meg choked back tears. "Simon did love his Madelyn."

It was an appalling image: a burning house, her mother lying dead, flames consuming everything. Then Vala recalled another fire, one she had ignited, forced by a deathbed command. In the end, Simon had followed his wife's fiery ending.

"She was a real beauty, your mother," said Fletcher.

"Very much like you, dear," Meg sniffled.

A tear escaped Vala's eye, and she brushed it away. "Why didn't he ever come back for me?"

"Oh, lamb!" Meg brushed her floury hands on her apron before putting a chubby arm around Vala's shoulders. "You were better off with your uncle. For Lugus and Ethan, sleeping in the wild, hiding and spying was a great adventure. I told him he was far too reckless with those boys." After a moment's contemplation, she added, "I think Simon was afraid, too. Afraid he would look into your eyes and see Madelyn."

Vala felt the weight of this possibility like a lodestone in her chest.

Meg smiled. "He'd tell fantastic stories to Lugus and Ethan of the beautiful young goddess secreted away on the edge of a far-off wood."

The tale was romantic and fanciful, not the sort Vala would have attributed to her father. Meg put a warm, fresh cup of braggot into her hands.

"What do you know of the Dumnonii?" Fletcher asked.

Vala sighed. "Very little."

Fletcher settled in. "The Dumnonii worship the old gods and keep their ways, but our numbers dwindle. The Roman church works diligently to convert this island to Christianity. They do it by means both subtle and rough. It is death to claim lineage from the Dumnonii."

According to Fletcher, the remnants of the Dumnonii lived an unsettled existence. Some traveled, selling charms and cures. Some huddled together for safety.

"These people are good, honest souls," Fletcher said.

Meg huffed. "All but Isolde."

"She is just a bit fanatical," said Fletcher.

"Ragnell is mad, and that son of hers gives me gooseflesh."

Vala experienced another moment of irritation. "Surely, that poor boy can't help his condition."

Meg shook her head. "It grieves me to speak ill of him, but Borghild is a product of his mother's tutelage. I'm told his chief entertainment is tormenting small animals."

"There is little to do here but gossip," Fletcher replied.

Meg huffed, then bustled off to collect some fresh herbs.

Vala cast about for a new topic. "What is it you make with all your tools?"

Fletcher grinned. "I make these," he said, going to the workbench. He handed her a hunting bow.

"Men in my village hunt with bows, but nothing so elegant as this."

"I feel the spirits in the wood, and they tell me how best to shape it. Always yew for a bow and hemp for the strings." He pointed to the drying plants hanging in the rafters.

"Remarkable," Vala said, admiring the various tools fashioned to aid in the bending and shaping of wood. There was a brazier for forming arrows and a wooden box of goose feathers ready to become fletching. Vala ran a thumb over a small carved symbol on the limb.

"That is the rune called 'Ur'. It encourages the arrows to true flight." He winked, and Vala was not sure if he was serious. "Would you like to shoot it?"

"Very much."

He led her outside to a target of deer hide tied between two trees. Against the cottage wall, he had a rack draped in oiled cloth which held a dozen bows and several quivers of arrows. "I test each bow before it goes to its new owner."

He chose one of the weapons and, applying pressure to the curved limbs, set the string in place. He deftly nocked an arrow and then, in one smooth motion, he raised the bow and released. The bowstring twanged, and the arrow struck the very center of the target with an impressive *thwop*.

"Now you." He handed Vala the bow and an arrow from the quiver.

"I've never actually—"

"No excuses. In learning, there is always the first time."

Her first arrow got away from her and flopped feebly to the ground. "Try again," said Fletcher with an encouraging wave.

Vala set a new arrow. On the second try, she released the arrow too soon, and it fell short of the target by a dozen feet. Vala was an impatient student, or so her uncle said. She wanted to excel immediately, so she plucked a third arrow from the quiver with determination. This time she managed to hit the ground beneath the target.

"Relax, my dear. Take a deep breath, hold it, and aim."

She set a fourth arrow, then sighted down the length of it until her arm began to tremble with the effort. The arrow pierced the target just inches below Fletcher's arrow. She whooped in excitement.

"You may have a talent!" he laughed, handing her a fresh arrow. "Try another."

The next morning was grey, with wispy threads of fog. Vala stood outside Ethan's hut watching the camp awaken. A plain-looking woman with mousey hair poking out beneath her cap approached with a hesitant step.

"Good morning, goddess."

"Good morning to you," Vala replied. "But please call me Vala."

"Breakfast is gruel," said the woman. "You can get a bowl over at the fire if you like. We make it from groats and milk."

"It sounds very good," Vala replied.

The woman looked at the ground and then blurted out, "Kale says you don't really have the Stone of Ansuz—that it's just Ethan trying to keep the old tales alive."

Vala drew out the chain hanging around her neck. The green stone did not sparkle as it might have in the sunlight, but it still possessed an inner glow.

The woman reached out but didn't touch it. "It's the talisman, just as Simon foretold. Thank you, goddess!" She made an awkward curtsey before hurrying away.

"Wait! Please call me Vala!"

Even though the woman spun and faced her for an instant, Vala could see that possessing the legendary stone put her above such familiarity. The woman scuttled to the fire and spoke excitedly to a gruff, balding man. It might be Kale—Vala could not recall—but most certainly by midday, the remaining doubters would be convinced.

Vala turned. Isolde was staring at her from across the clearing, and Vala nearly crossed herself as folk did when a ghost passed. Recalling where she was, she let her hand drop. With a swirl of grey robes, Isolde disappeared into her lodge, leaving her son, Borghild, standing alone with an absent look on his broad face.

Considering her options, Vala decided to accept Fletcher's invitation to break her fast with him and Meg. With a sigh, she went back inside and gathered up her precious books and treasures to show Fletcher. Vala was finding the Dumnonii a disappointment. Except for Fletcher, they seemed to revile her or esteem her beyond reason. She had earned neither response and wished Ethan would return to pave her way with these folk.

"Just in time!" cried Fletcher, beckoning her inside.

Meg fussed over her, seating her at the table and pouring her fresh milk, still warm from the goat. Fletcher served up porridge with crushed nutmeats and a humorous lecture on the best way to distinguish edible fungus.

When the meal was finished, Fletcher stood and rubbed his hands together. "I have a new bow I finished last night for Manning. I want to test it, and you can practice while I do."

An hour of shooting improved Vala's aim and technique. When her teacher called a halt to retrieve arrows and repair the goose feather fletchings, Vala rubbed at the soft skin on the inside of her forearm. It had grown a great purple contusion from repeated grazing by the bowstring.

"What's this?" Fletcher pulled up her sleeve and examined her arm. He dug in a sack and produced a leather arm guard. "It goes like this," he said, pulling it onto her arm and lacing it up. "That bruise is my fault. I should have padded your forearm." He examined the fingers on her right hand. "This bruising is normal," he told her. "Calluses will form." He paused, still holding her wrist. His eyebrows drew in in concentration. "You were wounded. It happened recently. It was on this side of your body."

Vala reached up to touch the knife wound. "How did you know?"

Eyes closed, he continued, "The man in black wanted your talisman and your life." He released her arm. "It appears you have some tales to tell, young Vala." He handed her another arrow.

Meg called them to eat, and fed them warm bread and hard cheese.

Settled in front of the hearth, Vala felt very much at home. "It is so kind of you to take me in like this."

"Nonsense!" said Meg. "Simon and Darian were the friends of our youth." Her gaze dropped to the floor. "When I think of the times the four of us sat around the fire long into the night—"

Fletcher clapped his hands together, breaking the dark mood. "Your books, my dear. Let's have a look."

Vala passed them over. "The one on top is from Glastonbury."

Fletcher opened it and ran his finger over the first page of text. "They just gave it to you?"

"They said it was of poor quality." She offered him the second one. "This one, I stole from Bishop De Roche," she admitted.

Fletcher chuckled. "A tale I'd like to hear." He leafed through the volumes and Meg mended a shirt as Vala told them how she had come to be in Glastonbury Abbey.

"Your Brother Phillip sounds like a kindly sort," Meg said as she pulled up a stitch. "It's fortuitous that the man was a healer, else you might have died."

"So many clerics think prayer alone will cure," said Fletcher. "You were lucky in this monk."

Vala was grateful they judged Phillip by his actions, not his beliefs, as Ethan had done. When Vala reached the point in her story where she learned the bishop had ordered her killed, Meg dropped her sewing needle and pressed her fingers to her mouth in horror.

"With both my father and my uncle dead, I knew I'd never learn the truth unless I had the box," Vala explained.

Fletcher and Meg stared at her, Meg's face pale as paste.

"Darian is dead?" Fletcher whispered.

"Yes," Vala replied. "He was attacked on the road."

"Darian was a good man," Fletcher said, his voice cracking. "A wise man. He'll be missed." He looked toward his sister. "Meg, are you all right?"

Meg nodded, wiping at her eyes.

Fletcher stared off in thought, shaking his head sadly before turning his attention to the books in his lap. "Can you read this one?" He held out the writings of Saint Gildas.

"Uncle taught me Latin," Vala replied, suppressing her own heavy sadness.

"Good." He set the first book aside and opened the second. "This writing is Frankish. Might I keep this and study it?"

Vala nodded. "I have these things, too." She pulled the small tapestry and the silver knife from her sack.

Fletcher peered at the decoration on the knife hilt. "You might ask Isolde to look at this." Meg huffed from her stool by the fire, but Fletcher ignored her. "It's more in her line of interest." Fletcher spread out the linen and ran a finger over the careful stitching. "Meg, look at this."

Meg rose heavily from her seat and came close. She fingered the border. "Beautiful workmanship. The thread is very fine, and the stitches are so neat and small. Look at the colors and the way the runes are worked."

"Does it mean anything?" Vala asked.

"It is the image of the goddess Morrigan," Fletcher said. "The border is made up of all the runes, but these three at the bottom are prominent. They represent earth, water, and air." He pointed as he spoke.

Ansuz, now familiar to Vala, was one of the three.

"The tree in the background is a symbol of life."

Vala touched the delicate stitching. The woman worked in thread gave her an enigmatic smile. "Why would anyone want to burn this?"

No one answered her.

It was evening, and Vala was sitting cross-legged on the floor of Ethan's hut next to a small peat fire. She took another stitch with the bone needle and length of thread she had begged from Meg. Her shift was a poor, threadbare thing, but it was the only one she had. If her mother had lived, Vala would have learned the rudiments of spinning, weaving, and sewing, and would have been well able to make such a garment, but her knowledge of womanly crafts was thin.

The angle was awkward, for she had not removed the garment before beginning her repair. She dipped her needle again, feeling the lumpy and snagged muddle of threads she had made. She tried not to think of the perfect stitches in the tapestry.

She bit the thread off as cries and shouts erupted from the clearing. Vala threw on her cloak and hurried toward the communal fire, where confusion reigned.

"Kale has been hurt!"

"Get Meg!"

Vala pulled her cloak more tightly around her shoulders. "What happened to him?"

Two men stood over Kale, whose thigh was bleeding copiously. "He fell from his flet and was impaled on a tree limb. We cut most of it away, but some is still inside his leg."

"Heat water!" Vala demanded, moving forward and kneeling next to the injured man.

The clearing went quiet for a moment. Vala looked up at the faces.

"Someone heat water, and someone get Meg," she ordered. "Tell her to bring spider web, garlic and..." She thought for a moment. "Honey."

Unsure looks met her glare.

"Quickly!" she shouted.

One of the young women broke off running toward Meg's cottage, while another went for the water.

Kale moaned, and Vala turned her attention to his wound. She probed it gently. "I'll do what I can for you," she assured him.

A broken branch about the width of a man's thumb protruded from the man's thigh. Vala felt around his leg. It had not gone all the way through, but the wound would be dirty. Her uncle had told her how worrisome that could be.

"I need a good sharp knife," she said to no one in particular. A knife appeared next to her, and Vala cut away Kale's blood-soaked leggings. He flinched each time she touched him. "Ale," she ordered. "Unwatered."

A jug was shoved toward her.

"Kale, we must pull the branch from your leg. It will hurt, so drink this." She brought the jug to the man's lips, and he gulped the strong brew. It occurred to her that Kale had never liked her much, and what she was about to put him through would not alter his opinion.

"Are you ready?" she asked.

Kale nodded.

She looked up at the assemblage. "Two of you must hold him down." Several men obliged her. Vala took a firm hold on the jagged bit of wood and closed her eyes, asking for strength. With as firm and smooth a motion as she could manage, she drew out the broken branch. Kale screamed in agony as blood gushed forth.

Vala pressed the hem of her shift against the wound to staunch it. "Clean cloth," she ordered.

Meg came panting up, followed by Fletcher, as women scattered in search of bandaging material. A kettle of hot water appeared, followed by a pile of linen scraps.

Meg dropped down next to Vala.

"Can you crush the garlic into the hot water?" Vala asked, pulling her blood-soaked shift back and pressing a pad of cloth over the wound.

Meg obliged, dipping a clean cloth into the liquid and handing it to Vala.

Vala cleaned the gash, picking out any bits of bark she could see. Kale swigged more ale.

"The bleeding is less," Meg said, inspecting the wound.

"I thought I'd use a honey poultice."

Meg nodded. They worked silently, covering the wound with honey and then spider silk. Over the poultice, they wound the clean strips of linen. By the time the women had finished, Kale was dozing. Vala accepted a blanket from Kale's worried wife and drew it over him.

"He should sleep here by the fire," Vala said, and Kale's wife sat, cradling her husband's head in her lap.

"Thank you, goddess," she muttered.

Vala rose and shook out her shift.

"Oh dear," said Meg. "You're covered in blood. Come along with me, and we'll get you something else to wear."

As Meg drew her away, Vala heard a silky voice say, "You ought to have called me immediately. An injury such as this calls for a strong charm."

Isolde moved into the firelight and gave Kale a poke. The man gave a loud snore, the ale having done its job.

Meg held firmly to Vala's arm and towed her off into the darkness as folk jabbered about what had happened.

"You did a fine job, Vala," Meg said.

Vala turned to look back at her erstwhile patient. "She won't tamper with the bandage? Will she?"

Behind them, Isolde began to chant in a raspy singsong.

*"A snake came crawling,*

*It bit a man.*

*Then Woden took nine glory-twigs,*

*Smote the serpent so that it flew into nine parts."*

"That's the Nine Herb Charm," Meg said, pulling Vala out of the clearing and down the path.

*"There apple brought this pass against poison,*

*That she nevermore would enter her house..."*

The witch's voice, singing its weird song, faded.

"The charm is a potion, coupled with a chant. The poultice is mugwort, lamb's cress, mayweed, nettle, fennel...well, nine specific herbs in all. You boil them with ashes and make a salve. Then you chant."

"Would she try to apply a poultice to his leg now?"

"Isolde rarely touches a wound. It's beneath her. Since Kale's wound is bound, she'll simply chant for a while. Of course, she will take the credit if he survives."

"And she will blame me if he does not," Vala sighed.

"You are wise beyond your years."

Inside their cottage, Meg rummaged in an old wood trunk. She pulled out a linen shift with long sleeves and a hemline edged in an embroidered pattern of leaves. She shook it out and held it up to Vala. Meg was a naturally rotund woman, so the garment was voluminous. But it was clean and not threadbare, nor stained with blood like the recently mended rag Vala dropped to the floor.

"This is very kind of you."

Meg tugged at the drawstring to tighten the neck opening. "I'm afraid it's a bit large," she tittered as she arranged the gaping neckline. "But we can take it in another day."

Vala pulled up a drooping shoulder. She slung on her cloak and with grateful thanks bade Meg good night.

A waning moon had risen large and orange, hovering over black treetops as Vala made her way to her hut. She considered checking Kale's wound again, but there was really nothing to be done until morning.

A gleam of white, waving gently in the moonlight, caught her eye. Vala moved to the edge of the overgrown path. She bent and took the curled flower petals in her hand. The blossoms of the night blooming catch-fly fanned open like little trumpets. She knew no medicinal use for the plant, but the flowers were very fragrant. She plucked one and breathed in its scent. If Phillip had been here, he would know its properties. He had not needed to chant to stanch and bind her knife wound, but perhaps he had said a prayer. A prayer was very much like a chant, she reasoned, but now she questioned their power to heal.

A dark shadow moved, blotting out the moonlight. She scrambled backward, for towering over her was a giant. Borghild stood silently on the dark path, looking down at her with dull eyes.

"You startled me," she gasped, climbing to her feet feeling foolish that the boy had unsettled her. She offered Borghild the flower. "This is catch-fly."

He opened a beefy hand, and she put the blossom into it, giving him a smile. Borghild crushed it in his fist and then lumbered off into the darkness.

Vala felt shaken. Anyone would have been, suddenly confronted by the slow-witted Borghild. She put a hand to her throat and smelled the lingering scent of the flower on her fingers. She must make an effort to treat him kindly.

Days passed, and Vala fell into the rhythm of the clan. She practiced with the bow under Fletcher's tutelage. She gathered wood, scrubbed and hung wash, and sat with the women at their mending. They began to accept her, and she found she felt less like an outsider. Kale's wound was healing well, which lent her more credibility. She rarely glimpsed Isolde.

In the afternoons, Vala liked to sit and read from Fletcher's hoard of books. Meg would putter about, preparing the evening meal and dispensing a liberal amount of gossip but refusing any help while insisting that Vala join them.

"We're having fresh trout. At the camp, they are having some sort of stew and stale bread," Meg would say with a grimace.

One clear day, Meg and Vala were hunting herbs. Meg led the way along a game trail away from the cottage and deeper into the wood.

"How long do you think Ethan will be gone?" Vala asked. "It's already been a fortnight."

"The boy will certainly not return until he has been successful. He is quite tenacious. Look, it's tansy!" Meg said, stooping to pluck some of the leaves. "Too early for the flowers."

"It's very good for the joints when steeped in water," Vala said.

"And good for worms in the gut."

"Do you think he'll kill Farley?" Vala asked.

"If this Farley killed your father, Ethan will kill him."

Vala spotted some bilberry and gathered the stems. "Meg, what sort of magic do you do?"

"Magic?"

"I've seen Ethan try to do magic, and Fletcher can read people by touch."

"Well, child, it's not so much a question of what I do, or what any of us does," Meg said as she pulled up a patch of moss. "We use the rhythms of nature to best advantage." She wiped the dirt from her hands on her apron. "For instance, Fletcher draws on the forces of air and earth to see a person's spirit. These forces exist, but most people ignore them."

"And you?" asked Vala.

"I can often tell the sex of unborn children. I can sense if they will come into the world well and whole." Meg stretched her back. "What we poor folk have mastered is nothing compared to the power you wield. You possess the ability to be a great seer."

"Ethan helped me use the stone, and I did see things, but not what they meant."

"Of course you don't, child. Christians raised you." Meg gave Vala an encouraging smile. "Don't fret. Beltaine is coming. We'll have a ceremonial fire, and you will use the talisman."

"I'm not afraid," Vala replied. She knew she sounded more confident than she felt. Using the stone had given her a brief but powerful sense of exhilaration, followed by complete exhaustion.

"Just keep clear of Isolde, if you can. Fletcher would say I'm being foolish, but now that you're here, she must be seething."

"Surely, she can do much more without a stone than I can with one," replied Vala.

"There are always those who seek more power than that which is freely given." Meg glanced into the spring grasses. "Oh, look. It's black bryony."

That evening, after an excellent dinner, Meg, Vala, and Fletcher sat quietly, watching the flames.

"The fish was very good, Meg," Fletcher said.

"Kale brought them to thank us for tending his wound."

Vala nodded. "I put on a fresh bandage yesterday. It is healing nicely."

Meg smirked. "He'll not be the last to seek your help. You will replace the old witch if I have anything to say about it."

"But I don't want to replace her," Vala said. "I certainly don't want to anger her."

"Oh, tosh."

"Meg, you'll scare Vala off." Fletcher retrieved a bow from his workbench. "What do you think of this one?"

The bowyer made beautiful weapons, slender and supple. This one was no exception. Vala pulled it and loosed an imaginary arrow. "It's exceptional. The owner of this will be pleased."

Fletcher grinned and took the bow back. He reached for an iron heating in his brazier and, with a deft hand, burned an image into the smooth wood. It was a small arrow pointing upward. "That is Tiwaz, the symbol for the hunt. The goddess of the hunt, Andrasta, is both a warrior and a seer."

"Who did you make this one for?"

"For you, child," Fletcher said, settling back on his bench.

Vala flushed. "But I couldn't—I mean, I've nothing to give for it, not for something so fine."

Fletcher laughed. "It's a gift. You wouldn't deny an old man the pleasure of making a gift to a young warrior goddess?" He winked at her.

Vala was thoughtful for a time. "The priests say there is but one god, not many."

"If you will, think about the idea of only one god," Fletcher said. "How would you explain why crops fail in one year but are abundant in the next?"

"God punishes men sometimes," she replied.

"He punishes everyone, including the good? The clerics say their god knows everything. If he knows all, why does he need to punish the good in such a way? No, my dear, there are many gods, and they are very much like us: good, bad, fickle, loyal. We resemble them because we have descended from their stock, so we live and fight and love just as they do. Crops fail because gods vie for dominance, they disagree, they are jealous, and they respond to the supplications of men."

"Father Cyril always said that God is merciful to the pure of heart," Vala argued. "So when he punishes all people, the holy folk will receive extra blessings when they die."

"Christians are always looking toward the afterlife, failing to appreciate the beauty of earth, water, and tree. What mercy do they need in such a wonderful and abundant world? They cry out that all things of the flesh are evil," Fletcher said, and Vala could hear the disgust in his voice. "*We* know that truly evil souls receive their justice by what they become in their next life."

Vala knitted her brow, unsure.

"The Dumnonii are fading," Fletcher sighed. "Few keep to the old ways. Few are descendants of the original tribe; most are just lost souls who have found us. Ethan is a prime example. We stand firm against the tides of change, but it is hard to fight this new church. Simon had a passion for it, and so does young Ethan." He paused. "In the north and across the Manx Sea, there are still strongholds where the Dumnonii resist the clerics and even kill them if they interfere." He stroked the edge of the bow in her hands. "Here, they kill *us*."

On a fine, warm afternoon, Vala sat with some of the women, mending garments. The conversation bubbled around her: husbands' idiosyncrasies, recipes, and the weather.

A young girl came up and whispered something to an older woman called

Calista, dropping her eyes in a blush. The others continued to talk amongst themselves, but Vala strained to hear the old woman's response.

"You don't need a love potion, child. Just pick seven cloves. Do you know what they look like?"

The girl nodded, wide-eyed. The rest of the women were now hiding their amused expressions.

"Grasp them tight in your right hand. This one here." The old woman squeezed the girl's fingers. "Think about the boy. Think on him hard. Then toss the cloves into the fire. He'll be yours within three days' time." The old woman raised three arthritic fingers.

"Truly?" the girl asked.

"I've known it to work miracles," said Calista.

The girl skipped off with a smile.

"A young one like that—don't need her drinking the swill Ragnell brews. Who knows what that old hag puts in her love potions," old Calista croaked. The other women nodded in agreement.

"Ragnell makes love potions?" Vala asked.

Calista frowned. "She says she does. It's a hard thing to make right. Some can do it, but Ragnell has no talent for it. She's like to kill someone one day. She's been making them for herself for years." There was general giggling, which subsided abruptly.

Vala looked up at the sudden rancid smell and realized Ragnell was at her side. The other women sat stone-faced as Ragnell raised herself up in a posture of self-importance. "Isolde wishes to speak with you." The stink was overpowering. "She'll be waiting on you."

As Ragnell flounced away, Calista blew out a breath. "I'm glad I'm not invited to visit with the goddess—alone. I'd be terrified."

Chapter Twenty-Four:
*"The bait hides the hook."*

Mint leaves steeped in water brewed in a dented copper vessel. Two stools sat near a window with a small table in between. Isolde fetched cups from the sideboard while her guest fidgeted on one of the stools.

"How do you find our little band, dear?"

"Everyone is very nice," replied Vala.

"I apologize for not welcoming you properly. But here you are now, and we shall have a nice long talk."

"I'm honored you invited me."

Isolde watched with lidded eyes as the girl took in the room: chock full of herbs, crocks of feathers, brightly colored powders, bowls of dried leaves, and dead beetles. Live birds and animals rustled in their cages. While the girl was thus distracted, Isolde tipped several drops of a dark red liquid into the taller of the two cups, careful to hide the little flask in her pocket. Smiling to herself, she filled the cups with the mint-infused water.

A cat streaked across the floor and pounced on a mouse. Isolde grinned. The earthenware mugs steamed as the old witch set them on the table, too hot to touch. Isolde brought the subject around to Vala's magical abilities.

"How do you like divination?" The girl looked confused. "When you look into the fire and see visions?" Isolde prompted.

"Oh!" Vala said. "I see things in the fire, but I don't understand it all yet."

Isolde watched the girl's fingers wrap around her emerald talisman. "Something to sweeten your drink?"

Vala nodded, and her hostess pushed a dish of golden honey toward her.

"You've looked into a scrying stone and glimpsed the future," Isolde said evenly. "You possess a great gift, one many would covet."

The girl sighed. "It could have been just a dream of sorts, couldn't it?"

The two cups continued to steep. Isolde avoided breathing in the vapor from the taller cup. "A dream? My dear child, you come from a long line of seers. Your father was a diviner of great renown, as was his father before him. Madelyn, your dear mother, was similarly gifted. Ethan assures me you have the gift too."

Vala sat up straighter. "Do you really think so?"

Isolde struggled to form a kindly smile. Yes, the damned girl was probably a seer. It was maddening, for the Dumnonii would follow this upstart, and worship her too. Simon's mystical progeny! Isolde might have used the girl for her own purposes if the slut had not lain with Ethan and however many others. By succumbing to base passion, she'd diminished her powers before she could even begin.

"It would be a surprise if you didn't have the gift," Isolde replied sweetly. "Of course your powers may be limited by your—uh—circumstances." She slid the tall mug toward Vala. "Be careful not to burn your tongue, my dear."

The girl needed to die. Without her virginity, she was worthless as a blood sacrifice in the ritual that Isolde hungered to try. That was a pity and a shame. If the girl remained alive, she'd usurp Isolde's place. Already, they'd named her 'goddess'. The time to strike was while Ethan was away. Isolde was clever enough that the death would appear natural, a sudden sickness—sad, but common enough.

Vala blew on her cup to cool it. "What sort of circumstances will limit my powers?"

"Well, I hardly like to say." Toying with her victim provided a bit of entertainment.

"Please, tell me."

Isolde pretended to hesitate. "Lying with a man will diminish your ability as a seer."

Vala set down her cup untouched. "I'm not married."

The idiot girl was dense as a stone!

"Perhaps I do not make myself clear," Isolde replied. "I too erred when I was young." She looked at her half-witted son curled up on the hearth. "The gods punished me by diminishing my power."

Vala's brow furrowed. "I've never been with a man."

The girl's tone lacked any guile or deceit. Isolde placed a restraining hand on Vala's wrist to keep the cup from the girl's lips.

"It's not a sin, you know. Ethan is quite handsome. Many a lass desires him."

"I've only just met Ethan, and I don't fancy him." The girl planted her cup hard on the table.

"Well, then, if you are a virgin, all is well."

The girl blushed, the truth plain on her silly face. She reached for her cup. Isolde jostled the small table, sending both cups smashing to the floor. Shards of cups lay amidst dark wet leaves and steaming liquid, seeping into the dirt floor. "Oh, my dear! Forgive my clumsiness. You might have been scalded!"

Vala stooped to pick up the broken crockery.

"I'll make a fresh batch, shall I?" Isolde asked.

"You had her here, and you let her live?" Ragnell groaned. "But I collected the roots and made the potion just as you asked."

"Yes, I let her live," Isolde said as she watched the girl enter Ethan's hut across the clearing.

"But you said the girl is useless and has to be killed," Ragnell recited.

Isolde raised a palm. "We may have been duped by that dog, Ethan."

"I like Ethan," Ragnell crooned.

Isolde gave her companion a slap on the head. "Our little Vala is fetching a silver knife with symbols on the hilt. She wishes me to look at it." Isolde tapped a finger to her lips. "You know, I never believed Simon's brat survived that fire. I was so hoping to see them burn the night the soldiers attacked." The old goddess shrugged. "At least I was well-paid for the information."

Ragnell giggled, scratching at a fleabite on her rump.

"Ah, well, there are any number of ways to skin the cat," Isolde remarked philosophically.

Ragnell delighted in the possibility of skinned cats.

Chapter Twenty-Five:
*"There's nowt so queer as folk."*

Vala strolled along the path to the horse paddock, feeling that all was right with the world. She'd met the dreaded Isolde in her lair and found the woman kindly enough. She'd been interested in Vala's silver knife, asking to keep it for study. So much for Meg's fretting.

With a carrot in her pocket for Thistle and a warm breeze wafting the scent of rosemary through the air, the only thing better would be news of Ethan and his friends.

She stooped to pick a few sprigs of wild spearmint. When she rose, she was not alone. Borghild stood motionless in the path.

"Hello, Borghild."

The huge lad had startled her again, and she strove to look unruffled, stepping to her right to pass him.

In a motion like a great wooden wain rolling downhill, he lunged, and she stumbled backward a few steps before he was upon her. Vala struggled wildly against his weight, twisting and writhing like an animal in a trap. His face was close enough for her to look into his small, vacant eyes. She tried to scream, but a beefy hand covered her mouth.

From beneath the trees, Ragnell came skipping with a flask held high.

"Good boy, Borghild. You win the prize!" She put a sweet cake into his mouth, and he chewed happily as Vala tried to wriggle free.

"Now, hold her nose shut," sang Ragnell.

Borghild moved his fingers to Vala's nose and pinched off her air. She opened her mouth to gasp for a breath, and Ragnell used the opportunity to pour the fluid from her flask down Vala's gullet. Before she could attempt to spit it out, Vala felt her limbs going warm and limp. Borghild's flaccid features went out of focus, and then all was blackness.

The rusty taste of blood was on her lips, and something bitter on her tongue. She couldn't focus, seeing only dancing orange lights in the darkness. Hours must have passed since Borghild's attack. Vala licked her lips, recognizing the unmistakable taste of hemlock. It was a powerful and dangerous sleeping draught. Her uncle had made it once for a villager who had lost a hand in an accident at the mill.

A raspy, excited voice said, "She wakes!"

"Good," another voice answered, silky smooth. "I wouldn't want our little goddess to miss this."

She knew that voice. "Where am I?" Vala croaked.

"The ring, the ring, the ring of Avebury," sang the first voice. Ragnell's face peered into hers. "You wanted to see it, didn't you?"

The woman's foul breath nauseated her. Dizzy as she was, Vala realized she was tied upright to something hard and cold.

Isolde floated into her line of sight. "Did you know that the Dumnonii are descended from an ancient and powerful tribe? But these who are left are a poor reflection of its glory." Isolde whispered something to Ragnell, and the crone bobbed out of Vala's sight.

Ragnell returned and placed something in Isolde's hand, and the old witch raised it high above her head. It glinted in the light of a torch held by Borghild. It was the silver knife Vala had brought from Bath. Isolde slashed it down savagely, barely missing her captive.

"You planned to unseat me," Isolde sneered. "And the rabble would worship you. But when I plunge this knife home, little seer, I will take your power into me, and I will be greater than any of them can imagine!"

Vala tried to keep her voice calm. "I never wished for that." She tried to swallow, but her throat was so dry.

"Quiet!" the old witch ordered, and Ragnell danced forward to stuff a rag into Vala's mouth. "Pile wood around her feet," directed Isolde.

"Won't the flames bring the others?" asked Ragnell.

"She'll be dead before help arrives," replied the old woman. "And I shall be immortal."

Vala fought her panic, struggling to see a way out of her situation.

"You didn't know what a prize you'd placed in my hands today, did you, child?" Isolde asked with smug condescension. "This knife is a Secespita, created for the sole purpose of magical sacrifice. It is imbued with demon magic." Isolde caressed the hilt, her face beaded with sweat. "Now, you will die by its blade." With that, Isolde whirled to face Ragnell and Borghild, the one in awe, the other staring dumbly off into space.

Vala cried, "I am no threat to you. Please, let me go!"

The mad witch ignored her. "Tonight, I will slay a virgin seer. Morrigan, greatest of the goddesses, will grant me your power and youth!"

Isolde began circling the stone and chanting in a strange tongue. Ragnell danced about holding a small beaten metal bowl, just within Vala's view. With demonic glee in her eyes, she mimed using it to catch Vala's blood.

The kindling at the base of the stone stank of rancid fat, ready to flame hot and high once Isolde stabbed her. Vala doubted the knife wound would be immediately fatal. Isolde would draw out her death as long as possible.

Vala tried a prayer, but it stuck in her throat. Whichever deity was watching now was about to allow the demented old witch to take her life. Tears trailed down her cheeks as she lifted her face to the heavens, rich and bright with stars. She felt the pressure of the knife tip press against her throat, and something warm ran down her neck.

There was a thud, and the knife fell away. Borghild, a rock clutched in his fist, stood behind his mother as she slumped to the ground.

"Your stupid oaf!" cried Ragnell. "You stupid, stupid—"

Her words were cut off by the backswing of the boy's powerful arm, which put her on the ground.

"Good boy!" he parroted placidly.

Vala swooned.

She awoke to bright firelight and a crowd of people pressing in around her. Someone was wiping away blood and wrapping cloth around her neck. She sat up. Borghild squatted nearby, watching the proceedings intently.

"He saved me," Vala croaked. "Borghild saved me."

"He did indeed," said Fletcher from behind her. "Unfortunately, Ragnell and Isolde are gone."

"But Borghild hit her with a rock, and—"

"Perhaps Ragnell dragged her mistress away. The men are searching the woods, but it is very dark. No moon."

The effects of the sleeping draught left her muddled and woozy. Meg helped Vala to Ethan's hut and into bed. She was asleep before the noise of the unsettled camp abated.

In a few days, with the administration of linen bandages and regular cleaning, Vala's wound began to heal. She still bore bruises from the assault, including a swollen lip. Her two tormentors had escaped, even though the men had spent a night and a day searching.

Fletcher took Borghild under his protection and made a place for him by the hearth in his own cottage. At first Meg resisted, but Borghild's devotion to Vala won the woman over. Soon, she was mending his tunic and cutting his matted hair.

"She'll have him looking like a lord if she keeps on," Fletcher told Vala with a wink.

As for Vala, she knew it was time to decide her own future. The Dumnonii would accept her if she wished to stay. Ethan would want her to stay, as would Fletcher and Meg. She was equally certain that the folk of Wistman's Wood would welcome her back. Yet, if she returned home, the bishop would eventually find her.

As Vala considered the events of the past days and her prospects, a group of mounted men galloped into the clearing. They slid from their horses to the whoops and cries of many voices. Vala threw on her cloak and pushed toward the center of the throng.

A hand grabbed her arm. "Goddess!"

"Manning!" she cried, turning to Ethan's friend. "I'm so glad you're safe!"

"As are we," he said with a grin. "I don't think I could have borne that saddle another day." He rubbed his backside. "And we've brought some prisoners."

Manning led her toward the center of the crowd where three men knelt on the ground with canvas sacks over their heads and their wrists tied.

Ethan's shaggy dark head turned. "Vala!" Ethan said, taking her hands. Then his jaw tightened. "Your throat! What happened?"

Before she could answer, Fletcher appeared. "What have we here?" He clapped Ethan on the back. "Our wayward friends, returned!"

Ethan grinned. "We found Farley, but best of all, we've captured the monk, Germain."

Fletcher scanned the captives. "What are you going to do with them?"

"Manning was all for killing them on the spot." Ethan jerked the sack off the first man. Farley the baker spat and sputtered, blinking at the light.

"This is the man who killed Simon?" Fletcher asked Vala.

"Yes, he is the poisoner," she said.

"I would never," the baker puffed, indignant. "I'm only a simple baker."

Manning cuffed him on the back of the head. "This one won't shut up."

"He was quite talkative in Bridestowe, too," Vala said.

Ethan grasped the hood of the second man, who was garbed in a black robe and fine boots. "Germain was with Farley. He put up quite a fight. He wounded Geoff, and Sig is dead."

The listeners in the circle gasped, and a woman let out a heart-wrenching sob. The Dumnonii began to jeer and heckle him.

The monk spat, "Pagan scum!" He turned his face up to Vala with nasty amusement. "And here is the little witch who flew off in the night. I'd have given you a quick, clean death, little witch, but not now."

Manning leveled a sideways blow at Germain's head. The monk slumped to the ground, unconscious.

Vala shuddered and turned away. Germain was a murderer, in the hire of a bishop. A lower form of life she could not imagine. Behind her, the Dumnonii were jeering and shouting threats at the prisoners. The children danced in and out, poking at them with sticks. Vala's gut churned, and she wanted to escape the turmoil.

The third prisoner began yelling. Vala didn't bother to listen, so deep she was in the blackness of her own thoughts. No form of death seemed to suit their crimes. She turned toward the persistent, muffled cries of the third man. Ethan was fumbling with the tie that secured his hood. The man was calling her name.

"Take a look at this one," Ethan shouted over the clamor. "We caught him poking around the ruins of Simon's cottage. He claimed to be Simon's brother, your dead uncle, so we knew he was a spy." As he ripped off the man's hood, a greying head turned toward Vala, eyes blinking in the sun.

Vala stared for a moment, dumbstruck. The crowd went quiet, or else it was the blackness closing in around her. She heard whispers like the rustle of leaves in the dark. "That's Simon's brother? Our Simon?"

Vala's eyes fluttered open. She was lying on the ground, and Meg was patting her hand and mouthing her name.

Fletcher pulled the dusty prisoner into prominence. He knelt by her side. "Vala, child, I feared I'd never see you again."

"It can't be!" she muttered. "It can't be you. I saw your grave!" For a crazy moment, she believed him an apparition, a ghost come back from death. His pallor was so grey. Vala raised a hand to her uncle's face. A tear coursed down his rugged cheek, streaking the dust, revealing the face of a living man.

"So, I decided to come and get you," Adrian said after a long sip of ale. He planted a fatherly kiss on Vala's brow.

Washed and dressed in borrowed clothes, Adrian was looking more himself. Fletcher had plied him with his best brew while Meg's shepherd's pie worked its restorative magic. Vala sat next to him, holding his hand, elated to have her uncle restored to her.

"I was attacked by a highwayman near Dartmeet. It was a nasty fight, and I killed him. I tried to move on, for I had grown ever more worried about you." Adrian nodded at Vala.

"It was a premonition," Meg stated.

"Perhaps," Adrian said. "But I'd injured my leg and had to stop and rest up for a day and night."

"The priest in Dartmeet thought he'd buried you," Vala said. "But it must have been the highwayman."

"I'm sorry, dearest, for giving you so much grief. You must tell me more about the fire in Wistman's Wood," Adrian continued. "And about how you came to meet Ethan and Fletcher."

"Sir," Ethan broke in. "Had I known, I would never have—I would never harm Simon's kin. Vala told me you were dead."

Vala scowled as Adrian patted Ethan's back. "You couldn't have known, my boy, and I was afraid to confide more until I knew your allegiance."

The feast Meg had mounted for them was being heartily devoured. Manning strummed a lute, concocting a song about the capture of the Black Monk. Fletcher was making everyone recount their part in the story, and the ale was heightening the jocular mood.

Vala stepped outside the cottage, sucking in a lungful of cool night air. She was overcome with happiness to have her uncle back safe and whole, no thanks to Ethan. Why did he always leap to conclusions? He might have killed her uncle, who was simply searching for clues as to her whereabouts.

Manning's clear voice drifted through the open window. "We caught the monk near Bridestowe town, darry-down, darry-down..."

It wasn't a very good song, but it was heartily sung and supported by many cheers. The clink of cups drew her back to the door. She had so many questions for Adrian. Somehow, they'd missed one another on the road, and she was no longer sure how many days had passed since she'd left Wistman's Wood. She grasped the door handle just as Ethan stepped out to face her.

"It was lucky we found your uncle," Ethan said, running his fingers through his tangled hair.

"Found him, bound him up, and towed him across country like a...like a...." Vala could not think of an apt comparison.

"I tell you, I am sorry about that," Ethan insisted. "I was certain he was lying. I might have killed him, but I didn't."

"Well, that was lucky," she snarled.

"I've apologized. What more can I do?"

Vala wrapped her arms about herself against the chill air. He'd treated her uncle just like Germain and Farley, a pair of vile monsters. It was difficult to forget.

Ethan changed tack. "You didn't tell me about that wound on your neck."

Vala's hand went to her throat and the blood-spotted bandage. "Isolde tried to kill me."

Ethan jaw tightened. "I'll rip her throat out."

"She's gone, Ethan. She escaped." Vala related the tale of the old woman's brutal attack and Borghild's timely rescue.

Ethan's face reddened. "I thought I'd fixed things," he mumbled.

"What do you mean?" asked Vala. "What did you fix this time?"

Ethan looked away. "Isolde needed a virgin seer, so I convinced her that you...that we..."

"You told her I was a fallen woman?" The pieces clunked into place. Isolde's remonstrance about her lost powers now made sense. "But it didn't fix anything, did it, because you didn't bother to tell me what you'd done." She put her hand over the bandage, shaking with rage. "You meddle in things without a thought, and this is the result."

Ethan let out a low growl. "I was trying to save you, you silly girl."

Before Vala knew what she was about, she landed a punch to Ethan's jaw, then spun on her heel and stormed off up the path. She heard Ethan curse but didn't turn around.

As she reached the clearing, she slowed. Firelight was dancing over the two prisoners who were bound to a tree. Germain had a dangerous look, even bound and bloodied. Farley hung limply from his bindings. She didn't like the look of the baker.

"That man looks like he's dead," she said to the guards.

One of the guards, a man named Reaga, touched Farley with his pole staff. There was no reaction.

"He was making noise just a bit ago," Reaga said.

"He's dead now," said the other guard.

"But, what happened to him?" Vala demanded.

"Well, you can see he's old," Reaga said. "And fat."

"Good riddance," the men agreed in unison.

The Dumnonii had been in favor of an immediate execution for both prisoners, but with passions running high, Fletcher had demanded they delay until all courses of action could be considered.

"Are you happy, witch?" sneered Germain, nodding toward the dead man.

"Farley poisoned my father."

"He's an idiot," said Germain. "A knife is so much faster."

In no mood to banter with the monk, Vala stalked off to Ethan's hut. Inside, she lit a small rushlight and then stoked the fire to life. Farley was dead, and Germain was in chains. At least that threat had been nullified. Fletcher and the others wanted their time with Adrian, and she did not begrudge them that. Soon, she'd have him to herself, and they'd have a good long talk.

Vala unwrapped her belt and removed her kirtle. The hut was chilly, so she swathed herself in a blanket. She was about to curl up on the sleeping pallet when the door opened and Ethan stepped inside. Vala could see the red mark on his face where fist had connected with chin.

"What are you doing here?" she demanded.

"This is my hut," Ethan replied.

She was the clear trespasser, but she was in a dark mood and intended to stand her ground. She lifted her chin toward the clearing outside. "You can sleep out there." She pulled off the blanket and threw it at his feet.

Ethan raised an eyebrow and took two steps toward her, backing her against the wall. "Do you think you would have lasted another day on the road with your precious monk if I hadn't found you?" His breath was warm on her cheek as his dark eyes drilled into her. "The bishop wants you dead!" He took hold of her shoulders. "And he was very close to succeeding."

She jerked out of his grasp, trying to think of a worthy retort, but the door banged open and Manning burst in, panting.

"They've found us! We have to get her away," he said with a nod at Vala. "Now!"

Ethan's jaw clenched in steely resolve. He bent and tossed her kirtle at her. "Dress and throw your things in a pack, quickly." Before she could reply, both men were gone.

Vala muttered fiercely as she wrestled into her clothes and hoisted her pack. She stalked outside, intending to find her uncle. The prisoners were unguarded and forgotten as people were scattering, clutching their few possessions. Vala started toward Fletcher's cottage when Ethan grasped her elbow, spun her and propelled her toward the horse paddock.

"Let me go!"

"Have you got the stone?" he asked.

"Yes," she said, struggling to get free. "But I need to find my uncle."

"Not now."

Manning came running toward them, four horses trotting at his heels. Without slowing, he scooped Vala up and slung her onto Thistle's back as Ethan steadied her mount.

Vala tried to rip the reins from Ethan's grasp. "My uncle—"

"Quiet!" Ethan hissed. "Do you want to get us killed?"

The men urged their horses to a gallop as soldiers crashed into the clearing. Germain was shouting to his compatriots as the trio plunged into the darkness. Vala struggled to slow Thistle, to stop this mad flight away from her uncle. Neither Manning nor Ethan heeded her, but with grim faces they pushed on until, by silent agreement, they veered off into the wood.

"I need to go back!" she cried.

Ethan stopped the horses abruptly and panted, "Don't you understand? The bishop's men are after you."

"I'll take my chances," she spat. "I've just found my uncle again. I'm not losing him."

"Fletcher and Meg will get Adrian away," Ethan said. "There was no time to follow them."

"They're all safer without us," said Manning. "Fletcher is an old hand at this. And frankly, small groups that do not include *you* will probably survive."

That brought her up short. She was Germain's quarry. She had brought the danger. "Are you sure the others are all right?" she asked.

Manning and Ethan exchanged a look. "Once we've found a safe place to hide, we'll scout out the situation," Ethan replied.

Vala wanted nothing more than to ride back and search for her uncle, but there was no sense debating the point, so she followed Ethan, with Manning bringing up the rear, as they picked their way through the dark woods.

Chapter Twenty-Six:
*"Needs must when the devil drives."*

For several miles, they traveled due south by the faint light of a clouded moon. When Ethan announced they would make camp, Vala slid off Thistle, unburdened her horse, and then rolled herself in a blanket on the ground. She dozed fitfully, disturbed by visions of those left behind.

The sky was dark beneath blue-black clouds when Manning shook her awake. "Can you take a turn at watch?" he asked with a yawn.

"I can do it," Vala mumbled as she got to her feet.

Ethan was sound asleep, letting out an occasional snore. Manning quickly drifted off. Vala walked over to the horses, hobbled near a large oak tree. Thistle radiated warmth as she leaned against him, giving his flank a pat. With both men asleep, she could easily slip away, but she had no idea where Fletcher would take her uncle. She would have to rely on Ethan to locate him again.

In the damp predawn hours, the men yawned and stretched awake. Soon, the trio was on their way again. Vala huddled in her cloak watching the mist in the hollows dissipate as they plodded south.

Both men were watchful and quiet all morning. Around midday, they halted, and Manning pointed to the east. "The crossroad is just over that knoll."

"I'll meet you in six days at Weyhill," Ethan said.

"Good fortune until then," Manning said, spurring his horse toward the road.

Ethan touched his amulet. "We need to stay hidden for a little while."

She could tell he was worried, but he said nothing, and the pair struggled up sheep tracks and down into thorny valleys. When the sun dipped below the horizon, they found shelter under a rock outcropping shielded by bracken.

Ethan insisted on taking the first watch. The rocky ground was uncomfortable, but Vala, overcome with exhaustion, fell into a deep, dreamless sleep.

She sat up when a ray of sun stabbed her in the eye. Ethan was huddled next to her, staring off down the draw.

"Why didn't you wake me?' she yawned. "I would have taken my watch."

"It's better if I watch," he replied, getting to his feet. "Manning shouldn't have given you a watch last night." His eyes were bloodshot, and his face was grim and pale. "We should go."

"What use will you be without any sleep? Do you think you'll be able to defend us when you're falling asleep in your saddle?"

He raised his chin but then fought down a yawn.

"I refuse to move from this spot until you've had a decent sleep."

Ethan attempted a glare. "We don't have time for this."

Vala returned his stare.

"Fine, a short nap, and then we go." He lay down and did not awake until midday. "You let me sleep too long!" he chided her as he stomped about, making ready to leave. However peeved he claimed to be, he looked much refreshed.

They set off down along the narrow cleft of land between two hills and hadn't gone half a mile when the ground became boggy. A tiny rivulet of water became a small stream. The stream increased in size and breadth, making footing treacherous. Soon, the choice was to walk the horses through the stream or to scramble up a rocky bank. Ethan was all for keeping to the stream.

Vala's feet were cold from the icy spring water. "I don't see as it matters. You don't know where we're going. Why not take the high ground? At least we'll be dry."

Ethan gave her a prickly look, but he had no better argument, so they began to urge their mounts up the incline.

The footing was treacherous, and their packhorse balked until Vala covered the beast's eyes. With some effort, they managed to struggle up the steep runnel and found themselves on the edge of a wood. From their new vantage point, they could see a road running east to west, crossing over the stream at a narrow ford in the distance.

"I don't like how open the land is around that road," Ethan remarked.

"Then it's good we turned aside."

The coolness of the tree canopy was inviting, with wildflowers covering the mossy woodland floor. Shafts of sunlight penetrated the gently waving leaves. Vala raised her head, taking in the scent of purple violets and pink lady slippers. Underfoot was a moss-covered path of stone blocks.

"We should get off this path," Ethan said, looking around nervously. "I don't fancy using a common way."

"See how the plants grow between these stones? No one has been this way for many seasons." Although the stones underfoot were set like a roadbed, thorny bushes encroached as the woods reaffirmed their supremacy.

They had followed the path for a short way when a wall of spiky barberry blocked the track. Ethan pulled out his short-bladed sword and began hacking the vines. The foliage put up a heroic fight, but at last, he broke through the hedge and tumbled to the ground.

"Damnation!" Ethan massaged his thorn-raked arm.

Vala clambered over the mess of hewn branches. A clearing opened before her.

Ethan scrambled to his feet, brandishing his sword, raking the clearing for an enemy, but Vala pushed in front of him.

"Oh my!"

"It looks Roman," Ethan said, stepping onto a courtyard of stone under an open sky. All around it, the woods closed in, but here, the stonework still held sway. A low wall ran along the flagstone quadrangle on two sides. Where the walls met, a stone block tower climbed above the courtyard. A low building adjoined the tower, girded in green ivy and lichen. The height of the trees surrounding the tower made it unlikely anyone would ever see the structure until they were upon it.

"It's like something from a fairy story," Vala said.

"Wait," Ethan hissed, grabbing for her arm.

She didn't heed him, running straight to an old wooden door at the base of the tower. Vala grasped the rusted iron handle and pushed with all her might. It gave way, scratching and groaning over the threshold until she could squeeze through.

Ethan had to push it farther yet to gain entry. "Will you wait?" he whispered. "Someone might be here."

"Unlikely," she said. "Otherwise, the door would still work. Why do you say the Romans built it?"

Ethan ran his hand over the stonework. "The Romans built in stone. They built for strength." He thumped the wall with his fist. "They had a talent with masonry. What they built can withstand the wind and ice, not like the daub and wattle we use. Look how the blocks are set."

"The courtyard looks unfinished," she said, pacing off eight steps across the circular room to where a narrow stone stairway hugged the wall, spiraling up to the next level.

A mouse scurried out the open door.

"It's very old," said Ethan.

Vala began to climb the stairs. They were so narrow that she leaned against the wall to steady herself. The second floor was an open room with a low ceiling and arrow slits to the west and east. Similar to the ground floor except for a smaller hearth, it too had a stair spiraling up to the next level. Vala began to climb again, brushing cobwebs out of her way. Ethan followed, puffing to keep up.

At the top was a wooden trap door. The wood was dry and cracked from age and weather, but there was a rather ingenious counterweight system that allowed Vala to raise the heavy panel with ease. She emerged into the open air of a crenulated platform.

"This is a good lookout," Ethan said, emerging behind her.

The tower, situated at the edge of a steep drop, gave an excellent view of the plain to the south, yet it would be nearly invisible from below. In the time since laborers had hauled the tons of stone to this promontory, trees had cloaked it from view. Ivy and woodbine had done the rest.

Ethan shielded his eyes and looked to the horizon. "We should go." He headed back to the trap door. "It's getting late."

"This is as good a place to spend the night as any. We'll be dry, and we can light a fire in the hearth."

Ethan shrugged.

While Vala settled the horses in the stable, Ethan used a tree limb to ream out the chimney so it would draw. Soon, he had a roaring fire.

They made a meal of a bit of bread and honey. The meal consumed, Ethan leaned back against the wall, legs stretched out in front of him. In the warmth of the fire, his head soon dropped to his chest, and he gave out a low snore. Vala was surprised he'd managed to stay awake long enough to eat. She covered him with a blanket, then pulled the heavy wood bar across the door. She felt safe within the tower and saw no reason to stand guard. Just before she curled up in her own blanket they wondered where her uncle was just now. Her thoughts grew fuzzy as she watched the fire burn down until sleep finally took her.

The morning sun filtered in through an arrow slit high up along the stairs. It felt decadent to lie and watch the light move along the wall in a perfect rectangle as the sun mounted higher in the sky. This tower would be perfect, she mused, if only the stream were closer. She would have to get up and fetch water for the horses.

Vala kept her blanket wrapped around her shoulders as she stepped out into the fine, cool morning. Between the outer wall and the trees that ringed the site was a narrow swath of land no more than a few strides wide. She strode along the wall's edge until she spied a neat ring of stone covered with a wooden hatch. She boosted herself over the wall and heaved the cover off. It was an old well with a wooden bucket dangling inside. She swept the bucket clean of spiders and then lowered it down. An echoing splash told her the well was still good.

She raised the leaky vessel full of cool, fresh water. She sniffed, then tasted it, then drank deeply. Vala made four trips to the well, fetching enough water to fill the horse trough in the stable. With a goodly supply of water, she set about cleaning and brushing out the dust and debris from the tower.

Ethan eventually opened his eyes and got dully to his feet. "How late is it?"

"Before noon, but not much."

Ethan scratched at the stubble on his chin. "Wait! We never had a watch? All night?"

"We're safe here," she said. "I know it."

Ethan's mood shifted suddenly from angry to animated. "You've had a vision, or seen a sign. I knew you would. I saw two magpies yesterday."

Vala rolled her eyes. "Magpies?"

Before Ethan could launch into a discussion of the meaning of magpies, she stomped off. In the stable, she discovered a heavy bench and dragged it out into the sunlight. Ethan had taken up a spot on the wall and was honing his short sword, polishing off the rusty bits, while Lugus strutted along the masonry, pecking at bugs.

The raven stopped and cocked its head.

"I see your pet has found us," Vala smirked.

Ethan scowled, "Lugus is no pet. He was keeping watch over you while I was gone to Bridestowe."

"Really? He wasn't all that much protection, was he?"

Ethan didn't defend the bird. Instead, he helped her heave the old bench inside the tower. Vala placed it before the fire.

"I don't know why you would bother with a bench," he said. "We'll be leaving soon."

"We need to find my uncle."

"Vala, Manning will try to locate him and Fletcher and the rest. You can't be seen right now. It would be very dangerous. I mean to keep you hidden."

"But—"

"This is what Manning is best at. Trust me."

That evening, from the top of the tower, Vala and Ethan watched the sky turn a dusky pink.

"The Dumnonii never got to gather at the stone circle in Avebury," Vala observed.

"We'll assemble once the danger has passed. I'll meet Manning and Kale in a few days. We'll decide then. We ought to leave here tomorrow."

Ethan had taken on the role of leader, although Vala doubted he'd realized it yet.

"If you find them, where will we all gather?" Finding the Dumnonii meant finding Adrian, which was worth a few more nights of sleeping in ditches and picking twigs from her hair.

"I think it will be the Knowlton ring." He pointed south. "It's not far, and it's a place we've used in the past."

Vala stared off in the direction he indicated. "How many rings are there?" she asked, looking up at him.

"Too many to count," Ethan said softly, staring into her eyes. He leaned a bit closer. "Sometimes we find a new one we've never seen before."

There was a moment of silence as they looked at each other, then Vala sat back against the wall, feeling suddenly embarrassed.

"The rings are curious too," Ethan continued, clearing his throat. "Some are just a few rough stones, some have a central stone, and others have chalk holes. There is a massive one to the north where the stones tower to the height of three men."

Before Ethan could lecture her about the rings he'd seen, she cut him off. "Since we are close to Knowlton, shouldn't everyone meet here? You could tell Manning and Kale, and they can tell the others. I'll stay here, and you can send them all to me."

"You can't stay alone."

"And why not?"

Ethan looked to the sky as though he could gauge such things by the weather. "It's a bad idea. What if soldiers find this place? The omens are not good."

"Omens, bah," she said. "This is a good plan. I'm staying."

"Even if you stay, I can't send folk here."

"What about my uncle? You could send him."

Ethan sighed. "Stay if you must. If I can, I will bring your uncle."

"As you wish," Vala said.

Ethan snorted. Having lost the argument, he sat in sullen silence as darkness fell, and wrapped himself in his blanket on the tower top, where he claimed to prefer to sleep.

In the morning, the sound of pounding woke Vala with a start. When she pulled the door open, she found Ethan standing on an upturned log, attempting to hang something on the lintel of the door. Ethan's ankle had a bare circle around it, not tanned like the surrounding skin.

She squinted up at his work, and the sun caught the glint of metal. His gesture tugged at her heart. "Ethan, that's your lucky amulet."

He shrugged. "It's extra protection while I'm away—against intrusion, storms, and wild animals."

Vala's reply stuck in her throat. He valued his amulet above all his possessions. She nearly reached out and touched him. Instead, she crossed her arms and watched.

Amulet affixed to the door, Ethan packed his satchel, all the while heaping on warnings and instructions. "Mind that you keep that door barred at all times. Don't leave things lying about. It should never look occupied." Then, with a final curse directed at her stubborn nature, he led his horse back down the stone path, vowing he'd be back in less than a week.

The days passed quickly for Vala as she worked around the tower. In truth, she began to think of it as her own. At least it was safe here; at least Germain didn't know of it. She spent her days busy with domestic activities. She wove a basket from woodbine and bark. She made a palliasse from a blanket and armloads of fresh rushes. To eat, she had a jar of honey and some dried apple slices on a string brought away from Avebury. She found berries aplenty in the woods, and she was able to snare rabbits with a bit of rope, using a trick her uncle had shown her as a girl. Each day, she made sure to practice with her bow and to take Thistle and their packhorse out to graze. By night, Vala read from her book by firelight and wondered if Fletcher had been able to decipher the one she'd stolen.

When she yearned for a diversion, she pulled out the green stone talisman. She sat squarely in front of the hearth, but no matter how long she looked into its emerald depths, she never had the sort of vision she had experienced on the hill above Ethan's house. Staring into the stone until her back was sore and her eyes stinging from the fire's smoke resulted in nothing more than vague daydreams.

On the fifth evening after Ethan's departure, Vala wrapped herself in her cloak and climbed to the top of the tower. A thickening haze filled the lowland, rolling and rising up like an earthbound cloud, until she was looking out over a sea of fog. She sat down and rested her shoulder on the stone crenulations, gazing over the edge into ethereal mist. Back in Wistman's Wood, it had been easy to consider herself daring and insightful. Over the past weeks, she'd proved both cowardly and stupid. She'd quailed in the presence of Bishop De Roche. She'd badly miscalculated the risk of riding out from Exeter unarmed. Isolde had almost murdered her, and she had completely misunderstood her father.

In the dark of the night, Vala awoke to the sound of Thistle rustling in his stall. The horse gave a loud whinny and she listened hard, trying to sort the ordinary night sounds from something foreign. When Thistle whinnied again, she scrambled to her feet and hurried down the stone steps on bare feet. The banked ashes in the hearth gave very little light.

She felt her way to the door. There was a swish of a branch and the scraping sound of something moving over the stone path.

Intruders, and they were close.

Her mouth was too dry to swallow as she reached for her bow. She tried to recall all of Fletcher's advice, particularly about shooting in the dark, as she edged over to the arrow slit in the wall. Swaying shadows played eerily over the courtyard, but she was sure there was movement on the path.

Lifting the bow, she silently nocked an arrow.

Chapter Twenty-Seven:
*"First deserve, and then desire."*

"The gods be damned!"

Ethan sprawled in the dirt, flailing his legs to untangle them from something that had snagged him on the dark path. He twisted up to a sitting position and yanked at...string? Where had string come from?

The zing of an arrow passed inches from his skull.

"Gods!" he cursed again, crabbing away from the path lest he be skewered by the next shot.

A door banged. A figure ran toward him, white shift billowing in the night breeze. "Oh, Ethan! I nearly—"

"Speared me like a wild pig?" Ethan snarled up at Vala.

"At the last instant, I realized it was you."

"And you shot anyway?"

"I'd already released, but I missed, didn't I? It serves you right, sneaking up like that."

"I wasn't sneaking anywhere. I was about to call out. And how could a person sneak up when you have that damned trip line in the path?" He rubbed his bruised knee. "Nice trick, by the way." He nodded toward the snag, and Vala grinned. "What made you think of it?" he asked, wincing in pain as he rose from the ground.

"My uncle used rope to make a temporary pen for our cow. He strung the rope higher, of course, but it gave me the idea."

"And to think I was worried about you." He limped toward the tower.

"Where is your horse?" Vala asked.

"Ran off."

Ethan hobbled through the door and sank heavily onto the bench by the dying fire.

Vala fluttered in behind him, shutting the door on the darkness. "You've been wounded," she cried. "I thought I missed!"

"You did," he groaned, pulling at his bloody sleeve. "I was riding in the dark when my horse threw me. I landed in pile of dead tree limbs and sliced myself open. I had to walk the last few miles."

Vala tossed a few faggots of wood onto the fire. She helped him strip off his shirt before taking a small jar from the shelf and lighting a candle. "Hold this, please," she said, giving him the candle.

He obeyed, watching her probe his wound. It was an ugly, jagged cut. "Ouch!" he winced as she made her examination.

"Sorry." She dabbed at the cut, cleaning away dirt and dried blood and then dipped her fingers into the small jar, scooping up some ointment. "This should help."

"That smells good." Ethan poked a finger into the jar and sniffed.

"Brother Phillip made it for me."

He hastily wiped his finger on his breeches. "Poxy monk! Probably has some sort of Christian curse on it." He didn't wipe it away from his wound, for it felt remarkably better from the application.

"Did you find Manning and Kale?" Vala asked.

Ethan nodded. "Kale has been back to Avebury. Everyone who fled that night has returned."

"Everyone?" Vala said hopefully. "What of my uncle, and Meg, and Fletcher? Are they safe?" She began wrapping his arm with strips of cloth.

"Meg and Fletcher are both fine. Everyone is fine, although your uncle left."

Vala stopped winding the bandage. "Where did he go?"

"Fletcher said that Adrian thought he knew of a way to help, and that he would return."

"He could be in danger!" she said, pulling the bandage a bit too tight.

"Be careful, woman!" he hissed through clenched teeth. "I asked Manning to try to find him."

Vala did not look convinced. "I suppose there is nothing more that can be done," she muttered, tying off her work. Her voice held the sadness of abandonment, and he looked up at her. "You should have kept your amulet. Then perhaps the horse wouldn't have thrown you," Vala said, now all business. "I'm nearly done."

Waves of honey-colored hair brushed his neck and shoulder as she bent over him. It was good that she was nearly done. He had told her how her uncle had gone off with nary a word, and she'd taken that better than he had expected. She leaned against him, inspecting his other scratches and bruises. He could feel her body's heat and smell the vague scent of wildflowers that she always exuded. The firelight flickered over her face, her throat. Ethan ran a fretful hand through his hair.

"It's fine," he said with a stiff smile and shifted away from her ministering fingers. "Did I tell you I had to avoid soldiers on the road? The bloody mercenaries are everywhere."

He hoisted himself to his feet. He needed to put a bit of space between himself and Vala.

"Will the others be coming here?" she asked.

"No, we set a time to meet at Knowlton ring." Ethan poked at his bandage. It stung like hell. "Ragnell, the smelly old carp, came back to camp with a tale that they were overtaken by soldiers, but her mistress escaped by turning herself into a wolf."

"The woman is completely mad," Vala laughed.

"It's not unheard of, you know," he said, looking up. "Some people are able to invoke a spell to change their shape. The goddess Ceridwen could do it, though it's difficult magic." Warming to the subject and grateful for the distraction, Ethan launched into a listing of animals suitable for such a transformation. Then, without warning, he swayed and put out a hand to steady himself.

"Have you eaten?" Vala asked, taking in his pallor.

"Not today," he admitted.

She pushed him back down and bustled around, setting out some cold cooked tubers and leftover pheasant.

"You must be quite good with snares to have gotten a fowl," he said, sniffing the pheasant with appreciation. It had been a nice fat one.

"I used my bow."

Ethan laughed. "A woman to be reckoned with, then."

"I'm not helpless."

She didn't look helpless. He watched her pour ale into a stoneware mug and then deftly wrap the hem of her shift around the top of the iron fire poker, plunging its smoking end into the mug. The liquid hissed and bubbled. She passed him the heated cup and bade him eat. He took a long, gratifying draught.

"Better?"

He nodded, wiping his mouth with the back of his hand. "It's very homelike in here," he remarked as he attacked the victuals.

"Yes," she said seriously. "I've claimed this tower until someone seizes it from me."

Ethan wolfed down the last morsel of pheasant. "It is well-hidden and not altogether indefensible. Still, it's much too remote. Until we go to Knowlton, I think you had better stay at the camp at Avebury." He said this with a full mouth and the confident conviction that his word would win out. With her standing at a distance, it seemed easier to think.

"Ethan, I appreciate everything you've done for me, but you will not tell me what to do nor where to go."

"I'm too tired to debate with you." If he looked on her now, silhouetted by the fire, hair undone, in nothing but her shift, his will might weaken, and not just on the subject of this tower. He crawled onto the sleeping pallet and turned toward the wall.

When Ethan awoke, he found Vala curled on the floor, asleep. It was only then he realized he had usurped her bed. His boots were standing near the door where hung his cloak. She'd removed his boots and beaten the dust from his cloak. His only hope was to make it up to her before she woke.

Ethan busied himself gathering firewood and taking the horses off to graze, and managed to bag a fat rabbit with Vala's bow. He reclaimed his amulet from above the door but tacked two ash branches over the lintel in its place.

"How did you sleep?" Vala asked pointedly from the doorway.

Ethan chose to ignore the barb. "I've put up these boughs. They will repel most bad spirits."

Vala's frown softened, fostering a hope that he was forgiven. Later in the day, as the odor of a savory stewed rabbit wafted from within, he was sure of it.

With a full belly, Ethan made his way to the top of the tower, where he sank down against the cool stone crenulations. The sky was softening to dusky mauve. It was nice here, he had to admit, and it was a distraction from his worries about the Dumnonii. He'd nearly come to blows with Kale when they'd met. The man could be an idiot. More troubling was the lack of information Manning had been able to gather. Manning had a small network of reliable snitches, but they had fallen strangely silent. The clerics were up to something.

Lugus whirled overhead, weaving and diving alongside another raven. Ethan leaned out over the edge to watch the birds swoop down into the trees where fireflies danced like tiny faeries. Vala was drawing up water from the well and singing a silly little song.

It was sad that he'd have to take her away from here. He understood why she liked the place. Still, it was his duty to protect her. Simon wouldn't have brooked the girl's dissension. He'd try again in the morning. She would just have to see reason.

He lowered himself back onto the stone floor and stared up at the first star of the evening, breathing a wish to it. He watched it until he nodded off.

Chapter Twenty-Eight:
*"It's easy to be wise after the event."*

The pounding of boots on stone roused Vala from a deep sleep. She stumbled to her feet in alarm as Ethan careened down the tower stairs two at a time.

"They're coming up the valley!" he cried, going for his leather scabbard. "It's an attack!"

Vala groped for her cloak. "How could an attack come that way?"

Ethan was already through the door. Vala grabbed bow and quiver, then dashed after him, her bare feet unsteady on the rough stones.

In the courtyard, Ethan hissed at her, "Shut the door! Don't let them see the light!"

Vala pulled the door closed, leaving them in near darkness. Overhead, long ribbons of tattered clouds obscured the moon. Tree limbs whipped wildly in the damp breath of a coming storm. The wind tangled Vala's long tresses in air that smelled of green sedges and rain. In the stable, the horses whinnied and stomped. Over this was the sound of hooves racing through the underbrush, tearing and rending it as they charged.

"Get the horses!" growled Ethan. "There are too many of them to fight!"

Vala slung her bow over her shoulder and raced to the stable, touching the stone talisman around her neck to reassure herself it was safe. When she looked back, Ethan had taken up a defensive stance, sword raised. She had barely reached the stable door when the attack came.

The warriors who had breached their security did not speak or cry out as they leapt the wall into the courtyard. Neither did they slow their pace. A bolt of lightning exploded in brilliant tendrils across the sky, revealing bright eyes wide with terror.

They stayed but a moment before thundering into the western woods.

"Deer?" Ethan cried in confusion.

Thunder boomed heavily, underscoring his question and vibrating the ground beneath their feet. A few stragglers bounded over the stone rubble and back into the darkness. Ethan spun to watch them.

Vala felt her own tension begin to ebb away. "The lightning must have set them running."

Ethan's taut shoulders relaxed. "Great Cernunnus protect us."

Vala tipped her head. "Who is that?"

"The god of deer."

Vala broke into laughter. Ethan tried to keep a stern face, but with a twitch of his lip, he too began to laugh. As relief flooded them, the heavens opened up and a roiling wall of clouds spilled down rain, hard and fast. Vala and Ethan raced for the tower, shrieking and laughing like fools. The old door would not budge as rain doused them. They both threw their shoulders into it and as the door gave way, they fell inside, water pooling around them. Ethan got to his knees and pushed the door shut.

Vala shrugged out of her sodden cloak, still laughing hysterically. "This is just like the first day we met," she said. "The two of us running from De Roche and drenched to the skin."

Ethan pulled off his boots and pitched them toward the warmth of the fire. "And again, the gods were smiling on us." He touched his lucky amulet.

"I should have shot. We could have had a good venison stew," Vala giggled.

"Fletcher always was a good teacher," Ethan said. "And you showed no fear." He stripped off his wet shirt and shook his head like a dog, splattering the room with water droplets.

"Stop it!" Vala shouted, jumping to her feet and shielding her face.

She stepped backward, and with a whoop of surprise slipped on the wet stones. Ethan scrambled to steady her, losing his own balance, which caused them both to slip to the floor in a renewed fit of laughter.

"I hope there are no more attacks tonight," Ethan said, disentangling himself from Vala.

Vala wiped water from her face. "The fire needs stoking, or we'll both take a chill." She turned toward the firewood.

Ethan belayed her. "You know, you're very beautiful like this."

Vala raised an eyebrow and looked down at the wet shift sticking to her skin. Ethan pulled her slowly toward him, his jovial demeanor shifting into another look entirely. Vala could not recall a man having looked at her in that way before, but there was no mistaking its meaning.

"I can't stop thinking of you," he said softly. "I know I should not. You are my goddess." His head bent toward hers, and drops of water from his hair ran down her cheeks.

Vala felt slightly dizzy. "No. Please," she whispered, struggling out of his arms. This was wrong. They were alone, they weren't married, and the image of Father Wulford's accusatory eyes bored into her head.

Ethan released her. "You're right," he muttered. "Of course you're right." His voice was barely audible over the whirl of wind strafing the trees outside.

Vala wrapped her arms around herself for warmth and propriety's sake. She took a step toward the fire, putting her back to him.

"It's wrong, isn't it?" she asked.

Ethan seemed to consider the question and then began to prattle away about the corruption of the power of a seer. "The power of a seer *must* come before everything else. Simon told me this many times—" His voice trailed away.

She turned. "That's not what I meant."

She found she couldn't finish her thought, recalling the heat of his body against hers. One slow step, and then another, and they were nearly touching. Ethan closed his eyes.

"I am not a goddess," she said quietly. "I didn't come with you because I wished to lead your tribe or see the future. I only wanted the truth about my family, and this stone." She touched the talisman hanging at her neck.

He bent his head, and his cheek, rough with stubble, rubbed against her neck. "Are you certain?"

Vala nodded.

At first, his kisses were hard and demanding. Vala raked her fingers through the wet tangles of his hair, pulling him against her, reveling in his warmth. When he drew back, breathing hard, he loosed the tie at her neck and pushed her sodden shift off her shoulders. His lips moved over the tender skin of her throat. It made her skin tingle. He smelled of rain and musky sweat as he lifted her and carried her to the sleeping pallet.

"*Tá mo chroí istigh ionat*," he whispered against her ear. "My heart is within you."

The wind had subsided, and the rain was no longer beating its tattoo against the wooden door. The scent of washed stone and wild heather filled the air as the last of the thunder rolled across the valley. Hours had passed, and Ethan was dozing, his breath warm against her shoulder. Vala lay listening to the sounds of the night.

After a time, she sat up, elated and a bit shaky. She knew what the women of her village whispered of a bride's first night, and she pressed her fingers between her legs.

Blood.

Ethan stirred and lifted her hand, turning her fingers toward the waning firelight. "A powerful charm can be made from the blood of a virgin."

Vala snatched her hand away. "You'll not be making this into an amulet," she said, wiping her fingers in the rushes.

Ethan laughed as he pulled her back into his arms.

Chapter Twenty-Nine:
*"A goose quill is more dangerous than a lion's claw."*

They stayed in the tower for another week. Ethan seemed to have lost his desire to go back to the Dumnonii camp. It was a golden time. They enjoyed sitting at the top of the tower long into the night, watching the stars spin in the heavens and snuggling together by the fire. Finally, Ethan announced that he had to meet Manning, and he rode off to find his friend, vowing to return quickly.

In the early morning two days hence, he returned, urging her to be quick and pack. The gathering was set, and they had to hurry.

Vala donned her leggings and tunic, tucking her hair up under a hood. Ethan insisted on the old disguise as a security measure, yet he gallantly helped her mount up, offering a protective arm. He even offered her an orange marigold he plucked from between the flagstones.

It was a pleasant day. They rode easily across the flat country south of the tower, not pushing the horses, but meandering along. They arrived at a wooded area a furlong from the Knowlton ring just at dusk.

The Dumnonii were milling about, chatting excitedly. Vala scanned the area, seeking Fletcher and Meg.

"Over there." Ethan pointed over the sea of faces.

Meg clapped her hands, and Fletcher exclaimed, "Vala, dear girl!" as she flew to them.

"I'm so glad you survived," she said. "I was so worried the night we left."

"Never worry about Meg and me. We're old hands at protecting ourselves."

"My uncle?"

"He insisted that he must leave," said Meg. "I was against it, but he would not change his mind. I think he was afraid that his presence would put us in more danger."

"Do you think that's true?" Vala asked.

"Don't you fret, dear," Fletcher said. "Your uncle is a wily, resourceful man."

Vala had never considered her uncle 'wily'.

The Dumnonii were staring at her and whispering behind their hands. She wished they would look away.

Fletcher didn't seem to notice as he patted his tunic. "I have something of yours," he said, withdrawing her book.

"Could you read it?" she asked, rifling the pages in excitement.

"Yes," he said. "At least enough to know why De Roche wished to burn it." Fletcher took her arm to pull her away from the group. "You understand that a number of men, and even a few women, have written the story of the Christian messiah? They love to tell the story of his death."

"Do you mean the gospels?"

"Yes, exactly. Your book appears to be one of that sort. A scholar who studied the writings of an apostle called Barnabas penned this work."

Vala could not recall Father Wulford ever mentioning St. Barnabas.

"This man, Barnabas, states that the Christ was a prophet, not a god, as the clerics maintain. Furthermore, he insists that the Christ rose up into the heavens without ever being crucified. According to Barnabas, an unfortunate associate called Judas was crucified in Christ's stead."

"That's heresy of the worst sort," she began.

Fletcher grinned. "Clerics want to suppress such reports, for they raise questions, and questions can be dangerous. They prefer for everything to be clear and in agreement."

"All the other apostles gave a different story."

"Clearly, not all the apostles have been heard from," Fletcher said with a wink. "What if—"

"Fletcher, may I have a word?" Ethan interrupted.

"Of course, my boy."

Vala drummed impatient fingers on the book. Barnabas must be a liar or a lunatic. She tried to remember how many other apostles had attested to the familiar version of the story. John, Paul, and Luke...

Ethan lowered his voice so that only the three of them could hear. "I have to ask something, for Vala's sake. Is it true that a virgin seer has more power than any other?"

The color rose in Vala's cheeks. "Ethan, leave off!"

Fletcher looked from Ethan to her.

"Please, ignore him," she said. If the legend was true, she wouldn't be able to see anything in the flames. It mattered little to her, for she didn't desire the worship of these people.

Manning loped toward them. "We should go soon. Everything is ready." He nodded toward Vala. "Hello, goddess!" He yanked down her hood playfully, spilling her hair over her shoulders. "Someone needs to mind the horses while we walk to the ring."

"Yes, the energy of the horses will disrupt the spirits, and we want Vala to have the best chance of giving us a prediction of the future," Fletcher said with a smile.

Vala wanted Fletcher's attention so they might discuss the story told by Barnabas. While she waited, she tried to recall gospel stories that varied so much in the details. She wondered how the Church selected the version they preached, and how would they choose? She weighed the small tome in her hand. It would be confusing if priests were to tell their flocks different versions of the death of Christ. Perhaps De Roche wanted this book burned to stop any misunderstanding, but that action was a suppression of information and possibly the truth.

"Meg is happy to stay with the horses," Fletcher was saying.

"I'll find her," Manning said. He nodded at Vala. "We are all looking forward to seeing you use the stone tonight, goddess."

She nodded as Manning trotted off.

Fletcher smiled solicitously. "Now, Ethan, what were you saying?"

Frustration filled Vala. She leafed through the pages of the book, wishing she could read the words for herself. An unexpected line of thought blossomed. If there were other apostles, there might be even more accounts of Christ's life waiting to be discovered and lost truths to be revealed. Brother Phillip sought a true miracle, and it would be a sort of miracle—or at least a great revelation—to discover a book that clarified the mysteries of the life and death of Christ.

Vala rubbed the leather cover of the treatise. Even if this version was flawed, others might not be. Her desire to be the discoverer of such truths made her fingers tingle.

Next to her, Ethan was repeating his pointless question.

"Ethan, it is not important," she said, her face going from pink to red.

"But it is important to *know*," he protested.

Fletcher raised his hands. "I cannot say if the old legends are true, but I've known a few great seers who would contradict the legend. Think of Simon, who was married, and Isolde was a fair hand at prophecy, but no virgin."

Vala gave Ethan a rueful glance, but he was clearly relieved. "I'll bring along the moonflowers, shall I?" he said, and was off at a trot.

The entire group began to shuffle toward a path into the trees. Clouds hid the rising moon as they walked the last mile to the ring. Vala found herself swept along as people she had met in Avebury took her arm, greeting her and pulling her into their groups. Deluged with questions about where she'd been and how she'd gotten away from Avebury, she smiled and gave the briefest of answers. Finally, on a half-mumbled excuse, she broke away, allowing the throng to pass by.

"You were going to tell me your opinion about the writings of Barnabas," she said as soon as she spotted Fletcher.

Before he could answer, Ethan came up, his arms laden with a large bouquet of flowering branches. Manning was loaded down with the same plant.

"You did well, finding so much," Ethan said to Fletcher. "It will be a good fire."

"We were lucky," replied Fletcher. "Meg has a nose for these things." He tapped his own with a gnarled finger.

With a distracted shake of her head, Vala began to re-state her question, when something clicked in her brain, and she gave the stalks in Ethan's arms a second and closer look. "That's not devil's snare, is it?"

"It's called moonflower," said Ethan. "It's an important part of the ceremony."

Vala took a stem of the stuff into her fingers. The shape of the flower alone convinced her. "This *is* devil's snare."

"That's one of its names," said Fletcher. "Thorn apple, moonflower, and by some, devil's snare."

"But it's dangerous," Vala said. "My uncle told me this would make a man go insane. It makes a person see things—mad things." She drew in a ragged breath as understanding dawned. "Oh my!"

"Your uncle possessed a remarkable store of herb lore, far beyond the ordinary," Fletcher replied by way of a compliment. "Simon often remarked on it."

Vala rounded on Ethan. "You put *this* in the fire when I used the stone."

"I used the seed pods," he replied. "I couldn't find fresh stalks."

"This is why I saw things in the fire." She felt the weight of discovery crush her.

Fletcher raised an eyebrow. "It's the way these things are done, child. The plant helps enhance our sensitivity and insight."

Vala fingered the plants.

Fletcher was unperturbed. "We believe that your affinity with the Stone of Ansuz, helped by the spirit of the moonflower, causes you to have visions that are more prophetic and insightful than the rest of us are able to achieve." Fletcher patted her arm. "Seers have always used such plants to commune with the spirits. We won't let you go mad."

He followed the others through the trees to the ring of stones. Torchlight illuminated each eager face that passed.

"We need to go," Ethan said, waving vaguely in the direction of the clearing.

"You go on," Vala said numbly. "I left the stone in my pack. I'll be along shortly."

"Don't be too long," he said as he dashed off after Fletcher.

She stowed the book in her boot, then put her hand to her chest and felt the stone hanging from its chain beneath her shirt. Whatever it was, the stone was not the magical talisman they all believed in. Her father thought it was a powerful object and had exiled her all the years of her childhood, thinking he was protecting her, believing she could wield it someday. Had he hoped that she would save the Dumnonii, inspire them to revolt, change the world? She knew in her heart that the secret to her visions was the burning of the plants and not the power of the stone. She could follow Ethan and the rest of them, sit by the fire, breathe in the fumes from the devil's snare, and she would certainly see things. It would be easy to fall in with the lie, but that wasn't why she'd come on this quest.

Vala edged around the outside of the grove of trees that surrounded the standing stones. She could hear Dumnonii voices, whispers in the dark. Soon, the light of a bonfire leapt skyward, and she stepped farther into the shadows. A chant went up, the voices of men and women entwining. She lingered just under the eaves of the wood, out of sight.

Ethan stepped to the fore and raised his arms. The people quieted, and as he pointed to the moon riding high above the clearing, they listened. He was probably telling them that the moon god was with them tonight or some such thing. Vala had shut her ears to it all. She clutched the stone in her fingers, saddened that the mystery and the magical possibility were gone, a truth revealed, a dream demolished.

The tribe rose and began to space themselves around the fire. Ethan stood back, watching the path, waiting for her. Manning fed the odious flower stalks into the flames, which blew back a smoky haze. Soon, they were dancing and twirling about with abandon, cloaks swirling and arms extended joyfully.

She could still do it. She could stride into their midst and dangle the emerald stone in the light of the fire and breathe in the smoke. They would take whatever she said as the greatest of prophecy, simply because she said it. She could pretend, and they would love her.

Vala ran her fingers over the stone in the dark. The faces around the bonfire were alight with excitement. She sank down on a log just far enough under the trees to hide her presence.

Something whooshed down from the sky and past her. Lugus flapped wildly, cawing out a warning. Vala spun around, hearing horses rustling in the underbrush.

Before she could shout out, Ethan saw the raven and began pulling the revelers back from the fire, urging them into the trees, extolling them to go quickly and quietly. Vala flung herself to the ground as horses pounded toward the ring from all directions. In horror she watched mounted soldiers bearing swords and spears invade the clearing. The Dumnonii screamed and cried out as they scrambled to escape. A great explosion erupted from the bonfire, sending sparks and smoke high into the air, startling the attackers and throwing them into confusion. Terrified horses careened wildly off into the trees, throwing their riders as the Dumnonii scattered into the darkness.

The unhorsed tried to capture skittish mounts while the few horsemen who had mastered their steeds shouted curses as they charged off to scour the dark woods.

A second explosion rocked the clearing. Vala was certain Ethan was using his fire powder as a distraction. She could see his hard grin as soldiers seized him. He took a punch to the side of the head as they dragged him toward a wagon, and then a kick to the stomach as they pushed him to the ground. They tied a sack over Ethan's head and bound his ankles and wrists before heaving him into the wagon, where he landed with a bone-cracking thud.

A second wagon trundled up, loaded with more captives, each one bound hand and foot with a sack tied over their head. A woman screamed and thrashed as a soldier hauled her by the hair from the trees. He dropped her near the fire, where he skewered her with his spear.

Vala fought shock and anger. She needed to reach the horses, warn Meg, and retrieve her bow. If she could get Thistle and Ethan's horse too, perhaps she would be able to rescue him.

She'd crept but a few yards before she had to flatten herself beside a fallen tree. The woods were crawling with the shadowy shapes of men beating the underbrush. The soldiers caught another man, an older man. He limped as they hauled him toward the wagon where Ethan lay. They trussed the man up, like Ethan, and flung him into the wagon. The man let out a low groan.

A loud grunt of laughter presaged a black-robed monk on horseback who emerged through the smoke like a demon from hell. Vala recognized the long scar disfiguring his face. Brother Germain. Red-hot hatred coursed through her, and she nearly leapt forward to run him through with a jagged stick.

All activity in the clearing stopped. Two men on horseback followed Germain along the edge of the ring, a troop of six soldiers and three hooded monks in tow. One of the riders wore purple. His companion was in emerald green, the rich fabrics rippling garishly in the firelight. They neared Vala's hiding place, but the stomping and stabbing of the undergrowth from behind told her she dared not move.

A few yards from where she hid, Bishop De Roche addressed the balding man next to him. "My dear Bertelli, I marvel at the speed with which you arrived. France can be a stinking mud hole at this time of year, and the crossing can be perilous."

"I had the blessing of His Holiness upon me, Bishop," was the thickly accented reply from a well-fed man adorned with heavy gold rings on his plump fingers.

"Here is your first lesson in dealing with these heathens," De Roche said to his companion.

Bertelli inclined his head to his host. "Pope John bade me watch and learn."

De Roche dismounted a few yards from one of the standing stones and flicked his horse's reins to an attendant. "Heed this, then." The bishop held out his arm and snapped his fingers. A monk rushed forward, handing the bishop a lit torch. De Roche brought it close to the stone. "When you find such as these, simply destroying them will not suffice, for the very ground they stand on is revered by the heathen."

Bertelli nodded.

"You must erect something else in its place—a shrine or a church."

Bertelli frowned, and then realization dawned on his round face. "So, the sacred nature of the heathen site is preserved, at least in the mind of the simple peasant. We replace it with an appropriate shrine to our Lord!"

"Exactly," De Roche said.

"But do they stand for this?"

"Peasants are weak-minded rabble," De Roche replied. "The church at Thornborough is constructed on the site of a circle of stones such as this, and then there is the abbey being built near Wandlebury Hill, another heathen place. Sometimes a simple shrine to the Virgin or some saint will be adequate, and much less costly. The peasants soon forget all, except that the spot is a holy one. In short, they will come to believe what we tell them to believe."

Ponto Bertelli beamed in appreciation.

"You might reuse these stones in the construction," said the bishop, swinging his torch around the clearing. "That will put an end to the devilry."

"It is a plan of sheer genius," Bertelli said. "His Holiness said you were a man of extraordinary brilliance, and I see that it is so."

De Roche patted the stone. "This will make a fine pathway if we break it into rubble, yes?"

The nearest monk clapped his hands, enraptured. "A pathway in the shape of a cross!"

De Roche mounted his horse, ignoring the cloying monk.

"What about your storeroom of pagan items, the moldy books, the bone carvings? Must I really bother with such trifles?" Bertelli gestured about the clearing. "I understand this. But as to the rest—"

"It is essential, my friend. We are waging a great battle."

"Forgive me, but if the plunder could be turned into gold, it would be another matter," Bertelli said, swatting at a moth.

De Roche brought his steed close. "We must wipe out all remnants of the old religions if we are to gain power over this land. The Church has set the Holy Year feasts to coincide with the pagan feast days, but this is not enough. We must root out the idols and symbols to which the peasants cling. We cannot hope to profit from the peasants' tithes unless they believe in their hearts that our way is the true way, unless they believe the very fires of hell are licking at their heels."

Bertelli nodded. "His Holiness said that your success could not be argued, and I live to do Pope John's righteous will." He crossed himself.

De Roche called out, "How many have we, Captain?"

"Six alive and three dead so far, my lord bishop."

"Two dead over here, Excellency," came a shout from the far side of the ring.

The captain jogged over to the bishop, a sword jangling at his hip. "I'm waiting for the rest of my lads to report in, Your Grace."

"Don't waste any more time with this. We only need a few alive as an example." He wheeled his horse toward the northwest. "Meet us back at the shire reeve's keep. Once they've confessed their sins, we'll hang the lot of them. I want it done by morning." He looked at Bertelli. "This hellish place is too damp. I want a warm fire and some food. What say you, Ponto?"

Ponto Bertelli nodded his agreement. De Roche signaled his entourage of monks and guards to follow while the soldiers stayed behind to finish up.

There was no time for caution. Vala had to free the prisoners before they were taken beyond her reach. She got to her feet, pulled her hood up, and drew out her knife, not much of a weapon against a soldier's sword, but it was all she had. She moved stealthily through the trees, around the edge of the clearing, making for the wagons.

Ethan was only a few yards away. His guard had his back to her and was alone.

The knife hilt was slippery in her sweating palm. Regardless of the outcome, it was now or never. She lunged forward.

Something caught at the back of her shirt, thwarting her reckless charge. An arm thick as a tree limb dragged her into a chokehold. She flailed against her assailant, swiping at him with her knife until he pushed the point of his sword into her cheek. She froze. A trickle of blood slid down her neck, and she let the knife slide from her fingers.

"One more here!" He smelled of ale and dirty straw as he dragged her into the open. "Young boy, this one," he called.

"Doesn't matter to the bishop how young they are. Heathens have to die for their sins," said the man guarding the wagon.

Vala's captor pulled a sack over her face and tied it at the neck, just as he had done with the others, then pushed her to the ground and bound her ankles. "Too bad there ain't more of 'em." He yanked her back to her feet. "The townsfolk love a good hanging."

He finished the job, binding her wrists in front of her, before pitching her headlong into the wagon. She slammed into another body. The groan of pain sounded like Ethan.

"Who's there?" Ethan coughed.

Before she could draw a breath to answer, she heard a thud and a gasp of pain.

"Stay quiet!" spat the guard. With a lurch, the wagon trundled off across the grassy clearing. Vala cursed herself for her foolishness, for they were both captives now.

## Chapter Thirty:
*"In a cat's eye, all things belong to cats."*

The beeswax tapers were very fine, the best the keep had to offer. Their scent reminded De Roche of summer flowers in the fragrant gardens of the Torre delle Milizie. Soon, he'd breathe the fragrances of Rome again, and to hell with this land of Celtic gods vying with him for the souls of the peasantry. In Rome, his talents would lead him to greater triumphs.

A light knock at the door brought him out of his reverie.

"Come," he commanded.

A serving boy pushed open the door, and Brother Germain stalked in. The uneasiness on the boy's face was clear as he stepped aside for the monk. Brother Germain had that effect on people. The bishop smirked.

"The prisoners will be taken to the dungeon as soon as the wagons arrive," Germain growled, sloshing wine into a goblet.

"Please see to the confessions," said the bishop.

"I shall happily encourage their true repentance," Germain replied, lifting his cup with a dangerous smile. The man appreciated torture and never needed coaxing.

De Roche strolled to the window. Below, torches bobbed as the rumble of noisy activity filled the courtyard below. "Here they come now."

Germain joined him. "I'll go see to the heathens. Then I'll make sure our good reeve has the gallows ready for the morning." Germain replaced his cup. "And I'll be glad to put a rope around the old hag's neck, too. I'm tired of her yowling."

"Watt thinks she is dying, but she must last till morning," the bishop insisted. "I want her kicking until the end."

His gaze shifted to the two covered wains that contained the contents of his household, standing in the shadows of the courtyard. "I've had a message that our ship is waiting at Swanage. I wish to be on the road before midday."

"It's well we're leaving. The effort of conversion tires me," replied Germain. "I'm sick to death of this place."

De Roche snorted. Brother Germain was a purist of sorts: kill anyone who stood in your path and sort the bodies later. The monk did not disdain torture in his quest for results. De Roche was not sure Germain believed in God. His zealotry bordered on insanity at times, but still, the man was a useful tool.

Chapter Thirty-One:
*"Everyone must row with the oars he has."*

Vala fought against her bonds until she tired and slumped back with a moan of despair. Even if she managed to roll off the moving wagon, she'd never be able to crawl, much less run away. The wagon was taking them nearer and nearer their deaths, and she could do nothing.

"Ethan," she whispered, pressing her shoulder against his chest. He wasn't moving, but she could feel him breathing. There were six or seven captives in the first wagon and three in this one. Women, children, and old men were all going to their deaths, just because they believed in moon gods, amulets, and prophecy. It was wrong.

"Ethan," she hissed again as the wagon jostled over a particularly rough patch of road.

There was a low groan. "What?"

"Are you all right?" she whispered.

"Vala? Is that you?"

"Yes, and I have an idea."

She did have an idea, but she was not at all sure it would work. "Listen," she whispered. "If my plan succeeds, you'll have to get the others away as quick as you can, in case the bishop changes his mind. Can you manage that?"

"Of course," he rasped. "Assuming I'm free of this." He lifted his bound wrists. "What are you planning?"

"You! In the wagon!" an angry voice shouted. "Keep quiet, or I'll skewer you on this spear!"

Vala shifted closer to Ethan, bracing her feet against the wagon's side and her back against Ethan's shoulder. She could feel his warmth as she fought to hold herself still in the rocking wagon.

"When we stop, I'll demand to see De Roche. He wants my family dead very badly. If the last descendant of Simon Finn Negus were freely and publicly to admit being in league with the devil, that should be worth something. I'll tell him I'll confess any sin he wants if he lets the rest of you go."

"No, Vala," Ethan growled painfully. "You mustn't!"

"It's the only way," she snapped.

She felt Ethan strain against his bonds. "Don't even think of doing this," he hissed.

"If he agrees, get everyone away quickly. They might still pursue you once I'm dead."

"I won't let you!"

"Stop the wagon, Gillian!" the soldier behind them shouted.

Vala and Ethan froze as they rolled to a stop. The wagon creaked and shifted as it took more weight. Someone kicked hard at Vala, separating her from Ethan. She heard a dull thud.

"No more talk!" bellowed the soldier, and he left the wagon bed.

There was no sound from Ethan as they resumed their trundling pace, and Vala didn't dare speak. Her side was aching from the soldier's kick, but she feared Ethan had gotten worst of it.

After a time, the wagon slowed to a jerky halt. "Who goes there?" called a gruff voice from high above, the sound reverberating in the night.

"The bishop's guard, of course!" was the irritated reply.

They must have been motioned ahead, for Vala felt the bumping of flagstones under the cartwheels. When they lurched to a stop, Ethan whimpered in pain. Someone began shouting orders. Vala was yanked from the wagon by her feet. She hit the ground hard, nearly banging her skull as she landed. Another body slammed into hers. Hands grasped her and raised her up.

"I must talk to the bishop at once," she shouted through the sack.

The response was immediate—a sharp blow to the side of her head.

Vala felt the bindings being cut away from her ankles. A hand clamped onto her forearm and dragged her forward.

"The bishop will want to hear what I have to offer!"

"Keep it up, and we'll kill ya right here," a voice snarled into her ear.

"This one isn't moving, Captain."

Vala feared they meant Ethan.

Her shuffling feet finally found themselves on smoother stone. She was sure there was a roof overhead. The enclosed space smelled of broiled fat and countless night fires. The guards herded the prisoners to the left, their steps echoing in the vaulted antechamber. The prisoners funneled, jostling and bumping, through a narrow opening. A heavy door slammed behind them, taking with it what little light the sack permitted.

A dank reek filled Vala's nostrils. Her guard restrained her for a moment, and someone behind her sniggered nastily, but she did not take it as a sign of mischief. Without warning, she was launched forward with a violent shove. Terra firma vanished from beneath her, and she plummeted into space.

"Lift your feet, heathen!" someone laughed.

Vala tumbled downward, step after rock-hard step, unable to stop or protect herself. When finally she landed on a cold stone floor, crumpled and broken, the world went black.

The damp floor was cool. There was the coppery taste of blood in her mouth. Vala ran her tongue over her split lip and struggled to open her eyes. Failing that, she sought to lift her head, but her brain refused to respond.

Something tugged at her leg, pulling it up off the floor and then letting it drop. Her knee hit first with a spike of pain. Vala twitched her arm, sliding her hand toward her side. She felt bare skin. With a supreme effort, ignoring the mounting complaints from every inch of her body, she pulled herself up to her elbows and blinked several times. The sack was gone, and she could see the dirty flagstones on which she lay. Nearby lay a sad pile of rags which looked very much like her clothing. A bedraggled rat scurried away along the wall and disappeared through a chink in the stone.

"Not much here," grunted a voice above her.

Vala tried to turn, but overwhelming dizziness forced her back down. She shut her eyes against the pain and nausea, then blinked at the sound of stone hitting stone. Her emerald talisman bounced onto the floor next to the rag pile. A pair of large boots tromped into view, ripe with the odor of horse dung. The owner dropped her leggings into the pile.

Vala slowly curled into a ball. Perhaps she could lie here undisturbed and die.

"Start with her," said a voice Vala recognized.

"Of course, Brother Germain, as you wish," said the first man. "You want any of this?" His boot toed the heap of clothes.

There was a sniff from the monk. "The bishop will want to see her. He will be here shortly."

The mention of the bishop kindled a flame in Vala's dulled brain. If that devil came to see her, she might still make a deal to free the others, but she needed her wits for that. She forced herself to focus. This was the keep's dungeon. Steep steps hugged the wall behind her, and a doorway led into a barrel-vaulted tunnel. She could hear moaning and coughs from that direction. Two men were hauling a limp figure away.

Her jailer approached and yanked her arms over her head. Vala screamed in pain. The man ignored her as he tied her wrists together.

"A trade," she rasped. "I have a trade to make."

The big man snorted as he brought over an iron hook attached to a rope. The rope extended up to an iron ring high in the ceiling. The man wedged the cold metal hook between her bound wrists.

"Did you hear me?" she demanded.

"You can squeak all you like, like a little mouse, but it won't do you any good." The huge brute took hold of the rope and began to haul on it.

Vala scuttled to her knees. Every bone and muscle in her battered body objected. She tried to slip the hook loose, but the man knew his business, hoisting the rope too fast and hard to allow her to jerk free. Vala somehow got her feet under her as a second man appeared in the doorway to the tunnel.

"I'm sick of watching over that old witch," he complained. He looked Vala up and down. "At least this one ain't old nor wrinkled."

Tears dribbled down her cheeks as she scrabbled at the rope like a hare caught in a snare until her heels left the floor. Vala shrieked as her shoulder sockets took the weight of her body. They were stringing her up like a piece of meat on offer at a butcher's stall.

The first man grunted heavily, hoisting her higher, until her toes barely brushed the floor. "At least make yourself useful, Alfred. Get over here and tie off this rope."

"What'd ya find on her, Watt?" Alfred asked as he wound the rope around a cleat affixed to the wall. "Anything valuable? Anything we could share out?"

Watt nodded to the pitiful pile of rags. "Nothing. Heathen nonsense, mostly."

"She has little enough on her, to be sure," chuckled Alfred. He moved away from the wall and reached a filthy hand toward her bare skin.

Vala clenched her teeth against her anger and fear. "I want the bishop," she said through the blazing pain.

"Shut your mouth, witch!" Alfred snarled, then he began to stroke her thigh. "Now, if you're nice, ol' Alfred, he'll be nice to you."

Vala shuddered.

"Leave off," Watt said. "We'll have our orders soon enough."

A door hinge creaked, and boots thudded on the landing above them. Vala twisted her head upward. A draft of air swirled the scent of rotting straw around her. Bishop De Roche sidled down the steps.

Watt removed his cap and bowed his head. "I'll have this one crying out for the Lord's mercy before ya know it, Your Grace."

Alfred just shrank back against the wall.

The look in the bishop's eyes gave Vala gooseflesh, but she spoke out. "Let the others go, and I'll confess to being a witch."

A hard slap to the side of her head left her seeing stars. "You don't speak to His Grace unless he asks you a question!" Watt warned.

De Roche smiled enigmatically and strolled around her. "You're quite the little fox, escaping me in Bath as you did. I underestimated your resourcefulness. Given the family history, I should have known better." He stopped, facing her. "Your father was a thorn in my side. The godless Celts were all but wiped out, yet your foolish father refused to let their pagan ways die."

"The Dumnonii," she gasped, her arms feeling as though they would pull out of their sockets. "They aren't godless."

Watt lifted a hand to strike her, but the bishop restrained him with a look.

"They worship the sun and the moon and the castings of worms, I suspect." His tone was sardonic. "Your father was their champion, defiling churches with heathen symbols and rousing peasants against the priests." He walked back toward the stairs and then paused. "The great Simon Finn Negus meant for you to take his place, didn't he? He nearly succeeded, too, for I didn't know you existed until you walked into my study and handed over your father's dearest possession." De Roche laughed.

She took a deep breath. "If the Dumnonii are heretics, they'll get their punishment in the next life."

"Don't presume to argue philosophy with me, girl. I am ordained by God."

Vala tried to reply, but the words would not come.

"Tomorrow you will die, and the rest will be Bertelli's problem."

The bishop beckoned to Watt, who lumbered to his side. The jailer's greasy head nodded as De Roche murmured his orders before departing the hellish dungeon.

Vala sank into despair.

"What'd he tell you?" Alfred asked in a hushed voice.

"His Grace says that a virgin seer is supposed to have special powers and that we're to make sure this one don't have any powers left when she goes to the gallows."

Alfred grinned.

Watt faced Vala. "The bishop, he likes to see a good lashing first. Penance, as it were. Then we'll see what heathen acts you have to tell our Brother Germain. After that—"

"Him?" Albert squeaked. "She'll be worthless once he's done with her."

"That might be, but orders is orders," said Watt. "Go see to the other witch."

Alfred protested before slouching off down the tunnel.

"Got some vinegar here," Watt said, sloshing a wooden bucket which he thunked down on the floor. "Do ya know what that feels like in an open cut?"

Watt dipped a fat hand into his bucket and smeared the strong-smelling liquid over the cut on her lip. Vala yelped as the wine, gone bad, penetrated her wound.

"It works wonders to get a good confession." Watt grasped her chin so tightly, she thought he'd break her jaw. "Not that Brother Germain needs any help. He's a man what knows his way around when it comes to persuasion."

Watt lumbered to the wall and took a coiled leather whip from a hook. "Ten lashes are the usual, but I can do what's needed—whatever it takes." Watt spat on the floor with a hoarse hacking noise. "The bishop gives me absolution beforehand, so I'll go right to heaven." He pointed toward the ceiling. "Straight up." He reached out and ran the knuckles of his hand down the length of her back. Vala gulped out a sob. "Pretty, pale skin, but not for long."

There was a sickening snap as Watt's leather thong whipped through the air, followed by immediate heat where the whip met her flesh. Exquisite pain seared her from neck to waist. Vala arched away, her fingers stretching upwards, and the muscles in her back seized in shock.

Watt put a huge hand on her leg to steady her flailing. The second slash cut across the first before she could prepare herself. Pain robbed her of breath. She could feel warm rivulets of blood trickling down her skin, and her eyes were damp with tears as she gulped for breath. A third cruel kiss of the leather whip slashed her from forearm to hip, curling brutally against her flesh. Vala screamed in misery. Sweat, tears, and drool trickled down her front as she tried to draw breath. She would swoon presently, and perhaps she'd not feel anything then.

The cell began to go dark around her.

"Master Watt!"

The lashes stopped, and Vala fought for consciousness. Feet pounded toward them from the tunnel, disgorging a boy dressed in a leather jerkin and skullcap.

"Come quick, Master Watt!"

"What is it?" rumbled Watt.

The boy stopped, taking in Vala's blood-streaked body for an instant.

"What is it, boy?"

"It's the old hag who told us where to find this lot. Alfred thinks she's dying!"

"She's the prize of the lot," growled Watt. "His Grace wants the old witch hung alive."

Out of the corner of her eye, Vala saw Watt swing up the bucket. The wine, now turned to vinegar, splashed over her body, into every cut and slice of the whip. She shrieked in inexpressible pain.

Watt up-ended the bucket on the floor with a loud thud, and he and the boy hurried from the room.

Vala blinked, fighting to ignore the pain. There was something important in what the two had said. She tried to grasp it, to understand. An old hag who'd told the bishop where to find them all? She closed her eyes, but that only made the agony worse.

Had they meant they had an actual witch? Could it be Isolde? Vala clenched her teeth. Was it possible the old hag had betrayed the Dumnonii? Hatred surged through her, firing her desire to escape and rescue Ethan and the others. It was a ridiculously foolish thought, she realized, bound and twirling from the end of the rope.

Vala squirmed, her arms and shoulders aching, her back on fire. Then she saw it.

The bucket.

It was quite close. If she could just reach it with her foot, she might slide it closer, close enough to stand on.

She tried to focus through the pain. Using her body like a pendulum, she threw herself backward so she could swing forward. She was able to extend her foot toward the bucket, almost touching it. It took a few tries, but, with a supreme effort, stretching as much as her stinging body could bear, she managed to get the edge of one foot on the upturned base. Pushing down on it with her toe, she slid it closer, a bare few inches. Then she slipped.

Vala stifled her tears, and with another hard effort, she worked the bucket over a few inches of the rough floor and under her dangling legs. Careful not to let the damned thing tip and roll away, she slowly let it take her full weight. With the extra inches of height, she was just able to release her wrists from the iron hook.

Her weakened arms dropped, the bucket skittered out from under her, and she crashed to the floor. Nearly spent from the effort, she fought to remain conscious. The pain in her back took her breath away, but she had to ignore it. Using her teeth, she tugged at the knot of cord around her wrists. It gave enough to allow her to wrench her right wrist free.

With shaking fingers, she pulled on clothes, wincing as the rough fabric abraded her flailed skin. With an effort, she managed to pull on her boots, then stuffed the small treatise of Barnabas down inside. Lastly, she lifted her emerald from the filth.

"Not so lucky, are you?" she whispered to the talisman.

The clever thing, the intelligent thing, would be to climb the stairs and sneak out of the keep before Watt returned. It was tempting. Vala wiped blood from her swollen lip and limped to the darkened tunnel. She peered into its maw. She could make out voices down at the end, punctuated by a woman's screams and moans. She moved inside as silently as her aching body could manage.

Cells lined the tunnel, barely of enough height for a man to stand. Inside the first was a body, dead eyes staring at the ceiling. She recognized the greying bristly hair but could not recall his name. In the next, a man was shivering in the straw on the floor, hands and feet bound, with a sack tied over his head. An amulet encircled his ankle.

Vala slid back the bolt and pushed her way inside.

"Ethan!" she groaned, kneeling with difficulty. She pulled free the sack covering his head and gasped in horror. If she had not known it was Ethan, she doubted she'd have recognized his bloodied and bruised face. One eye was a slit, puffed up and going purple.

He tried to push himself up but sagged at once back to the floor.

"Don't try to stand." She fumbled with the ropes, fighting to ignore her own pain. Ethan writhed in agitation and rasped something she could not understand. "Lie still, will you?" she hissed at him, working frantically at the knot. "We have to do this quickly if we want to get away."

Ethan mumbled through swollen lips and snatched at her sleeve.

"Speed will not avail you," said a cold voice.

Vala spun to find Brother Germain's robed form filling the narrow doorway. He stepped inside, allowing the door to close behind him. "You have some luck on your side, girl." He pulled his hand from inside his robes, drawing out a long knife that gleamed red in the torchlight. He ran a finger gingerly along its edge. "But your luck is at an end. You and I will have a little talk. Confession is good for the soul." He grinned nastily at her. "And after I've finished with you, I'll have a go at this one." He toed the sole of Ethan's boot.

Vala knew with sickening certainty that Watt's methods would be nothing compared to Germain's ministrations.

"It's unfortunate that your brother and father are already dispatched. Your family would have made a nice row of scarecrows on the gallows."

Enveloped in a black rage, Vala lunged with wild fury toward the monk. Germain recoiled, staggering and stumbling to the floor, and Vala was upon him, hammering at the monk with her fists. She barely registered the ping of steel against stone.

"Knife!" Ethan wheezed as he flung himself toward Germain's flailing legs. He grabbed for the monk's robes but received a kick that sent him tumbling into the wall. Ethan could barely crawl, but he clawed his way back toward the fray.

Vala saw the knife glinting in the filthy straw. Both she and the monk lurched toward it. In the scrabbling of fingers, Germain reclaimed his weapon and pushed Vala down against the rough stone floor, pressing his forearm against her throat. The pain in Vala's back was so exquisite, she nearly passed out. She heard movement behind the monk.

Germain glanced behind him. "Move, and she dies." Ethan froze and then sank against the wall, breathing hard.

"Why don't you just make an end of it?" she cried.

"Perhaps I ought to let the guards have you for an hour or so," Germain hissed in Vala's ear. "Or I could tie you to a post in the courtyard and slit you open so the birds can peck at your innards. You'll be able to watch! It might take days for you to die." Germain moved into a crouch next to her, grabbing a handful of her shirt. "On your feet," he ordered.

As he rose, Vala grasped his ankle and yanked hard. The monk lost his balance, stumbling sideways. Vala fumbled for Germain's flailing knife hand and received a slice to her palm before she grasped his wrist. With all her strength, she twisted his arm, and in the ensuing scuffle, Germain went sprawling to the floor.

The cell door crashed open, and Vala skittered backward, shielding Ethan from the two new monks who pressed inside. They bent their hooded faces over Germain, who looked up at them with wide, terrified eyes, his knife buried to the hilt in his chest. He gurgled out an incomprehensible word before slumping lifeless against the wall.

The black-robed monks turned toward Vala.

She watched dark blood soak Germain's robes. She bowed her head and waited for the sword thrust or the blow that would snap her neck. It would be better than hanging. It would be quicker, at least.

Ethan coughed out a word. "Phillip?"

"Keep your voice down!" ordered one of the monks as he extracted a black bundle from beneath his robes.

"Good work, my dear!" said the second monk as he lowered his hood. "Brother Germain looks wholly surprised by the turn of events."

"Father Guillard?" Vala said in astonishment. "How did you—where have you come from?"

Guillard put a finger to his lips.

The other monk lowered his hood. "We heard they intended to raid a Dumnonii ceremony at Knowlton ring." Phillip shoved the black bundle at her. "Here, put this on."

Vala winced in pain as she struggled into the monk's habit.

"We might use these," Guillard said, touching Germain's gory robes. "But they might be a bit of a giveaway."

"No, I think not," said Phillip. He caught sight of Vala's bloody shirt. "My blessed Lord!"

"I'm fine," she replied stoically.

"Then we'll bring your friend along and think of something once we reach the courtyard," said Father Guillard.

Ethan yowled in pain as Phillip lifted him. "Lean on me," said Phillip.

Father Guillard pulled the knife from Germain's chest and handed it to Vala. "You may need this, my dear."

Grim and grey-faced, Ethan limped forward, putting a hand on the old priest's shoulder for support. Phillip allowed Vala to pass, then closed the cell door on the dead monk. They both turned as the sound of screaming echoed from the far end of the dark tunnel.

"The others," Vala said. "We can't leave without the others."

"This place is crawling with De Roche's men," Phillip said. "We'll be fortunate to escape ourselves."

Vala shook her head adamantly.

"Of course," Phillip sighed. "You're right."

"Check all the cells," Vala ordered, pointing to the right side of the tunnel.

She took the left-hand side, peering into each cell in turn while trying to suppress her urge to fly from this hell and never look back. The uproar from deep within the dungeon continued as Isolde shrieked and guards shouted. They would send someone for the bishop soon.

The cell beyond Ethan's held four men, sacks over their heads and roped together along the wall. Vala slipped the bolt and moved silently inside, cut their bonds and murmured to each to keep quiet. She recognized Kale among the men when he nodded his gratitude. Although they bore signs of beatings by the guards, they were able to walk and moved quickly back toward the stairs.

Phillip joined them with two women and a sobbing young girl. Vala bent to the lass. It was the same child who'd asked about a love charm back in Avebury.

"You must be brave and quiet," Vala told her. "Can you do that for me?"

"Yes, goddess," the girl replied, wiping at her tears with her sleeve.

Phillip chivied them all toward the stairs, but all eyes were on Vala. They expected her to save them.

"Go to the top of the steps and wait by the door," she told them, but she had no idea what to do beyond that. She turned to Phillip and Guillard, "We need a plan."

"One may present itself," Guillard replied, as though this were an expedition to discover mushrooms in the woods. Then he pointed behind them. "You might start by barring that door."

Phillip and Vala turned as one and lurched for the tunnel's door, pulling it shut with a thud. Phillip lowered the heavy wooden bar, trapping their captors inside. Once their jailers realized what had happened, they could halloo and shout until the noise brought help, but it would give the escapees time.

At the top of the stairs, the Dumnonii huddled against the door. Ethan leaned weakly against the wall for support.

"Outside is a gallery that runs the length of the keep," Phillip said.

"We should have a look," replied Vala.

The two climbed the steps and squeezed past the prisoners and through the narrow door. The reddish glow of firelight streamed from a wide archway in the left-hand wall, twenty or so feet ahead. The corridor was deserted, most of the inhabitants being asleep at this hour.

There was a small door to the right, and Vala opened it carefully. It was a dark, narrow room smelling of tack and iron, a dead end. She crept further along the gallery, Phillip at her elbow. The gathering hall held sleeping people stretched out along the walls.

Opposite the hall was an archway opening on the courtyard. Vala shrank into the shadows of a stone pilaster. Across the yard was the gate. The portcullis was up, and two guards were slouched against the wall, sharing a wineskin.

"How did you plan to escape?" she whispered to Phillip.

"Walk out with our heads bowed and our hoods up," he said. "We thought no one would question Brother Germain's monks coming and going."

Vala felt a flood of gratitude. Phillip had risked so much to come for her. She was jeopardizing his life and Father Guillard's too by insisting they rescue all the prisoners. She looked about the courtyard hoping for an inspiration that would save them all. "Perhaps there's another gate?"

"Just the one. This place was built for defense," Phillip replied.

Vala's heart fell, and then suddenly, there it was, in the darkest corner of the yard. Vala grabbed Phillip's arm and pointed. "Those wagons covered with tarpaulins."

"But we don't have horses, and besides, they are full of the bishop's household possessions," he replied.

"There must be a stable," Vala said. "We need to find it. With luck, we can just drive the wagons through the gate. We'll say," she continued as the idea blossomed, "the bishop ordered us to take his things on ahead."

Phillip gave her a skeptical look.

"We have to try something," she said. "There is no need for you and Father Guillard to come. If you stay behind, you can blend in with De Roche's retinue."

Phillip's eyes narrowed. "Do you really think I'd throw in with that man once I found out what he was?" His face flushed with anger, and he took a deep breath. "I could never condone his actions, even if he were the pope himself."

Vala tried to smile, but her swollen lip hurt, so she reached out and squeezed his arm.

There wasn't much time. The guards would soon discover the empty cells and rouse the keep. Vala opened the door and saw the cluster of worried faces searching her own.

"Follow me," she whispered, ushering the group through the door. Vala hoped to herd them all into a dark corner of the courtyard and then go in search of horses, trusting to luck that they would not be noticed. They shuffled into the gallery, and Vala had begun to chivvy them forward when Guillard put out a halting hand.

The sound of feet moving through the high-ceilinged hall echoed out into the shadowy gallery. Vala spun, pushed open the door to the small tack room, and drove the group inside. Kale was the last inside just as a servant with a torch stepped into the gallery. Phillip, Guillard, and Vala stood in a tight group blocking the doorway.

Vala bowed her head low so her hood would obscure her face, hoping fervently that the man would go on his way. The servant nodded to the group as he lit the torches along the wall. Phillip smiled, nodding at the man, who disappeared down the gallery.

"What now?" Phillip groaned.

Before Vala could answer, Kale appeared from the shadows of the small room where the prisoners were hiding.

"There is a door in this room. It opens on a passage between this hall and the kitchens."

Grateful for any possibility, Vala followed Kale inside. The narrow antechamber was dark as pitch, and she was surprised he'd discovered anything.

Kale led her to the end of the room, dodging the others huddled along the wall. She heard a faint click, and a door swung inward, revealing an open-air passageway.

Vala leaned out and sniffed the strong odor of onions and lamb. No one was in sight. She pulled her robes tightly around herself and sprinted down the passage between the buildings. She could hear Phillip hissing her name in the darkness, but there was no time for discussion with the fate of all the prisoners in her hands. If there was a kitchen, there was a garden, and what better place for the animals than behind the garden?

The smell of horse stalls hit her as she reached the shadowy kitchen garden. To the right was a low barn. No one was in sight, not even a dozing groom. No one must have reckoned that the small band of Dumnonii was likely to present any danger, so the lord of this keep had sent his servants to bed.

She'd need two horses to pull the wagon. She took a torch from its bracket and hurried to the barn, where she inspected the beasts tied in their stalls. There were two sturdy carthorses, heavily muscled, with large hooves. Vala coaxed them from their stalls and led them down the passageway, making as little noise as possible.

"What are you doing?" demanded Phillip, who was waiting near the tack room door. "You might be seen!"

"We needed horses, so I found some."

"If they catch you, they'll kill you."

Vala nodded toward the door. "And all of them as well."

"Dear God, help us," Phillip muttered. He beckoned to Kale. "Can you hitch up the horses quietly?"

Kale nodded and gestured to another of the prisoners. The two took the horses' reins from Vala and led them through the dark yard to the wagons. Phillip and Vala followed. Kale efficiently backed the horses into the staves of the far wagon. Luckily, a few other horses were tied in the courtyard, and their snorts and stamping covered any sounds from the pilfered steeds. Vala folded back the tarpaulin, and with Phillip's help, began to remove boxes, chairs, and small barrels to make room to hide the prisoners. The silent parade of objects was swiftly stacked along the wall, hidden from view by the second wagon.

Once Vala judged that the opening in the wagon was large enough, Phillip returned to the tack room and began to send the prisoners, one at a time, across the courtyard, keeping to the deepest shadows. The captives hunched and crowded themselves into the wain. When they were all inside, she handed up a few boxes to hide them in case of an inspection at the gate. With trembling fingers, she tied down the tarpaulin, for although the entire operation had gone as flawlessly as she could have hoped, time was passing far too quickly.

Vala rushed back to get Phillip and Guillard so they could leave. *And Ethan.* She had forgotten Ethan! They would have to reopen the tarpaulin to get Ethan inside.

Vala pushed open the door to the tack room. The torch sputtered over Father Guillard's head. He was tending Ethan, splinting his swollen ankle with some broken bow staves he'd scavenged.

Vala went to Phillip. "We have to open the wagon again." She nodded toward Ethan.

"Quickly, then," said Phillip. "I can hear voices in the gathering hall. It sounds like the relief guard waking up." He edged the inner door open a bare slit. "We ought to go before they come on duty. We don't want extra hands at the gate when we try it."

"The ones on duty have been drinking, and so are less of a threat," remarked Guillard, who joined them at the door. As they spoke, two fresh guards ambled into the gallery, arguing over a bet they had and in no hurry to relieve the gate.

"It's no good." Phillip glanced at Ethan. "We'll have to wait until the gate is relieved and only two are on duty again."

"Go without me," Ethan said, clutching his leg. "You'll have the best chance that way."

"Ethan, no," Vala said. "I'm not leaving you behind with these beasts."

"I completely agree, young man," said Guillard. "If you stay, it will be your death warrant. And yet, we cannot afford to wait, for I fear someone might spot the wagon." Guillard put a finger to his forehead and grinned merrily. "I have a plan to solve two problems at once." He hurried to where Ethan sat.

"A plan?" Vala said to Phillip. "What could it possibly be? The old man is a dear, but—"

Phillip cut her off. "Guillard is brilliant."

Vala turned in time to see Father Guillard pulling off the black monk's robes. The old priest had not bothered to wear his usual robes and was now clothed in nothing but a sort of loincloth. Vala gasped and spun back toward Phillip in embarrassed surprise. Guillard had gone insane, and they were all going to die.

"Father!" breathed Phillip. "You must put your robe back on."

"No, silly boy. I'll just totter on back to my rooms, and no harm done. Here, help this poor lad to dress."

"But, Father," Ethan said as Guillard tossed the robes into his lap.

"Father Guillard, wait!" Vala cried as the old priest squeezed past her and set off down the corridor. Phillip made a grab in his direction, but too late.

A shout came from the gallery. "Who goes there?"

Vala and Phillip exchanged a look of alarm.

"Father Guillard, is that you?" one of the soldiers asked. "What's happened? Let me help you."

"Just out for a stroll," the old priest replied in a quavery voice.

"Father, please, take my cloak," the first soldier insisted. "Where are your clothes?"

"Clothes?" Guillard wondered vaguely.

"Let us help you to your chamber," said the other soldier.

"What nice lads you are," said the old priest. "What are your names?"

"I'm Dirk, and this here is Gilbert," said the first, shooting his companion a look. "Father, we've met before."

"Have we?" Guillard sounded confused. "Have you been to France too?"

"No, Father," the man replied. "You ought not to be wandering at night like this."

Their voices trailed away as they led Guillard off.

Phillip said quietly, "Guillard used himself as a diversion, and now Ethan can pass for one of Germain's monks, too," he said with a shake of his head. "Brilliant."

Vala was speechless.

"That old priest is very clever," Ethan agreed as he struggled into the disguise. It was the kindest thing Ethan had ever said about a man of the church.

Phillip helped Ethan to his feet, and the three made their way to the door.

"We may need a distraction when we get to the gates," Phillip said in a low voice.

"What do you have in mind?" Ethan asked, hobbling between them.

Phillip shook his head pensively.

"Weapons?" asked Vala. One corner was full of them. She spotted a rack of bows and took the shortest one she could see, along with a quiver of arrows. She tossed a sword in a worn scabbard to Phillip and another to Ethan.

Phillip gritted his teeth with grim resolution and belted on the blade. "These might be a threat, but not a diversion."

"Ethan," Vala said. "Your fire powder."

"I'd forgotten." He dug under the black robe, wincing with pain as he did.

"What are you planning to do?" he asked, extending a small amount in his fist. "Throw it at them?"

Vala wrinkled her brow in thought.

"What is fire powder?" asked Phillip.

Ethan began explaining his concoction, and Phillip bent over it, holding the candle carefully away from the volatile granules.

"Could we use the powder to send the guards off to deal with a fire while we drive through the gates?" Ethan wondered. "What we need is a way to light it, but not until we reach the gates. Something that would burn, but not too fast."

"Like a candlewick?" Vala suggested.

Phillip pulled out his knife and sliced through the hem of his robe. He pulled free several strands of wool. "We can twist these together and place one end in the powder. If we light the other, it should give us time to reach the gate before the flame ignites it."

Ethan leaned against the wall for support and accepted the wool strands, which he twisted together. Phillip gathered up some dried rushes as tinder to spread the fire.

"This isn't going to burn properly. Not like this. We need—" Ethan said.

"Oil," said Vala, finishing his thought. "Wet the wool with oil."

She rummaged in the sword rack and found a jar of oil used for cleaning the metal and keeping away the rust. Ethan dipped the wool strings into it and rubbed them to saturate the wool. "It might go off too soon," he said.

"Or not at all," said Phillip.

"We should go," Vala said nervously.

Phillip nodded. "We'll put this in the second wain. De Roche deserves to lose his worldly goods."

Vala had to help Ethan limp across the courtyard. He could barely put weight on his injured leg. Once they reached the wains, Phillip placed the handful of fire powder with its oil-soaked wool fuse just inside the back of the second wain, then arranged bits of tinder amongst the booty so it might burn once the powder had ignited. He asked for forgiveness for this sin while praying for its success.

"Get into the wagon," he ordered. "I'll set the wick alight."

Ethan hobbled to the first wain and hauled himself into the seat. Vala tried to climb onto the back of the wagon, but pain shot through her back and she nearly tumbled to the ground.

"Allow me," Phillip said, then lifted her gently up until she could grip the wagon sides.

"Thank you," Vala gasped.

His hands lingered on her waist, and then he strode to the front of the wagon and took his place on the wagon seat. He glanced at Ethan. Thankfully, it was dark, for the man's face was swollen and bruised.

"Pull your hood lower," Phillip snapped as he clenched his fingers around the reins. Then he muttered, "I'll need my confessor if we ever reach safety."

"Don't stop the wagon, even if they call you back. Just take the left-hand road outside the keep and go as fast as you can. We have friends outside Knowlton," Ethan said.

"I'm going to stop at the gate as though everything is above board," replied Phillip. "And we're taking the road through Cranbourne."

"Are you mad? Just drive straight through the gate. They won't question the bishop's men, surely."

"We must stop. It would be suspicious if we didn't," Phillip shot back. "And stopping will give your powder time to ignite. Then we escape in the confusion, and no one is the wiser."

Ethan grumbled as they trundled across the courtyard.

Phillip wasn't about to explain to this pagan, but if all went to plan, he would have one more surprise waiting.

The wagon rolled under the stone archway, the noise of it causing one guard to shamble to his feet. "What do you think you're up to?"

His fellow jerked upright with a bleary grimace and rubbed at his jaw, staring up at them in confusion.

"Do you not recognize this robe?" Phillip demanded, plucking at the black wool on his chest. "We are Brother Germain's men, the bishop's personal servants."

"Why are you moving this wagon? That's what I want to know," the guard said, un-cowed.

"The bishop's ship awaits. He intends to leave in the morning, but wagons do not travel with the speed of men on horseback, so he is sending us ahead."

"What's on the wagon?"

"Is that your business?" Phillip asked in a haughty tone.

The second guard strode to the back and pulled up the edge of the tarpaulin. "Boxes and such," he replied with a yawn.

"I don't like it," said the first guard. "No one told me of this. I should send someone to check."

"You want to wake the bishop?" the second guard asked. "Because I do not."

"Why don't you wake Brother Germain?" suggested Phillip.

"Rather wake the devil himself," muttered the second guard.

Vala watched Ethan cast a glance back toward the dark corner of the courtyard and the bishop's other wagon.

"I have my orders," Phillip said curtly, urging the horses forward while the two guards argued, their voices rising over the rumble of the wheels.

This would have been a fine moment for the second wagon to erupt in flame, but it did not. The first guard turned and made for the keep, so Vala screamed, "Drive!"

Phillip snapped the reins hard, and the horses hurtled full tilt down the narrow road toward the village, the wain swaying and creaking. The women hidden inside shrieked in terror, and Ethan clung to his seat with great difficulty.

Phillip spared a glance toward a thick band of woods a hundred feet off the road. As if on cue, a man erupted from the trees on horseback, trailing a pack of horses. The horseman sped toward them.

"Phillip," Vala cried, pointing at the phantom rider in confusion.

Instead of driving the horses harder, Phillip pulled up and slowed the team. Shouts muffled by the night resounded from the keep. In front of them was the village of Cranbourne, where the execution was set for the morning. Phillip gave quick instructions to Ethan, who cursed as he accepted the reins. Phillip leapt to the ground and ran to the back of the wain.

Ethan gave the reins a hard shake, and at the same moment, Phillip gripped Vala's wrist and pulled her from the wagon. He caught her, keeping her from landing hard on the ground as the wagon gained speed. Vala stared at him, astonished.

Chapter Thirty-Two:
*"If you want a thing done well, do it yourself."*

Ethan gritted his teeth as he drove the team. He was light-headed, but he couldn't afford to let that affect him, not at this moment.

He repeated Phillip's words over to himself. "Get the people to safety. We'll hold off the pursuit." All his bones ached from the beatings he had taken, and the kick to his head had muddled him badly. "Get the people to safety."

He disliked the monk, but the important thing just now was to cooperate. He glanced behind the wagon, unhappy that Vala had stayed with Phillip. Even though she had the talisman to protect her, she ought to have remained with the wagon. If it would not endanger the lives entrusted to him, he'd go back and demand she come with him. As it was, he'd have to trust her to Phillip if he had any chance of saving his own precious cargo.

He did not slow the team as they passed through the sleeping village. As the houses dwindled on the far side, Ethan swerved to the left, taking the westward fork in the road, not the straight path north. This road, much less traveled, was familiar to him. It ran through heavy woodland for many miles. He still believed he was right to tell Phillip to turn toward Knowlton, but Phillip's plan had merit.

Ethan looked around at the dark countryside and suddenly knew how he might help. Perhaps his head *was* clearing.

He knew a spot where a game trail led into heavy undergrowth. No horseman would be able to follow that track. Phillip had intended that he take the wagon well away, but this would be better than keeping to a road.

Ethan brought the wagon to a rolling stop. The ground was hard and should allow the prisoners to get away unnoticed. In the light of day, canny trackers would pick up the trail, but not by night.

"Kale," he called, "Get everyone into the woods." The tarpaulin flew up, and dark shapes began to emerge behind the wagon. "Go straight west until the trees end, and then make for the hills."

"Aye," said Kale as he helped folk to the ground. "We'll be fine, Ethan. But what about you?"

"Don't worry about me. I'll find you soon. And cover your head, man!"

Kale pulled his hood over his shining bald pate with a wink. After the last of the Dumnonii had faded into the trees, he swept the footprints from the dusty roadway with a fistful of arrow grass.

Ethan felt relieved that his people were safe. Now, he needed to help Vala.

Chapter Thirty-Three:
*"God helps those who help themselves."*

"What are you doing?" Vala sputtered as she regained her balance, feeling afresh every bruise and hurt on her body. The wagon rattled off into the darkness without her.

"Your horse is coming," Phillip said, turning her and holding her attention with the intensity of his eyes. "Take it, and get as far from here as you can. Go east. We'll create a diversion."

"And leave them?" She tried to gesture toward the retreating wagon. "I'm not leaving you and Ethan to die when I can help."

Her words were lost in the sounds of hooves and snorting animals. The horseman reined up next to Phillip, jerking and twisting to bring the rearing beasts under some control. She looked up at the newcomer, who tossed Phillip the reins of two of the horses dancing between them.

"Uncle Adrian!" she cried, but Phillip spun her toward a horse.

"Not now," Phillip said. "There is no time. Mount up and ride!"

He shoved the reins of a big mare into her hands, and she clambered into the saddle. Phillip was right. There was no time for pleasantries, because a band of mounted pursuers from the sheriff's keep thundered out of the darkness toward them. Vala extracted the bow from beneath her robes and slung the quiver over her head, ignoring the ache as it bumped against her wounded back. Without further conversation, the three of them galloped for Cranbourne, three riders, and four horses.

She realized the extra horse had been for Father Guillard. At least *he* was safe.

Chapter Thirty-Four:
*"As you sow, so shall you reap."*

"I'm sorry, my lord bishop," Watt panted as he wiped sweat from his red face. "I've never had an escape before."

The keep was in turmoil. A handful of guards had gone after the fleeing prisoners while Watt awakened De Roche.

"Incompetence!" raged De Roche. "Where is Brother Germain?"

"I'd gone to find him when I discovered the prisoners had scampered," Watt explained, "The old witch was bellowing, and I'd been at whipping that young one," he stammered. "But she's disappeared, and the rest of 'em too. And they locked us in."

Lord Fagen, a balding man with a slight paunch, came puffing up. "Your Grace," he said, head bowed. He had hoped the bishop's stay would be brief and uneventful, for the man terrified him. Unfortunately, one did not refuse entry to a bishop of Rome.

"Wasn't anyone on guard?" demanded De Roche, his face a livid red.

"There were guards at the gates," said Lord Fagen. "But the prisoners escaped using one of your wagons. I understand they dressed like your men."

De Roche narrowed his eyes as an unnatural roar went up in the courtyard outside, orange light exploding in the darkness. Shouts of "Fire!" filled the air. Lord Fagen and his men sprinted toward the disturbance. De Roche followed with long, purposeful strides.

His wain, filled with his possessions, spewed flame into the night sky. Heat rolled across the flagstones, fanning his rage.

"Your Excellency," Watt mumbled, taking hold of the hem of the bishop's sleeve. De Roche scowled at the cringing jailer. "He's dead," said Watt.

"Who is dead?" barked De Roche.

Two men were hauling a body along the gallery. Something dark dripped from it as they made their shuffling progress. Watt shrank away. De Roche intercepted the bearers as they passed beneath a bracketed torch. His finger touched the pale, bloodless scar that disfigured the cold cheek.

"Get me a horse!" he bellowed.

Chapter Thirty-Five:
*"Fortune favors the brave."*

Phillip slapped his horse's flank as they entered Cranbourne. Vala found the jolting gallop almost beyond endurance, but she had to keep pace. The three riders were bait for the bishop's soldiers, drawing his forces away from the innocents in Ethan's wagon. Phillip was probably seething that she'd refused to escape, but Vala knew it was a brilliant piece of work to have had the horses standing by. She wondered how Phillip and her uncle had found each other.

Phillip led them toward the west road, which dove through thick woodland, providing some cover. That was a blessing, for without it, they were doomed. Vala turned and counted five in pursuit. The horses' flanks pumped, hooves pounding rhythmically, gaining some ground on the chase. They crossed a large swath of moonlit road, and Phillip pulled his horse to a stop just beyond it, motioning for Vala and Adrian to join him.

"Alright," Phillip said. "Vala, you must ride into the woods as fast as you can. Catch up with the others. We'll hold off the guards here."

"No," she replied curtly.

"If my original plan had worked, we'd be far from here by now."

"But we had to rescue the others," Vala insisted. To demonstrate her resolve, or perhaps her foolishness, she nocked an arrow. "We ought to hide over there." She nodded to her right. "We'll attack them when they reach this clearing."

Phillip took hold of her horse's bridle. "We cannot win this fight. Don't you see? The soldiers outnumber us. We can only give the others time."

Before she could reply, the creak of wooden wheels startled them. A large wain lumbered out of the darkness. Ethan pulled the team to a stop next to Phillip and smiled weakly.

"Can I help?"

When the soldiers rounded the bend, their horses reared to a halt, throwing the troop into momentary turmoil. A high-sided wagon blocked the road.

The men mastered their mounts with curses and insults to the driver who sat slumped in the seat.

"Move that wagon!" the leader ordered.

"I'm sorry?" said the driver, as though he was hard of hearing.

Two soldiers drew their swords and closed in around the wain. The leader flung out his arm. "Move the wagon!"

The wagon driver raised himself up, and with lightning speed, flung a fist-sized rock at the nearest rider. The man took the full force of the blow on his temple and toppled from his horse. At the same moment, an arrow zinged through the air, striking another soldier in the shoulder. The injured man completely lost control over his horse, which reared and threw him.

Phillip and Adrian galloped from the trees, swords drawn. Adrian swung his blade with the skill of a practiced swordsman. It clanged against the flat side of the leader's blade as he struggled to block the attack. The men pushed away from each other with grunts of exertion, and each took another swing. The soldier's blow went wide as Adrian lunged, thrusting his blade under the soldier's guard. With a scream of pain, the soldier fell.

Phillip was battling one of the pursuers close in, trading teeth-grinding blows. The man Vala had wounded writhed in pain, trying to pull the arrow from his shoulder. She nocked another arrow and held her breath as she pulled her bow up on the remaining horsed soldier. He lunged toward Ethan, but her shot took the man square in the chest.

Vala pulled a third arrow from her quiver, trying not to think about the men she had hit, trying to remember her lessons with Fletcher. She shook her left hand to relieve the cramp in her arm and then surveyed the battle scene. Phillip required no assistance; he was wielding his sword with admirable skill. He unhorsed his opponent and then leapt to the ground to finish the fight. Ethan slipped from the wagon and limped toward the battle brandishing a knife. Vala tried to raise her bow again, but the strain on her bruised shoulders was nearly unbearable. She wondered how she had managed to shoot, and even to ride up until now. She gritted her teeth and tried to draw the bow again but could not do it.

Too late, she glimpsed the shadow leaping toward her. Her assailant knocked her to the ground before she could cry out.

The face above her had a hideous bleeding lump protruding from his temple, where Ethan had hit him with a rock. He slammed his forearm down on her chest and raised a long, wicked knife. Vala tried to scream, but the man's weight took all the air from her lungs. She struggled, kicking and swinging wildly.

The blade came down as she wrenched herself aside. Vala cried out in agony, her torn back jabbed by tree roots. The man wrenched his blade free and swung. Vala tensed in expectation of the killing cut.

The man's head snapped forward with a crack, and he slumped to the ground. Phillip held the sturdy little club he always carried in one hand and a bloody sword in the other. The knife was stuck in the earth an inch from her ear. Phillip flung away his gory blade in disgust and helped her to her feet.

"We have been lucky. More will be coming soon," Ethan gasped, breathless.

Phillip nodded, pulling Vala to her feet.

Ethan scrambled up into the wagon and yanked hard at the carthorses to turn them. Pale and wobbly, he ought to be lying in the wagon rather than driving it. Adrian must have thought so too, for he whipped his horse around and caught hold of the carthorse's bridle, then steered the team forward as Ethan clutched at his leg.

Vala shambled, bruised and exhausted, to her own horse. She wished it were Thistle. She had no idea where they were and was not sure she could keep her seat in the saddle. She'd wounded a man and probably killed another, not counting Germain, whom she had certainly killed. Now that it was over, the thought brought bile to her throat.

She wiped at her cheek, but her hand came away sticky with blood. Shaking uncontrollably, she gripped the reins tighter.

"Are you all right?" Phillip asked as he rode past her.

Vala nodded.

On they rode through the darkness. Vala wanted to rest and to let the pain surging through her body a chance to quiet. She wanted to stop eating the dust kicked up by the horses. She wanted water. More than all these, she wanted to lie on firm earth and feel safe again, but they never slowed. After a time, she trailed so far behind that Phillip fell back and led her horse.

"If they don't find us tonight, they'll stop looking," Phillip said as they finally brought the horses to a halt.

"Why would they give up?" Ethan asked, his voice weary. "They were quite keen to kill us all, just a few hours ago."

"De Roche wants you dead, I agree, but the bastard is under papal command to return to Rome, so he'll not lose another tide."

"You seem to know a lot about it," Ethan mumbled.

"And knowing what I know saved your skin," Phillip said.

Phillip and Ethan were destined to disagree, and Vala was too tired to mediate. She slid from her horse's back and sank to the ground, dizzy and sick. Waves of exquisite pain surged down her back, shooting through her arms and legs like white-hot lightning. What a comfort a small fire would be, she mused as she curled up in a ball on the ground, heedless of horses or men. Even if the hounds of hell had been on her heels, she could stay awake no longer.

Iron-tight fingers hauled Vala to her feet.

A fire with flames of orange, purple and green licked at the darkness. A cacophony of voices shouted, and men scuffled at the edges of her vision. Phillip was bound to a tree, his head lolling to one side. Blood dripped down the side of his face onto his cowl. Ethan was struggling with two black-robed figures. Vala twisted, trying to wrench her arm from the man holding her, but she was too weak and his fingers were strong, digging into her bruised flesh.

A tall figure appeared just beyond the blazing fire. He spread his arms, his green robes and golden cross sparkled garishly in the flickering light.

De Roche smirked. "You and your heathen friends have caused me to lose a night's sleep."

Vala's stomach tightened. They were all going to die. She could see it in his black, ravenous eyes.

"Your sorceress's wiles bewitched a son of the church." He nodded toward Phillip, whose body hung limp, while black-robed monks, like hovering vultures, were taking it in turns to beat Ethan.

Vala tried to scream, but only a thin whine escaped her throat.

The bishop stepped across the fire like a demon emerging from hell. He towered over her, and she detected the scent of brimstone. "Squeak all you like, but you will still die."

"No! Oh, no!" she gasped in horror as the monks sliced Ethan open from throat to waist. A hand grasped her shoulder, and she flailed against it, choking back the sob in her throat.

"Vala!"

She didn't want to die, but struggling hurt so much.

"Vala!"

She batted at the air in confusion.

"Vala! Wake up, girl!"

She vaguely recognized the voice.

"Calm yourself, child."

She was lying on her side, held down by someone with a strong grip.

"Just a moment more. It's nearly done."

"You're hurting her!"

"Just one more *moment*," was the growled reply.

Vala twisted, trying to get free, until she saw it was Ethan holding her still. "It's all right, Vala," he soothed.

Her uncle smiled down at her over Ethan's shoulder.

"Am I dead?"

"Not yet, child."

Her uncle knelt and smoothed back her hair. "Hold still while the good brother finishes dressing your wounds."

Phillip dabbed at her back, the scent of coneflowers wafting about them.

"We had to wet down your shirt to peel it free from your torn skin," Phillip said. "The wounds inflicted by the whip are ghastly." The monk laid a clean strip of cloth over her flayed back and draped a blanket around her shoulders. "We will have to make a sticking plaster of honey as soon as we can, but this will do for now."

Vala turned her damp face to him and nodded her thanks.

Her uncle wiped her cheeks with the frayed corner of the blanket. "I didn't realize you'd been whipped and beaten." he said. "You should never have stayed with us to fight."

Ethan nodded. "You should have taken a horse and fled."

Phillip snorted.

"I had such a bad dream," Vala muttered. "It was so real."

"A dream?" Ethan asked, his eyes agleam through a battered visage. "What did you see?"

"It wasn't that sort of dream," she said.

Ethan raised his eyebrows. "You can't be sure. Dreams are powerful passageways to the world of spirits."

"I hope not," she muttered.

Ethan gave her a regretful look, then found himself a place to lie down on the other side of the fire.

Vala turned her attention to her uncle. "Where have you been?"

"Have some of this warm ale, and then I'll tell you everything. Although I am sure your story is much more thrilling than mine."

He passed her a cup and then got to his feet to put more deadfall on the fire. The scent of Phillip's salve, subtle but distinct, was still floating in the air. The harsh sting of the lashes had already subsided, replaced by a dull, nearly tolerable soreness. Vala took a small sip and relaxed.

They were on a hill, but lying low in a hollow. The horses were drowsing, tethered to a nearby tree. Ethan was already snoring. Phillip shook out a blanket and settled himself on the ground with his head on his pack and his back to the fire. Vala huddled in the blanket and watched her uncle set the camp in order.

"After the raid, I left Meg and Fletcher and went to Bath to seek out Guillard. There, I learned that De Roche was sending his soldiers to Knowlton." He held out his hands toward the fire, flexing his fingers and rubbing them together.

"You went looking for Father Guillard?" she asked.

"He always made me laugh, that one. He and I have corresponded for many years."

"Father Guillard?"

"We communicate by pigeon," he said. "You know that I got messages at times. I kept most of the news they brought to myself. If I had let you handle the birds, you would have wanted to turn them into pets and send messages of your own."

Vala wanted to question him on the subject, but instead, she asked, "How did the two of you meet?"

Uncle Adrian sighed. "When I was a boy, I was restless. My family lived in a small Dumnonii community, and they practiced the old ways. They worshipped the Celtic gods, they brewed herb potions, they charted the stars, and they read the rune stones. Simon followed them in their beliefs unquestioningly. I was the quarrelsome one. I had questions. I was young and full of myself, I think."

Vala cringed. It sounded like he was describing her.

"I ran away from home at fourteen and traveled to France, working at anything that would earn me food or a bit of silver. I joined the forces of Count Odo when Siegfried and his Northmen besieged Paris. There, I took a spear to the thigh." He rubbed his leg.

With regret, she said, "I never thought to ask why you had that limp."

Adrian squeezed her hand. "One rainy evening, as I was seeking shelter for the night, I stumbled upon the monastery at Cluny. The priests fed me and gave me a bed for the night. They were a learned group, and I enjoyed their discussions of politics and religion, for they were open-minded and forward-thinking. A night became a week, and then a month. It was there that I met Pier Guillard. We became instant friends. Guillard and I got up to a great deal of mischief in the years I stayed in Cluny." He grinned.

"You trained to be a priest?"

"I told the fathers I was a Christian, which they easily believed. They wouldn't have been so quick to accept me had they known I'd never been baptized. I was content there, but when it came time to take my final vows, I found I could not. I enjoyed the life, but I could not reconcile myself to their beliefs. Guillard and I stayed friends and kept up a running correspondence, even after he went off to devote himself to the Vicomte De Roche."

Vala's mouth hung open. "How could he devote himself to such a man?"

"Not Bishop De Roche, but his father, the elder De Roche. A man of foresight and honor. The son hasn't his father's principles."

It was all so fantastical. "I never knew any of this," Vala said.

"Precisely as I planned," Adrian replied. "Your father, regardless of his supposed safeguards, was erratic and extreme. I needed to protect you even if he did something foolish. In the end, all our precautions failed."

Vala nodded. "I hope Father Guillard is all right. I'm worried that the bishop will discover his role in the escape."

"Bishop De Roche is no match for Pier Guillard, my child." He tapped a finger to his nose. "Have no fear."

She glanced toward Phillip, and then Ethan. They'd all risked so much. "Thank you for coming to find me," she said.

Adrian chuckled. "You were doing quite well without my help."

Vala sighed. "You didn't like my father, did you? You weren't happy that day you said we were to go to see him."

"I loved my brother. I disliked his cause and his belief in the stone."

Vala drew it from her pocket and held it up to the firelight, where it spun at the end of its chain, flashing its emerald radiance.

"It's a powerful object," Adrian replied. "If only because his people believe in it so strongly."

Vala fiddled with the chain before securing it around her neck.

Adrian yawned and stretched. "I'm feeling my age, I fear. We'd best get some rest." He wrapped himself in a blanket and curled up on the ground.

Chapter Thirty-Six:
*"Action is the proper fruit of knowledge."*

"They tied her to a pole in the marketplace and sliced her open so the birds would pick at her entrails," Manning recounted.

He'd been loitering at a crossroads, for it was the meeting place he and Ethan liked to use, gambling that his friend would come that way or leave some token. When their party rode into view, Manning galloped to greet them.

"They'd tacked a sign over her head saying, 'Here Stands a Witch'." Manning framed each word in the air with his hands. "Isolde was already dead, but De Roche will have his revenge."

Vala was sickened by the story, even in the light of Isolde's treachery.

"I never liked the old hag," Ethan replied in disgust.

"Still, we ought to pray for her soul," said Phillip.

"Perhaps we should just raise her from the dead," laughed Ethan.

"Only our Lord could rise from the dead," Phillip muttered in contempt.

Ethan smirked. "Anyone can rise from the dead." He sat up straighter on his horse, warming to the subject. "You must catch a unicorn on the Solstice. Then you cut off its horn and grind it into a powder..."

"Utter nonsense! Have you even ever seen a unicorn?" Phillip demanded.

"Have you ever seen the trinity of ghost beings you pray to?" Ethan asked.

Phillip's face flushed red-hot, and Ethan narrowed his eyes in defiance.

"There's no need to quarrel," Vala interrupted.

Manning spoke over the fray. "There was a report that the escaping pagans stripped an aging priest of his robes and beat him."

The group went silent.

"He was found wandering senseless and naked in the keep."

"Is the priest all right?" Ethan demanded.

Phillip cut in, "Did you see him?"

Manning scowled. "You lot didn't really hurt an old man?"

"No!" replied Vala, Ethan, and Phillip in unison.

"I didn't believe it could be true," Manning said. "The old priest was riding in a wagon this morning. Off to Swanage, they say. He looked fine to me."

Vala and Ethan grinned while Phillip crossed himself and whispered a prayer of thanksgiving.

Manning snapped his fingers. "I nearly forgot! There was a fire at the keep last night. The fire spooked the bishop's horse. The beast threw him, and he broke his leg. So he couldn't join the pursuit, and he had to ride in the wagon, too."

"What about our people?" Ethan asked.

"I sent Meg and Fletcher back to Avebury. They will watch for others."

Ethan told the company about Vala's tower, and they made for it, as the closest place of safety. Before long, Ethan and Manning were chattering like magpies, planning their next move.

By midday, they had reached the hill below the tower. They hid the wagon deep in a copse of bracken. A few items had survived the wild ride over the dark roads: an ornate chair, a small cask of wine, a wooden crate. These, they tied to the carthorses. Under the driver's seat, wedged in the corner, Vala found a small strongbox edged with leather and metal studs. She strapped it to her saddle, and the group moved toward the gully and the trail up the hill.

There was general disbelief when the men breached the thick undergrowth and glimpsed the vine-covered tower and its courtyard. Vala left them to their discussion of the merits of Roman architecture while she tied the horses. By the time she'd finished, they'd all drifted inside for a look around.

"It's amazing to find something like this." Manning ran a hand over the weathered stone. "It's completely hidden."

"Go up to the top, why don't you?" suggested Ethan. "The lookout is well-placed for a guard tower."

Adrian, Manning, and Phillip all clambered up the winding stairs, remarking over the wonders of stone engineering. Once they were out of sight, and their voices were muffled by the thick floors, Ethan took Vala's hand and pulled her to him.

"I have to go immediately," he told her.

"Surely not. Your leg needs time to heal," she said.

"There is much to do. I'll be back to get you very soon. A fortnight at the most."

Vala raised an eyebrow.

"Well, I thought I would ask your uncle to stay here with you until I returned." He scanned her face with a quizzical look. "I must see what's happening."

"I know all that. But I've no plans to leave," she countered.

Ethan's lips thinned, but he quickly composed his features. "I thought you'd live with me. We can even marry if you like, goddess." To punctuate his invitation, his lips grazed hers with a kiss.

"I'm no goddess," she whispered, closing her eyes as he moved on to her neck.

"Many innocent people owe you their lives."

"You and Phillip as well," she sighed.

"Just come with me. I'll protect you. While I find the rest of our people, you could stay with Fletcher and Meg. They dote on you."

"Ethan," she said with a firm push against his chest. "I won't be the baggage you tow about behind you and set down when it becomes too troublesome."

"People count on me, Vala." Ethan's eyes glinted. "A little inconvenience should be an honor to you. You'd be fulfilling your father's dream."

Vala narrowed her eyes. "I want my own life, not your idea of a life, or his."

"Well, then, shut yourself up in this tower like a nun in a cloister," Ethan sneered.

"Like a *what*?"

"Maybe your monk friend can stay behind. Perhaps he'll pray over you at night."

Vala pointed to the door. "Go!"

Ethan's bravado waned, and he took a step backward. "I didn't mean that." He looked down at the floor, breathing hard. "I just want—I just thought you'd come with me."

Even though she liked Ethan, wanted him, even, she wanted her freedom more. There were many unanswered questions to ponder, books to read, and the possibility of returning to Glastonbury's library. She wanted to learn her father's history from her uncle and to sit with Fletcher to discuss the story of Barnabas.

They stared at each other in silence until the scrape of Manning's sword against the stonework announced the return of their companions.

"I'll have to remember this place. You can see for miles up there," Manning said with a grin.

Vala wiped a tear from the corner of her eye. There was nothing else to say.

"You'll be safe, I think," Ethan muttered. "Set your snags before dark, will you?"

Vala nodded.

"I will be back—before Beltaine."

She nodded again.

Manning looked from one to the other. Then he sighed and went to get the horses. Ethan clasped Adrian's arm and gave the monk a nod, which Phillip returned. Without a backward glance, Manning and Ethan mounted and disappeared into the trees.

Phillip shielded his eyes. "That man would make a formidable enemy."

"But a good ally," Vala replied.

Adrian and Phillip set about hauling the bishop's possessions inside. While her uncle worked at prying open the wooden crate, Vala inspected the small, leather-bound casket. Metal straps bound its stout sides together, so she prodded the lock with her knife. The knife slipped, slicing her finger, and Vala yelped.

"You've cut yourself." Phillip came over to where she sat.

"It's nothing. I've opened it!" She sucked at the gash while lifting the lid with her good hand. "Look."

The strong box held a goodly quantity of gold and silver coins, loose gemstones, and jewelry. Lying on top was a roll of parchment tied with a red ribbon, its heavy wax seal broken.

Phillip lifted the document. "May I?"

Vala nodded, and he strode over to the window for better light. She probed the remaining contents of the box, which included an object Vala recognized at once. It was the ornate gold crucifix from De Roche's study. She lifted it out, turned it over, and ran her fingers over the jewels that encrusted the surface.

"A pretty thing," remarked Uncle Adrian.

"Damn him to hell!" Phillip's face blistered with anger. "This is a letter from Pope John himself." He slapped the parchment with the back of his hand. "Apparently, His Grace the Bishop is not content to kill Britons, but is off to put an end to the pope's mother." Phillip read the letter aloud to them.

"I am always amazed by the lengths a man will go for power," said Adrian, returning to the crate he was trying to break open.

"Yes, power," Phillip mumbled, his face set hard as stone. He looked up. "I must go."

"But the bishop will be at sea by now," Vala said.

"I know, and good riddance to him," said Phillip. "But it's not over as long as Rome can send us such a one as that."

"Couldn't you stay just a day or so? I have so many questions," Vala asked unhappily.

"I'd like that," said Phillip. "I'd like that too much, I fear. Once you're rested, you'll be going home with your uncle to Wistman's Wood?"

"I plan to stay here," she said. Why did all these men assume she'd run for home or cling to them for safety?

He frowned. "I'll try to come back in a month or so. Just now, I need to get to Glastonbury and find Brother Cuthred. The night we dined at the abbey, he expressed his concerns about the bishops that Rome selects for us. I thought the old man a bit of a fool, but now I see he was right." Phillip held up the letter. "This proves that the rot goes very deep. Perhaps we can do something if I can convince a few highly placed friends. May I have it?"

"Of course," Vala said, blinking at Phillip's zeal.

Phillip stuffed the parchment inside his robes and headed for the door. "Take care of your wounds," he ordered. "Remember, honey poultice."

She nodded.

Phillip shook Adrian's hand. "You are a brave man, sir," he said. "I see where Vala gets her spirit."

"No less than you, my son. You went against your superior when you found he was corrupt. That takes much fortitude. I salute you." Adrian bowed to the monk, and Phillip's ruddy face went even redder for a moment.

As he rode off, ducking under the low-hanging branches, Vala wondered how soon she would see her companions again.

Adrian put his arm around Vala and led her back inside.

"You know," he began as he resumed prying on the large crate, "young Ethan was very worried about your condition. I had to force a double portion of ale down him to get him to calm himself."

Vala did not look at him. She understood his meaning. "He feels he must lead the Dumnonii now that my father is dead."

"A pity," Adrian said as he pulled his sword from his belt and applied it to the box lid with a concentrated effort. The lid finally gave way, revealing some useable goods. There were a few well-crafted earthenware bowls, a feather bed, and several cassocks woven of fine linen. Someone had laid lavender in the folds of the garments, and the scent of it rose from the crate to fill the room. Beneath the clothing, to Vala's delight, was a heavy book.

Adrian glanced at the pages as she turned a few. "*Vetus Latina.*"

"Old Latin?" Vala asked.

"Yes. It's what the scholars call translations of the gospels into Latin. There are many versions of the gospels, of course, and every one of them is slightly different, as you might imagine." Uncle Adrian went to the hearth, where he fed the remnants of the broken wooden box lid into the fire.

Vala closed the book with a sigh. It was astonishing to think of all the possible accounts of one event there might be. Could any of them be counted as the true one?

She laid the book aside and fingered the gilt filigree of the cross and then the rough edges of the stone of Ansuz, hanging at her neck. Someone had to save the remnants of history from scribes who might change the meaning of a book with a stroke of a quill, or fanatics who would burn it out of existence, and even from those who would hide bits of truth away to fade and molder. Texts like the gospel of Barnabas needed protection, even if the book was sheer madness. Who knew what would prove important in the future?

"What are you thinking, child?"

"Oh, nothing," she mused. "And everything. Just think about the books that are locked away, that no one ever reads. At Glastonbury, the monks love books, yet the worms devour them faster than they could ever copy them. Someone has to save them."

"I admit I've never thought of it."

"What if I tried to recover some of them, so they are not lost forever?" She realized how ridiculous this sounded.

Adrian fixed his niece with a hard stare. "Recover, or steal?"

To be honest, she had no idea how she would lay hands on those books. Books were incredibly expensive, and with the exception of the caches the church hoarded, they were rare and precious.

"Most lasses aspire to be wives and mothers, not book thieves."

"How dangerous could it be?"

He sighed. "The Lord knows I went off to seek my own fortune. I learned the hard lessons of honor and truth, so I would be a hypocrite to attempt to convince you otherwise. However, as one who loves you as a daughter, I fear for your safety."

A large raven fluttered down onto the window ledge.

"Merlin?" it croaked.

Adrian moved to shoo the bird away, but Vala stayed his hand. "Uncle, do you believe that souls can come back and inhabit animals?"

"It's a doctrine that my parents embraced, but I do not."

"Ethan believes that raven is the embodiment of my dead brother." She gave a respectful nod to Lugus. "Or perhaps it's only an annoying bird. We can't know the truth, can we? Not as long as men twist the truth to suit their own plans and plots."

Adrian raised an eyebrow.

Lugus edged along the window to peck at a battered leather hat hung on a peg in the wall. Adrian's sudden whoop of pleasure startled the raven into flight. "You really did save it!" Vala grinned as her uncle smoothed the brim and pushed his favorite old hat back on his head.

Look for the continuing adventures of Vala in *Bloodstone* (no release date), as she becomes a parchment buyer in order to lay hands on old manuscripts, preserving what has been written from destruction. However, it is her skill in healing that leads her and her friends into danger and death.

You can find out more at www.lauriewipperfurthauthor.com or on Facebook @lauriewipperfurthauthor

Made in the USA
Columbia, SC
04 May 2019